7

8

The Daughter

The Daughter

Caroline Gray

Except where they can be historically identified, the characters in this novel are invented, and are not intended to portray real people, living or dead.

This title first published in Great Britain 1992 by
SEVERN HOUSE PUBLISHERS LTD of
35 Manor Road, Wallington, Surrey SM6 0BW
First published in the U.S.A. 1992 by
SEVERN HOUSE PUBLISHERS INC of
475 Fifth Avenue, New York, NY 10017–6220.

British Library Cataloguing in Publication Data
Gray, Caroline
  The daughter.
  I. Title
  823.914 [F]

  ISBN 0-7278-4347-8

Typeset by Hewer Text Composition Services, Edinburgh
Printed and bound in Great Britain by
Billing and Sons Ltd, Worcester

Geli von Uderstadt believed that she was the only person alive who knew the true identity of her father. But she was wrong. The result was tragedy.

PROLOGUE

1944

THE MOTHER

The single-engined upper-wing monoplane began to drop through the clouds, and Helene von Uderstadt clenched her fists inside the thick, fur-lined gloves she had been given to wear. The weather had been fine when they had left Tempelhof, but now she could see nothing.

She had a desperate urge to lean forward and touch the pilot on the shoulder, ask him if he knew where they were. But that would be stupid. Of course he knew where they were – he was descending.

Helene had only flown once before, when her brother Ulric had taken her up for a spin, soon after he had been given his wings. That had been four years ago.

Four years ago had been another world. Four years ago had been one of the finest summers in recorded history. And not only weatherwise. Four years ago had seen the ultimate triumph of the Wehrmacht, and, in the beginning, of the Luftwaffe. Four years ago, in April, every German in uniform had been a hero. Within six weeks they would be masters of the continent.

Four years ago, she had met Hitler for the first time. Which was why she was here today, she supposed. Papa had introduced them, when the Führer's party had stopped at the Schloss on their way to his headquarters in Aachen, just before the offensive which would knock France out of the war had begun.

"Helene," Hitler had said, after kissing her hand. "You remind me of someone. But her name was Geli."

Geli Raubel, of course. Helene had only been twelve when Geli Raubel had committed suicide. Nobody knew

9

why, which had naturally merely fuelled endless rumours. That Hitler had been in love with his glamorous niece was certain. After that . . . no one could be certain whether his unwanted advances, as he had moved toward power, had been resistible except by the oldest and most final of weapons, death, or whether, as some people whispered, he had been so unnatural in his desires that Geli's young mind had snapped.

Within a year, when he had become ruler of Germany, in form if not yet in name, no one had dared ask. And in the spring of 1940, twenty-year-old Helene von Uderstadt – the same age as Geli Raubel when she had died, with the same dark hair and pretty face and sparkling eyes, the same trim figure, and, unlike Geli, all the trappings of the Uderstadt wealth at her shoulder and on her back, barking around her feet and towering above her head – had had no desire to ask. To bask in the favour of the Führer was as high as her ambition could possibly soar.

At twenty, a von Uderstadt woman was essentially innocent. Not for her the Strength Through Joy movement which had so liberated German girlhood – and caused a dramatic rise in the birthrate. Helene had certainly been brought up to the Germanic ideals of health and strength and beauty through the active open air life. But when she swam in the nude it was with her parents and brothers in their own pool, shut away from prying eyes. Masculine lust had not been evident, feminine lust non-existent.

There had of course been men, and an engagement. This was a necessary part of being a member of the Party, of showing the country, and the world, one's mettle. Freddie had been a dear boy, and as by then the war had become rather more serious than parades and instant victories filmed by the newsreel cameras, she had felt it her patriotic duty to yield her virginity on the night before he had left for Russia. That had been a distasteful business, although Freddie had appeared overwhelmed: the pretty girl of twenty had by 1942 become a quite beautiful, tall, dark-haired woman of twenty-two, the slightly large features fitting the voluptuous figure to perfection.

Helene had looked forward to marriage to Freddie, to a deeper understanding of the mysteries of sex, and possibly even an enjoyment of them as time went by. But Freddie had been on Paulus' staff, and only a year ago had disappeared into the fiery maw of Stalingrad. She did not even know if he was alive or dead. But she was sure he was never coming back.

The clouds thinned, but Helene could see nothing. Beneath her was impenetrable darkness. Yet the pilot was dropping lower and lower. She could tell this both from the altimeter in her cockpit and from the way her stomach seemed to be jammed against her throat.

And then she saw a flare, and another. Five minutes later, the plane was bumping over a grass strip, and was surrounded by armed men.

The pilot waited to assist her down; she moved awkwardly in her leather flying suit, and gratefully pulled the helmet from her head. "That wasn't too bad, was it?"

"It was exhilarating. Will you be piloting me back?"

"Of course. Whenever you are ready." He gestured towards the waiting Mercedes.

Helene had not met Hitler between April 1940 and April 1943. Then she had attended a memorial service for the men who had fallen at Stalingrad, and had been one of those presented to the Führer after the ceremony.

"Helene von Uderstadt," he had said, holding her hands and peering into her face with that benevolent and slightly bemused smile which to any loyal Party member made a nonsense of those people who would describe him as a bloodthirsty warlord. "Freddie Dietrich was your fiancé?"

"Yes, my Führer," she had replied.

"This war brings tragedy for us all. We can only hope to atone for it when we have gained the victory. But you

. . . so young, so beautiful, so alone . . . I also am alone. A leader is always alone. If I sent for you, would you come to alleviate my loneliness, Helene?"

Helene had been able to do nothing more than smile her agreement, before escaping as soon as she could, and seeking the advice of her mother.

"He is our Führer," Helga von Uderstadt had said, reverently. Papa and Mama had been amongst the earliest supporters of the Nazi Party, simply because it had promised some relief from the ever-mounting burden of taxation which the socialists had seemed to find necessary. The Uderstadt companies had poured money into Hitler's campaign funds, and Johann von Uderstadt had never regretted it, even if the war now seemed likely to end in a stalemate rather than a sweeping German victory. "It is possible to see a great future for you, Helene."

Neither woman considered the morality of the matter at all; that was not a Nazi attitude.

"He is old enough to be my father," Helene had argued.

"And young enough to be your husband."

"Oh, Mama, how can you even think that? What of Eva?"

"A common slut. A photographer's model. My God! Could such a woman ever be the wife of the ruler of Germany? Whereas you, Helene . . . there is the best blood in your veins. You should be proud."

Well, Helene supposed, she was proud, even as she had reflected, with some relief, that such a summons was very unlikely ever to materialise.

But it had, and she was here.

The road was very dark, but the Mercedes followed its headlights into the gloom with complete confidence. The young officer sitting beside Helene gazed rigidly in front of himself.

"Is it far?" she asked, less from curiosity than because she was growing more nervous by the moment.

"We have arrived, Fraulein," he replied, and a moment later the Mercedes drew up before a gate set in a high wire fence. Here there were several soldiers, and the officer had to produce a pass, while flashlights were shone into the interior, and over Helene's face.

"The Führer is very security conscious," the officer explained.

"Of course," Helene agreed, feeling more nervous yet.

Now there were buildings, mostly low and built of wood, but few lights. When the car stopped again, she could hear the soughing of the wind in the pine trees. It was difficult to accept that she was in the very nerve centre of the German army, the German nation.

The lieutenant held the door for her, and she got out. Another door was opened, and for a moment there was a gleam of light, instantly doused as she stepped through and the blackout curtain was dropped into place behind her. Facing her was a woman wearing a nurse's uniform. "Fraulein Uderstadt?" she asked.

"Yes. Yes, I am Helene von Uderstadt," Helene said, beginning to feel a little piqued at the way these people were treating her as if she were some menial come to apply for a job. "Where can I change my clothes?"

"In here, Fraulein." The nurse opened an inner door and Helene entered a rather spartan bedroom. It contained two bunks, one above the other, a table and two straight chairs, and a washbasin. She turned and watched her valise being brought in by an orderly. He placed this on the table and left again without a word.

Helene looked at the nurse, who closed the door and remained standing before it. They stared at each other for several seconds, and then the nurse said, "Will you not undress, Fraulein?"

"When you have left."

"I am required to stay, Fraulein. Until the examination is finished."

"The examination?"

"You must be searched, Fraulein. And then examined."

"And suppose I refuse?" Helene demanded, her pique turning into anger.

"Refuse?" the woman asked, genuinely bewildered.

Because, presumably, Helene realised, if she was here at all, she was knowingly subject to all the rules that surrounded the warlord. Nor could she now decline to accept them. She had come, and she was not going to be allowed to leave until she had completed her function.

She pulled off the fur-lined boots, unbuttoned the leather flying jacket, let it fall to the floor, then stepped out of the leather trousers. Underneath she wore slacks, a blouse and a sweater. She gazed at the woman as she removed these in turn, and the woman gazed back, impassively. Helene hesitated.

"The underclothes as well, Fraulein."

Helene removed her camiknickers, and then her stockings. "Am I now permitted to dress?" she asked, keeping her voice low and hopefully controlled, but it trembled with a mixture of embarrassment and outrage.

"I must search you."

"Well?"

"You must bend over the table."

Helene's jaw dropped. "You would not dare!"

"I must, Fraulein. Or would you prefer it if one of the guards did it?"

Helene bent over the table. My God, she thought, what I am going to tell the Führer? But he was the man who would have ordered this dreadful humiliation. Or was he not just a victim of his own bureaucracy?

"Thank you, Fraulein." The nurse washed her hands in the basin. "Will you open the valise, please."

Still trembling, Helene obeyed. All manner of thoughts were tumbling through her mind. It was not merely the touch of those impersonal fingers . . . even if she could still feel them. It was the feeling of helplessness in the face of overwhelming power. Once, just before the war, she had been at a very drunken party which had broken up with shrieks of laughter as they had decided to drive up to

14

Ravensbrück Concentration Camp, just north of Berlin. Helene had never been to a camp before, but most of her companions apparently went regularly.

She had not known what to expect, although she had been told that Ravensbrück was an entirely female camp, which contained all the women who had been convicted of trying to bring down the Reich. She had therefore not been prepared to feel any sympathy for the inmates. Yet she had been appalled. They had arrived just after dawn, in time for roll call, and women, of all ages and sizes, and wearing the most ridiculous pyjama-like garments, shapeless sacks which concealed every feminine attribute and yet were somehow embarrassingly inadequate,had come running out of their barracks to take their places in the line and stand there, rigidly to attention, chivvied by their female guards while the roll had been called with terrifying deliberation. Knees had given way or inmates had lost their balance and brushed shoulders with a neighbour, in every case to be rewarded with a terrifying flick of a rubber truncheon which had some on their knees, vomiting, whereupon they had been hit again until they recovered.

Helene's companions had found this enormously entertaining; she had felt sick herself. It had been less the physical mistreatment than the sheer helplessness and terror of the women, their obvious awareness that they had no rights whatsoever . . . their total surrender to the forces surrounding them.

She had gone home thanking God she was Helene von Uderstadt, and not some enemy of the Party. But now she had, unthinkingly, placed herself in the Party's power, and was as helpless as any of those inmates.

Had Hitler known of it? She still refused to believe that, any more than she believed he knew what was happening to her at this moment.

The nurse had finished going through her things, and had picked up the telephone receiver from the wall mounting. "Whenever you are ready, Herr Doktor," she was saying.

15

Helene selected her clean camiknickers. She had intended to change them anyway, before seeing the Führer, but now it seemed absolutely necessary.

"You must not dress," the nurse said. "Not yet."

"I am to see the Führer like this?"

"No, no. You must see Dr Morel first."

The doctor arrived immediately, and it was the most distressing event of what was turning into a thoroughly distressing evening, thus far. He was short and fat, bald and myopic, unshaven and had not recently bathed. While he had most certainly recently dined off garlic. He was also the first man she had ever stood in front of, naked; her night with Freddie had been dark and they had always been half-dressed.

"Fraulein von Uderstadt," he said. "What is your sexual experience?"

"My . . .?" But as she was caught up in this madhouse it seemed pointless now to lose her temper. "I am not a virgin, Herr Doktor."

He waved his hand. "How many?"

"What do you take me for, a prostitute?"

"How many?"

"I . . . I slept with my fiancé. Once. Before he went to the Russian front."

"Hm," he said disbelievingly. "We shall see. Get on the table."

"The table?"

"The table, you stupid cow," he shouted. "Lie on your back. Quickly. I do not have all night. And neither does the Führer."

As it was already midnight, that remark did seem to have some point. Helene climbed on the table, and lay on her back.

"Legs up," Morel commanded. "And apart."

Hardly believing that she was being that subservient, Helene obeyed, and had her knees grabbed and held by the nurse, to make sure she stayed the way the doctor wanted.

16

He didn't even wash his hands, before or after, and hummed as he went about his business. "You are not diseased," he said, sounding slightly surprised. "And you are most certainly sexually inexperienced." That seemed to surprise him even more.

I am Helene von Uderstadt, she wanted to shout, but decided against it. There didn't seem much point.

"Get dressed," he said. "The Führer is waiting."

Helene had chosen a silk dress printed with flowers, modest at both bodice and hem, but which gave off a gentle swish as she moved. She had had her hair done before she left Berlin, and it lay in dark waves on her shoulders. Now it was just a matter of checking her make-up.

"You are very beautiful," the nurse remarked.

Helene glanced at her, suddenly curious. "Do you have many women to . . . examine?"

"Not so many," the woman said. "The Führer is very busy."

"Oh. Yes, I suppose he is." She was dying to ask if Eva Braun ever came to Rastenburg, and if she did, whether she had to undergo such an experience every time, but she decided against it.

The nurse actually opened the door for her, and in the outer room there were two guards, one of whom held a greatcoat to put round her; the early April night was chilly in East Prussia.

Then she was hurried through the darkness, to the house occupied by the Führer.

It was dawn when the aircraft landed at Tempelhof, chilly and misty. Helene was led from the plane to a waiting-room where she could discard her flying gear, and then a car took her to the Uderstadt town house.

This had so far escaped structural damage from the Royal Air Force or the Americans, although all of the valuable paintings and objets d'art had been removed to

17

the cellar, which had been fitted up very comfortably, and where the family spent a good deal of its time, and indeed, every night. Thus, this early in the morning, Helene was reasonably sure that the apartment itself would be empty.

She let herself in with her latchkey, went to her room and turned on the bath. There was only a trickle of water, and it was not very warm, but she waited patiently until she could totally immerse herself except for her cap-protected hair. She was still lying there, beginning to feel chilled and not the least clean, when the door opened and her maid, Ilse, came in.

"Oh, Fraulein!" Ilse's voice squeaked: she was only sixteen and very excitable. "I did not know you were here. I did not know you were back."

"It's time I got out anyway," Helene said, and did so.

Ilse handed her mistress her towel, but her cry had alerted the entire household, and a moment later Helga was in the room.

"Helene! My poppet. But . . . what happened?"

Helene merely looked at her.

"Off you go, Ilse. Find yourself something to do," Helga ordered.

Ilse scuttled from the room.

"Now," Helga said eagerly. "Tell me what happened."

Helene looked at her mother again. Tell you? she thought. That would be quite impossible. "Nothing happened, Mama."

"Nothing? But . . ."

"I have slept with the Führer."

"And you call that nothing?"

Helene shrugged.

"What did he do to you?"

"Oh, for God's sake, Mama."

"There must have been more than just . . . well, love-making."

Love-making? Helene thought. My God! I was a receptacle. Nothing more than that. However could anyone get the idea that love could possibly enter into a summons, a requirement, a dismissal?

But she had to say something. "We talked."

"About what?"

"The war. At least, he talked, and I listened."

"What does he think of the situation?"

"He seems to be quite happy with the situation. He says that we will start winning again when our secret weapons are ready, and that will be quite soon."

"Well, that is good news. How do you feel?"

Cheap, Helene thought. Like hell. There had been nothing the least bit perverted or obscene about either Hitler or his sexual habits. It was simply that she could have been anyone. She had prostituted herself, and not even been paid for it with a single red rose.

"When will he send for you again?" Helga asked, eagerly.

"I have absolutely no idea, Mama."

Hopefully, never.

"Well?" Helene demanded.

For the past week she had been afraid to think.

Dr Allding was the Uderstadt family physician. He was in his sixties now, and would have retired but for the war. He had known Helene all of her life, having, indeed, delivered her.

He sat beside his desk and gazed at his notes. "One month is meaningless, in these times. I will test these samples, of course." He gazed at her. "You have reason to believe that you *could* be pregnant?"

"Yes," Helene said.

Allding sighed. Modern youth. Of course one expected it of the Hitler Youth girls; they took pride in it. But Helene von Uderstadt . . .

"Come back in a month," he told her. "If you have missed another period . . ."

"It is very important that I know, at the earliest possible moment," Helene said.

19

"Ah. Your lover is married."

"You could say that," Helene agreed. To his country, she thought.

Helga was sitting in front of the radio, listening to the news of the battle for the Normandy beaches, when Helene came home from her next visit to the doctor.

"It's terrible," she said. "There has never been anything like it. So many men and ships . . . of course we are going to defeat them. It is going to be the biggest disaster ever suffered by the British and the Americans. The Führer says so. But still . . ."

Helene sat down. "Would you turn off the set, Mama? I have to speak with you."

Over the month her nerves, and her acceptance of the situation, had slowly come together. She had had no doubt she was pregnant when she had missed her first period; she had never missed a period before. It was the enormity of it, the possible ramifications, which had been unacceptable, in the beginning. Her mental solution had been to skip the immediate problems, and think only of a year from now, perhaps, when she would be the mother of Germany's future Führer. On that high cloud she had resided for four weeks; it had quite made up for the calamity of the visit to Rastenberg itself.

And it had been her secret. She had always loved having secrets, looking at other people, even her own family, and thinking to herself, they don't know.

She had never possessed a secret quite like this.

But now it was necessary to leave the cloud, and come down to earth. And she had simply no idea how to begin.

Dr Allding had asked the name of the father, and she had refused to tell him. That had left the poor old chap with the impression that there could be more than one possibility, and he had shaken his head sadly.

But Allding would have had hysterics if he had known the truth; Helene had never been quite certain that he was as good a Nazi as he pretended.

There was no equivocation where Mama was concerned. "What on earth can be more important than the Allies invading France?" Helga demanded.

"If you will turn off the set, I will tell you," Helene said.

Helga turned off the radio. "Well?"

Helene drew a long breath. "I am pregnant."

"Oh, Helene! How could you? I really am ashamed of you. I had hoped you would keep yourself for the Führer. Now . . . he will not wish to send for you again."

"Mama, I have slept with only two men in my life. One was Freddie, two years ago. And the other *was* the Führer, two months ago."

Helga's mouth formed a huge O. "Oh, my God," she said. "Can it be true?"

"It is true."

"But . . . what are we to do?"

"I am hoping you will tell me that."

"My God," Helga said again. "What will your father say?"

"I do not think Papa should be told, as yet. But should we not tell the father of the child?"

"But how?"

Helene looked at the telephone. If Fraulein von Uderstadt were to telephone Rastenberg and insist on speaking with the Führer, she did not think she would be too vigorously resisted.

Helga snorted. "You do not understand, my darling. This is no ordinary baby."

"Well, of course it is not."

"I mean, it may well be the heir to the Reich."

"I have thought of that."

"Have you? Have you considered that there must be quite a few people who already see themselves as heirs to the Reich? What of Goering, who has been named? That slimy toad, Bormann. Goebbels! My God, Goebbels!"

Helene stared at her mother. That aspect of the situation had not occurred to her.

21

Helga got up and began to pace the room, suddenly a woman with the power to rule the German universe. "We must think very carefully about this."

"I must go to Rastenberg and see Adolf, and explain the situation to him," Helene said.

"Ye-es," Helga said, without conviction. "But once you do that, it will become public. And the conspiracies will begin. We both know how preoccupied the Führer is with the military situation, and now that there is the fighting in France as well . . . we must choose our ally, our supporter, in advance."

"You are making it sound like a conspiracy. I am pregnant. By Adolf."

"Himmler," Helga announced.

"Eh?"

"I don't like Goering. He may have been a hero once, but now he is a fat slob. Goebbels gives me the creeps. Himmler is the man. We can trust him."

"Trust Himmler?" Helene disliked the SS chief even more than Goering or Goebbels.

"Yes. He knows *he* can never succeed. The others would never stand for it. It is his pre-ordained fate to be a power behind the throne. This will be his opportunity to secure his position. Yes, he will be our support. I will telephone him today and arrange a meeting."

"I do not understand," Helene said. "You wish to tell Himmler about this, *before* Adolf?"

"Yes," Helga said. "It will be best. We need the support of the SS."

"Hm," Heinrich Himmler remarked. "Hm." His face always wore an apprehensive expression, as if he was unsure where the next blow was going to fall. Perhaps, Helene thought, he had once been attacked by a rampant hen during his chicken-farming days. But his eyes were disconcertingly invisible behind the thick lenses of his spectacles.

22

Now he moved his forefinger up and down from the hand resting on his desk, as he looked at Helga. "The Führer is not a eunuch, Frau von Uderstadt." He glanced at Helene, "As your daughter must know."

"Well, of course." Helga prepared to bridle.

"He is a man of fifty-five," Himmler said. "And to my knowledge . . ." He paused to leave no doubt that his knowledge was complete. "He has never fathered a child."

"Well, he is going to father one now." Helga von Uderstadt was not going to be browbeaten, even by the head of the Schutzstaffel. She pointed at the papers on the desk. "There you have the doctor's confirmation."

"It is a question of believing that the Führer is the father," Himmler remarked.

"Are you questioning the Führer's potency?" Helga inquired, gently.

"Of course I am not," Himmler snapped. Although he had just done so, Helene reflected. She was finding the whole thing very embarrassing. "But I have to know who else the Fraulein has slept with during the period that she might have conceived."

Now Helene was both embarrassed and angry, but she had an adequate champion.

"How dare you?" Helga shouted. "How dare you? My Helene has not known a man since the death of her fiancé, Fredrich von Dietrich, until the Führer sent for her in April."

Himmler looked somewhat flustered. "It is my duty to be sure, Frau von Uderstadt."

"You have my assurance," Helga said grandly. "Do you not think I know what my daughter is up to?"

"I am sure you do, Frau von Uderstadt. I am sure of it. Now . . . who else knows of this?"

"That she is pregnant? No one, save us three, and the doctor. But he does not know the name of the father."

Himmler nodded. "And he must not."

23

"I should think my maid, Ilse, suspects," Helene said.

"Your maid. Is she trustworthy?"

"I do not know, where something like this is involved."

"Hm," Himmler commented.

"I must have a maid," Helene pointed out.

"Oh, quite." He did not appear convinced. "Can this woman have any idea of who the father might be?"

"No. I do not see how she can."

"You do not exchange confidences with your maid?"

"No."

"Well, see that you do not. No one must know about this until I have spoken with the Führer."

"You?"

"It is best that I handle this affair. You may be certain that I will have your interests at heart. I will attend to it immediately."

He stood up to indicate that the interview was at an end.

After that it was simply a matter of waiting, and growing more and more excited . . . and more nervous, as day succeeded day and there was no word. Of course, Helene understood that the Führer must be terribly busy, as the Allies were not after all hurled back into the sea to suffer that irreversible defeat, but instead consolidated their bridgehead. Yet surely the prospect of a son was of greater importance even than this temporary setback?

She began to suspect that Himmler was deliberately suppressing the news, and after a month had passed without any word from him, determined that she would give him one more week and then insist upon seeing Hitler herself. But then catastrophe struck. Just before the week was up, the radio buzzed with the news of the attempt on Hitler's life, and Berlin was turned into an armed camp.

Helga had taken Helene down to their country house in Bavaria, far away from the bombings and the excitement, for the good of the baby, she had said. Therefore they

24

only learned of the assassination attempt through the radio. Helga immediately tried to get Himmler on the telephone, to ascertain exactly what had happened – there were rumours that Hitler, if not actually dead, was too badly hurt to continue as head of state – but that was impossible: the Security Chief was far too busy arresting people. Helene wanted to go to Berlin, but Helga opted against that.

"Anything might happen," she declared. "You must never forget the precious burden you are carrying."

She was more excited about the baby than Helene was. But it was disconcerting to hear no news about what really mattered, from anyone, and Himmler remained unobtainable. However, at the beginning of August two very official-looking cars arrived at the Schloss, and several armed policemen got out, together with two men in plain clothes.

"We are here to question everyone who visited the Führer's headquarters at Rastenberg this year," one of the men in plain clothes announced. "You were there, Fraulein von Uderstadt, on . . ." he checked his notebook, "April the tenth."

"Yes," Helene agreed. "I was there."

"Then you must accompany us to headquarters."

"Am I under arrest?"

"We wish to ask you some questions."

"Are you mad?" Helga demanded. "Do you realise who you are speaking to? Don't you know . . ."

"Mama!" Helene said sharply. "I am sure these gentlemen have nothing to ask me which I cannot answer to their satisfaction. It would be better if you got hold of Uncle Heinrich."

Helga stared at her for some seconds, then realised who she meant. "Yes," she said. "I will do that."

Helene was not the least afraid of the Gestapo, for all its sinister reputation. Besides, these were local people who had all known the Uderstadts for years.

Not that this apparently mattered.

"There are very many high-ranking officials involved in this plot," the Oberleutnant who interviewed her told her.

"Well, I am not involved in any plot," Helene retorted. "I was summoned to Rastenberg by the Führer himself." She gazed at the embarrassed young man. "The purpose I leave to your imagination."

He swallowed. "We will get to the bottom of it," he said, and summoned one of his female assistants to take her away.

She was locked in a small windowless cell which stank of disinfectant. "Why am I being treated as a criminal?" she asked.

"Because you may be one," the woman said.

"And how soon will I find out if I am a criminal or not?"

"I do not know. As soon as the Oberleutnant has completed his enquiries."

"You will all regret this," Helene contented herself with saying.

Helga must have got through quickly this time, Helene thought, for the apologies started that very afternoon, when she was released by the Oberleutnant himself, very humbly, and taken downstairs to a waiting car, in which she was driven home. There was an official Mercedes outside the Schloss, and Himmler was inside the castle.

"Fraulein!" He kissed her hands. "I can only apologise for the zeal of my men. You are not harmed?"

"I need a bath. A hot tub."

"A hot tub?" He looked concerned. "No, no, Fraulein. Hot baths are not good for someone in your condition."

"Oh, come now. You mean I can't have a bath for the next six months?"

"Cold showers," Himmler said primly.

26

"I will ask Dr Allding."

"You will do no such thing."

"All right. You can check with your doctor."

"I read it in a book," Himmler told her. "Anyway, there is no time. You must leave here immediately."

"Leave the Schloss? To go to Adolf?"

"No, that is not possible at this moment."

"It is orders from the Führer," Helga said eagerly.

"I do not understand," Helene protested.

"I have spoken with the Führer," Himmler explained. "I have told this to your mother. Adolf is delighted with the news. I have never seen him so pleased. But this plot . . . it is very disturbing. We no longer know who to trust and who is a traitor to the cause. The Führer is concerned that an announcement at this time might place both you and the baby in danger. He is even afraid that without an announcement you will be in danger the moment you begin to . . . ah . . . show. There are many people who know that you went to Rastenberg, and the date. Therefore he wishes you to leave the Schloss and go to a secret place where you will be safe, and where the baby can be born. Of course, once all of the traitors have been found and eliminated, then he will immediately make it public that you are the mother of his child. There is even talk of marriage . . ."

"Marriage," Helga breathed. "To the Führer!"

Helene gave her an impatient glance. "Is there no message from Adolf?" she asked.

"I have given you his instructions."

"I was thinking of something personal."

"He sends you his love, of course. But he is very busy. Busier than he has ever been in his life before."

"We are to go with you," Helga said eagerly. "There is nothing to be afraid of."

"Where is this place we are being sent?" Helene demanded.

27

"Somewhere safe," Himmler promised. "You will be accompanied by my most faithful people."

"May I take Ilse as well?"

Himmler's eyes were as usual hidden from view. "Why not, as she is your maid?" he asked.

Helene supposed they were being sent to Bertschegaden as they were driven south into the Bavarian Alps. She would have enjoyed that. It would have given her a sense of confirmation, that Adolf really was pleased about the baby – she had only Himmler's word for it at present.

But instead of Hitler's own home, they were taken to a remote farmhouse set in a high valley. It was really very beautiful, far removed from the war – if they saw planes from time to time, these were always on their way to or from some other target – and still an active concern, operated by the elderly farmer, his wife, and two French prisoners of war who seemed quite happy with their situation. The arrival of three women, no husbands, and four SS guards caused some consternation at first, but everyone soon settled down. Herr Bendt and his wife were naturally curious as to the reasons for two obviously aristocratic ladies being boarded with them, and to be so well guarded, but as the guards did not know the reason themselves and neither Helga nor Helene were willing to reveal it, they and their neighbours were forced to be patient. Although as Helene's stomach began to swell, it all became quite obvious, even if no one dared make any suggestions as to who the father might be.

Ilse was most intrigued of all. Undoubtedly she had observed several months ago that her mistress was no longer menstruating, but had been mystified because there had been no great explosion of either joy or anger on the part of Helga, and equally because there had been no immediate preparation of a layette – this had actually been on Himmler's instructions.

Thus she had been forced to wait until the facts of her

28

mistress's lapse from grace became known. To be treated like royal prisoners had taken her breath away, and left her at once frightened and discontented, as Helene still refused to talk about it . . . or the father.

Clearly Ilse presumed it was Himmler himself.

For Helene it was a trying period. It would have been, anyway. She was a socialite, and had always indulged herself in parties, the theatre and opera, the good things of life. Even at the Schloss there had been her horses and her dogs. At the farm there was nothing. There were horses and dogs, to be sure, but these belonged to other people, and in any event riding was out of the question. Thus she was left with just her mother for company, and throughout her life Helene had always endeavoured never to spend more than half an hour a day in Helga's company. She missed her father badly. Sometimes she thought she was going mad.

They were both depressed by the news, which went from bad to worse that summer as the Allies surged across France and the Russians surged across Poland.

"Where are these secret weapons Adolf promised?" Helga asked.

The launching of the V rockets on London of course made a great splash, but did not seem to be having the slightest effect on the Allied war effort or on their will to fight.

"He should send them against the Russians," Helga complained.

There was no telephone at the farm. The only news from the outside world, apart from what they could pick up on the radio, came when the guards were changed, which happened every month. But the guards knew as little about what was going on as the two women, and nothing at all about anything which might have interested Helene. They could tell her that the Führer seemed to have recovered from the injuries he had received in the explosion, and the radio told them that the search for the conspirators was continuing, with many arrests and executions already having taken place. These included some very high-ranking people indeed.

"I must get down to the village and telephone Himmler," Helene decided.

But the guards would not let her.

"Do you realise we are prisoners?" she stormed at Helga.

"Now, my dear girl, we are doing what the Führer wishes," Helga insisted.

"Are we? Or are we doing what Himmler wants?" Helene inquired savagely.

"Whichever it is, we mustn't complain," Helga insisted. "We are safe, we are well looked after, and your time will soon be here."

That at the least was true, as the autumn drew on. Winter was early, and by mid-December there was heavy snow. It was then that the news was broadcast about the huge German offensive in the Ardennes, which would drive the British and the Americans out of the war and enable Hitler to concentrate all Germany's strength on dealing with the Russians. They celebrated with a hearty dinner, too hearty, because next day Helga was taken ill. She just gave a little groan and collapsed, quite without warning, and then, although she still breathed, couldn't speak or move.

Herr and Frau Bendt put her to bed, looking very anxious.

"We must send for the doctor from the village," Helene told the SS sergeant.

"That is forbidden," the sergeant said.

"My mother has had a stroke, you great oaf," Helene shouted. "She is paralysed. She could be dying."

"There will be a doctor," the sergeant told her. "Soon."

To her surprise, he was right. The next day an SS doctor arrived, his car slithering through the snow.

"Oh, thank God!" Helene cried.

He frowned at her. He was a precise young man with a pencil moustache. "You have not been well, Fraulein?"

"Me? I am as fit as a horse. It is my mother. I think it is a stroke. She cannot move."

The doctor hurried to Helga's room, took her pulse, peered into her eyes. "Yes," he said. "A stroke. She is paralysed."

"Then we must get her to the hospital, as quickly as possible."

"That is a waste of time. She will not recover. She has had a very severe stroke. I do no think she can live more than a couple of days."

"But she is my mother!" Helene shouted.

"I know, and I am sorry, Fraulein. But there it is. Anyway, it is not possible to go anywhere in this snow and ice. I was lucky to get here myself. But now that I am here, there is nothing for you to worry about."

"Nothing . . . my God! What are you doing here, anyway?"

"I have come to deliver your baby," he said.

Helga died that afternoon. She had been unable to speak since her stroke, and Helene did not know if she had been aware of what was going on. Her eyes had remained open, but they had not shown any response to stimuli, not even when the doctor had pricked her arm with his needle.

Helene had never felt so alone. Her mother was dead. Ilse did nothing but weep, noisily. She had no idea where any of her brothers were, or her father. She had had no word from either Hitler or Himmler . . . and yet, Himmler must have been very aware of her and the date to have sent a doctor to her in this remote place.

"You must try to relax," Doctor Zeitler told her.

"Relax," she snorted. "When is my poor mother to be buried?"

31

"We can do it now."

"Just like that? In the back yard? There must be a priest."

Zeitler considered.

"There is a priest in the village," Helene told him. "It is a Catholic community."

"We will have to wait for the snow to melt," Zeitler decided. "We will put her in one of the outbuildings for the time being. In this weather she will be perfectly preserved."

Helene stared at him in horror, but he seemed unaware that he might have said anything distasteful. "Now please, Fraulein, it is time to think of your baby."

"How can I think of my baby with my mother lying dead?"

"You must. It is a very important baby."

"Do you know how important?"

"No, Fraulein."

"Then why are you here?"

"I am acting on instructions from Herr Himmler, Fraulein."

She wondered if he was lying. But she was glad he was there, and more so when she began to have labour pains on New Year's Day.

"It is too soon," she gasped.

Zeitler nodded. "According to the dates I have been given, you are premature. Probably your mother's death is affecting you. But all will be well, Fraulein, Have faith in me."

Amazingly, she did. He was terribly efficient, put Frau Bendt and Ilse to work as well as the two Frenchmen, and although Helene took a long time and thought she was going to die, delivered her of a daughter on the afternoon of 2 January 1945.

"A daughter?" She was aghast.

"She is a strong, healthy babe," Zeitler assured her.

A daughter, Helene thought. What on earth can Adolf

32

do with a daughter, at such a time? But then her natural optimism surfaced. As Himmler had pointed out, Hitler had never fathered before. But he had by her. Therefore he could do so again.

Her milk came in twenty-four hours, and Zeitler was pleased. "There is some sign of a thaw," he said. "I must leave."

"And I must bury my mother."

He nodded. "I will see to the priest."

She held his hand. "I thank you, for everything."

"I was obeying orders, Fraulein."

"Then you will be reporting to Herr Himmler?"

"Yes. I will tell him all is well."

Clearly he also thought the child was Himmler's own.

"If I give you a letter for him, will you deliver it?"

"Of course, Fraulein."

Zeitler left two days later, and that same day Father Jorge came up from the village. Herr Bendt had already prepared a coffin – a very plain wooden box – and in this Helga's body was placed. Out in the woodshed, as Zeitler had promised, she was as well-preserved as the day she had died. The guards had the two Frenchmen dig a grave on the slope of the hill looking down into the valley, and there she was buried.

Helene insisted upon attending, although she still felt somewhat weak. She also felt more lonely than ever before in her life. News was trickling in that the Ardennes offensive had failed, and the German armies were being hurled back to the Rhine.

Helene asked Father Jorge to come back with her to the farmhouse and have a glass of wine. She closed the bedroom door very carefully and sat with the babe in her arms, while Father Jorge sipped his wine and waited, somewhat apprehensively.

"A funeral, and then a christening," Helene said.

"That is God's way, my child," Jorge said.

"Will you do this for me?"

33

"Of course. As soon as you are strong enough to come down to the church."

"They will not let me come down to the church, Father."

He frowned. "You are a prisoner?"

"Can you not see that?"

He pinched his lip. "I do not understand."

Enemies of the state in Nazi Germany were not usually kept in extreme comfort in remote farmhouses.

"It is my child," Helene said.

"I do not understand," Jorge repeated.

"I shall call her Geli," Helene said.

"A pretty name."

Indeed, she thought; he does not understand. "Father," she said, "may I regard this as a confessional?"

"If you wish it to be so, my child."

Helene drew a long breath. "Then Father, forgive me, for I have sinned . . ."

Telling Father Jorge seemed to lift an enormous weight from Helene's mind, even if the poor man was clearly terrified by her revelation. She felt she had a friend, or at least a confessor.

Geli was christened a fortnight later. But by then the fronts were collapsing east and west, and even south, as the Allied armies stormed through Italy. Helene became quite desperate. Had Zeitler delivered her letter to Himmler? In it she had begged to be allowed to be re-united with the Führer. Now she wished even more to be at his side, but February drifted into March without a word. When next the guards were changed, she gave the sergeant another letter.

The new guards were alarming. They were very young, and very nervous. They told Helene and the Bendts of the gradual breakdown of civilisation in the Reich, and certainly, with their undernourished bodies and ill-fitting uniforms, as well as the way they tore at their food, they hardly suggested the elite of the German fighting forces.

"The Russians are marching on Berlin," they told her. "The British and the Americans are marching on the Elbe."

"Where is the Führer?"

"He is in Berlin. He will defend it to the last."

And I am here, Helene thought desperately. She began to think of escaping. But she knew that was impossible. Geli was only two months old, and she had no money, no passport . . . nothing to see her to safety. And in any event, where was safety?

She could do nothing but wait . . . until on 10 April Himmler himself appeared at the farmhouse.

"Heinrich!" Helene drew him into her bedroom. "What an anniversary."

He gave his cold smile, and stood above the cot to look down at the baby.

"Do any of these people know the name of her father?"

"No," she said. "No one."

He glanced at her. "What about the priest who christened her?"

"Of course not," Helene lied.

"He has disappeared."

"Father Jorge?"

"Yes. He suddenly left his church, three weeks ago, and has not been seen since. Why should he do this?"

"I have no idea," Helene said, heart pounding.

"He will be found," Himmler said. "He will be shot. But you . . . you must leave this place. Immediately."

"To join the Führer?" Her heart pounded harder than ever.

"That will be impossible. The Führer is in Berlin."

"Then that is where I wish to go."

"Berlin is surrounded by the Russians. Do you wish to be raped by a Russian?"

"I wish to be with the father of my child."

"It is the Führer's decision to remain in Berlin. It is my responsibility to look after the safety of your child

35

and yourself. This country is in a state of collapse. I do not know what the outcome will be. But I do know that the Reich will rise again. It always has before, and it will do so again. When that happens, Hitler's daughter must have a part to play. It is your duty to ensure that she lives to play that part. Now, I have here a passport for you and some money. My guards will take you to the Swiss border, and you will cross, and go to Zurich. There you will call on a man named Walther Schmidt. I will give you the address. He is my personal agent, and is expecting you. He will finance you and see that you reach a place of safety. There you will wait until you receive a summons from the Führer, or from me, or from someone else you know you can trust. I give you this nut-cracker. You see it is a brass figure of an alligator, made in two parts. It is unusually made, and the parts fit together as you see, their edges serrated. You will take one half, and I will keep the other. The messenger who will summon you to return to Germany and your proper place will bring you the other half. Is this understood?"

"Yes," she said. "But I do not wish to leave Germany. I wish to go to Berlin. That is my proper place, now. At the side of the Führer. I insist upon it, Heinrich."

Himmler's smile was colder than ever. "That is not possible, Helene. The Führer does not want you in Berlin. He has sent for Eva. I believe he intends to marry her."

1992

THE DAUGHTER

CHAPTER ONE

In April, the wind sweeping down from the Black Sea was cold and brought with it a succession of rainsqualls. Dark water-curtains drifted across the Bosporus, obscuring the Asiatic shore, rattling on the bridge named after Mehmet the Conqueror and then shrouding the fortress he had built, five and a half centuries ago, to assist him in wresting the city from the Byzantines.

Then it had been called Constantinople. Now it was Istanbul.

The rain splattered across the Topkapi Museum and the Blue Mosque, raised echoes within the vast interior of St Sophia, and hurried on down Ordu Street, encompassing on its way the Mosque of Suleiman and the university. The secluded harbour of the Golden Horn became a place of hooting sirens as the ferry-boat captains and fishermen peered into the rain mist.

Istanbul shivered.

In the environs of the city, beyond the ruined Wall of Theodosius, it felt even colder. Geli Littler hugged her coat more tightly around herself as she made her way up the pathway between the neat gravestones in the little Christian cemetery. It was an expensive coat, and she wore expensive boots: both were at the moment sadly tarnished by the weather. Geli Littler was forty-seven years old, a slender, attractive woman, just below medium height, with dark hair and somewhat clipped features. Her clothes and perfume, the confidence with which she walked, the fact that she was in the Christian cemetery at all, delineated her as exactly what she was: a member of the ever-expanding expatriot business community based in Istanbul. Her exact nationality would have been less easy to determine, for she spoke several languages fluently. A look in her handbag would have discovered a Swiss passport, but that, too, would hardly have been conclusive.

Geli Littler was, in fact, almost as Turkish as anyone she passed on the street; she had lived here ever since she could remember.

She reached the headstone she sought, stooped to place flowers on the grave, then straightened again, the rain dampening her headscarf. She gazed at the inscription, which was very plain: HELENE SCHMIDT, BORN 12 JULY 1920, DIED 10 APRIL 1965. Too young. But Mama had been living on borrowed time for years. That she had stayed alive just long enough to see her only daughter successfully married had been an act of will.

"Bless you, Mama," Geli said, and walked back to her car. She wondered if Mama was still afraid.

Mama had died of cancer. So many people died of cancer. But Geli had always felt that the cells which went mad within the body needed an outside prod, some kind of mental catalyst to start the destructive process. Many doctors agreed with her that cancer was often the result of a lengthy period of stress. Mama had lived in fear all of her life. Fear of discovery, of somehow being dragged back to Germany to face anger and humiliation, perhaps even trial. With every year Mama's paranoia had grown, even as she had studied every newspaper coming out of Germany, seeking the death of anyone who might have shared her secret. Eventually there had been only one known to be left, Walther Schmidt. There was still only one.

All the others had perished, or might reasonably be supposed to have done so. Himmler had committed suicide. Both Zeitler and Father Jorge had simply disappeared in the chaos that had been Germany in 1945: even Mama had eventually recognised that they must be dead. Nothing had been heard of the farmer and his wife, or the two French prisoners-of-war. After forty-seven years surely they too must be dead, and in any event, none of those *knew*. They could only suspect.

Even Papa, when he had gone through that weird and somehow blasphemous ceremony of marriage with Eva immediately before killing himself, had apparently died without telling anyone, even his new bride, about his daughter.

Mama, of course, had developed a theory about that which had made her more bitter than ever: she was certain that Himmler had never told the Führer at all, had been keeping her, and her baby, a secret for his own personal use at some future date . . . and had been overtaken by the total collapse of German civilisation.

Mama could well have been right. But it had been backwards thinking, surely, for her to regret it. Had Himmler told the Führer, she might have been summoned to Berlin and died there, with her baby, as the Russians had swarmed through the stricken city.

In which case, Geli thought as she got behind the wheel of the Volvo estate, I wouldn't be here . . . and neither would the children. Horrible thought.

Each death had been a source of relief to Mama, yet each had left her wondering, and worrying, about those who might not have died. Of them all, only Ilse, the maid, had in any way troubled her. It had been Himmler's decision that they should abandon Ilse when they had fled for Switzerland. Ilse had wept and begged to be taken with them, so Mama had said. Mama had had to harden her heart and refuse, relieved because Himmler had promised to take care of the girl. It was only later that Mama had started to worry just what that sinister phrase "take care of" might have meant.

Then it had been too late.

Having been brought up in Istanbul, Geli did not find Turkish driving habits the least alarming. Traffic signals were a comparatively recent innovation in the city, and a

41

large proportion of the population still seemed to think the multi-coloured lights had been added as decoration rather than for any functional purpose. One drove with one hand resting on the horn, and one's eyes sliding back and forth, and up to the rear view mirror. Concentration was the key. To have a car more than a year old in Istanbul without a dent in it somewhere was a sign of extreme ability. Geli was proud of her driving; Hans had put a dent in his new Mercedes within the first week after its delivery.

But then she was through the city and driving north on the road beside the Bosporus. The Littlers lived at Telibaba, almost on the Black Sea. It was quiet there even if, at this time of the year, the wind seemed to bring with it all the chill of the Russian steppes. Now it was possible to drive quite fast behind the whirring windscreen wipers, and to relax.

Geli wondered if there would be the usual telegram from Walther. He never forgot the date of Mama's death, just as he never forgot *her* birthday, either. He was actually more of a father to her than anyone, even if she had only seen him a few times during the past twenty years.

She had always known him as Uncle Walther, and she could first remember him visiting Mama in the 1950s, when she had been a very little girl and they had lived in a small apartment in the very centre of Istanbul. She had never been sure of the exact relationship between Mama and Uncle Walther. Mama had been a beautiful woman before the cancer had reduced her to a shell, and Uncle Walther had been a handsome man thirty-five years ago. There had only been one bedroom in the apartment and when Uncle Walther visited, Geli had been required to sleep on the living-room settee while Uncle Walther had shared the bedroom with Mama. So almost certainly they had been lovers. Uncle Walther had certainly been their sole means of support, although Geli now knew that the money came not from him personally, but from an investment trust set up for her mother, and inherited by herself, in a Swiss bank. Apparently she could never touch the capital, but the income had been sufficient to keep her very comfortably, and it had grown to match inflation. As a lawyer, Uncle Walther had managed the trust.

He had never admitted to her who had set it up – but she had her suspicions, even if she always accepted the monthly cheque.

Uncle Walther was now eighty, and retired from his law firm. But he still managed the trust. It was a disturbing thought that this could not last much longer. Would there then have to be someone else in the secret? No doubt his nephew, who had the same name and was now the senior partner.

That thought would have driven Mama half mad with worry, but Geli really did not think it mattered, at this distance in time, save that Uncle Walther, as a lifelong admirer and supporter of Mama, and as administrator of the trust, had to have been a Nazi sympathiser. And probably still was. But even that was surely irrelevant, after forty-seven years . . . except in the context of the Littler household.

Geli drove the Volvo into the garage beneath the house and listened to the doors sliding shut behind her. She got out and went up the internal stairs into the utility room.

"Oh, madam, you are very wet," Shiera remarked.

"I will change. Has the post been?"

"Yes, madam," said the Turkish woman. "And there is a telegram."

"Ah!" Geli took the envelope, slit it open with her thumb.

"THINKING OF YOU WALTHER"

She went up the next flight of stairs to her bedroom, put the slip of paper in one of the drawers of her bureau. Hans would of course know there had been a telegram from Walther, because there always was one on the anniversary of Mama's death, but he would not wish to speak of it or

43

to know what was in it, and Geli had no desire to upset her husband.

Hans had no doubt at all that Walther Schmidt had been either the lover or the secret second husband of Helene, which was why Geli bore his name before her marriage. They certainly weren't blood relations.

Hans was fifteen years older than Geli, and could thus remember so much more of Nazi Germany: Geli's memory did not begin until 1950, and her knowledge of the period was based upon books and upon what Mama, poor dreadfully lonely and frightened Mama, had told her. No doubt a psychiatrist would claim that Helene had gone a long way towards ruining her daughter's life by those confidences. But Geli had always possessed a strong streak of practicality and pragmatism, which was her greatest strength. She did not believe in psychiatry, but rather in the business of getting on with life. If it was exciting to think that Hitler had been her father, it was both salutary and satisfactory to realise that he was dead, as were all the others – and she was alive, fit and well, a successful wife and mother. If to maintain herself in that happy state she had to keep an enormous secret from her husband and her children . . . that was the hand fate had given her to play.

And she knew it was a hand that had to be played to the end. Every time she needed to go to Mama's safe deposit box in the bank in Istanbul, and saw the half of the brass crocodile, she was tempted to throw it away. But she never had. That was the tangible reminder of the secret which must accompany her to her grave.

And if her secret had led her to turn in upon herself, to shun even an intimate woman friend who might one day have found out the truth, that too she was prepared to accept until the day of her death. Only her family mattered; the protection of them from the knowledge of their own ancestry.

And the preservation of the love and respect of her husband.

Hans claimed – and she believed him – to have always been an anti-Nazi, as had his parents. He had been conscripted as a boy of fourteen in 1944, but had used the first opportunity to surrender to the Allies. That had not saved him from being separated from his family and nearly starving, but the contacts he had made had taken him eventually to Istanbul and a successful career, beginning as clerk in Schiller and Company, then as shareholder, and finally as principal shareholder and Managing Director.

He had accomplished all of these things at a very early age, and had already been top of the tree when he had proposed to her, twenty-five years ago. His decision had caused some ripples within the large German community in Turkey. Having finished her studies Geli had gone to work in Schiller and Company as a stenographer, thus it was from his own office floor that Hans Littler had plucked his so much younger bride.

There had immediately arisen the question of Geli's antecedents. Mama had then lived in Istanbul for twenty years, and was well-known to everyone, while at the same time *known* to no one; even more than her daughter had she shunned friendships. She had told a reasonable version of the truth from the beginning, that her husband had died in the war and that she and her babe had been fortunate enough to escape Germany and find refuge with an uncle in Switzerland. Keeping secrets in Istanbul was a difficult business. If no one had ever been able to penetrate Helene Schmidt's German background, everyone knew that she received money each month from a bank in Zurich, and that she lived quite well, if not extravagantly. Hans Littler had obviously wished to know more.

But by then Mama had already been very clearly dying, and Hans was too much of a gentleman to make her last weeks more painful than necessary. He could tell that she was relieved to have her daughter married, and to a successful man who was also a German, and that was gratifying. But he could also tell that the whole concept of Geli being married at all, being forced to experience

45

the immense intimacy of a husband, had also frightened the dying woman.

Thus his questions to Geli had been slightly more probing, but here again he had been hindered by being desperately in love with this so attractive young woman, and by Geli's transparent honesty – something she had cultivated since that unforgettable day Mama had told her who she really was.

"I never knew my father," she explained. "He was in Berlin at the end, and I was only three months old when Mama escaped to Switzerland."

"Berlin," Hans had said thoughtfully. "He was a soldier?"

"An officer, Mama always said," Geli had replied.

"And his name was Schmidt?"

"That is the name on my passport," Geli had said.

There had to be hundreds of German officers named Schmidt, and Hans knew about Mama's income, if not whence it arose. He had not pursued the matter. Obviously, if Geli had been born just as the Nazi Empire had collapsed, she could not have been a member of the Party herself, and if her mother and father probably had been, one was dead and the other dying. There are few men who can resist the temptation to take a young girl and remould her in an image they have chosen. Hans assumed he had done that, and Geli was content that it should be so.

The temptation to tell him the truth had, from time to time, been almost irresistible. Partly it had been caused by her reluctance to have *any* secrets from her husband. He had been good and loving to her, and she felt she had been a good and loving wife in return. They had three splendid children and an enviable lifestyle. But Geli could not help but wonder if she would have had any of those things, or have them now, if Hans ever discovered she was Hitler's daughter.

Equally, however, she had been tempted by loneliness. Having a secret is of no great use unless someone else

46

knows you possess it. Uncle Walther filled that requirement, of course. But Uncle Walther was eighty. She realised that the thought of his death quite frightened her, and hastily rejected it. She had seen what fear could do to her mother.

Geli had a hot shower and put on dry clothes, a pants suit, went downstairs for her early evening aperitif, prepared expertly by Shiera, and waited for the arrival home of the children. She sat in the windowseat and looked through the enormous sheet of plate glass at the rainswept Bosporus. She loved her home and had spent a lot of time, and some money, on making it exactly as she wished. She went in for modern furniture and even more modern paintings; her choice of wall paints was for deep colour rather than pastel shades. She supposed there might be some psychological link with her past in that . . . which made it the more disturbing that her children reckoned the past had come full circle, to their advantage.

Paul was first home. He was the tallest, although the younger of the two brothers; he took after the Uderstadt side of the family, although with the Littler colouring. Just under six feet tall, with fair hair and twinkling eyes, he might have been a changeling, and perhaps for that was her favourite. He attended the university and was hoping to be a schoolmaster. But not in Turkey, in view of recent events.

It was a looming crisis which would have to be resolved some time quite soon.

"Still raining," he commented, and went off to change.

Helene and Herrmann arrived together; they were very close, and Helene invariably drove into the city with her older brother. These were more recognisably Geli's children. Helene, just seventeen and still at school, was dark and pretty; her already busy social life suggested that it could only be a short time before she found a permanent partner. But she too wanted to go "home", as they called Germany, even if none of them had

47

been born there, just as soon as she completed her studies.

Herrmann, twenty-three, was the shortest as well as the eldest. He was also the most disturbing, in that there were distinct facial resemblances to his grandfather. But as long as he did not grow a moustache only Geli saw them. Like Paul, he was still at university, which they attended as day students as their home was so close.

"I had a meeting with Herr Bennigsen today," he announced enthusiastically.

"What about?"

"There is definitely a place for me in his firm. In Stuttgart."

Geli gave an involuntary shudder.

"Mama?" Helene put her arm round her shoulder.

"I think I must have caught a chill at the cemetery," Geli said.

"You must take more care." Helene was the only one of the children who in any way understood how desolated her mother always felt on the anniversary of her grandmother's death.

"So I will be going home," Herrmann said. "As soon as I get my degree."

"Oh, yes? Have you spoken with your father?"

"He has raised no objection. He understands. I am German. Being born in Turkey is irrelevant. Our re-united Germany is going to dominate Europe. That is where the future lies."

"I seem to remember certain people saying that once before."

"Oh, really, Mama, that is old hat."

"There are still Nazi sympathisers in Germany," Geli said fiercely. "As there are in France and England. You read about them every day."

"So?" Herrmann demanded. "Then surely every good German should return to his fatherland and help to combat these people."

48

Geli sighed. "We will talk about it with your father, when he comes home."

*

"Herr Brauer to see you, Herr Allendt," said the secretary.

Joachim Allendt looked up from the copy he was studying and smiled at her. Inga was a pretty girl, with masses of yellow hair. A very Aryan young woman.

He fully intended to bed her in the not too distant future, but had just not yet found the time. Now his day was spoiled. What moment of weakness had led him to give Gustave Brauer an appointment? The fellow was always so vehement, so certain he had discovered the secret of something or other.

Joachim Allendt was a large, stout, falsely jolly man; he earned his living from depicting the misery of others, and thoroughly enjoyed it. Gustave Brauer was one of the few people who had the power to depress him.

"Well," he said, "you had better show him in."

Inga departed and returned a moment later. "Herr Brauer," she said, and closed the door behind him.

Allendt had known Brauer for many years. The time had been when Brauer was one of the leading investigative journalists in West Germany. He had always chosen to work freelance, but there were few newspapers or magazines, from *Der Spiegel* down, which had not been happy to receive an offered story from the typewriter of Gustave Brauer.

Then had come one divorce, and another, and a general malaise had crept in, accentuated by the drinking . . . Brauer had become an embarrassment. Yet, for old times' sake . . .

"Gustave, how good to see you." Allendt came round the huge steel and chrome desk to shake hands, gestured to the steel and chrome armchairs with their black leather cushions. "Sit down, my dear fellow, sit down. You'll take a drink?"

"Well . . ." Tall and thin, with a drooping moustache

49

which matched his drooping raincoat and generally drooping figure, so oddly set off by the gleaming eyes above, Brauer drooped in his chair.

"I am having one." Allendt returned behind his desk, opened his drinks drawer, took out a bottle of Hine Antique, quarter-filled two goblets and pushed one towards the journalist. "To success." He allowed the alcohol to brush his lips, set down the glass. "You spoke of a scoop."

Brauer drank, deeply. "The scoop of the second half of the century."

"Oh, yes? You have information that China is not going to take over Hong Kong?"

Braur gave a contemptuous wave of his hand. "Is that of any importance to us? I am speaking of Germany."

"Well?"

Brauer finished his brandy, set the goblet on the desk as he leaned forward. Allendt obligingly refilled it.

"You will know that I am working on a biography of Himmler," he said.

"I did not know," Allendt confessed. "For which publisher?"

"I do not work on commissions," Brauer said scornfully. "This will be the definitive study on one of the most evil men of our time, so cunningly concealed beneath that mild chicken-farmer's exterior."

"I seem to have read that somewhere before."

Brauer ignored the jibe. "In the course of my researches, I have come into possession of Himmler's secretary's appointments diary, from the summer of 1944 to the end."

A frown flitted across Allendt's face, then he gave an elaborate sigh and raised his eyes to heaven. "Really, Gustave. Is that what you are expecting me to buy? An appointments diary? After that fiasco with Hitler's so-called diary?"

"This diary is genuine. But it is not for sale," Brauer said.

Allendt gazed at him in disbelief.

"Nor would it be of the least interest to a tabloid . . ."

50

again contempt crept into Brauer's voice, "such as yours. It is nothing but a list of dates and appointments, trains caught and people seen."

"Then why are you here?" Allendt began to grow irritated.

"It is how various diary entries relate to other pieces of information I have obtained that is interesting," Brauer said, taking a very dog-eared-looking desk diary from his briefcase. "The entry which first puzzled me was one dated the tenth of April nineteen forty-five. On that date Himmler drove into the Bavarian Alps, to a village called Nissing. He went to a farm beyond the village owned by a Herr and Frau Bendt, to see, according to his secretary's entry, HvU/b." He placed the opened book on the desk in front of Allendt.

"So?" the editor asked.

"Does that not strike you as odd, Joachim? The tenth of April nineteen forty-five? Germany was collapsing in ruins. The Allies were streaming across the plain, the Russians were at the gates of Berlin. Himmler, we know, was intriguing to assume command of the Reich. And yet he takes the trouble, and a very time-consuming drive, to seek out a certain HvU/b."

"Hm," Allendt commented. "The small 'v' is clearly a 'von'. He was conferring with some general." His voice was non-committal, but Brauer could tell he was more than just a little interested.

"In the Bavarian Alps? As far away from any actual fighting as is possible?"

"At that time Eisenhower was convinced the Reich was setting up a huge defensive bastion in those mountains. Perhaps there was some truth in it."

"But you and I know there was *no* truth in it," Brauer pointed out. "However, that entry caused me to examine the diary even more closely." He leaned over Allendt to turn the pages backwards. "Here we have the entry for the twenty-fourth of December nineteen forty-four. 'Contacted Zeitler. Unhappy, but obeys. Will be at Nissing

26th. HvU not due until second week Jan, but H does not want to take any risks.'"

"That is definitely arranging a meeting," Allendt commented.

Brauer sighed; how did someone this thick become managing editor of one of Germany's biggest newspapers? "I hunted through the files," he said. "The only Zeitler connected with Himmler was an Albert Zeitler, a gynaecologist. A pretty unpleasant character, known to have carried out experiments on live foetuses cut from their Jewish or Russian mothers. That's not relevant here. What is important is that Himmler sent Zeitler to this remote farmhouse, where this HvU was staying, to make sure all went well whenever she became due."

"You think this HvU was a woman?"

"Yes. I have a name for her as well. Helene von Uderstadt."

"I remember Uderstadt," Allendt said thoughtfully. "Industrialist. Fanatical Nazi. The Russians shot him in nineteen forty-five. And you think this HvU was his daughter."

"I am sure of it."

"Who was carrying Himmler's child? Well, who would have thought it of that dry stick? At least it will give your book some human interest. But I'm afraid it is of no great importance in the context of today's situation."

"Joachim," Brauer said, picking up and closing the diary, replacing it in his briefcase and then sitting down in front of the desk. "I do not think that Helene von Uderstadt was bearing Himmler's child."

"Don't you? Pity. It would certainly improve your book."

"You are aware, I suppose, that from time to time Hitler had young women taken to Rastenberg?"

Allendt's frown was back.

"I have obtained an almost complete list of these ladies," Brauer went on. "None of them is the least important. They visited the Führer, and then they disappeared. Save for Helene von Uderstadt."

"She was one of them?"

"Helene von Uderstadt visited Rastenberg on the night of the tenth of April nineteen forty-four. So her baby was due in the first fortnight of January nineteen forty-five. Would you like to use your calculator?"

"There is no record of Hitler ever fathering a child."

"Is there any record that he *couldn't*? I would say it is more likely that he did not wish a child, and that any woman he impregnated was either forced to abort or was done away with. But it is my opinion that this Helene von Uderstadt did not go to Hitler when she discovered her condition. I think she went to Himmler, I can't say why, and he buried her away up in the Bavarian Alps. Why? Until she, or her child, could be of use to him? Himmler certainly knew that Hitler's physical condition, the amount of drugs he was pumping into himself, or were being pumped into him by that quack Morel, meant he wasn't going to live very long, even if Germany had won the war."

"It is all very circumstantial."

"Yes? Well, here are three more 'circumstantial' pieces of supportive evidence. Himmler went out to this farm at Nissing on the tenth of April nineteen forty-five, a year after Helene von Uderstadt's visit to Rastenberg."

"Pure coincidence."

"It may amuse you to think so, if you happen to believe in coincidences. I do not. Two: Helene von Uderstadt bore a striking resemblance to Angela Raubel."

"I do not find anything very startling in that. Going by her photographs, Geli Raubel was a rather typical example of a good-looking Bavarian brunette."

"Indeed? Finally, I went to the Nissing parish church. It had survived the war intact, although the parish priest, a Father Jorge, disappeared in nineteen forty-five and there, Joachim, I found the birth recorded." He produced a notebook and read. "'Helene von Uderstadt, spinster, female child, born 2 January 1945, christened 5 January 1945' – somewhat unseemly haste, would you not say? – 'Names Geli Helga.'"

Allendt stroked his chin. "There is no mention of the father's name."

"For God's sake, Joachim, would you expect there to be?"

"The second of January is too early to fit your theory."

"The child was premature, and I will tell you why: there is an entry in the death register of the Nissing church recording the death of Helga von Uderstadt, wife of Johann von Uderstadt, in Nissing, mind you, on the twenty-sixth of December nineteen forty-four, aged fifty-three. Helene's mother was with her at the farm, and it was her death brought on the premature delivery."

"Fanciful. There is not one shred of direct evidence save that this woman visited Hitler once."

"The name, Joachim. The name." Brauer raised his hand and began ticking off the fingers. "One, it is generally acknowledged that if Hitler ever loved any woman, it was Geli Raubel. Correct?"

"It is generally acknowledged." Allendt agreed.

"Two. When Geli killed herself, his chances of domestic happiness were finished, except with people like Eva Braun. Correct?"

"There is no proof of that."

Brauer refused to be distracted. "Three. When Hitler needed to spend long periods out at Rastenberg, he sent for company as and when he needed it. Four. We need not go into the question of how many of them got pregnant. The fact is, only one ever gave birth, so far as we know. And how do we know it was Hitler's child? The name. Geli. Geli is not a name. It is a diminutive, for Angela. Helene von Uderstadt knew that, and she was determined to make sure Hitler knew it too."

"Only it would appear he never did know it."

"Because of Himmler."

54

Allendt drank some of his brandy. "That story is too nebulous to print."

"Suppose I were to produce the girl? Or woman, I suppose she would be now."

"After forty-seven years? Yes, I would say you could describe her as a woman. And you think you can find her, after forty-seven years? She would almost certainly have perished, either in nineteen forty-five or forty-six. Things were very bad. You should be able to remember."

"I do. They were very bad here in Germany, and anywhere else the war had been fought. But not in Switzerland."

"Switzerland?"

Brauer turned some more pages of the diary, presented it once again. "'22 April 1945. S reports HvU/b arrived Z safely.'"

"S?"

"I would say that is Walther Schmidt, a Zurich lawyer. He apparently handled various matters, including the investment of funds, for the SS in general, and Himmler in particular. It is the obvious place for Himmler to send Uderstadt and her daughter. We know *he* was himself trying to escape to Switzerland when he was captured. Obviously he planned to join them there."

"And you think you can trace this Walther Schmidt? It is a very common name."

"I think I can trace him."

"How?"

Brauer actually smiled. "I have an address for him. Or at least the address he was using in nineteen forty-five. He is probably still living there if he is alive. It will certainly provide a starting point."

"The address is in that diary?"

"Yes."

Allendt stared at him for several seconds. "Show me."

Brauer's smile widened. "After you have bought my services and paid for them, Joachim."

Allendt considered for a few moments. Then he asked,

"You think this Helene von Uderstadt and her daughter are still in Switzerland?"

"That I cannot say. The mother would be seventy now. But the daughter will only be forty-seven. If she survived the end of the war, there is every possibility that she is still alive. And if she is, I can find her. I know I can."

"Then do so. Until you do, and can prove who she is, there is no story."

"I agree. But as I have said, I will need financing."

"Ah. How much?"

"I cannot say. If she is not in Switzerland but has fled someplace else, it may be quite expensive."

"You wish me, Gustave, to give you an open-ended cheque? In the present economic climate? And for you to drink yourself to death?"

"Joachim, if I can produce Hitler's daughter . . ."

"It will be a great scoop. I agree. But it is the longest shot in history. Why has she not come forward before?"

"Would you, were the Führer your father? Anyway, she may be ignorant of that fact."

"And you propose to enlighten her. I am sorry, Gustave. The whole thing sounds like a cock and bull story to me. If you would like to leave that diary with me, so that I can make one or two investigations of my own as to its genuineness . . ."

"Do you take me for a fool?"

"I take you for what you are, a desperate man clutching at the straws of a once-great career. Be honest with me, Gustave; you would do anything to break back into the big time. But you must come up with something better than this. I have made you an offer. Let me have the diary, and if it stands up to my investigations I will offer you a modest financing to find this woman."

Brauer put the diary back into his briefcase. "If I let that diary go, I have nothing."

Allendt leaned back in his chair. "You are saying that you do not trust me."

"I am saying that I do not intend to let that diary

out of my sight. I am quite willing to work with your investigators, although they will only be going over ground I have already covered."

"You do not trust me," Allendt said again. "And yet you expect me to trust you. Tell me something, Gustave: how many people have you aproached with this story?"

"Approached. Well . . ." Brauer finished his drink.

"I see," Allendt said. "You have attempted to sell this story all over Germany. Is that not the truth?"

"Well . . ."

"And at last you have come to me. Why is that, Gustave? I will tell you why. None of the quality papers or magazines will buy your absurd theory, so you come to me because I am reputed to have, shall we say, 'right wing' views. You think I am a soft touch. Well, you are wrong. I am not a soft touch. I think you had better leave."

"I intend to." Brauer stood up. "You have just thrown away a big opportunity, Joachim. I will find someone who is more interested."

"You do that," Allendt said. He did not rise to see Brauer out. He waited for five minutes, gazing at the closed door. Then he picked up the office telephone. "Has that man left, Inga?"

"Oh, yes, Herr Allendt."

"Then give me my private line."

"Yes, Herr Allendt."

Allendt listened to the click, then punched out the number himself. "Hello? I would like to speak with Frau Bruening, please. It is very important."

When Brauer left the newspaper building, he headed for the Liebe Bar. He did this instinctively because he had always drunk in this bar, as did most journalists in the city, and he was always treated as some kind of legend there. Well, he supposed he was. But legends needed sustenance as much as real people. Just as they needed money, and support.

"Your usual, Herr Brauer?"

57

Brauer nodded, waited for the brandy to be poured and retreated to one of the booths. He felt sick. Allendt had been his last hope; the scoop he was sure he had uncovered was simply not wanted. He had tried the best. Only the previous day Carl Uhlmann had been especially interested, and Brauer had always felt that Uhlmann, with his well-known extremist views, was a strong possibility. But after some consideration, Uhlmann had turned him down. Thus he had had to try the worst. Allendt, with his scandal-mongering and his often-sleazy reportage, was about the worst there could be. But his attitude had been the same as everyone else's: there was no proof, and no one was quite sure the story would be of sufficient interest, forty-seven years afterwards, anyway.

Brauer had no doubt that it would be. He could see a book, he could see a movie. He remembered the furore caused by the Grand Duchess Anastasia . . . or not, as the case might be: they had still made a movie about her. He was talking about the daughter of one of the most infamous warlords who had ever lived. It was a story which could earn him a fortune. More important, it could earn him that fame he so desperately wanted to regain.

But to write it he had to find the woman. And to find the woman he had to have financing; at the present moment he was having difficulty with the rent, much less being able to consider a jaunt to Switzerland, and perhaps further than that.

He drank deeply, leaned back against the plush cushions and gazed at Charles Hunt, standing beside the booth. For a moment he couldn't remember the Englishman's name, although he recognised his face immediately.

"Gustave Brauer!" Hunt said.

Charles Hunt was chief European correspondent for the *London Globe*. He was young for such a responsible position, but at forty-two he had already had a distinguished career which had begun with those amazing reports from Vietnam, followed by his coup in getting into Russian-occupied Afghanistan, and out again after actually recording an interview with a Russian soldier.

Tall and powerfully built, with craggy features and heavy shoulders, he looked what he was – a one-time second row forward. Nowadays he had to watch his weight, but he did not take that too seriously. Eating well – and drinking well – went with the job.

"Charles!" Brauer extended a hand. "Good to see you. What brings you to Hamburg?"

"The Environment Conference. What are you drinking?"

"That is very kind of you. Brandy."

Hunt signalled the waitress, sat opposite. "How're things?"

As if he couldn't see at a glance, Brauer thought. Hunt's forte was observation: a threadbare suit, over-used tie and down-at-heel shoes would tell him all he needed to know.

But at the same time, the sight of Hunt's equally obvious affluence, the realisation that he worked for one of the world's great newspapers and, equally, the warmth of his greeting, had Brauer's brain ticking over at speed. It had not occurred to him to attempt to sell his story outside Germany, but the British remained fascinated by World War II: it was the last time they had dominated the international stage.

"Pretty good," he said. "Although they could soon be a whole lot better."

"Great," Hunt said, and drank some of his lager.

"But I need help with my story," Brauer said, studying him.

Hunt gazed back. "From me?"

"If you are interested."

"Try me," Hunt invited.

Brauer talked and Hunt listened. After an hour the pair of then went out to lunch together.

"Do you think your paper might be interested?"

Hunt had been looking through the diary. "Yes. I think

59

they might. I think they might certainly be interested in this diary."

"That is not for sale."

Hunt nodded. "Quite. Without it you have no leads. Okay, Gustave, I assume that if you do get at this story, you want it under your name."

"Is that so unreasonable?"

"Not unreasonable at all. It's just that, well . . ." Hunt was well known for straight talking, even if he sometimes caused offence. "It's easier to lose a reputation in this world than make one. It's even tougher to get one back."

"Meaning your people will feel I will merely drink whatever they pay me," Brauer said sadly.

"Meaning if they decide to finance this operation, they'll want one of our boys working with you."

"To steal my story."

"Now, Gustave, we can't do business with a paranoiac. You reckon the lady is in Switzerland?"

"I think she was taken to Switzerland. Whether she is still there or not, I do not know. Everything depends upon finding this man, Schmidt."

"And you have his address?"

Brauer patted his pocket.

Hunt grinned. "Which you're keeping close to your chest."

"Until there is sufficient money up front. Am I being unreasonable?"

"Not at all," Hunt agreed again. "How much?"

"Twenty-five thousand pounds, up front. All expenses. And seventy-five thousand when I deliver the goods."

"I know we live in an inflated age, old man, but that is a lot of money."

"It is a lot of story. I also wish to work with someone I can trust. And who is prepared to trust me."

Hunt nodded. "Me."

"You? My dear Charles, that would be magnificent. But . . . will they let you?"

"I'm in the happy position of being able to choose my work, unless an international crisis crops up. And it'll be a package. If my editor is prepared to fork out a hundred grand, he's got to believe it's something big. If he believes that, then I'm the man for the job. Right?"

"When will you know?"

"I'll telephone right away. Where can I find you?"

"You'd better came to my flat." Brauer wrote out the address. "Do you think they'll go for it?"

Hunt grinned. "I did. Do, I should say. Keep your fingers crossed."

"I shall." Brauer finished his brandy. "This is very important to me, Charles. A matter of life and death."

"I understand," Hunt said. "Expect me this evening. We'll have dinner together. It'll be celebrations all round."

After Hunt had left Brauer sat at the table for some time. Then he called for some writing paper, wrote a brief letter, sealed it and put it in his pocket.

He had always liked Hunt. Not everyone did. Hunt could be abrasive, he was arrogant, he could be very tough, and there were elements in his past that had left people uncertain of his politics, and indeed, his ethics. Some people regarded him as not quite trustworthy. But, Brauer thought ruefully, beggars could not be choosers. Besides, he had no doubt he could handle Hunt's idiosyncracies. He thought their chance meeting had been a very fortunate stroke. He grinned to himself: one of those coincidences in which he did not believe.

Certainly if Hunt could produce the necessary money.

He went from the restaurant to the post office to mail his letter, and thence to the bank: there was just time before it closed.

He had reached a stage in life where heavy drinking lowered a blanket over his mind, yet did not impair his essential faculties. He would not of course pass a breathalyser test, and that was as it should be: his reactions

61

were too slowed to cope with a sudden emergency. But as he didn't possess a car, that didn't matter. But the blanket did not in any way lessen his understanding of the dog-eat-dog world in which he lived, or what needed to be done to survive in it. He *might* be prepared to trust Hunt, to a certain extent, where there was so much money involved. But there were a great many totally untrustworthy men about, especially where a scoop like his was concerned.

Men such as Joachim Allendt.

The diary had been a necessary piece of armament to prove that he did have something. Now it might well have fulfilled its role, for the time being. Until the money came through.

Until then it had to be in a safe place.

Brauer was feeling sleepy by the time he got back to his flat, situated in a somewhat poor part of the city: it was all he could afford. His drowsiness was from a combination of all those brandies and a lurking elation. Why hadn't he thought of someone like Hunt before? Hunt was a go-getter, a positive man who believed that ideas, possibilities, were there to be explored, not rejected out of hand. And a man who could command an awesome amount of support: the resources of the *London Globe*.

Brauer had no doubt at all that Hunt would deliver the money. What he now needed to do was have a good nap so that his brain was in full working order when Hunt called that evening.

While he climbed the stairs he took out his latchkey. By the time he reached the landing he was out of breath, his hands trembling so that he had to steady himself by leaning against the wall, and he needed to hold the key in both hands as he pushed it into the lock.

As he did so, he was surrounded. Someone grasped the back of his raincoat, someone else threw an arm round his neck and pulled his head back, preventing him from uttering a sound. A hand reached past him as his fingers released the key, turned it and threw the door open. Still unable to speak, his mind too fuddled to understand what was happening, Brauer was thrust into the room, right across it, and then forced to his knees at the settee, his face pushed into the cushions by the iron hand on the nape of his neck.

Vaguely he heard the door close, and then hands were inside his own clothes, slipping here and there, searching him with brutal efficiency. He gasped, and inhaled perfume – it was not worn by the men holding him.

"He's clean," a man's voice said.

"Get him up," said a woman.

Just in time, Brauer thought: he was nearly out of breath. He was jerked to his feet, turned round and thrown on to the settee. His head snapped against the back and he thought he might have broken his neck.

He blinked at the people standing round him. The woman registered first. She wasn't young, in fact he thought she might be in her sixties, but she was very well groomed, tall and slender, her grey-black hair neatly waved, her face clean-fleshed and handsome. Her green eyes were cold. She was also very well dressed, in a quiet suit, and she wore that expensive perfume. She stood immediately in front of him. To either side of him there was a man, each much younger: one was in his early twenties, chunky and bearded, the other somewhat older and more heavily built. This man was now picking up the briefcase which Brauer had dropped when first attacked.

Brauer got his breath back. "Just what the hell do you think you're doing?" he demanded.

The woman glanced at him. "If he speaks again, hit him," she commanded.

The younger man moved closer.

Brauer took another deep breath, but kept his mouth shut. He wished his brain were more clear, more able to determine the situation, who and why and how . . . and what to do about it.

The man placed the briefcase on the table and the

woman went to it. "I need the key," she said. Her voice was quiet.

The other man came towards the settee. Strong hands seized Brauer's arms and twisted them behind him. The bearded man bent over him to thrust hands into his jacket pockets. Brauer kicked him on the ankle. He gave a little gasp of pain, then raised his leg very high and stamped the shoe on to Brauer's groin. Brauer gave a shriek of agony, and his body twisted to and fro while the man sat beside him and continued to go through his pockets.

"We don't want too much noise, and remember he's not very strong," the woman remarked. "I may need to speak with him."

"He's alive," the man assured her, and found the briefcase key. He threw it to the woman at the table, and remained sitting beside Brauer, staring at him. Brauer returned the stare through tear-filled eyes as the huge pain which was swelling through his entire abdomen began to subside.

The woman unlocked the case, threw up the lid, riffled through the contents.

"Yes," she said. "I will need to talk with him."

The bearded man smiled.

Hunt took a taxi to the address Brauer had given him; he didn't know the back streets all that well. He paid off the driver and climbed the stairs, nose wrinkling at the various unclean odours that surrounded him.

But twenty-five thousand pounds would enable Brauer to move. And if they could really find this woman who might or might not be the daughter of Hitler, another seventy-five could just set him up for life – Hunt certainly intended to make sure the old boy got the money if they found their quarry. He hoped that would be the case. He had always admired Brauer as a journalist, and while he recognised that his was a case of pure self-destruction, he could not escape the reflection that there but for the grace of God . . .

The naked bulb in the hall was not more than twenty-five watts, and he had to peer at the list of names to find the one he wanted. He climbed the stairs and rang the bell, waited and rang it again. Then again.

His first reaction was annoyance. Was the old fool such a lush he could not even wait in for so important a visit? Then he reflected that Brauer had known, and stated, how important a visit this would be. He rang the bell a fourth time, then went downstairs.

"I think my friend may be unwell," he told the concierge.

"That Brauer? He is always unwell. He is always drunk."

"I really would like to see him. He's expecting me."

"If he was expecting you, he would have answered the door."

"Not if he was drunk," Hunt pointed out, and laid a twenty-mark note on the counter.

The concierge took out his keys and climbed the stairs, muttering. He rang the bell, knocked and shouted. There was no response.

"He must be very drunk," he remarked.

"I think we should open the door," Hunt said. He spoke calmly but there were alarm bells jangling in his brain.

"I will hold you responsible," the concierge said, and inserted the key. The door swung inwards. "Is there anyone there?"

Hunt inhaled the various odours in the room and knew what had happened. "You had better turn on the light."

The concierge thumbed the switch, and gasped. Hunt stepped past him, stood above the body for a moment, looking down on the anguished features. He had no need to stoop and examine closely, or feel for a pulse; he had seen death too often not to recognise it instantly. He picked up the telephone.

"What are you doing?" the concierge muttered.

"Calling the police," Hunt told him.

*　　*　　*

65

Hunt sat in a corner of the room while the policemen went through their routine. He had already analysed his feelings. Firstly, there was the excitement of a newspaperman who knew he was on to something very big – but he had had no doubt of that from the beginning. Then there was the disgust that any human being, or group of human beings, could have so mistreated another, especially in the light of what his highly trained powers of observation had told him the moment he had entered the room. Then there was pity for an old man who had sought only rehabilitation and had it snatched from his grasp.

There was also anger. Many people considered Charles Hunt a cold fish because he had done so much, seen so much, experienced so much, and written so much, that getting an exclamation mark out of him, much less a superlative, was a difficult job. Well, he supposed in many ways he was indifferent to the crimes and follies of mankind, recognising that most wounds and misfortunes were self-inflicted. That could certainly be said of Gustave Brauer. But to his knowledge Brauer had never wilfully hurt a soul. Yet there he lay, his pants around his ankles, his features a mask of terrifying despair and agony . . . death had not come to Gustave Brauer with dignity, and that surely was the ultimate catastrophe that could befall any human being.

But above all, there was irritation. Presumably Gustave Brauer's murderers had obtained what they wanted before killing the old man. Therefore they were one complete march ahead of him. All he had was a name, and he shuddered to think how many Walther Schmidts there might be in Zurich – supposing the SS lawyer was still there at all. Thus they had left him with no lead, until they were caught.

And he did not even know what exactly they were after. Or who. He only knew that he had a job of work to do.

The police inspector sat beside him. "Lorenz."
"Hunt."

66

"This I know. We have met, but you do not remember me."

"I'm sorry," Hunt said.

"You are a busy man," Inspector Lorenz remarked. "As well as a famous one. So was Herr Brauer, in his day. Thus he was a friend of yours?"

"More an acquaintance," Hunt said.

"Did he know you were coming here tonight?"

"Yes."

"On business?"

"Yes."

"Would you care to tell me what this business was?"

"Frankly, Inspector . . . no."

"But it seems to have been business that interested someone else. You know that Brauer was tortured before being strangled?"

"Yes."

"Rather unpleasantly tortured?"

"Yes."

"But the concierge claims to have seen no one and heard nothing."

"There were professionals, Inspector. They just walked into the building and waited for Brauer to come home. Look at the marks round his mouth. He was gagged while pressure was applied, and then invited to speak, probably with a knife at his throat to dissuade him from shouting when the gag was taken away."

"And eventually he told them what they wanted to know. You agree with me?"

"He told them something that satisfied them. The apartment has not been searched."

Because they had found what they were looking for. Brauer's briefcase lay open on the table – the appointments diary was gone.

"Exactly," Lorenz agreed. "You keep saying them."

"There was more than one person. It needed more than one person. Besides, one was a woman."

Lorenz raised his eyebrows. "How do you know this?"

67

"The scent has faded now, but it was quite strong when I entered the room."

"You recognised the scent?"

"Adoration."

Lorenz wrote in his book. "Expensive."

"Yes."

Lorenz closed the book. "You understand, Herr Hunt, that without knowing what these people wanted from Herr Brauer, I am lacking a motive, and a policeman without a motive is like a man with a wooden leg attempting to take part in a hurdle race. You know what this motive is. I have the right to take you in for questioning."

"And I have the right to refuse to answer your questions, Inspector." Hunt smiled as he spoke. "But I want to nail Gustave's killers as much as you. He had been investigating the life of Heinrich Himmler with the view to writing a book on him, and I know he felt that he was possibly unearthing facts about people who may not have been Nazis, but who may well have had links with the Nazi Party which they would be reluctant to have publicised."

"After forty-seven years, Herr Hunt?" Lorenz was sceptical.

"Even after forty-seven years."

"And you think Herr Brauer was tortured to reveal some of this information?"

"Yes."

"After forty-seven years, so to kill a man?" Lorenz was more sceptical yet. "But you and he were working together. Therefore you have the information yourself."

"No, I do not," Hunt told him. "Herr Brauer mentioned certain names and possibilities to me, nothing more. And none of the names could possibly have been those of his murderers."

"But you *were* working together."

"Look around you, Inspector. Herr Brauer desperately needed money. He approached me to obtain an advance from my newspaper to enable him to continue his researches. As I have said, he told me enough of what he had discovered to interest me. I told him I'd see what I could do. As it happens, my paper was also interested. You can, if you like, call the London office of the *Globe* and check that out. My editor is named Halliday. Having got Mr Halliday's agreement, I came round here tonight to tell Herr Brauer the good news. Only someone got here first."

"I see. May I ask just how much money Harr Brauer wished?"

Hunt gazed at him. "Twenty-five thousand pounds."

"Hm. Does it not occur to you, Herr Hunt, that these people may be aware of your business dealings with Herr Brauer, and may have been looking for the money? Twenty-five thousand pounds is a sizeable sum. Perhaps they expected to find you here as well, with the money. Now, they may well be after you?"

"I doubt that."

"Why?"

"Firstly because the money is being transferred from London to Herr Brauer's bank here in Hamburg: it will never be anywhere as cash. And secondly, because I have none of the facts on which Herr Brauer's story was based. He was a cunning old bird. The deal was he'd provide the facts when my editor came up with the cash he wanted. But when he died, he didn't even know that I had succeeded in getting the deal approved."

Lorenz nodded. "As you say, he was a cunning old bird. Perhaps too cunning for his own good."

Hunt returned to his hotel room, ordered a Room Service dinner, then telephoned and cancelled the meal he had laid on for two at the best restaurant in Hamburg.

He wasn't very hungry but he felt like a drink and had a double Scotch. Then he made a telephone call.

"Damnation!" said the voice on the other end of the line when he had finished. "What happens now?"

"We keep looking," Hunt said. "We know she's there. I'm going to hang on to the money, right?"

"Certainly," the voice said. "But keep in touch."

"I will." Hunt hung up and dialled again.

"Problems?" Halliday never minded being called at home.

"Did you send the money?"

"Your man can collect it in the morning."

"I can send it back, you mean." Hunt told him what had happened.

"Oh, hell!" Halliday commented. "What a way to go. Do you really think he had something?"

"Yes, I do."

"So?"

"I think I'll take a ride down to Zurich tomorrow."

"Do you have any idea how many Schmidts there must be in Switzerland?"

"I have an idea the people who killed Brauer also have his name, so this particular Schmidt may not be able to keep his head down. Have someone keep watching the fine print over the next couple of days. Whenever the name Walther Schmidt crops up, he may be our man."

Layton was called from the dinner table to take the telephone. He was annoyed about this, but when he heard that the call was from Halliday he listened attentively, his finely chiselled features settling into hard lines while the fingers of his left hand stroked the lapel of his dinner jacket.

"That is very interesting," he commented. "You are quite certain Hunt did not murder this man?"

"I suppose it is possible," Halliday said. "But the German police have not arrested him."

"Hm," Layton remarked. "Do you believe he is really on to a woman who may be Hitler's daughter?"

"I believe he thinks he is. What is more important, someone else believes it, very strongly."

"Who?"

"Whoever sent him to the Liebe Bar. Hunt forgets how much I know about my people. When he tells me that he

70

happened to stop in at the Liebe Bar and there, by golly, by gosh, is old Gustave Brauer, well . . . Hunt has never patronised the Liebe Bar. And when he also tells me that he wishes to handle the assignment himself, when it could be a wild goose chase . . ."

"Just what are you trying to say?"

"That he was sent there, by someone who knew that Brauer *did* patronise that bar, at the precise moment that it was known Brauer would be in there drinking, and desperate to raise money for his scoop."

"You're taking it very calmly," Layton remarked. "Doesn't it bother you that one of your top correspondents may actually be working for someone else?"

"I've known about Charles Hunt's politics for a long time. They don't concern me, so long as he produces the stories, and he has always done that. But now . . . I have a feeling that he may be looking for this woman, if she exists, for a far more serious reason than a scoop."

"Hm," Layton commented. "Well, thanks for calling. I really do appreciate it."

"Aren't you going to do anything about it?"

"Oh, I think we shall have to. I'll have to speak to one or two people. Leave it with me."

"Hunt is planning to go down to Zurich tomorrow. He's not an early riser, but I wouldn't leave it too late."

"I understand. Where is he staying?"

"The Hotel Atlantic."

"Good. Good. By the way, I am assuming that Hunt has no idea that you, ah . . . keep in touch with us."

"None at all."

"Good. Keep me informed. And again, thanks for calling."

Layton replaced the telephone and returned to the dining-room.

"Not some new crisis, darling?" Janet enquired, and the dinner guests pricked up their ears.

"Some young woman has got herself lost, that's all." Layton smiled as he sat down. "Not really our business at all. But you know what the FO is like nowadays, always in a twitter about something. I have no doubt at all that she'll turn up, in due course."

Hunt had another Scotch and slept heavily. Next morning he breakfasted, shaved, dressed and was about to leave when there was a tap on the door.

"Come," he called.

"Letter for you, Herr Hunt," said the bellboy.

Hunt raised his eyebrows, tipped the man, sat down to slit the envelope. Inside there were two sheets of paper: one addressed to him, one to the manager of a Hamburg bank.

Hunt read it, then called London again.

"I know it's early," he said. "But we're an hour ahead of you here."

"Yes," Halliday said, wearily.

"I just wanted to say, as you were. I won't be returning that twenty-five grand immediately. I may need to use some of it."

"Don't tell me Brauer isn't really dead?"

"Even dead men can talk," Hunt pointed out. "If they have the foresight."

CHAPTER TWO

Geli lay against Hans in the warmth of their big bed. They
needed a big bed because Hans was a very big man, over
six feet tall and heavily built. When they had first married,
she had been afraid of him for more reasons than just her
virginity: her rib cage had seemed at risk as well. Now
she liked nothing better than to snuggle into the warm
protectiveness of his strength. Even at sixty-one he was
the strongest man she had ever known.

He stirred, and she knew he was awake.

"Herrmann says he has spoken with you," she mur-
mured, watching, though the window, the sun beginning
to rise out of the Anatolian peninsular; she always slept
with the curtains open so that she would be awakened by
that glowing globe.

"Yes," Hans said.

"And that you are not opposing his return to Germany."

"He is twenty-one years old, my love. If he is determined to go, there is nothing we can do about it. And in
many ways he is perfectly right in saying that Germany is
where the future lies. This reunited Germany has got to
be the dominant factor in the European Community, in
all Europe."

Geli hated to hear anyone talk like that. But she took
another tack. "But you're not thinking of returning? I
mean, permanently."

"No, no," he assured her. "I am too old to think of
starting all over again."

"You wouldn't have to, would you? If you sold the
business, you could retire."

"I suppose so . . ."

"But not to Germany."

"Probably not."

She breathed a sigh of relief, but he was still talking.

"There are things . . ."

She sat up. "What things."

"Well . . . I didn't wish to upset you."

"Tell me."

"A man was murdered in Hamburg yesterday afternoon. It was on the news last night, after you had gone to bed."

"Someone you knew?"

"No, no. I did not know him personally. Quite a well-known journalist, though. The suggestion is that he was murdered because of associations with the Nazi Party."

"Oh, God! Don't tell me it's starting up again."

"I don't think it's ever really gone away, Geli. I mean, think of all the Nazi-style demonstrations we read about. Which is why I have no intention of going back. I suppose it's all right for young people like Herrmann, who don't remember and have no connections with the past . . . but . . ."

No connections with the past, Geli thought desperately. "He is at an impressionable age and could easily get sucked into that kind of politics," she said. She felt quite sick.

"Well . . ." Hans grinned and pulled her down for a kiss. "We will have to trust in the upbringing we have given him, eh?"

After they had all left the house, Geli dressed and attended to various chores. But her heart wasn't in it. They had a satellite TV and she listened to the news every hour. Gustave Brauer's death was mentioned several times, as he had apparently been quite famous in his time.

"The police have no direct leads to the killers," the newscaster read. "But a spokesman has said there are

74

links with the past and members of a neo-Nazi Party may well be involved. We have learned that Herr Brauer had been working on a biography of Heinrich Himmler, the infamous head of the Schutzstaffel, who committed suicide upon his capture by Allied troops in 1945."

Geli clasped both hands round her throat.

"The implication is that Brauer discovered some fact, or facts, which may have linked Himmler or one of the organisations he commanded to someone who is alive today, who may have been connected with the Nazis, and who has evaded detection for the past forty-seven years. Such a person would necessarily have had to be very close to the Nazi heirarchy, and speculation is rife as to who it could be as all of the principal German leaders of World War Two have long been accounted for. However . . ."

Geli switched off the set and sat in silence for several minutes, her hands clasped on her knees. Of course, the chances that it was anything to do with her had to be remote. Save for the mention of Himmler. And if this man Brauer *had* turned up anything about her . . .

"Are you all right, madame?" asked Shiera.

Geli's head jerked. "Oh. No, I am not feeling very well. I will lie down for a while."

She hurried to her room, locked the door and picked up the phone to call Switzerland. It took some time to get through, and then she got the ansaphone. Damnation. But in Switzerland it was eleven o'clock on a Friday morning. Uncle Walther had every reason to have gone out.

"This is Geli," she said. "Have you heard the news from Germany? I wish you to call me the moment you get in."

She hung up, then dialled again, the office of Schmidt and Schmidt.

"No, madame, Mr Schmidt senior has not come in today. But then, he only comes in once or twice a week now he has retired."

"I know," Geli said. "It's just that I called his apartment and he wasn't there. I wondered if you might have any idea where he might have gone?"

"It is a nice morning here in Zurich, madame," the woman said. "Herr Schmidt might have gone anywhere. He is probably having a coffee and looking at the lake. Did you leave a message for him to call you?"

"Yes," Geli said. "Yes, I did."

"Then I am sure he will do so when he returns to his apartment. Good day to you, madame."

Geli spent the rest of the day in bed. What on earth had this Brauer man turned up that could have led him to be killed? But the feeling was hardening that it could only be about her. Or was she developing her mother's paranoia? She had always been determined that would never happen. But if Brauer *had* turned up something . . . and someone had killed him to find it out! God, God, God!

After forty-seven years! Oh, why didn't Uncle Walther ring?

She waited until just before the children started arriving home, then telephoned again. And got the ansaphone again. Was he spending all day out?

"Uncle Walther," she said. "Have you not heard the news from Hamburg? You *must* call me, immediately."

Then she realised he might already be on his way to see her; the situation might be too grave for telephone conversations or a wire. How she hoped he was coming to see her.

Equally she realised he might just have cut and run.

Inevitably, that evening the conversation turned to the Brauer murder and the possibility that there might still be a prominent Nazi at large.

"I cannot see who it might be," Hans declared. "Anyway, he would have to be very old. Certainly not less than seventy-five. I cannot see what all the fuss is about. No matter what crimes these people may once have committed, forty-seven years is too long to keep hunting them down."

"Well, whoever it is must be bothered," Herrmann argued. "And he must still be pretty powerful, to have that journalist bumped off just for finding out about him."

Geli felt sick all over again. Because that was the truly terrifying asspect of the situation. Whatever Brauer had found out, someone had regarded it as important enough, and dangerous enough, to murder him for it. Then if that person, or persons, could ever catch up with her . . . But who? And why? They were all dead. She had been so sure they were all dead.

She went upstairs, ostensibly to go to the toilet, dialled Zurich again. The phone rang, and she waited for the ansaphone to cut in, then a man answered.

"Herr Schmidt's apartment."

He was speaking German but it was not Uncle Walther. Geli stared at the telephone as a rabbit might stare at a snake.

"Who is this?" the man asked.

"I would like to speak to Herr Schmidt, please."

"Herr Schmidt is not here at this moment. If you will give me your name and telephone number, I will ask him to call."

Geli gulped. Something had happened. Something terrible, because everything was suddenly terrible.

She hung up.

*

The bank manager studied the letter Hunt had placed on his desk.

"I assure you it is genuine," Hunt told him.

"I have no doubt of that, Herr Hunt," the manager said. "And it is perfectly true that Herr Brauer deposited a packet here yesterday afternoon for safe-keeping, with instructions that it was to be released only to him or to someone authorised by him."

"Well, then?"

"Well, you see, Herr Hunt, since then the situation has changed. Dramatically. Herr Brauer is dead. It is at least possible that he was murdered for something in that sealed packet. Therefore it could be regarded as material

77

evidence, and should go to the police."

"I would say that your first duty is to carry out the instructions of your dead client," Hunt said.

"Well, yes, on the surface . . ."

"If it is of any help, I will guarantee to hand over anything which may be of value to the police in their investigation," Hunt said. "Should I find such an item."

"Well, of course, if you will do that." The manager rang through to his secretary, and a few minutes later the packet was produced. "Would you care to open it in my presence?" he invited.

"Surely." Hunt cut the badly tied string, on which the bank's seal had been imprinted, and unwrapped the diary. "Well, what do you know . . .?" He feigned surprise. "A desk diary."

The manager looked puzzled. "Herr Brauer's?"

Hunt flicked the pages. "I would say so."

"But . . . is it valuable?"

"It doesn't look valuable."

"But it may contain some clue as to who he has interviewed in connection with this book of his. One of whom may be the murderer."

"You're absolutely right," Hunt agreed. "But I can't tell that until I've read it."

"Ah."

"I propose to do that immediately. Do not worry, Herr Peters, you have my absolute assurance that the moment I have read it, I will hand it over to the police. Until then, however, I'd prefer it if you did not mention the diary to anyone. Especially the police."

"Of course. I am a bank manager, not a gossip. But . . . do *you* think it contains anything important?"

"I hope it does."

"And you will give this information to the police? I have your word?"

Hunt nodded. "Shouldn't take too long. Now, regarding the money that arrived for me this morning . . ."

"There were two transfers. One from England, in the

amount of twenty-five thousand pounds. And one from Munich in the amount of sixty thousand Deutschmarks."

"That is correct."

"Do you wish it now?"

Hunt had already made his plans. He himself very seldom used cash, preferring to rely upon credit cards and Eurocheques, which were in any event a more efficient way of presenting his expense account. But he was prepared to bribe his way to his goal, if necessary. "I'll take the twenty-five thousand pounds, in pounds. Hang on to the rest until you hear from me."

"You will have to open an account."

"If you wish."

Peters nodded, called his secretary and gave the necessary instructions. She went off and returned with various forms for Hunt to sign, as well as the English money, a considerable wad. "I will need a receipt," Peters said.

"Certainly."

"And your address and telephone number."

Hunt raised his eyebrows, but obliged. "I'm not promising how long I'll be at the hotel," he pointed out. "Nor do I have any idea where I shall be going when I leave."

Hunt returned to his hotel and carefully locked his bedroom door. If the diary was what Brauer's murderers were after they hadn't got it. That was why they had held the match or the cigarette lighter to the poor old fellow's genitals. But the torture had been successful, otherwise they would have searched the apartment instead of merely strangling him and taking their leave. So what had Brauer told them to make them leave? The whereabouts of the diary? Or the address of Walther Schmidt in Zurich? If the latter, they were already nearly twenty-four hours ahead of him and there was nothing he could do about that. If the former, they would be hunting for Hunt. They had probably followed him from the bank. In which case . . . but even if they had only wanted Schmidt's address, and

had obtained that, they would still be wondering where
the diary had got to, because it would contain the clues
which could send others in pursuit.

He sat down with the diary. Had Brauer known he was
going to be murdered? Or at least, interrogated, with all
the terrible connotations that word could raise? Either
way, he had elected to trust Charles Hunt more than any
other living creature. That was quite a compliment.

Speculation as to Brauer's motives quickly ended as he
turned the pages and realised that Brauer had put his
facts together very neatly and very well. But he was most
interested in discovering the address of this man Walther
Schmidt, and there it was, in Zurich.

As was his habit, he made two telephone calls. The first
to Munich, the second to London to put Halliday in the
picture.

"So you're off to Zurich?"

"Well, I was going there anyway, remember? This just
makes my journey worthwhile. I have to say that I take
off my hat to old Gustave."

"And what happens after Zurich?"

"That depends on this fellow, Schmidt. Presuming he's
still alive. I mean, if he was senior enough to have control
of some SS slush fund in nineteen forty-five, well, he can
hardly be under eighty."

"But Brauer evidently thought he was alive."

"That's right. So wish me luck."

"Keep in touch," Halliday told him. "If Schmidt's
address was what those murderers were after, and they
got it, I want to know where you are, and how you are,
every minute of the day. Come to think of it, I wonder if
you shouldn't have some support."

Hunt had already arranged support. But it might well be
a case of the more the merrier. "Might be an idea. Look,
I want to get down to Zurich right away. Have someone
meet me there."

"Where?"

"Oh . . . the Baur au Lac will do."

Halliday blew a raspberry. "Isn't that the most expensive hotel in Zurich?"

"In Switzerland," Hunt assured him, and hung up.

Halliday telephoned Layton. "I know it's early, but . . ."

Layton listened. "I think that is very good," he remarked at the end. "Very convenient."

"Hunt is expecting this back-up to be waiting for him in Zurich."

"I understand that. What are Hunt's sexual proclivities?"

"Oh, heter. And how. He is the ultimate MCP. Most women hate him the moment they get to know him."

"That agrees with my own file on the gentleman. Covering Mr Hunt, if you will excuse the *double entendre*, will obviously be a time-consuming operation."

"Yes, but what do you want me to do?" Halliday asked. "About this back-up?"

"Obviously it must be one of your own people, and known to Hunt, otherwise he may become suspicious. However, this person must be absolutely trustworthy from our point of view, and will need to be thoroughly briefed. He or she – and in view of Hunt's reputation it should be a she, I feel – will also have to be capable of taking instant and, if necessary, difficult decisions. From what we know of Hunt, it may even be necessary to take an executive decision. But of course this must only be in the last resort, and in any event should not be considered until after Hunt has found his quarry. Have you got such a person?"

"Ah . . . yes, I think I can find one."

"Then do so," Layton told him. "But remember that Hunt is not to be stopped. He is, indeed, to be assisted. Until he finds this woman. If she exists."

"And then? I didn't really involve you in order to have my best foreign correspondent done. Contrary to most, I like the fellow."

"What happens then depends on what Hunt is really after. I do assure you that we are not in the assassination

81

business. Except, of course, unless the interests of this country and her allies are at stake. You may leave that with me, John."

"Meaning you have already placed one of your own people on Hunt's tail. Are you sure your man and my woman aren't going to trip over each other?"

Layton smiled at the telephone. "Quite sure, old man. Oh, quite sure." He hung up.

Hunt ordered Room Service lunch as he had no desire to leave his bedroom and thereby expose himself until he was ready to leave the hotel itself. Then he called the Baur au Lac, booked himself in, and packed his travel case. If he left immediately after the meal, he would be in Zurich that evening. The address was an apartment, so it was clearly Walther Schmidt's home. Supposing he was still alive.

However, Hunt could not see any great merit in rushing around like a chicken with its head cut off. The woman who wore Adoration perfume had watched Brauer die some time around four o'clock yesterday afternoon. If Brauer had told her what she wanted to know, presumably Walther Schmidt's address, she and her henchmen could have been in Zurich by midnight. He had not read the diary for another twelve hours. Whatever was going to be done was already done. He could only pick up the pieces and trust that Walther Schmidt had been a harder nut to crack than Gustave Brauer. If Schmidt had indeed been a paymaster for the SS, Hunt did not doubt that he would have been, and probably still was, a very tough nut indeed. Supposing he *was* still alive. But as the odds were that he was by now dead. Adoration and her pals would have come to a dead end. Catching them up in that state might well be interesting.

He felt pleasantly excited. It was a long time since he had actually been on the chase, as it were. And this one had the most promising ramifications. As for instance, the character of the woman Hitler herself. If she existed. Or indeed, had ever existed. But the more he considered

82

the diary entries, the more sure he became. He could understand Brauer's excitement.

He did not doubt he was going to be able to find her. But dealing with Adoration came first – that became more of a personal matter every time he remembered Brauer.

There was a knock on the door. He opened it and a chambermaid appeared, pushing the lunch trolley. Hunt raised his eyebrows in surprise, but she looked very efficient. She was also decidedly attractive, tall and blonde, her figure accentuated by the form-hugging black uniform with its white apron; the skirt was short enough to indicate that she also had good legs. Her face was too blunt for beauty, but she had a splendid smile and excellent teeth. Her hair was pinned up beneath her cap, but enough strands were peeping out to indicate that it was a very pale yellow, and probably quite long.

"Good morning, Herr Hunt," she said, closing the door behind herself before wheeling the trolley into the centre of the room.

He liked her voice, too.

"And the same to you, Fraulein. What's happened to Dieter?"

"Oh, we are so busy today," she said, expertly removing dish covers. Then she uncorked the wine, and poured a glass for him to try.

"Just what the doctor ordered."

"If you will sign the account, sir."

Hunt took account and pen, bent over the table to write his name. "I'd like my bill prepared as well," he said. "I am leaving immediately after luncheon."

"For Switzerland, Herr Hunt?"

Hunt raised his head, looked into the barrel of an automatic pistol at the same time as he realised that it had indeed been a long time since he had been on the chase, to have been so completely relaxed as to have been caught out by something like this.

"And that will be the famous diary," the woman said.

83

"I think I will just remove it to keep temptation from your way, Herr Hunt."

"I thought you'd got what you wanted from Gustave Brauer," Hunt said, speaking quietly while his brain seethed. The odds were very long, especially when supported by the pistol. When he made a move, if he made a move, it was going to have to be very fast and very violent. The temptation to do nothing was enormous. But if this woman had been one of those who had murdered Gustave, in the coldest of blood . . . after holding a burning cigarette lighter to his genitals . . . then he realised that if she was, she had changed her perfume.

"Poor Herr Brauer. He tried to be so careful," the woman said. "Even to the extent of sending you the diary in case of his death. Have you read it?"

"Not yet. I was hoping to do so over lunch."

"You'd find it boring, I'm sure." She picked the diary up, put it in the pocket of her apron. The movement caused some of her perfume to drift past him, and his nostrils twitched. But it was definitely not Adoration.

"Now, Herr Hunt, I would like you to undress. Everything, please."

"Are you serious? Up till now our meeting has been so disappointing."

"Just do it," the woman suggested.

Hunt stood up and she moved back about four feet. But the pistol was still levelled. He took off his jacket and tie. "Next thing, you'll be telling me you're good with a cigarette lighter, too," he remarked.

"A . . . hurry up," she said.

She had not understood the allusion. Hunt was reassured; he was now practically certain she had not been involved in Brauer's murder, and he was glad of that – she was simply too attractive. On the other hand, she knew of the existence of the diary . . . and he reckoned she was fairly ruthless.

84

He undressed, smiling at her as he did so. She smiled back, but it was not a reassuring smile.

"Now, lie on the bed, on your face, Herr Hunt, and do not move. This pistol is levelled at the back of your head."

Hunt obeyed. The odds still had to be considerably improved before he could chance anything, and for the moment they had worsened, at least psychologically – it was a stupid fact of life that being naked when one's assailant is clothed induces a tremendous feeling of inferiority. Disappointingly, he supposed that was all she had in mind.

He listened to movement about the room, and ripping sounds. Out of the corner of his eye he could see his valise being emptied on the floor. The woman knelt beside it and went through every garment.

"What are you going to do with these English pounds?" she asked.

"Spend them."

"I think I will take them. Then you can tell the police, if you wish, that I came to rob you. So if you choose, you need not tell them about the diary at all."

She placed the money in her apron pocket as well. He continued to watch her from the corner of his eye as she then tested various of his ties for strength. The woman who had murdered Brauer had not thought of ties.

She selected five of the ties, and then came towards the bed. "Now, Herr Hunt," she said. "I would beg you to do nothing foolish. Not only am I armed, but I am an expert in unarmed combat. And you will agree that you are not in the best of condition."

"Would you really say that?"

"You are overweight," she told him, severely. "Your stomach is flabby and too big. Too much beer, eh?"

"You could be right," Hunt agreed, wondering if anyone had ever told her that she talked too much.

"Now, I would like you to bring both your wrists behind your back, and put them together," the woman said.

85

"Don't I even get to know your name?" Hunt asked.

"No," she said. "Your wrists."

She was standing at the side of the bed, immediately next to his left ankle. She could not reach his wrists from there, would have to kneel on the bed to secure them. When she did that, she would also have to pocket the gun, or at least lay it down, for the few seconds that would be necessary to bind them together.

She was utterly overconfident, perhaps because he had so far made no effort to resist her . . . and because of that assumption that he was past physical combat.

He brought his arms together behind his back, felt the bed depress as she knelt beside him, waited until she touched his wrists and then rolled over, at the same time swinging his arms and legs with all his strength.

Immediately he was struck a paralysing blow on the neck and although the momentum of his roll continued and he found himself on his back, for the moment he knew only pain. But the force of his movement and his kick had also tumbled the woman right off the bed on to the floor, and for that same moment she sat there, winded.

They rose together. She reached for the pistol in her pocket, but he discounted that and leapt straight at her. She drew the gun, but was gazing at the huge naked form flying through the air at her rather than attempting to level it. Instead she rolled to one side, and as he landed on his hands and knees with a crash which seemed to shake the hotel to its foundations, kicked him in the thigh with the toe of her high-heeled shoe.

He gasped with the pain and rolled, but made himself move towards her again. She now pointed the pistol but he was against her ankles, throwing both arms round her knees and bringing her heavily to the floor. Before she could recover, he had swept his hand sideways in a slap which made her gasp, and had then struck down in a karate chop on her wrist which sent the pistol to the floor.

She moaned with pain while Hunt reached his feet again, panting, and kicked the pistol across the carpet. It came to rest against the far wall, but instead of following it, Hunt crossed the floor and turned the key in the lock. Just in time, as there came an urgent knocking.

"Herr Hunt? Are you all right?" It was the usual chambermaid.

"Oh, yes," Hunt said. "I just fell out of bed."

"Ah!" the girl said, and he listened to her feet receding.

Hunt stood with his back to the door and looked at the woman. She was on her knees, and she was looking from the gun to him. They were about equidistant from it, but he didn't think she could have any hope of reaching it before he did.

"I think we should now deal with each other as equals," Hunt suggested.

The woman licked her lips.

"So . . . shall I dress, or will you undress?" he asked.

She looked at him, her eyes as cold as ice.

He sighed. "I thought you'd take that attitude, Fraulein. Well . . . for the sake of European unity . . . but, I do not wish you to move. If you do, I am going to throw you on the floor, knock you senseless, and then rape you until you fall apart. Understood?"

This time the woman's lip curled, but he thought she got the message.

He went towards his clothes, dressed himself, never taking his eyes from her face. He was now between her and the gun, and felt totally in command of the situation.

"Are you a fool or a madman?" she asked.

"Which do you consider the most likely?"

"I could have shot you."

"Yes, you could. But you didn't. And you were never going to. I knew that."

She frowned at him.

Hunt knotted his tie, pulled on his jacket and felt at ease with the world, if a trifle hungry. He sat at the trolley, drank a glass of wine and tried the coquilles. They were only lukewarm, but still edible.

87

"How did you know that?" she asked.

"Let's say that, regrettably, I have been around longer than you have, Fraulein. Had you really meant to kill me, you would have come in here and shot me without all the palaver. Had you been *prepared* to kill me if I did not do what you wished, you would have told me so, perhaps, and then done it. But you would not have added that you were an expert in unarmed combat. Unless one party is very foolish, or the other is very good, that is an unncessarily difficult way of killing someone when one possesses a gun. As it turned out, I am not very foolish . . . and let's face it, you are not very good."

She glared at him, and he grinned at her.

"You have also managed to spoil my lunch. Aren't your knees hurting? You can get up if you like. Slowly."

She stood up, uncomfortably, straightened her skirt and apron. Her cap had come off and her hair was slowly uncoiling from its various pins; as he has supposed, it was long and straight. She was obviously shaken, and there was a trace of blood on her lip. Her wrist was also clearly very painful.

"What are you going to do?" she asked.

"Finish my lunch. Would you like a glass of wine?"

"No, thank you."

"Well, sit down. There." He pointed at the chair at the side of the trolley farther from the gun. "What happened to Dieter?"

"I asked him to allow me to take his place."

"And you can be very persuasive, I'm sure. But you don't really work here, do you?"

"It is a large hotel. There is always staff coming or going."

"So who do you work for?"

"That is my business."

"Unfortunately, you have just made it mine, Fraulein. Look, I really don't want to have to harm you, or hand you over to the police, but if you don't co-operate, I will have no choice."

"If you touch me I will scream."

"Be my guest. Then the police will have the pleasure of interrogating you. And locking you up afterwards."

"They have nothing on me. It will be your word against mine. I will say I delivered your lunch and you assaulted me." She was beginning to breathe heavily.

"Won't work, Fraulein. You are a false waitress. So you will say you inveigled your way in here to interview me, perhaps, and then I assaulted you. But what about the gun? I have not touched it. Therefore only your fingerprints will be found on it. Therefore when I tell the police you threatened me with it, they will believe me and not you." He finished his meal, drank the last of the wine, wiped his lips with his napkin and stood up. "And if you have one or two bruises about you, and I claim it was self-defence, they will believe that also."

"I already have bruises," she said, massaging her wrist.

"I was thinking of one or two more." Hunt stood in front of her, but out of range of any sudden kick or lunge. "Look, let's be friends. We haven't even introduced ourselves. I'm Charles Hunt."

"That I know."

"And you are?"

"My name is Leni."

"Leni what?"

"Angstrom."

"Leni Angstrom. All right, Leni Angstrom, tell me about your friends, who murdered Gustave Brauer."

Her head jerked. "I know nothing of Brauer's murder."

"Oh, come now. They were after the diary, and now you are after the diary."

"I know nothing of Brauer's murder." Her voice rose an octave. "You have just proved that I am not a murderess."

"So I did." He had merely wanted to watch her reactions. He was pleased, but not actually relieved because if she was telling the truth, and he was sure she was, then there were two other parties involved, one prepared to kill and the other – this woman's employers – prepared at least to use strong-arm tactics to reach Hitler's daughter before anyone else. Then how far was *he* prepared to go? "All right," he said. "We'll agree that you have nothing to do with Gustave's murder. So, you were sent here . . ."

"I was not sent here. I came here."

"Okay. You came here, to relieve me of Brauer's diary. But someone must have told you I have it. And there is only one person in the world apart from Brauer's killers who could have done that, supposing they knew it themselves. That person is Herr Peters. What is the connection between you and him?"

"It has nothing to do with Herr Peters."

"Convince me."

She stared at him. "I will tell you the truth."

"Super." He sat on the bed.

"I am a journalist, like you."

"My respect for my profession grows. What paper?"

"Freelance."

"My respect for you diminishes, Leni. I can check that out, you know."

"It is the truth. Listen, I sometimes provide copy for Joachim Allendt. Do you know him?"

"You're going down all the time."

"Okay, so he's not a very nice man. But he pays well. I was there yesterday morning, not with Allendt but speaking with one of his sub-editors about a piece I had done, and I saw Brauer go in to his office. I was interested because Brauer is a has-been. You know this?"

"Was a has-been, darling."

"Well, yes, I am sorry about that. Well, I am fairly well acquainted with Allendt's secretary, so when Brauer left I asked her what was the reason for his visit. She told me he was trying to get backing for some crazy idea he had that Adolf Hitler had actually had a daughter, and that she could be alive somewhere. He was trying to sell this information. Well, Herr Allendt was not interested . . ."

"Joachim Allendt was not interested in a story like that?"

"He virtually kicked Brauer out."

Hunt stroked his chin.

"While I, I went to the Liebe Bar because I knew that was where Brauer spends most of every morning."

"No, you didn't, darling," Hunt pointed out. "I was in the Liebe Bar yesterday morning and you were not." He grinned at her. "I'd have noticed you."

"I know. I didn't wish to go in. I waited outside until Brauer came out and then I spoke with him."

"You knew him?"

"Oh, yes. Well, we were acquaintances. I told him I knew of his project and would get the backing he needed for his search, if he would let me share in the credit. Well, I have my career to make."

"I'm sure you do. And he agreed?"

"No. He turned me down. Because he had already struck a deal with you, I suppose."

"He told you that?"

"Well, not in so many words. But he did say that if anything ever happened to him, the diary was coming to you, and you'd know what to do with it."

"He always did talk too much," Hunt said easily. "And this was yesterday morning, after he had left the Bar?"

Leni Angstrom hesitated for a moment and then nodded. "Yes."

The problem of what to do with her was growing every moment. Whoever had briefed her had been so lacking in accurate information that her story was ludicrous, if only because her tutor had not known that when Brauer had left the Liebe Bar it had been in his company, and they had lunched together . . . nor had the matter of the disposal of the diary even been discussed at that point – because there hadn't been a deal at that point.

So he was no nearer finding out who she worked for. But he did not suppose that knocking her about was going to elicit an answer, even if he was the sort of man who enjoyed knocking women about. While handing her over to the police would involve a considerable delay while Lorenz asked questions . . . and he was already too far behind.

Yet he couldn't just throw her out. She would continue to follow him, or worse, someone he didn't know would take over. And they would again try to get hold of the diary. He wasn't sure handing her over to the police would improve the situation because someone had told her of the connection between Brauer and himself, and the field was limited.

Besides, she was an attractive young woman. The idea of allowing her along was growing on him.

But he was not a man who took risks lightly. "I assume if you are a journalist you are a member of the union?" he asked.

"Of course."

He picked up the phone. "Then you won't mind if I check?"

"Not at all."

Yet she was tense. Hunt dialled. "Pieter? Charlie, here. Oh, pretty good. And you? Fine. Yes, you can do me a favour. I assume you have easy access to a list of every registered journalist in Germany? Good. Will you look up a Fraulein Leni Angstrom? Yes, I would say definitely of Swedish descent. I'll wait." He smiled at Leni over the receiver. She licked her lips. "Pieter? Oh, good. I'll just make a note of those. Age twenty-seven. Right. Height five feet nine inches. Right. Hair, yellow . . ." He smiled at Leni again. "Do you mean natural yellow? Oh, I see. Yes, if I can I'll look at the roots. Eyes grey. Right. Freelance. Yes. You wouldn't have the bust measurement, would you? You don't do that? Well, I don't suppose we do that in England either. Pieter, you've been a dream, as usual. And . . . would you repeat that?"

"Left-handed," the man named Pieter said.

"Oh, quite," Hunt said. "I'm sure you're right. Thanks

92

a million. I'll be in touch." He replaced the phone. "He says you are known to have a way with men."

"Do you know that you are the sort of man every woman loves to hate?" Leni asked.

"It's a cultivated vice. Is your hair real, or natural?"

"It is real, Herr Hunt."

"And what is your bust measurement, anyway?"

"Ninety-four centimetres."

"That does it. Leni, how would you like me to make you a proposition?"

"Forget it, Herr Hunt."

"You gay?"

"I just don't like you."

"That's not exactly an answer to my question. But actually, my proposition has nothing to do with sex, at least in the first instance. You want to find this woman, Hitler's daughter, right?"

Leni gazed at him.

"Well, so do I," Hunt said. "And I have been backed by my paper. Unlike poor Gustave, I don't have a reputation to re-create. I also have the information. It may at this moment happen to be resting against your undoubtedly delightful pubes, but I'm going to have it back. With my money. The question is, would you like to tag along?"

"With what in mind?"

"It would take too long to outline that, darling. Just say I'm generous, and you have a pretty face. Yes or no?"

Leni hesitated. "I get to write the story?"

"*We* get to write the story. But your name will appear on it. Below mine."

"And the payment?"

"Seventy-five, twenty-five." He held up his finger as she would have spoken. "All I'd have to do is turn you over to the police and you wouldn't get a bean. Whereas, in addition to twenty-five per cent of the take, you get to print your name, below mine. That's worth twenty-five grand for a start. How about it?"

They looked into each other's eyes and he thought –

and certainly hoped – that he could read her mind. This man is a fool, she would have to be thinking, made so by his lechery.

"Why are you being so generous?" she asked. "When, as you say, you could just hand me over to the police?"

"What, close on one hundred centimetres? Darling, I'm hoping you're going to be generous too."

Still they stared at each other, and he almost felt sorry for her. It was not an offer she could refuse, and she must be certain that when she obtained whatever it was she wanted, she would be able to ditch him, or do him, with the minimum of trouble. But, as with the facts of yesterday, equally she was unaware that he had any back-ups joining him in Zurich. Or that he knew she wasn't really Leni Angstrom: she had held the gun in her right hand.

"Well," she said. "I will have to think about that. However . . . what do we do first? Read the diary together?"

"That won't be necessary," Hunt told her. "I know where we're going." He held out his hand. "But I'll have it back, if you don't mind. And the money."

Leni hesitated, then thrust her hand into the apron pocket and produced the diary and the bundle of notes.

"Thank you," Hunt said. "Now, I am going to repack that bag, go downstairs and check out. I assume you have some proper clothes to put on. You can't go traipsing across Europe dressed as a waitress; people might take one look at you and want servicing."

"I have a valise in the Ladies, on the ground floor."

"Well, I suggest you go change, and meet me in the downstairs car park in ten minutes. Not a moment longer, or I shall leave you behind. I am driving a dark blue Peugeot 505 estate. You can't miss it."

Leni frowned. "You are letting me go?"

"Why not? You are going to be there, aren't you? Or there's no story. However . . ." He got up, spread a large handkerchief on the bed, then took one of the knives from the trolley, went to the corner and picked up the pistol by thrusting the knife through the trigger guard. The pistol he placed in the centre of the handkerchief, which he then folded over it. "I'll just hang on to this, shall I?"

"How do I know that the moment I leave you will not just drive off without me?"

"Darling, don't push your luck. I have invited you to come along. I'm not going to welsh on that. You now have nine minutes, Fraulein. I would start moving, if I were you."

Leni hesitated, then got to her feet and almost fled from the room. Hunt supposed she would spend most of her nine minutes on the telephone, asking for help. But then, he had some calls of his own to make.

"I do not like it," Munich said. "The odds are becoming too great, Hunt."

"I'm supposed to be getting additional help from London. How're we fixed in Zurich?"

"Someone is waiting for you at the hotel. His name is Carl. He will keep out of sight until and unless you need him. Who is this London help? Someone who will know everything?"

"Who will know everything, save what really matters. And who will be in the employ of the *Globe*, and therefore above suspicion, and who will also do exactly what I tell him to, because I will be the boss. Stop worrying. If I need more, I'll call for help. Meanwhile, *cherchez la femme*, eh? If you'll excuse the language."

"Which *femme*?"

"I'll worry about Fraulein Hitler. You work on Fraulein Angstrom, or whatever her real name is. I want to know who and what she is, and who she is working for. I'll call you from Zurich."

Hunt then called London, and brought Halliday up to date.

"There are other people involved as well," he told his

boss. "I would like all the information you can get me on the political views of Joachim Allendt . . ."

"For God's sake, don't tell me he's mixed up in this."

"He could well be," Hunt said. "I want his real views, not those expressed by his newspaper. There is also a bank manager named Peters, also based here in Hamburg. I want to know if either of those two have any affiliation with any neo-Nazi, or equally, any virulent anti-Nazi, groups. You can send the data to Zurich, but I would like it by lunchtime tomorrow."

"This is starting to read like a serial," Halliday commented. "We'll get on to it. You're still meaning to visit this chap Schmidt? With your blonde girlfriend?"

"I'm going to have a go. My trouble is I don't know whether or not Brauer's friends got the address out of him before he died. In which case . . . my next call may well be from a Zurich morgue."

"Just so long as you're not the chap on the slab," Halliday told him. "What time do you expect to get there?"

"Well, obviously I'm running late. I won't be there until suppertime."

"That's all right. Corinne will be waiting for you."

"Corinne? For Christ's sake . . ."

"You're looking for a woman, right? You may just need a woman to sniff her out. And if and when you find her, again a woman may come in handy. And incidentially, Corinne is useful when the chips are down: she has a black belt. She can cope with your friend Angstrom if she starts to act tough again. She also speaks fluent German."

"Cheer me up. I've worked with Corinne before, you know."

"I remember, Charlie. She seemed quite keen on working with you again. And on spending the night at the Baur au Lac."

"Shit," Hunt commented. "When does she get in?"

"In a couple of hours."

"Okay. I intend to be on the road by then. Give her a call and tell her I'll be in touch."

Hunt took his suitcase downstairs and settled the bill. By then he had parcelled up the diary, with a covering note explaining how it had come into his possession, but making no mention of the strange appearance of Leni Angstrom, and addressed it to Inspector Lorenz, and this he now gave to the reception clerk to mail; he had every intention of remaining on good terms with the German police.

He had a lot on his mind. Top of the list, of course, was the cold-blooded, vicious, and rather horrible murder of Gustave Brauer. Last night he had been aware only of emotion, a combination of hatred for the killers, anger that Brauer should have been robbed of his scoop, and disappointment that an assignment to which he had been looking forward, and which he regarded as important, might not now be going to materialise.

Today had so far been all instinct. He could no more have omitted to go to the bank with Brauer's last letter than he could have stopped breathing. If he had always known the diary was what the killers were after, it had not occurred to him that they could in any way know he was about to come into possession of it – unless Brauer had told them that.

If Brauer had confessed his ploy, Leni was a natural concomitant. But Leni was not part of them. Which, as Munich had pointed out, made the situation more complicated, and double-headed, as it were. Not only did he have to find out how Leni had come to know about the diary – and who she really was as well as for whom she was working – but also how the killers had done so. He had no doubt at all that Joachim Allendt was responsible for one lot. He hoped it wasn't Leni. But would even Allendt have sent a hit-squad to get hold of a diary he could easily have bought?

And that still left Leni. Because now he had had a chance to think about it, there was a good deal more to

Leni than met the eye. Principally there was the point that what had happened this morning had almost been scripted. He had been assaulted, but not hurt, given the opportunity to respond, violently, and found her an easy target. If that were truly so, then he was wading in some very murky waters – and he could be taking along as a semi-prisoner someone who had always intended to go.

And overlaying all of those considerations was the thought of the bloody Corinne. Mind you, he thought he would thoroughly enjoy the sight of Corinne, six feet tall and an ex-England soccer centre-forward, having a set-to with Leni. It was the thought of Corinne having a set-to with him that frightened him. She might be a forceful investigative reporter, but when she had had a few drinks, as he remembered from the previous occasion they had worked together, she was inclined to become amorous.

It is very difficult to resist a fourteen-stone woman black belt who is also a committed feminist unless one is prepared to exert considerable physical force of one's own. On the other hand, he could pull rank and forbid her to drink. He wondered how she would react to that!

Leni was waiting for him, equipped with an overnight bag. She had changed her waitress's black dress for a pale blue pants suit, worn with an open-necked white shirt, and her hair was loose. She looked very good.

Hunt unlocked the car and she got in. He sat beside her. "How's the wrist?"

"Painful. How is your neck?"

"Sore. Your boss happy with the situation?"

She turned her head to look at him. "I do not have a boss, Herr Hunt. Where are we going?"

"South."

He drove out of the garage.

It is just over four hundred miles, as the crow flies, from Hamburg to Zurich. By using the Autobahns it is possible to drive considerably faster than a crow can fly, and the route is almost as direct.

It would not even have been greatly quicker actually to fly, allowing for the inevitable check-in and check-out delays, and passenger lists could be investigated by any would-be pursuer. Hunt intended merely to disappear, and surface in Zurich. If Leni Angstrom had arranged support, they would have to find him all over again.

He got away from the hotel at three o'clock, took the E4 round Hanover, the E45 down to Kassel, and then the E70 to within striking distance of the border. After Ulm the pace dropped, and there was a brief delay as they showed their passports at the Swiss border, but it was only just after seven when the Peugeot pulled to a halt in the Baur au Lac forecourt.

Leni got out as one of the doormen opened the door for her, looked up at the building, and then out at the lake. "You travel in style, Herr Hunt."

"Expenses."

"You mean I am being paid for by the London *Globe*?"

"Enjoy it."

He signed the register. "Is Mrs Grundy here yet?"

"Indeed, sir. Mrs Grundy arrived at three o'clock." The under-manager looked past Hunt at Leni, waiting patiently by a potted palm. Hunt presumed that he was reflecting that this man was a glutton. "But . . ." He glanced at the key in the pigeonhole. "She is presently out."

"That's fine."

"Shall I inform her that you have arrived, sir? When she comes in?"

"No," Hunt said. "No, I wouldn't do that. Just give me her room number, and I'll call her later on."

"Very good, sir."

The bellhop was waiting to take them up.

"This place is really something," Leni commented.

"I like it."

The door was opened for them, the lights switched on,

the two valises placed on the stand. Hunt tipped the boy and he left.

Hunt wondered if he had yet met his number one back-up. But that he had arrived would be simple enough for anyone to ascertain.

Leni was regarding the bed.

"Did you *request* a double?"

"As a matter of fact, yes. Are you a restless sleeper?"

"I'm sure you are." She went to the window to look out at the view. "Do you suppose I could sue you for sexual harrassment?"

"Ah . . . no. Not as you agreed to come along in the first place. And certainly not in your precarious legal position."

She turned. "Do you still have my gun?"

"I put it in a safe place. Leni . . . we were going to be friends, remember? I know you don't like me, but you simply have to co-operate with me. I mean, I'm co-operating with you: I haven't even asked you yet what you spent your ten minutes off doing, this afternoon."

She gazed at him in that disturbingly direct fashion she had, then shrugged and took off her jacket.

"Not now, darling," Hunt told her. "Regrettably. But in my business we work first and play after. We have a call to make."

Leni put her jacket on again.

The doorman summoned a cab and Hunt gave the address.

"Who are we going to see?" Leni asked.

"Brauer's Swiss contact. A man named Schmidt."

"Tell me about him."

Hunt looked at the back of the driver's head. "Later."

Walther Schmidt's apartment was in a very prosperous-looking building on a very prosperous-looking street. If he had been a Nazi paymaster he had clearly also had sticky fingers.

"Is it easy to get a cab around here?" Hunt asked as he paid the driver.

100

"It is not difficult. Just walk to that corner and you will see them passing. Or you can telephone. Here is the card of my company."

"Thanks." Whether or not he could telephone would depend upon how well he got on with Herr Schmidt. He looked at the list of names, pressed the bell, and again.

"All of this way," Leni commented. "To find that he has gone away."

"It's the fact that his name is still on the door that matters," Hunt reminded her. But he was beginning to have a sinking feeling that he had experienced this before, because he had: last night. He pressed the ordinary bell, and after a few minutes a voice requested his business.

"I am here to see Herr Schmidt," Hunt explained. "But he does not answer his bell. Can you tell me if he is out?"

There was a brief hesitation. "Yes, he is out. If you will give me your name and address, I will ask him to contact you."

Hunt felt better. For a moment there he had felt certain Brauer's killers had got here first.

"My name is Charles Hunt, and I am staying at the Baur au Lac Hotel."

"All right. I will tell Herr Schmidt to contact you there. When he comes in."

Hunt and Leni walked to the corner, waited for a taxi.

"Tell me about this man Schmidt," Leni said.

"The woman Brauer was looking for, Helene von Uderstadt, who may or may not have been the mother of Hitler's baby, was sent out of Germany, with her child, in April nineteen forty-five, to this man Schmidt."

"Forty-seven years ago? And you still expect to find him?"

"Darling," Hunt said. "I have just found him. That diary is the key."

"If it is the same Schmidt," Leni pointed out. "That concierge was lying to you."

101

Hunt frowned at her. "What do you mean by that?"

"What I said. He was not telling the truth when he said Schmidt was out."

"How do you know that?"

"Call it a woman's instincts."

"I stopped trusting those years ago."

Leni shrugged. "Do you still have the diary with you? We may need it."

"It's in the hands of the Hamburg police."

That gave her something to think about. Hunt waved his arm and a cab stopped. They rode back to the hotel in silence, but her remark had him worried. The problem was, if she was right, what to do about it?

He went to the desk for the key.

"Mr Hunt?" enquired the clerk on duty.

"That's right. Any messages?"

"Ah, no, sir."

The young man looked terrified.

"Mrs Grundy back yet?" Hunt asked.

"Ah, yes, sir. Would you like . . .?"

"No," Hunt said. "I'll call her when I'm ready." He collected Leni and they got into the elevator. "There's something going on I don't much care for," he said.

"About Schmidt, you mean?"

"I don't know." He unlocked the bedroom door, stood back to allow her to enter. She did so, switching on the light in the same movement, and stopping, immediately inside the door, so that Hunt bumped into her as he too tried to enter.

He looked past her at three men waiting in the centre of the room. The sinking feeling was back, even as he wondered whether he should throw Leni at them and try to get away.

The middle of the three men spoke in English. "Mr Hunt?"

Hunt's fingers had already closed on Leni's arms, but the man's voice made his pause; he had heard voices like that before, far too often.

102

"We are police officers, Mr Hunt," the man said. "We wish to ask you some questions."

"What about?" Leni asked, revealing another facet of her character, as she also spoke English – very well.

The police inspector looked at her.

"My assistant," Hunt explained, brain racing. "But she has a point."

The inspector nodded. "Will you come in, and close the door, Mr Hunt?"

Hunt eased Leni forward, pushed the door shut.

"It is a murder investigation," the Inspector said. "We wish to speak with you about the death of Walther Schmidt."

CHAPTER THREE

Geli replaced the phone. She was shaking. Because now she was sure something had happened to Uncle Walther. That what had happened was connected with the death of the man Brauer seemed equally certain. There was a force advancing towards her, tracing her movements from when she had been a babe in her mother's arms, and then ruthlessly eliminating each link.

But there were no remaining links between Uncle Walther and herself!

There was so much needed doing, she was certain, and she could not make herself move.

When she returned downstairs, the others were watching the news, but even if she accepted the worst, that Uncle Walther was dead, the death of an elderly Swiss lawyer was not international news in the way the murder of Gustave Brauer had been. Therefore she did not even know, as yet, if Uncle Walther had been murdered. Only that there was a strange man in his apartment. Geli shivered, went to the bar and poured herself a brandy.

"You all right?" Hans asked.

"I'm fine," she said, and sat with them to watch a movie.

What was she to do? Tell Hans? That was an impossible thought. She simply could not imagine what his reaction would be. Whatever was happening on the other side of Europe, it might well mean the end of her marriage. Her so happy, so contented marriage.

Besides, she tried telling herself, if there was no intermediate link between Uncle Walther and herself, there was a sizeable gap.

Except that Uncle Walther would undoubtedly have her address, and if he had been killed, his murderers would be going through his files . . . She poured herself another drink, spilling some as her hand was shaking.

But surely he would not keep her address at the apartment? It would be in his office, where it would be difficult to obtain. And anyway, hers would not be the only address on file in the office of a busy man like Walther.

Save that he had retired. Perhaps she was his only remaining client. She took great gulps of her drink, holding the glass in both hands.

The telephone rang and she spilled her drink again as she leapt out of her seat to get it before any of the others could. "Hello?" she shouted. "Hello? Who is this?"

"Geli?" The voice was high and excited. But this voice was always excited.

"Oh, Freya," Geli said, in a mixture of disappointment and relief.

"Geli? Are you all right, Geli?"

"Yes. Of course I am all right, Freya."

"But you were coming to play bridge this evening. And you were not here," Freya pointed out with devastating logic.

"Oh. Was I? Oh, Freya, I am terribly sorry. I'm afraid I am not very well."

"You forgot," Freya accused.

"Because I am not well," Geli insisted. "Listen, I will call you in a day or two. I do apologise, Freya."

"You should send for the doctor," Freya said severely, and hung up.

Geli started to bite her nails.

*

"I told you that concierge was lying," Leni said, sounding rather like an irate schoolmistress. "He knew Schmidt was dead. And he was just waiting to telephone the police."

"Exactly," the Inspector said.

"He was murdered?" Hunt asked.

"We are treating the death as murder, yes."

"Do you know who did it?"

"Why, no, Mr Hunt, not yet. We are hoping you will be able to assist us in our enquiries. Why do you not sit down?"

Leni was the first to obey the request. Hunt sat beside her. If his brain was tumbling, he was, as with Brauer, principally aware of anger.

"My name is LeCompte," the Inspector said. "And this young lady?"

"Leni Angstrom. Can you tell me if Schmidt was knocked about before death?"

"Knocked about? Ah, you mean tortured? Yes, it would appear that he was. That is why we are treating it as murder. Herr Schmidt actually died of a heart attack while being questioned."

"How was he being questioned?"

The Inspector gave Leni a rather anxious glance.

"She's a big girl," Hunt assured him. "But you can tell that by looking at her."

Leni put out her tongue at him.

"I'm afraid it was very unpleasant," the Inspector said. "They held a naked flame to his private parts."

Leni swallowed.

"When you say a naked flame, would you suppose it may have been a cigarette lighter?" Hunt asked.

"Why, from the nature of the burns, I would say that is very probable. Why?"

"Then I can tell you who did it," Hunt said.

The Inspector raised his eyebrows.

"I suggest you contact Inspector Lorenz of the Hamburg police," Hunt said. "He is leading the investigation into the murder of Gustave Brauer."

The Swiss Inspector stroked his chin. "You think the two are connected?"

"Same MO, Inspector. Same reason. Brauer was actually strangled. Your man was probably luckier."

106

"I see. May I ask where you fit into this?" He glanced at Leni. "And the young lady?"

"I have told you, the young lady is my assistant," Hunt told him. "May I put my hand in my pocket?"

The Inspector nodded.

Hunt gave him a card.

"The *London Globe*," the Inspector said thoughtfully. "And you were also anxious to interview Herr Schmidt. May I ask you why?"

"I would prefer it if you didn't."

The Inspector pointed. "You turned up, knowingly, at the scene of a murder. I can hold you on suspicion. You may even be the murderer. They often do come back."

"Oh, really, Inspector. If you want to play games, I suggest you telephone the Atlantic Hotel in Hamburg. They will tell you I left, by car, at three o'clock this afternoon. The desk downstairs will tell you I arrived here just after seven. You try doing it faster than that in a saloon car. My assistant was with me all the time. Just when was Schmidt murdered, anyway?"

"It was at some time last night or very early this morning, Mr Hunt. Before dawn, certainly. Have you an alibi for then as well?" Again he glanced at Leni, who gave a little snort of derision.

"I was in bed at the Atlantic," Hunt told him.

"Can you prove that?"

"The hotel car park is locked at night, Inspector. If I had wanted to drive down here, and then back again so that it would look as if I had spent the night in my room, I would have had to make special and rather public arrangements."

"Mr Hunt, I am quite sure that you did not cause Herr Schmidt's death. But I am also quite sure that you have a fairly good idea of why he was murdered. Without this information my investigation is hampered. Therefore, from my point of view, you are a very material witness. My only material witness. I have every right to hold you for further questioning, unless you are prepared to co-operate."

107

Hunt's brain had been working overtime during the exchanges. Brauer's killers had obviously got Schmidt's address from the old journalist before killing him. They had thus come down here, immediately, gained access to the lawyer's apartment and set about torturing him for more information on the whereabouts of Hitler's daughter. But Schmidt had proved of tougher material than Brauer and had died without telling them what they wanted to know: the Inspector had said quite definitely that he had died under interrogation. Had he told his tormentors what they wanted to know, they would merely have strangled him as they had Brauer.

Therefore their quest had come to a dead end. Therefore . . . they would most probably know about him. Because if Brauer had reached the stage of giving answers, he might well have told them of the plans he had made for the diary. But if Leni was truly not connected with them, that had interested them only in so far as they needed to have made their next move before the diary could be collected from the bank. From their point of view it contained nothing of value, as they already had the address of Schmidt.

Presumably it had crossed their minds to eliminate the only other man who could possibly obtain that address, but they had discarded that idea, partly because they reckoned they had something like a twelve-hour start – and they assumed that was sufficient – and partly because to plan and carry out the murder of an internationally known correspondent, in one of Hamburg's best hotels, would have been to undertake an unnecessary risk.

That all made logical sense. But now, with Schmidt dead, he was their only possible lead. He actually knew nothing about how the quest for Hitler's daughter was to continue, but they would have to hope that he did, that perhaps there had after all been something in the diary to help him take the search a stage further.

That meant they had to be still in Zurich. That they had probably been watching the apartment building this evening. In which case they probably knew where he was right this minute.

And also that he was closeted with the police?

He had a distinct feeling that the hairs on the back of his neck were prickling.

"Well, Mr Hunt?"

"Okay, Inspector, I'll do a deal with you. I'll tell you what I am after, and what the killers are after too, if you will let me take a look in Herr Schmidt's apartment."

"It has already been thoroughly searched."

"I'd still like to take a look."

"Very well. When?"

"Well, time is of the essence, Inspector."

The Inspector sighed. "Very well. We will go there immediately."

"Wait just one moment," Leni said. "When do we eat? It's gone eight and I'm starving. I didn't have any lunch, remember," she told Hunt.

"Well, I offered you some," he countered. "We'll eat as soon as we've had a look at the apartment. Work before play, right?"

She gave one of her little snorts.

The Swiss policemen had been waiting patiently.

"Now you tell us what you are after?"

"It's very simple, from my point of view. Herr Brauer was compiling data for a new biography of Heinrich Himmler, and he claimed to have come across information that there is still a prominent Nazi at large. This person he proposed to track down, but he lacked the funds to carry out an extensive search by himself so he approached my paper. The *Globe* agreed to take part, and I was assigned to the job."

"With your assistant," the Inspector put in. Hunt began to realise that he was not by any means as slow as he wished to appear.

"With my assistant, of course," Hunt agreed.

"And the name of this man you are seeking?"

"I do not know," Hunt said, truthfully. Geli Hitler

would hardly be living under that name now. "Brauer merely knew that the man Schmidt would have information which should help us. However, there appear to be some people who wish to find our quarry even more urgently than we do."

"So they tortured and murdered Herr Brauer, and then came down here. But how can you be sure Herr Schmidt was not the man they were looking for? We do know that he had Nazi connections during the war."

"Well, you could be right, Inspector. But if these people were merely looking for Schmidt, why, having found him, should they torture him until he died?"

"Hm," the Inspector commented. "Unless it was not Schmidt, or any human being, they were looking for, but something which they felt Schmidt possessed and which he would not give to them."

"I still go for a human being, from what Brauer told me."

"And you think you may be able to find something in the apartment that will tell you about this missing man?"

"Or woman," Hunt said. He did not wish at any stage to be accused of lying to the police. "Yes, I am hoping to find something. So . . . let's go."

The telephone rang and five heads turned.

"You'd better answer it, sir," the Inspector suggested.

Hunt knew who it was going to be, and had to form a plan of campaign very rapidly. He picked it up. "Hello?"

"Charles? Charles! Just what the hell is going on? I'm told you're here but that I'm not to contact you, that you have some kind of blonde floosie in tow, and now that you are here you're being interrogated by the police. I thought we were down here to work, Charles!"

"I'm sorry," he said. "But you have the wrong room."

He replaced the receiver. "Let's go." Before she gathers her wits and rings again, he thought. Or comes along here in person.

"Who did they want?" the Inspector asked as they went into the corridor.

110

"Someone called Robert Browning," Hunt told him. "Does that name mean anything to you?"

The Inspector stroked his chin as he watched Hunt close and lock the door. "The name is familiar, yes. But I cannot place it."

"The phone is ringing again," Leni pointed out.

"Probably the same mistake," Hunt assured her and hurried them along the corridor to the lift.

Disappointingly, Schmidt's apartment had been aired: there was no perfume to be smelt. No doubt fortunately, there were no other odours left as well.

"The apartment had been searched by the murderers," LeCompte explained. "It was in some disorder."

"Do you think they found anything worthwhile?"

"I do not think so. Although Mr Schmidt was a very old man, he remained senior partner in his law firm and even, I understand, continued to handle one or two old clients. All that confidential information is kept in the computers in the law office. This one . . ." he tapped the little PC, "seems to have been used for letters and household accounts. The hard disk is being analysed now by our people. But I ran it through quickly this morning myself. There does not appear to have been anything of importance on it. We have of course already contacted Herr Schmidt's nephew, who is now the senior partner in the firm."

"And what did he have to say?"

LeCompte shrugged. "He wishes to say nothing on grounds of client's confidentiality. But I am obtaining a court order forcing him to allow us to inspect his files tomorrow morning."

"When you hope to make progress. But do you mean the disk was still in this machine when you arrived? The killers didn't take it?"

"No. Which is not to say they didn't examine it. According to the concierge they were up here for several hours."

111

"And he had no idea what was going on?"

"None, Mr Hunt. They rang the apartment street bell, spoke with Mr Schmidt and he allowed them upstairs. There was no reason for the concierge to be the least suspicious."

"Until when?"

"Until this morning. Herr Schmidt was apparently in the habit of taking an early morning walk, and this time he did not. The concierge felt he might have overslept and called him on the telephone as he was instructed to do in such circumstances. When the phone was not answered he came up and let himself in with his passkey. He was quite shocked by what he found."

Hunt wondered if poor Schmidt had been desperately trying to keep alive until the precious telephone call.

"And what time did the killers leave?"

"The concierge does not know. They did so when he was asleep. Now, Mr Hunt, I have answered all of your questions and, like your assistant, I think it is time we had some supper."

Hunt looked at the telephone and the ansaphone. "Were there any messages on the phone?"

"No."

"Your people played it through?"

"I played it through myself, Mr Hunt. There was the call from the concierge. Nothing else."

"Where is the tape?"

LeCompte raised his eyebrows. "Still in the machine."

"Mind if we play it through again?"

"There was nothing on it."

"When you played it back. What time was that?"

"About eight o'clock this morning."

"And did you have someone in the apartment for the rest of the day?"

"No. We locked it up and sealed it at ten o'clock when our forensic people were finished. The concierge was instructed to telephone us if anyone attempted to see Mr Schmidt . . . and this he did when you appeared."

"Therefore the apartment has been sealed since ten o'clock this morning."

"That's right."

"Don't you think someone may have telephoned since then?"

LeCompte frowned. "You mean after Schmidt was already dead? Why should the murderers do that?"

"I am not thinking of the murderers. But it will still be interesting to listen to."

"I doubt that. But . . . put the machine on, Sergeant."

The sergeant flicked the switch and they listened to the woman's voice. And then a second time.

"As you say, that is quite interesting," LeCompte observed. "A woman called Geli who is alarmed about Brauer's murder."

"And who knew Schmidt well enough to call him Walther," Hunt suggested.

"Uncle Walther," Leni corrected.

"That is true. Do you know of such a woman, Mr Hunt?"

"I know dozens of women called Geli," Hunt told him. "As to whether any of them knew Schmidt . . .?"

"Still, as you say, it is interesting. I will certainly have it checked out. Well, Mr Hunt, are you satisfied?"

"Oh, indeed. You have been most co-operative, Inspector."

"Well . . ."

The telephone jangled.

Hunt and the Inspector gazed at each other.

"I think someone should answer that," Hunt suggested.

LeCompte picked up the receiver. "Herr Schmidt's apartment," he said in German. He waited, listening, for a moment, then he said, "Who is this?" This time there was apparently a reply because he said, "Herr Schmidt is not here at this moment. If you will give me your name and telephone number, I will ask him to call." Then he raised his eyebrows. "The person hung up."

"Do you know who it was?"

113

"Oh, yes, Mr Hunt. It was the same woman who called earlier. The woman on the ansaphone."

Hunt wondered if she wore Adoration perfume. But that was ridiculous. The women who wore Adoration knew Schmidt was dead.

"Can you trace that call?"

"It was brief. But with the other calls, we should be able to do so. And what are your plans now?"

Hunt smiled at Leni. "I think they had better concern food or I am going to have a strike on my hands."

"But you will keep in touch."

"Oh, certainly," Hunt assured him.

"Food," Leni said as they got out of the police car in the forecourt of the Baur au Lac. "I am so hungry I could eat anything."

"Well, I just have to pee. I don't think I'll make the room. Listen, here's the key. Why don't you order from Room Service at the desk? It'll be quicker. I'll just go and do what I have to do, and I'll see you upstairs."

"All right. But I don't know what you want."

"Anything you want, darling. And some decent wine."

He ran in the direction of the Gents, then doubled round a couple of potted palms. Leni had both elbows on the desk and was studying the Room Service menu with a helpful clerk. Hunt went up the stairs two at a time. By the time he reached the third floor he was willing to concede that Leni could be right and he was out of condition.

He took a couple of deep breaths and knocked on Corinne's door.

It opened immediately and he was the recipient of an icy stare, as well as a powerful hand which seized his jacket lapel and almost jerked him into the room.

"You are lucky I am still here," Corinne told him. "I damn near caught the evening plane back out."

Hunt closed the door behind himself and gave her a hug and a kiss on each cheek. "I would have been desolated. My, you look good."

114

Corinne always surprised him. It was in fact one of the great disappointments of his life that he had never watched her playing soccer, with presumably her long legs muscling out from her tight shorts, her magnificently tight bum rotating madly as she galloped up and down the field, black hair flowing in the breeze like some latter-day Valkyrie, even, perhaps, small breasts jouncing beneath her shirt.

That was, regrettably, fifteen years in the past, but Corinne remained a distinctly athletic woman, even when wrapped up in a blood-red house robe and, he suspected, nothing else. Her legs were still long, her hair still black, her features still boldly challenging, as if the entire male sex was an opposing goalkeeper who required flattening, by fair means or foul.

Hunt had often thought that being shipwrecked on a desert island with Corinne would probably be very close to paradise, if only because she would instinctively do most of the work when it came to building huts or fishing or climbing coconut trees.

"I watched you getting out of the police car," she growled. "Who's the blonde?"

"That is something I want us to work on."

Corinne raised her eyebrows. "You're double entendring very well tonight. But I presume you have already done some research on the subject."

"Not enough. I haven't had the time. And I don't have much time now. Listen. Did Halliday give you any kind of briefing?"

"It was brief, if that's what you mean. Brauer, Himmler, murder, some female who could be Hitler's daughter."

"Then check this." Hunt brought her as fully up to date as he could. "Now what I want you to do is this: get hold of Richement, remind him he is the paper's local correspondent and that the time has come to earn his keep. I want, just as rapidly as possible, all the information he can get on the woman who telephoned Walther Schmidt three times today."

"What information can be possibly get in these automated days?"

"If he knows the right people, he can certainly find out
where the calls originated, and even the number from
which they originated. In addition to being automated,
they're all automatically recorded and billed."

"Well . . . all right."

"He'll have to be careful because I suspect the police
will be after the same info. right this minute."

"I'll tell him. What are you going to be doing?"

"Having dinner."

"With your little blonde bit."

"If you really did see us getting out of the car you'll
know she isn't that little. Now, Corinne, listen. I don't
want her to know you're my back-up. That is very
important. As I told you, we're dealing with two separate
groups here, as far as I can determine, and it's our business
to remain one jump ahead. You get me that information,
and contact me the very moment you do."

"Won't I be interrupting something?"

Hunt grinned at her. "Hopefully not. Now, you understand what I want?"

"I suppose so."

He took her in his arms, sniffed. "How many?"

"Well . . . there didn't seem much else to do."

"Listen, sweetheart, this is a twenty-four hour a day
assignment. Stay sober or get a replacement."

"Holding you like this," Corinne remarked dreamily,
"I could knee you in the balls so hard you really wouldn't
enjoy your evening."

Hunt gripped her shoulders and stepped back. "Get
me that info. and call," he reminded her. "Don't pay
any attention to what I say on the phone. I'll be right
down." He closed the door behind himself.

Leni was standing at the window, looking out. She
turned as he came in. "You must have the bladder of
a camel."

116

"I got caught short the other way. Where's dinner?"

"On its way." She came towards him. "Hunt, what happens now?"

"I'm thinking about it. But I do that better on a full stomach."

"Do you think the woman on the phone is the one we want?"

"Yes."

"Then you think she is here in Switzerland?"

"No."

"Why not?"

"Because if she was, and she was that agitated by Brauer's death that she simply had to get in touch with Schmidt . . . had she been within driving distance she would surely have come to see him. And there is nowhere is Switzerland which isn't within driving distance of Zurich."

"Ah. You seem able to think of everything."

"I thought you didn't like me?"

"I don't. That does not mean I cannot respect your professional expertise."

"Well, I'm quite good at some other things, too."

"I know. Unarmed combat."

"It comes in a lot of shapes."

"I am sure. Here is dinner."

The trolley was wheeled into the room and Hunt realised that Leni hadn't been exaggerating when she had said she was hungry. He watched two ounces of caviar disappear as if it were soup, and bent over the remains. "That's not Danish."

"Russian," Leni explained with her mouth full.

"For Jesus' sake. And what's to follow?"

"Fillet steak."

Hunt looked at the bottle of claret. "Château Batailley seventy-five," he remarked.

"There's not a lot of the seventy-five left, nowadays," Leni explained. "You have to drink it whenever you see it. Of course, it's a little pricey. But you told me you wanted decent wine."

"What do you specialise in as a journalist – food and drink?"

"Do you know," she said thoughtfully, "I never have. When we have tracked this woman down, I might do a series on the good things in life."

The caviar was finished and the waiter hurried forward to uncover the steaks and offer the wine.

"I'm not sure my editor is going to appreciate this," Hunt remarked.

Leni smiled at him. "But you are, Hunt. I certainly am."

They ate, slowly and luxuriously. It was all very good. And there was Hine Antique to finish, with their coffee.

Leni sighed as she leaned back in her chair. "Now I at last feel good. How long do we stay in this hotel?"

Hunt was inspecting the account before signing it. Halliday was going to blow his top. "Not a moment longer than I can help." He watched the trolley being withdrawn and the door closed. "However, there is such a thing as paying the piper."

A meal like that always made him feel randy.

"Of course," she said. "I understand. And after a meal like that I might even do it." She got up, strolled about the room as she removed her jacket and then her shirt. "But are you sure an old man like you can manage it, after such a meal?"

Leni did not wear a bra and there could be no argument about her attractions. Hunt sat up. "I'm sure."

"Well . . ." She kicked off her shoes, released the waistband of her pants and slid them down to her thighs, revealing the skimpiest briefs he had ever seen on a woman . . . and the telephone buzzed.

"Oh, fuck it." But he had the presence of mind to reach the handset before she could.

"I thought you were going to fuck me," she remarked.

"Hello," Hunt groaned.

"Did I interrupt something?" Corinne asked. "I hope."

"Oh . . . Yes," he said.

118

"Has she got her knickers off yet? Or am I being naive?"

Hunt looked at Leni. The pants were off, anyway. She looked good enough to eat. But he believed in his own motto: work first and play after. "All right," he said. "I'll be right down."

He replaced the handset.

Leni had her thumbs into the elastic waistband of the briefs. Now she regarded him with arched eyebrows.

"That was the porter. Some question about the car. Look, I'll be back in five minutes. Why don't you just slip out of something more comfortable and get into bed?"

Leni shrugged and switched on the television.

Hunt hurried along the corridor, more than ever aware of being both overweight and a trifle overage for this kind of thing. He'd been absolutely crazy to have that second brandy.

"You look all hot and bothered," Corinne commented.

"I am all hot and bothered. Give."

"You mean you haven't had her yet?"

"Where was the woman calling from?"

Corinne sat at her dressing-table and checked her notes. "Istanbul."

"Istanbul?"

"It's a town in Turkey."

"Yes," Hunt said.

"I even have her name and telephone number. A Mrs Hans Littler."

"You have been efficient."

"Thank you. I assume you wish to get to this woman just as fast as possible?"

"I do."

"That's what I thought. I have checked with the desk. We can catch a plane at ten o'clock tomorrow morning which will land us at Istanbul at one o'clock local time; they're a bit ahead of us, time wise."

"If the flight isn't fully booked."

119

"There'll be seats, first-class. Do I book for two or three?"

"Cheer me up. I think I used up all my expenses on dinner. Okay, I'll leave that with you. Get three tickets first thing tomorrow morning and leave my two at the desk."

"I will get the tickets now," Corinne said. "The desk serves as a travel agency as well, for hotel guests. The boy said he could make them up for me whenever I wish."

"So be super-efficient. Remember, we don't know each other."

"How long does this go on?"

"Until we find Mrs Littler, or until Leni shows her hand."

"Is it her hand you're after?"

He kissed her. "Sleep tight."

"In my lonely bed," she said. "And guess what, I haven't had a drink since dinner."

"Stay with it."

He closed the door behind himself, went up the stairs. Mrs Hans Littler. Was this the mother or the daughter? He rather went for the daughter. At the very least, the mother had to be past sixty-five. The daughter would be twenty years younger than that, and the voice on the ansaphone recording had been young and strong . . . although, he reminded himself, she would still be older than himself.

And the mother might very well still be alive. What secrets might she hold locked away in her brain?

He hurried along the corridor on the fourth floor and checked when almost at his bedroom door. His nostrils twitched. Adoration!

In the corridor!

He stood at the door and listened. Not a sound came from inside. Leni had been about to watch television. But maybe these were very solid doors.

He moved back along the corridor as quickly as he could without making a noise, went down the stairs and knocked on Corinne's door.

This time the blood-red robe had been very hastily put on. But she looked pleased to see him. "Don't tell me, she's done a bunk."

"Listen," he said. "I don't suppose you have a weapon?"

"I have lots of weapons," Corinne said, shaking her hips at him.

Hunt stepped past her, looked round the room. Hotel bedrooms were so indefensible. He dropped to his hands and knees and looked under the bed. No luck.

"As a matter of fact," Corinne said, "there is one. In the bedside cupboard."

"Well, I suppose beggars can't be choosers. Corinne, I wish you to do something for me."

"In the chamber pot?"

"With the chamber pot. Unless you possess anything more lethal hidden away somewhere. I think there are nasties in my room."

Corinne raised her eyebrows. "With the blonde bit?"

"Yes. Now, I may be wrong. However, if I'm right I'll need support. You."

"Me," Corinne said sadly.

"So I am going to go back up there. You will give me ten minutes, then you will come up and knock on the door. Now I want you to listen very carefully because you have to get this right. You will come up carrying your chamber pot, and when the door opens you will hit whoever opens it on the head, as hard as you can, without any hesitation whatsoever. Unless, and please remember this, it happens to be me."

Corinne's eyes were wide. "You mean I can hit your friend?"

"If she opens the door, yes."

"Whoopee. Please let her open the door."

"Listen! I don't know how many of these people there are. Having eliminated one, I wish you to enter the bedroom and cause as much mayhem as you can, right? Until they are all out of action."

"Sounds like fun."

121

"I should point out that these people are almost certainly armed and highly dangerous. To my knowledge they have killed two people already."

"If they are that dangerous," Corinne said, "and you have been playing tag with them for the past twenty-four hours, how come *you* aren't armed?"

"I am, sweetheart. But my gun is in the bedroom and I don't know if I am going to be able to get at it."

"Oh, big deal," she remarked. "I wonder what James Bond would say about that."

"So, don't forget what you have to do. And also don't forget that you and I are strangers."

"So why am I knocking on your bedroom door with a potty in my hand?"

"Because you're drunk and have lost your way."

"Ah," Corinne said.

Hunt returned up the stairs. He'd been gone rather a long time and he reflected that if Leni had allowed herself to be nobbled, they might have got tired of waiting for him to come back. On the other hand, even if she had been suffering a bit, she couldn't tell them anything more than that herself . . . and she had wanted to come along.

The temptation to call up Carl as well was enormous. But he had to keep an ace in the hole and if Corinne was still as good as she used to be, he wouldn't need him.

He slowed up as he approached his door to get his breathing under control. He was not a man who ran away from trouble, but how he hoped the door would be opened by Leni, in her brief briefs and all ready for bed. After all, the woman who had tortured Brauer and Schmidt was not the only one in the world to wear Adoration.

He stood at the door, knocked. There was no sound from inside.

"Leni?" he called. "Leni? Open up."

Still there was no sound.

He frowned and tried the handle. It turned in his hand

and the door swung in. The room was dark and if the scent of Adoration was present, it was shrouded in a great many other scents.

Hunt took a long breath and reached for the light switch. As he did so his arm was seized and he was jerked forward. He didn't go very far as he ran into someone who was waiting for him and hit him very hard in the stomach. Hunt gasped and sank to his knees while stars spun in front of his eyes, and he heard the door close as from a great distance.

Then the light was on and he was staring at trouser legs and an automatic pistol, equipped with a silencer, which was being pointed at his head.

"Co-operate, Hunt," the man said in German.

Hunt raised his head and gazed at his captor. He turned his head, looked at the younger, bearded man who had pulled him into the room. He looked to his left, at the woman smiling at him. He knew at once, and had it confirmed by his nostrils, that she was Adoration, and found himself surprised and disturbed by both her age and her elegance.

Then he looked past her at Leni. She lay on the bed, bound hand and foot and also gagged, so that she could make no sound. She did not appear to have been harmed but they had taken off her briefs, or maybe she had done that before they had come in. The important thing was that her pale pubes were unsinged . . . so far.

"Don't you people ever sleep?" Hunt asked.

"You think it is some kind of a game," Adoration said. She sat down in one of the two chairs in the room. "No, don't get up. Stay there on your knees." She smiled. "You may need to be in that position to pray."

Hunt waited. He reckoned about half of the ten minutes were up. But even Corinne's interruption was going to be difficult to capitalise on while he was kneeling facing a pistol. He could only hope that her entry would indeed be with all her talents in action.

"I am sure you understand the situation, Hunt," Adoration said. "We are both seeking the same object. But your quest is merely for front page news, and possibly some lucrative rewards. Ours is a much more serious affair. Therefore you will understand that we do not think it is a game at all."

"Oh, quite," Hunt said. "But we are both now in the same boat. Thanks to your overheavy methods, we have lost all our leads."

"Have we, Hunt? I do not think so. I think you may have more information than us. I think you should tell us about it. Firstly, I would like the diary."

"The diary is in the hands of Inspector Lorenz of the Hamburg police," Hunt told her. "As he is in charge of the investigation, should you care to go and collect it from him, I know he will be pleased to see you."

Adoration studied him for some seconds. "Perhaps you are telling the truth," she said. "But it is no matter. You have read it and therefore you know what is in it. I wish you to tell me where we can find Fraulein Hitler."

"There was nothing in it about Fraulein Hitler," Hunt assured her, as usual carefully telling the truth: the diary had been about the girl's mother. "Brauer believed that Walther Schmidt, who, you may or may not know, was an SS moneybroker during the war, was the man who looked after the removal of a certain lady from Germany in the spring of nineteen forty-five and who, presumably, kept her in funds after that. Therefore, Schmidt would know where she was. With her daughter, if she had one. Well . . . you have gone and finished Schmidt. So I would say we all go back to what we were doing before this caper began."

Adoration regarded him for several seconds.

"He is lying," the older man said.

"Oh, indeed," Adoration agreed.

"Let me have him," the younger man requested.

Presumably he was the smoker in the party.

124

Adoration considered. "He is quite tough," she commented. "And overweight. It is a bad combination. We do not want him dying of a heart attack. We will do better with the girl, while he watches. I think that may break him down more quickly. He is obviously very fond of the girl."

The younger man shrugged, a trifle petulantly, felt in his pocket and took out a gold-plated cigarette lighter. This he flicked, and then carefully adjusted the flame to its greatest extent.

Leni gave a little moan and a wriggle. While Hunt thought this was the longest ten minutes he had ever experienced. What in the name of God was Corinne doing?

The younger man knelt on the bed beside Leni. "This may hurt a little," he said.

Leni's moan was almost a shriek, even through the gag.

And there came a tap on the door.

Five heads turned together.

"Are you expecting someone?" Adoration asked Hunt.

"I wish to God I was."

"Get up," she said.

Hunt obeyed, for a moment hit by the dreadful thought that he might be commanded to open the door. But Adoration merely gestured him away from the direct line of vision. "Stand there," she ordered. "And do not move. Heinrich, get rid of whoever it is."

The older man nodded and went to the door. He opened it, allowing it to come in only a few inches, and a chamber pot, apparently delivered with an overhead swing, crashed on to his head.

The thick porcelain shattered as Heinrich hit the carpet without a sound other than the thump of his collapsing weight.

Adoration gave a startled exclamation and reached for her bag. The younger man was quicker, dropped the lighter on to Leni's stomach – fortunately it went out as

125

he released the cap – levelled his pistol and fired in one movement. He had in fact been too quick, however: the bullet smashed into the woodwork beside the door while Corinne was still outside, and before he could squeeze the trigger a second time the room was filled with a blood-red and black explosion.

Corinne had found two more weapons. In her right hand she carried, by the neck, a bottle of Johnnie Walker Black, and in her left, also by the neck, a bottle of Smirnoff. The Scotch thudded into the side of the young man's head. He had got his arm up and wasn't laid out, but he fell heavily against the wall and dropped his pistol.

Adoration had by then drawn hers but that too went flying as the vodka, coming in a backhanded sweep, struck her arm. She fell right across the bed and on to the floor.

"Get her!" Hunt commanded, as Corinne seemed to have momentarily run out of steam, mainly because she was gazing with a stricken expression at the two broken bottles and the cascading liquor.

He himself went for the young man, who was back on his knees and reaching for his pistol. Hunt hit him a swinging right-handed punch, and he fell away from the gun. Hunt reached for it in turn and was struck a savage blow in the middle of his back, which again flattened him. He got his head up in time to see Adoration's legs disappearing as she left through the open door.

"Shit!" Corinne commented. She had dived right across the bed after her quarry, kneeling on a gasping Leni as she did so, but Adoration had rolled away.

Hunt reached his knees and the young man kicked him in the chest. He fell backwards, and was struck another blow on the back. This time it was Corinne, again on her feet and starting a hot pursuit. Now she fell right over him, landing on her hands and knees with a shock which again shook the room. Before either of them could recover, the young man was also through the door.

"For Jesus' sake," Hunt commented.

Corinne stayed on her knees as she crawled forward, firstly to retrieve the young man's pistol, which she thrust into her waistband, and secondly to peer at Heinrich.

"Oh, Lord," she remarked.

"Oh, God!" Hunt agreed, kneeling beside her. There was a lot of blood, and when he put his fingers on Heinrich's temple there was no pulse.

"Well," Corinne said. "You told me to come in swinging."

"Oh, quite," Hunt agreed. "I had no idea I was unleashing Attila the Hunperson."

"Do you think there'll be trouble?" Corinne asked anxiously.

"Of course not," Hunt said. "I mean, hotels like the Baur au Lac have at least one corpse a day lying about. Don't they?"

"He was a thug. Surely we can prove he was a thug?" Corinne said defensively.

"I'm sure we can, during the next six months. Which isn't going to do us much good. Close the door." He seized Heinrich's ankles and pulled him into the room.

"Mmmmm," Leni remarked.

Corinne brushed the remains of the chamber pot into the room and closed the door.

"Do you suppose anyone heard the noise?"

"Give or take a hundred. Depends how full the hotel is." Hunt surveyed Heinrich's lifeless body. His brain was going round and round.

The phone jangled.

Corinne and Hunt looked at each other.

"Mmmm," Leni said urgently.

"She's not very lucid," Corinne remarked.

"I would say someone heard the noise," Hunt said, making some very quick decisions.

He picked up the phone.

"Mr Hunt?"

"Yes."

"This is the Duty Manager, Mr Hunt. I am afraid there

127

have been several complaints about the noise coming from your room."

"Complaints!" Hunt shouted. "Of all the bloody cheek. Complaints?"

"Well, sir, there seems to have been an unusual amount of noise. I will have to ask you to be more quiet."

"Oh, yes?" Hunt demanded. "Or what will you do?"

"Well, sir, if that is your attitude, I will have to ask you to leave, as soon as is convenient, tomorrow."

"If that is *your* attitude," Hunt told him, "I will leave now!"

There was a moment's astonished silence. Then the Duty Manager said, "It is midnight. Where will you go?"

"Anywhere will be better than here," Hunt pointed out.

"My dear sir, if you will only be reasonable . . ."

"I am leaving now," Hunt insisted.

The Duty Manager sighed. "Very well, sir. I will send up a porter for your luggage . . ."

"Forget it," Hunt said. "I travel light. Just get my bill ready for when I come down." He replaced the handset. "There goes my reputation at one of the best hotels in Europe. Get out of here and back to your room, Corinne. Now listen very carefully. Do you have a car?"

"I hired one at the airport. I thought it might come in handy."

"Good girl. Where is it parked? In the hotel park?"

"No. On the street out there."

"Better girl. Can you get out of the hotel without anyone knowing?"

"I imagine so."

"Right. Give us time to leave and wait for things to settle down, then leave the hotel, get into your car and take the road to Baden. Ten kilometres out of Zurich there is a turn-off on to a B-road for Weiningen. Turn down there. A kilometre down that road we will be waiting for you. Got me?"

"Yes. But what about him?"

"You never saw him in your life, and you have not been in my room tonight. Unfortunately, everyone in the hotel knows you came here to join me, but you have not even seen me yet and you have no idea what I have been up to. Right?"

"Right," Corinne said doubtfully. "I wish you'd explain to me what you're planning to do."

"I'll explain when you pick us up. Now get to it."

"Mmmmmm," Leni commented.

"I would keep her gagged," Corinne suggested, and went to the door. "When?"

"One hour."

Corinne nodded, turned to the door and froze as there came a knock.

Damn, Hunt thought. If Carl had waited just another two minutes.

"What are we going to do?" Corinne whispered, staring at Heinrich's body.

"Leave this one to me." Hunt opened the door a crack, gazed at the man who stood there wearing the uniform of a bellhop.

"Good evening, Herr Hunt," the man said. "My name is Carl. Is there anything I can do to help?"

"You'd better come in."

Carl stepped into the room, looked at Corinne and then at Leni, still lying bound and gagged, and naked, on the bed. He looked at Leni for several seconds. Then he looked at the man on the floor. "Is he . . .?"

"Absolutely. You know we are checking out?"

"That is why I am here."

"How long will we have?"

"Not very. There will be someone in this room almost immediately."

"I need time, Carl."

Carl nodded. "There is a vacant room two doors away. If we put him in there, he will not be discovered until the chambermaids go in, and that will not be until ten o'clock tomorrow morning. This morning, I should say."

"Right. Is the corridor clear?"

"Yes."

"Then let's shift him."

Carl looked at Leni again, somewhat longingly. "And the woman?"

"She's with me."

"Ah." Carl was clearly disappointed. But he stooped and grasped Heinrich's shoulders. Hunt held his legs and they lifted him from the floor.

Corinne, who had been left speechless by Carl's appearance, recovered. "There's blood on the carpet."

"Pour water on to it," Carl recommended. "Then the maids will not immediately understand what it is."

The two men carried Heinrich's body into the vacant room and laid it on the bed. Then Carl carefully locked the door behind them. "Will there be anything further, Herr Hunt?"

"I think you want to forget you ever saw me."

"Oh, I shall do that. I am sorry I could not offer actually to dispose of the body. But . . ."

"I should have asked for more support. You've done everything you could, Carl. I won't forget it."

"Thank you, Herr Hunt. And . . . good hunting."

Hunt returned to the bedroom.

"Hunt," Corinne said, "just what the hell is going on?"

"Carl is my second cousin, twice removed," Hunt explained. "He is a bellhop in this hotel. Which is why I am staying here."

Corinne snorted.

"I wouldn't knock it," Hunt suggested. "Seeing as how it was you actually did for poor Heinrich. Now you know what you have to do. Do it."

Corinne looked as if she would have liked to argue some more, then she went to the doorway, regarded Leni for several seconds, said, "Have fun," and left.

"Mmmm," Leni commented.

Hunt knelt beside her, released the gag.

130

"Water," she gasped.

He released her wrists and ankles, filled a tooth mug from the bathroom.

She drank greedily.

"Now get dressed," Hunt told her. "We have to move."

"Do you honestly think we'll get away with it?"

"Long enough."

"Long enough for what? What good is a scoop if we're both in prison for murder?"

"Look, are you getting dressed or are you coming like that? I am leaving here in five minutes."

Leni swung her legs off the bed, and checked. "Who were these people, anyway?"

"The heavy mob." Hunt was looking round the room. The place stank of liquor, naturally, but there wasn't a lot he could do about that. In fact, the stench and the broken crockery should distract any maid from the brown stain on the carpet. It might even stop her noticing the bullet holes.

He picked up the two remaining guns, dropped them into his overnight bag.

Leni was dressing, slowly. She had a lot on her mind. "Then who was that woman? The one with the chamber pot?"

"A friend of mine. I ran into her when I had to go down to the car just now, and when I realised there was going to be trouble, I asked her to help."

"Hunt," Leni said severely, "you are lying to me."

"It's a habit I got into as a small boy," Hunt confessed. "And nowadays I'm finding it increasingly difficult to break."

"You expect me to believe . . ."

"It doesn't matter a damn what you believe, darling," Hunt said. "If Corinne hadn't agreed to pitch in, this bedroom would presently be filled with the smell of singeing rather than liquor, and you would probably be dead. She's also going to help us get out of here without any unpleasantness from LeCompte. So for Christ's sake shut up and get on with it."

131

Leni got on with it but she was still brooding. She repacked her overnight bag, stepped into the corridor, watched Hunt carefully lock the door and pocket the key.

"You said you knew there'd be trouble," she said thoughtfully. "How did you know there'd be trouble?"

"I smelt it," Hunt said truthfully.

She brooded on that, as well, while they rode down in the elevator.

The Duty Manager was waiting for them. "There really is no need for you to leave, Mr Hunt," he protested. "Where are you going to go at this time of night?"

"To the airport. You have plane tickets waiting for me, to Istanbul."

"Yes, I have." He gave Hunt the envelope. "But the flight does not leave until ten in the morning."

"We'll sleep in the airport lounge. Have you got my bill?"

"It is here, sir. But really . . ."

Hunt paid by Eurocheques; he didn't want to wait while they obtained clearance for his card.

"Tell them to open the garage doors," Hunt said as he escorted Leni towards the elevator.

The Duty Manager sighed. "Of course, if you will not change your mind. Oh, Mr Hunt . . . the key, please?"

Hunt handed it over. "Good night to you. Or is it morning?"

The elevator doors closed. "Do you suppose this charade is going to fool them, or the police, for more than an hour?" Leni asked.

"Carl says we have until ten o'clock this morning."

"And then we're going to have every policeman in Switzerland at the airport, looking for us. And there's another thing. Who is this man Carl who so obligingly came out of the woodwork? And don't give me any bullshit about second cousins."

Hunt started the engine and drove out of the park as the gates swung up. "You wanted to come along."

"You don't think I'm entitled to know what's going on?"

"No."

"Well, at least tell me where we're going to hide."

"Well . . ." Hunt appeared to consider. "It won't be at the airport."

CHAPTER FOUR

"Why don't you tell me what the matter is?" Hans asked as they lay awake in the dawn.

"The matter? Nothing is the matter," Geli protested.

"You are upset. You have been upset since you heard of the death of that man, Brauer," Hans asserted.

"Oh, nonsense."

"Did you know him?"

"Know him? How was I to know him? I left Germany when I was three months old."

"Well, yes, but he might have come to visit you here. He might have been a friend of your mother's. Like old Walther Schmidt."

Geli sat up. "Hans, I had never even heard of Gustave Brauer before you mentioned his name yesterday morning."

"All right. Then why are you upset?"

"I am not upset," Geli shouted, scrambling out of bed and running for the bathroom before he could pursue the matter.

She could hardly wait for them all to get out of the house: she wanted to be alone.

But would they go out? It was Saturday. She could not remember what they all had on. Fortunately they slowly drifted away, one after the other. Hans was playing golf. Herrmann was going to the library. Paul was playing tennis. And Helene was visiting a girlfriend. They were an active family.

When Geli closed the door behind Helene she gave a huge sigh of relief. Shiera did not come in on Saturdays, and she was entirely alone. She could sit down and think. Rationalise. Regain control of her nerves, hopefully.

Last night had been flat panic. A strange man in Uncle Walther's apartment. Today, common sense, surely. A telephone call to Walther's office. That would put things right. On a Saturday? But young Walther was a workaholic. He always went in on a Saturday.

She looked at her watch. Half past eight. That meant it was half past six in Zurich. She would have to wait until at least nine o'clock, local time, eleven o'clock in Turkey. She might as well go shopping.

She put on her best smile, her most efficient bustle, and drove into Istanbul. She went to the supermarket and then to the bank – in Turkey Saturday was a full working day. She stood in the line for the teller. She normally cashed a hundred thousand lira to see her through the week; with inflation running at some sixty per cent in Turkey, the sum was slowly escalating. But then, so was the value of her monthly transfer from Zurich. Would the transfers stop if something had happened to Uncle Walther? But of course nothing had happened to Uncle Walther.

Still . . . she could not shake off a gut feeling that she might need more ready cash than usual. She wrote out a cheque for three hundred thousand and then asked to be admitted to her safe deposit box. There was little in there except for a few bonds she had bought . . . and her half of the brass alligator, bequeathed to her by her mother. She took it out and looked at it. Then she put it in her handbag.

She was acting purely on instinct, obeying some sixth sense which suggested that if Uncle Walther had been murdered by the same people who had murdered Gustave Brauer, and that they were in fact looking for her, the half-alligator might act as some kind of a talisman to ward them off.

Or bring them to heel?

She got home at half past ten. Then it was a case of waiting, watching the minutes ticking by, until five past eleven.

135

She dialled, watching through the window the breeze whipping up whitecaps at the north end of the Bosporus.

"Schmidt and Schmidt? May I speak with Mr Walther Schmidt, please? This is Frau Geli Littler calling."

There was an almost audible gulp at the far end of the phone. "Did you mean Mr Walther Senior, or Mr Walther Junior, madame?"

"Well, senior, if he is in."

"Will you hold the line one moment, madame?"

Geli waited. It really wasn't important if Schmidt & Schmidt traced the call: they know where she was to be found, anyway.

But the girl had almost made it sound as if Uncle Walther might be there.

"Madame? I'm afraid Mr Walther Senior will not be in this morning but Mr Walther Junior would like a word."

"Thank you." Progress at last. But her momentary optimism had faded. Something had definitely happened to Walther Senior.

"Frau Littler?" The voice was relatively young, and strong.

"Yes."

"Frau Littler, thank God that you have called. I was about to call you."

"Yes."

"I'm afraid something rather dreadful has happened."

"Yes?"

"Uncle Walther has died."

"Died?"

"Well . . . the police seem to think it was murder."

"Murder?"

"It was actually a heart attack but he was, ah . . . being ill-treated at the time."

"Yes." Poor Walther. They had been questioning him about her. They!

The man at the other end of the line had waited for a few moments, perhaps wondering at her lack of emotion.

136

Now he said, "Frau Littler, the police have been asking questions about you."

"Me?"

"Did you telephone Uncle Walther yesterday?"

"Well, yes, I did."

"More than once?"

"Well, yes. I wished to speak with him. But he was not there."

"I'm afraid he was already dead, Frau Littler. The police were able to trace the calls, you see, and they feel that you may have information which may possibly lead them to the killers."

"Me?" Geli's voice rose an octave.

"They asked me about it, you, of course, last night after they had traced the calls," Walther Schmidt Junior told her. "But I refused to discuss a client's affairs. However, I believe it is possible that they may send someone to speak with you."

"Oh!"

Why, oh why, had she telephoned?

"They cannot suspect I had anything to do with your uncle's death?"

"I am sure they do not, Frau Littler. Not directly. But I believe they may well mean to obtain a court order to look at our books. In which case they will find out all about you."

"All about me?" Geli's voice had risen another octave. "What do you mean?"

"Well . . . as I said, I was going to call you this morning, anyway. It is about the money, you see."

"Money?"

"You do not know about the money?"

"What money?" Geli shouted, her nerves at last giving way.

"Do you not know that my uncle was administering a trust fund in your name?"

"Well . . . I know he sent me money every month."

"From this trust fund, Frau Littler. I am afraid that

137

what I have to say to you may come as a considerable shock."

"Yes?" Geli's voice was now faint, even as she reflected that it did not really matter, financially, if her allowance were to cease with Uncle Walther's death . . . but Hans might well want to know why.

"My uncle was the sole administrator of this trust fund," Walther Schmidt Junior continued. "It was set up by certain parties who are now long dead. I do not wish to go into details over the telephone, but I believe their identities are known to you, Frau Littler."

"Your uncle told you this?"

"No. He never discussed it with me. However . . . I was informed yesterday morning of my uncle's murder. The police then naturally wished to examine his papers. I resisted this, both on the grounds of clients' entitlement to confidentiality and because I was able to explain to them that my uncle had retired and was no longer actively engaged in the business. The police seemed to accept this at the time but since then, as I have said, they have come back to me twice, last night at home, about your telephone calls. The last time they spoke with me they informed me that they would return this morning with a court order as they feel that there may be some clue to my uncle's murderer, or murderers, in his papers. I am bound to say that I now feel they may be right. That is why, first thing this morning, I came down here to go through them myself – I am his sole executor, you understand – and I came across this trust fund. Frau Littler. I must tell you right away that my uncle did not properly administer this fund. In the first instance, he remitted to your mother and then, after her death, to you, only a fraction of the income arising from the capital."

"Oh!" Geli said. "It always seemed such a lot of money."

"It was, a lot of money," Walther Schmidt Junior agreed.

"Far more than either your mother or yourself ever

138

apparently suspected. Or anyone else in the firm. When it was set up, of course. Uncle Walther was senior partner and in fact virtual sole partner. There was no one to ask questions and as your mother and yourself were always regarded by my uncle as especially his clients and no one else's, the matter has never been questioned to this day. However, the fact of the matter is that some three-quarters of the income arising from the trust fund was never remitted to either your mother or yourself. I am sorry to say that some of it, at least in the early days, was appropriated by my uncle for his own purposes. His lifestyle was always very good and no one questioned that either. In more recent times he had a legitimately high income and so the entire amount was re-invested, less such moneys as he remitted to you. Presumably he was afraid that if he suddenly started sending you greatly increased sums of money, you might start asking questions."

Geli discovered she was quite breathless. "Why are you telling me this, Herr Schmidt?"

"Because it is my duty to do so, Frau Littler, as I have just discovered this, ah, fraud, and because it is my duty to inform the police of it. You may think it proper to sue my firm for the return of the misappropriated moneys, and you would be within your rights to do so. Obviously I cannot advise you in this matter. However, my uncle, although I have just confessed that he has from time to time been a dishonest man, was not a bad one. The reason I discovered the fraud, which might otherwise have remained undetected for years, if not for ever, is that he himself confesses it in a letter addressed jointly to you and to myself. In this letter, which was only to be opened after his death and of which I am sending you a copy, he confesses to his irregularity and instructs me to wind up the trust and transfer all the funds to you. This I now propose to do. Have you any instructions regarding the disposition of the money?"

It was some moments before Geli could speak; her throat was dry.

"Is it a large amount?"

"I would describe it as a large amount."

"How much?"

"Well, if you do not mind my telling you over the telephone . . ."

"How much?" Geli asked again.

"Approximately three million Swiss francs."

"Three million?"

"Yes. That would be approximately three and a half million German marks, or one and a quarter million English pounds, or twelve million French francs, or two and a quarter million American dollars, at current rates. I am not quite sure of the amount in Turkish lira because the rate changes every few hours, but in any event I would strongly advise against transferring it into Turkish lira."

"Yes," Geli said absently. Three and a half million marks! Once again her brain seemed to have mounted a roller coaster. There were immediately so many imponderables . . . so many more imponderables than even a few hours before.

"Frau Littler?"

"Isn't it possible for the fund to remain as it is?"

"It is, Frau Schmidt. But it will be difficult for you to administer it from Istanbul."

"Can you not administer it for me, as your uncle did?"

"My uncle gave explicit instructions in his letter, Frau Schmidt, and those instructions I must carry out."

Geli got the message: he wanted out, just as quickly as possible. He had already indicated that he knew the fund had originally been set up by the SS. Now he knew that his uncle had been murdered. By people attempting to reach her. Why? Because someone knew she was Hitler's daughter? Or because someone knew about the fund? People would commit murder for a lot less than three and a half million marks.

Her throat was quite dry.

"Frau Littler?"

Geli pulled herself together. "You must give me a little

140

time, Herr Schmidt. I have had quite a shock this morning, as you can imagine."

"Of course."

"Now I feel I must discuss the matter with my husband. How long can you wait before you start winding up the investments?"

"Well . . . I suppose, on Monday morning . . ."

"I will call you back this afternoon. Will you be at the office?"

"Ah . . . yes, there will be someone here to take your instructions. However, Frau Littler, I must tell you that I will have to reveal the existence of the trust and its contents to the police if they do indeed arrive with a court order."

"I understand. There is no risk they may be able to freeze the funds, is there?"

"Only if they can definitely connect you with the death of my uncle. But this is another reason for haste: I believe they may well try to do so. In view of the telephone calls, you see. May I ask why you made those calls, Frau Littler?"

"I will call you back this afternoon with my instructions," Geli said, and hung up. He knew too much as it was.

She spent the next half an hour staring at the wall. But she knew this was something far too big for her to handle on her own any larger. She was going to have to tell Hans. Everything. She got goose pimples at the thought.

But there was no point in delaying it. The net, whatever was inspiring it, was starting to close round her.

She telephone the golf club, left a message for him to call the moment he completed his round. As he had started very early he would be in by twelve, but it was his habit to lunch at the club with his friends. Well, today would have to be different.

He called back at twelve fifteen. "Geli? Is something wrong?" She had never called him at the golf club before.

141

"Yes," Geli said. "Hans, I must speak with you. It is most terribly urgent."

There was a brief hesitation at the other end of the line and she knew what he was thinking: that he had invited her to speak with him that morning and she had refused.

"Very well," he said at last. "Why do you not come into the club and meet me for lunch?"

"I would prefer to talk with you in private. Can you not come home?"

"For lunch?" With you, he had almost said, she knew.

"It is most urgent."

"Oh, very well. I will be there in half an hour."

He replaced the phone rather heavily; he was not amused. She dared not think what he was going to be when she had finished her confession. Still, three and a half million Deutschmarks . . .

*

Hunt found the lane he wanted. As he had told Corinne, a kilometre short of Weiningen. He drove down this for half a kilometre, then turned into a pasture, bumped his way some distance across it until the Peugeot simply refused to go any more: it had sunk to its axles in earth.

He got out, surveyed the road: it was about four hundred metres away and they were hidden by several trees. "I think we should be all right here for a while," he remarked.

"A while!" Leni snorted. "Come daylight, a helicopter will find you in five minutes."

"Us, darling. The word is us," he reminded her. "I'm sure you are right. But according to Carl they aren't going to start looking until after ten o'clock. And then they will first of all look at the airport. And we have an hour or so to first light. Let's get back to the road and wait for Corinne."

"Your friend."

"You are starting to sound a little peevish."

"I have never been on the run for murder before."

"It's something that most people only experience once

142

in a lifetime," Hunt agreed, taking out their overnight bags.

"Do you joke about everything?"

"Unless I'm actually crying about something, it seems the best way to get through this dreary old life. Coming?"

Leni got out of the car and Hunt locked it.

Leni shivered. "God, it's chilly."

"It usually is at about two o'clock in the morning. I'll do something about it when we get within sight of the road."

"Oh, yes? What makes you think she will come? Why should she get involved?"

"Simply because she is more involved than either of us. She hit the poor lad, remember. Anyway, she happens to be working for me at this moment." Up to a point, he thought.

"I think you should try telling me the truth," Leni suggested as they stumbled across the pasture and on to the lane.

"About what? You know who I am, who I work for and what I'm doing."

"And this person?"

Hunt decided she might as well realise how the odds were stacked against whatever it was she had in mind. "Oh, well, when you butted in I felt I needed a back-up, just in case you turned out to be a baddie."

"So you sent for Corinne."

"No. I sent for an assistant. They sent Corinne."

"But now that you are convinced I am not a baddie, as you put it, why do you not send her home?"

"Because I would say we need her more than ever, right now. Wouldn't you? We certainly would have been sunk without her back at the hotel. Now, be quiet. I need to think."

There was a great deal to think about. As it was Saturday morning, and he had mailed the diary after lunch yesterday, presumably there was a chance Lorenz would not receive it until Monday morning, therefore

143

unless the German police had made great strides, and he doubted that with the evidence they so far possessed, there was nothing to connect the dead man at the Baur au Lac with Brauer's killers. The connection would of course be established on Monday, but until then Heinrich was simply someone who had been murdered in an hotel bedroom. But Hunt did not suppose it was going to take Inspector LeCompte a great deal of thought to decide that Herr Hunt, who was anyway involved in some funny business, and who in addition had left the hotel just after midnight, was involved with this death as well. LeCompte would most certainly then decide to bring him in and would put out a general call for that purpose. Much would depend upon how far he could get by ten o'clock.

But the Swiss police would also by now know that the telephone calls had been from a Frau Geli Littler in Istanbul. They had no evidence to tell them who Geli Littler was, or even to link her to Schmidt's death, but it would certainly cross their minds to check her out as possibly the person everyone was looking for, and that included himself.

Then there was the question of what Adoration and the Beard were going to be doing. What, in fact, they were doing at this moment . . . and what kind of back-up *they* possessed.

But as far as he could determine, they had blown it.

"Here is the road," Leni remarked. "I see no car."

Hunt dropped the bags. "Well, it'll probably take her a little while. Why don't we sit down and let me warm you up?"

"I can warm myself up."

"Really? I thought you were getting quite horny back at the hotel."

"That was back at the hotel," she reminded him. "Before I was assaulted by a bunch of thugs. And," she added, "before you started lying to me. Anyway,

144

here on the ground? Ugh! Do you know how long it is since I have done that? I was twelve."

"You shock me. Last year, was it?"

"Here is a car," she said.

"Get down." Hunt put his hand on her shoulder and pressed her into the grass. They lay with their heads together as the car approached at great speed and then stopped at the turn-off with a squealing of brakes. The headlamps died and the left-hand front door opened.

"Late, as usual," Corinne commented.

Hunt stood up, pulling Leni with him.

Corinne peered at them in the gloom. "Oh, shit!" she remarked. "She still around? I thought we were here to work, Hunt."

"I would love to be able to do that," Hunt assured her. "Have you had any problems?"

"I do not have problems," Corinne pointed out.

"Point taken. Now, let's get the hell out of here."

"Back to the airport, right?" Corinne asked, getting behind the wheel.

Hunt put Leni in the front beside Corinne and he got into the back with the overnight bags – Corinne's was already there. That way he felt he could keep an eye on her and besides, he had work to do. "Not the airport."

"Why not?"

"Simply because, a, thanks to your super-efficiency last night, everyone knows that's where we're going; b, we cannot fly out to Istanbul until ten; and c, very shortly after ten every airport in the country is going to be swarming with police looking for Leni and me. As they know where we are going, and the flight number, they will certainly be able to have a reception committee waiting for us in Turkey."

"Ah," Corinne said. "So you reckon it would be safer to go back to Germany?"

"No," Hunt said. "For how long did you hire this car?"

"I took it for a week. I thought that might be useful."

"Corinne, you are a treasure."

Leni snorted.

"So drive for the Austrian border," Hunt said. "It's only about fifty miles. We'll be there by dawn."

"They'll want to look at passports."

"They'll still have no reason to hold us and we'll be out the other side by ten o'clock. Let's move it."

They drove as due east as possible, circling round the various mountains. While they did so, Hunt opened all three of the overnight bags and took out the assorted hardware: Leni's pistol and the three weapons dropped by Adoration and her friends. These he unloaded and then took the guns themselves apart with the screwdriver attachments to his pocketknife. The separate bits, including the bullets, he then wrapped up in various pieces of underwear, stowing one in Corinne's bag, one in Leni's and the other two in his own. All the bullets he placed in his.

Leni turned round in her seat to watch him. "Can you put those back together?"

"Given time."

"But until you do, we're unarmed."

"So the war's over, remember?"

Hunt opted to cross at Bangs, the small town where Switzerland, Austria and Lichtenstein came together, and where he hoped there would be no great border checks.

He was right: the sleepy Austrian guard hardly glanced at their passports. And they still had four hours in hand. It all was so easy he began to worry.

"What time does the maid do your room?" he asked Corinne.

"I hung a 'Do Not Disturb' on the door before I left. I shouldn't think anyone's going to bother about me until this afternoon."

"And you're quite sure no one saw you leave?"

"Absolutely. I used a fire door."

146

"So unless a missing person call is put out for you, with a description, you're in the clear."

"Yeah," Corinne said, her tone suddenly doubtful. "Then they're going to want me for murder."

"No one except us knows you came to my bedroom last night. And Adoration, of course. But she's unlikely to go to the police. If you keep denying that you have any idea what I was up to, and are pretty mad at me for standing you up . . ."

"That won't be difficult," Corinne remarked.

"Quite. Therefore, all they'll want you for is sneaking out of the hotel without paying your bill. On the other hand . . ." His brain was whizzing.

He had Geli Littler, or Geli Hitler, in his sights. He had no doubt at all that the woman who had been so agitated by Brauer's death and his quarry were one and the same. He was also out of Switzerland and he intended to be in Turkey by that evening at the latest. What happened tomorrow was irrelevant. All he needed was twelve hours to complete his mission.

Now was therefore the time to dump Leni. She would regard it as a double-cross and it would be that, but he couldn't really allow that to influence his decision – he was feeling pretty chauvinistic towards her at the moment, anyway, after her change of mood. And Corinne had been sent to help him cope with Leni.

Because now he was so close to home it was necessary to dump Corinne as well.

"I think we should find some breakfast," he suggested.

"Oh, that's a brilliant idea," Leni said. "And I simply have to pee."

"Then we're agreed. Next likely looking place."

Corinne found a village with an open café.

"Breakfast?" said the host. "My pleasure."

"Back in a flash," Leni said and hurried off.

"I think she has a good idea," Corinne said.

"In a moment," Hunt said. "Let's talk."

Corinne sat opposite him.

147

"I know you're worried about being blacked in every hotel in Europe because you've run out on the Baur au Lac," Hunt said.

"Am I?"

"Well, you should be. Where are you going to go on your honeymoon? Once you get on an international credit black list, you've really had it."

"You don't think my husband will pick up the tab for the honeymoon?"

"The man who marries you won't be able to afford anywhere as good as the Baur au Lac," Hunt pointed out. "I think you ought to return there just as quickly as possible. Before anyone gets the idea you've gone AWOL."

"Yeah?"

"If you drive like a bat out of hell, you can be back for lunch. Tell them you sneaked out for a date which took longer than you thought."

"And what are you going to do for wheels?"

"We're out of Switzerland now. I am going to get myself to the nearest airport, and fly. I make that Innsbruck."

"I see. With your popsie."

"Ah, no."

Corinne gazed at him.

"I rather think you should take her with you. She can be a bundle of fun."

Corinne continued to gaze at him.

"Of course, there is the point that she knows it was you who bopped our young friend on the head. Therefore it would probably be a good idea for you to unload her before you regain the Baur au Lac."

"Unload her?"

"I'm not asking you to hit her as well. Then you'd be getting a reputation. What I want you to do is take her with you, after a couple of hours make another comfort stop, and when she's ensconced with whatever it is you girls do, drive off."

Corinne smiled. "It'll make her mad."

148

"I thought you might enjoy that. But if she doesn't know where you're going, and she doesn't know where I've gone . . ."

"But she will know where you have gone. Turkey."

"Maybe she will. But as I intend to remove all of her finances, she won't be able to do much about following me."

Corinne considered. "And you don't reckon she'll go to the police?"

"She's an accomplice in a murder. She's also playing a game all of her own. I don't think she wants to get involved with the police any more than we do."

Corinne was still unhappy. "There could well be a bulletin out on her, out on you both, by now."

"If there is, we're in trouble. I'm hoping there isn't as yet. But in any event. I'm the only one they can properly identify. Leni's just a unfluffy blonde. And they'll be looking for my car at Zurich Airport. Although it won't be there. I imagine they will find it pdq, but I will have disappeared. My bet is that they will start searching from the car outwards because they simply will not know that I had any other transport available. That's what makes it very important for you to be back at the hotel, all sunshine, light and ignorance, by the time they start asking questions. As for Leni, if you dump her soon enough, I mean, in Austria, your problems are over."

Corinne considered some more. "I was sent along to back you up," she remarked. "The police are going to brood on that. Also, it was me booked your ticket to Istanbul."

"I told you to do so on the phone. But you have never been to my room. They can't prove you have."

"Carl?"

"Is on our side and totally reliable."

"What about my ticket to Istanbul? It's still at the desk."

"Tell them you overslept. They'll have to cancel your seat. Then, when you're done, check out, say this evening,

149

in an orderly fashion, and *then* take a flight to Istanbul. I'll leave a message for you at the airport, telling you where to find me."

"Will you, Hunt?" For a moment she looked almost wistful.

"Cross my heart and hope to die. Well, at least to have hiccups. Don't let me down now. There is no better way to back me up than to get rid of Leni."

Corinne brooded some more, and then sat up straight. "Hell! She's been a long time in the loo."

"Probably diarrhoea. But you'd better get in there and find her. I'll be seeing you."

Corinne hesitated a last time, then headed for the toilet. The host was just producing sausages, rolls and coffee.

"My, that looks good," Hunt said. "I'll be back in a moment."

He went to the car, got out his overnight bag and opened Leni's as well. She had credit cards and a wallet in there. He took them both. When she got stranded, he wanted her to be stranded.

Pity, he thought, she could have grown on him. But, as he had told her so often, work before pleasure.

He toyed with the idea of taking her passport as well, then changed his mind. She had to have some identification. But he looked inside the wallet in which it resided for several seconds, thoughtfully, before replacing it in the bag.

He walked along the road to the taxi rank. "I wish to go to Innsbruck," he said.

"That is eighty kilometres. It will be very expensive."

"That's my worry."

The driver shrugged and got in.

"The airport," Hunt told him.

He was in Innsbruck at eleven. This was really the crunch if the news of what had happened at the hotel in Zurich, and his name, had been released to the international media. But there was no comment when he produced his passport

150

and credit card, and he was booked on the afternoon flight to Istanbul.

He had three hours to kill so he thought he might as well have a leisurely lunch: he hadn't actually had one of those for forty-eight hours and he had recently missed breakfast.

It also gave him time to do some more thinking.

In the first place, there was no point in worrying about what the Zurich police might be doing. They would probably have found the car by now, and they would know he had not used his air tickets. They would surely be concentrating their search in the area around Weiningen, and have decided that their quarry had abandoned all idea of flying to Istanbul. He had to believe that. It would, of course, have been safer to fly somewhere else and enter Istanbul by car, but the nearest international airport was Ankara and that would involve a drive of some three hundred kilometres, which was simply too long, especially as the Istanbul flight left earlier.

And there were a great many other things to be considered.

He thought about Geli Littler first and felt a surge of real excitement. There could be no doubt of her identity. She would have to prove it, of course: but he felt sure she would be able to do that as well.

And then? He would have to play that by ear. But by this evening he would have all the answers, he was certain.

And then? Well, that would depend on a great number of imponderables. The woman herself, to begin with. But there were other factors. The woman Adoration, for one, and her bearded friend. They were killers, and they were killing their way towards their goal. But what was their goal? Geli Littler? Or the money?

And who were they representing? He thought he might enjoy obtaining that information from Adoration. But he was extremely unlikely to have the opportunity. He did

151

not see there was any way she could possibly now know, or discover, where Geli Littler was to be found. When they had run out of the Baur au Lac last night they had run right out of contention, so far as he could figure it out.

And lastly, he supposed, finishing his beer and calling for another, he should spare a thought for Leni Angstrom. He still had no idea for whom she was working, or what her game was, but she was a cute little number who had laid her plans very carefully – the way she had got him to take her along had been a stroke of genius, even if he had seen through it quickly enough – but she had strayed into something which was entirely out of her league.

Poor little Leni Angstrom. Or whatever her name really was.

"Oh, there you are, Daddy," she remarked.

Hunt spilled his beer as he sat up. Leni carried her overnight bag, and was accompanied by a rather anxious-looking taxi driver.

"Would you mind settling up for me, Daddy?" Leni asked. "I seem to have mislaid both my money and my cards. I think it comes to the equivalent of fifty English pounds. But he says he'll take sterling."

Hunt produced the money. "Where have you come from?" he asked, trying to think.

"Nenzing," the driver explained.

"And you trusted this young woman, my, ah, daughter, all the way from Nenzing to here?"

"Well, she has a pretty face." The taxi driver receded.

"Are we lunching?" Leni asked. "Thank God for that. I'm starving."

"It appears to be a permanent condition. Are you absolutely sure you're not pregnant?"

"I probably would be, if I had surrendered to your male ego last night. Or was it this morning?"

"Yes, we are lunching," Hunt decided. "And when we have done that I am going to exercise a father's privilege, take you somewhere private, drop your pants and beat the living daylights out of you. Fathers are entitled to do that sort of thing in Austria, aren't they? And I know you'll enjoy it."

"Look," Leni said, sitting down and calling for a Bloody Mary. "I am the one who should be angry with you, you fat louse. Running out on me like that."

"Am I allowed to ask how you knew where I was going to be?"

"Well . . ." Leni gave one of her little shrugs. "Corinne told me."

"Corinne told you? Just like that?"

"Well . . . we had a little chat and she decided to co-operate. She really is a very nice person."

"Is?"

"Oh, yes."

"But lying in a ditch someplace, is that it? God, I thought she could take care of herself."

"I'm sure she can," Leni argued. "I mean, you saw how good she is with a chamber pot."

"Only she didn't have a potty handy when you got to her?"

"Well . . . no."

"Leni, if you have killed Corinne I am going to break every bone in your body before impaling you on a coat hanger."

"Of course I have not killed her." Leni drank half of her Bloody Mary and seemed to feel better. "I told you, we had a little chat and . . ."

"You will have to do better than that."

"Ah," Leni said. "The menu. Did I tell you I was starving?"

"Yes, you did. Do you ever think about anything save food?"

"No caviar. Bother! I'll have the steak, medium rare."

"Make that two," Hunt said. "Tell me about Corinne."

"Tell me why you ran out on me. And what time we leave for Istanbul."

Hunt had had time to think. "I ran out on you because I suppose the old instinct overcame me. Scoop and all that."

"You really should give up lying: you're so terribly bad at it. However, I should be grateful if you will give me my cards and money back, and if you will come downstairs with me to collect my ticket."

"I'm flying first-class."

"So am I, Hunt. There was one seat left."

"And you think I am going to pay for that?"

"No, no. The *Globe* is. We're partners. remember?"

"Not any more."

"Oh, you beast. Very well. I shall stand on this table and start shouting about everything that has happened, including the body in the Baur au Lac. Someone is sure to notice."

Short of strangling her there and then – and that would certainly be noticed – Hunt realised he would have to go along with her until he could get her quite alone . . . and presumably that would not be until Istanbul. In fact, he reflected, it might be more convenient in Istanbul. So he bought her ticket.

"Now tell me about Corinne," he said over lunch.

"Well, we got to talking and then to . . . other things. We became very friendly. Did you know she was like that?"

"No," Hunt said. But he supposed it was possible: Corinne was fairly omnivorous. However . . . "And she told you all?"

"Well, I convinced her that you had really played me a very dirty trick, all for the sake of a story, and she saw my point of view."

"All this happened in between gasps of ecstacy?"

"Well . . . afterwards, really."

"Was this before breakfast? Or after breakfast?"

"Oh, after breakfast. I find it very difficult to make love on an empty stomach."

"And you have the nerve to call me a poor liar. I meant

154

what I said, about what I was going to do with you if you have bumped her off."

"Well . . ." Leni looked at her watch. "I think Corinne will have regained the hotel by now. Why do you not telephone her?"

Hunt regarded her, and she swallowed some steak and smiled at him.

"I might just do that. Don't go away."

"Hunt, I am never going to let you out of my sight again for a second."

"Sounds promising." He went to the telephone, dialled.

"Hotel Baur au Lac."

"May I speak with Mrs Grundy, please?"

"May I ask who is calling, please?"

"I'm her boss."

"Ah. Will you hold the line, sir?"

A moment later a woman said, "Hello?"

It sounded like Corinne but he had to be sure.

"I imagine you know who this is."

"I imagine I do."

"Then identify yourself without using names."

"Well . . . shall I say that I expect you are calling from Innsbruck Airport?"

"Right. Now tell me, is there any police activity at your end?"

"There are what I would assume to be a couple of plain clothes men in the lobby, but they are being very discreet."

"Now tell me what the hell is going on between you and Leni and why the hell you told her where I was and then let her go."

"I think you should ask her," Corinne said, and hung up.

Hunt stared at the phone for several seconds. He had never encountered a situation like this before. Corinne had been nobbled. How one nobbled a woman like Corinne he simply did not know: it was obviously an absurdity to suppose that she and Leni could have become

155

lovers in the five minutes or so which was all the time they could possibly have had between breakfast and Leni setting off in pursuit of him, or that Corinne would have changed sides even if they had. Therefore Leni had to have pulled some whopping ace out of her sleeve . . . or they had to have been working with each other from the beginning.

From long before the beginning.

But he had asked for assistance from London . . . he snapped his fingers: Halliday had said Corinne had virtually volunteered for the job.

He called London while looking out of the telephone booth at his table where Leni was contentedly chomping away, apparently without a care in the world.

"Hunt!" Halliday said. "Where the hell are you?"

"Innsbruck. It's a long story, but our quarry appears to have gone to ground in Turkey."

"And you're in Innsbruck. Charlie, I'm getting some bad feedback about you."

"Such as?"

"A telephone call from a Swiss policeman named LeCompte."

"I hope you were co-operative."

"I told him I didn't think you were a murderer, if that's what you mean. And I regard that as sticking my neck out."

"Self-defence."

"So you claim. Look, are you sure you know where your woman is?"

"I'm sure."

"Then get there. I want you to wind this thing up just as fast as you can, before it gets really nasty."

"It's already got pretty nasty. Listen, I asked you for some information."

"And you have it. I sent it to the hotel."

"I haven't been in that hotel since one o'clock this morning. There's just one really important point. Leni Angstrom."

"Ah . . . Leni Angstrom. Yes, the German reporter of Swedish descent."

"That's on the level, is it? You've checked descriptions, backgrounds, the whole thing?"

"Oh, indeed. She appears to be perfectly genuine. Is she still with you?"

"Have you ever had a close encounter with a leech? There's one more thing: Corinne has gone sour."

"In what way?"

"I'm not sure, yet. Maybe she always was."

"Corinne? I can't believe that."

"I find it difficult, too. But facts are facts. Tom, I need another back-up. In Istanbul. Do we have someone on the ground?"

"Of course we do. Roger Trenton."

"Right. I shall be landing, with Miss Angstrom, at seven o'clock local time. I wish to be met by someone who will take care of the young lady for me. I want her out, urgently. Can you do that?"

"Well . . . yes. I hope you're not suggesting we, ah, do the young lady?"

"I wouldn't dream of it. I just want her removed from my hair long enough for me to get our exclusive."

"All right. I'll work something out."

"Thanks a bundle, old man. I'll call you the moment I've spoken with Mrs Littler."

Now what the hell is Halliday playing at? he wondered as he slowly replaced the phone. Claiming Leni was genuine? But he wasn't going to know for sure until they landed in Turkey. Then some hands were going to have to be revealed. But, fuck them, he thought: if that's the way they want to play it, that's the way it's going to be played.

He made another phone call.

"What did Corinne say?" Leni asked, delving into her flan. "It was an awfully long phone call."

"She told me that she felt sorry for you."

157

"She's a dear, sweet girl," Leni agreed.

"You need glasses. However . . . we'd better go along to departure."

"How're we going to get the guns through? Even in pieces they're going to make our luggage sound like the piccolo section."

"By checking our bags as hold luggage. They only spot check those, and little bits of steel lying around could be razors. As long as we're on the plane with our bags, they'll be happy."

"But . . . don't you think we may need them?"

"Not on the flight, darling. Be reasonable."

"I hope you're right," Leni said pessimistically.

She cheered up after her second glass of champagne. "Pity it's a daytime flight," she remarked, looking down at the Alps.

"Safer," Hunt grunted.

"I was thinking of the six-mile club."

"Oh, yeah?"

"Look, I'm sorry I stood you up back there. I was peeved. Anyway, on the ground in the open air . . ."

"You made that point."

"Sex should be the unanticipated result of a romantic interlude," she said dreamily.

"So send for a blanket. But I am going to sleep."

At least he knew where she was all the time, and that she couldn't get up to any mischief. In fact, he slept heavily: he needed it after the previous night. He didn't awake until they began their descent into Yesilkoy.

"What do we do now?" Leni enquired as they collected their bags.

"Do you mean to say Corinne didn't tell you?"

"She only told me where to find you."

Maybe he'd been maligning her. "Well, having nothing else to do, I'm going to read a telephone book." He went to the nearest free booth and thumbed the pages. Littler, Hans. In a village called Telibaba.

158

"Any joy?" Leni asked.

"I hope so. We're going to take a little drive up the Bosporus. It's very beautiful this time of year."

"I'm sure it is, if we can see it. It's pouring with rain out there."

She was right. The evening had turned distinctly gloomy. It was seven o'clock Turkish time and was going to be dark in a few minutes. For a moment Hunt was tempted to telephone the Littlers to make sure they were there and to check as to whether or not the Zurich police had been in touch as yet. But he decided against it. Geli Littler would undoubtedly have been watching the news, and she was probably in a state of agitation anyway. He needed to get to her just as rapidly as possible . . . and before she had the time to consider what she was going to do about him.

He had to assume that she was quite capable of coping with the police or any of the problems she must have anticipated all of her life.

"Come on," he said.

They went outside and immediately a taxi pulled up in front of them.

"Here's a stroke of luck," Hunt said. "Our first, wouldn't you say?"

"I don't like strokes of luck," Leni said. "Let's wait for another."

"In the rain?" Hunt already had the door open. "In you get. Do you speak English?"

The driver, a very typical Turk, grinned at him. "I speak English very good."

"What is your name?"

"Achmed."

"That figures. Achmed, we want to go out to a place called Telibaba. Do you know it?"

"Oh, yes, sir. But it is a long way. Thirty kilometres. It will be expensive."

"That's all right," Hunt said and wrote down the address: he didn't want Leni being able to follow him.

Achmed pocketed the piece of paper and engaged gears.

159

The car moved out of the airport and into the glare of searchlights from the adjoining military establishment.

"I hope you know what you're doing," Leni grumbled. "This pick-up was just too quick."

"You wanted to come along, darling."

"This is the first time I have been to Istanbul."

"So enjoy it."

Now they were approaching the city itself. Hunt would have thought it would have been quicker to go round the centre rather than through it, but presumably Achmed was acting under orders and he had himself only been to Istanbul a couple of times before, so he didn't really know enough about it to argue. He looked at the lights instead, and the cars looming through the rain to either side.

"Do we get to see a belly dancer while we're here?" Leni asked. "I've always wanted to see a genuine belly dancer."

"We'll see what we can squeeze in," Hunt promised.

"Where are we staying?"

"I haven't sorted that out as yet."

"Hunt, we're right at the beginning of the tourist season. We could wind up on the beach. In the rain," she added as an afterthought.

"We'll find somewhere," he promised her. "But we have to see somebody before we do anything."

"You know who?"

"That's right. If I'm right."

"You know I'm quite excited?"

"So am I," Hunt said, truthfully. "So . . ." The taxi turned down a very unsalubrious-looking street and stopped. "What the hell . . .?"

"We're going to be mugged!" Leni snapped as Achmed opened the door and ran out into the rain, rapidly disappearing.

Hunt hurled himself over the front seat to gain the wheel, but as he did so Leni shouted and he realised the car had been surrounded by several youths. If this

160

was Halliday's idea of discreetly removing somebody, the world had gone mad.

"Lock the doors," he said, but it was too late. The rear door had already been pulled open and several pairs of hands were dragging Leni out. They weren't finding it easy, and one of them was already kneeling on the road, clutching his groin, but there were too many of them.

Hunt realised he would have to help her or she might well be beaten up: Halliday's local man seemed to have gone right over the top. He sighed and opened the front door to slide out.

Instantly, two of the youths attacked him. The other four appeared to be attempting to bundle Leni to the pavement, presumably with rape in mind – someone was going to be fired for this.

But first things first. Hunt kicked his lead attacker in the genitals as he got within range, and as he fell to his knees with a grunt of pain, kicked him again so that this time he fell backwards against the legs of his companion, who fell forwards over him and on to Hunt's hands, clasped together and swinging from left to right, which slammed into the side of his head and sent him staggering against the wall. He slipped down this without a sound.

"Hunt!" Leni screamed.

They had got her down at last and there was a tearing sound as her pants were ripped. More important, one of her assailants had seen what had happened to his friends and turned away from her, drawing a wicked-looking knife as he did so.

The man Hunt had first kicked was just getting back to his knees.

"Sorry, lad," Hunt said, picked him up and threw him. The man with the knife couldn't get either himself or his weapon out of the way, and the blade sank deep into his friend's side. The dying man uttered a fearsome shriek and fell back to the pavement.

The man thrown against the wall was just regaining his feet. He took one look at the situation and ran away. So did the knifeman, leaving his weapon still embedded in his friend's side. The other three released Leni and also took to their heels.

A police whistle blew.

CHAPTER FIVE

Hans came into the house having apparently made up his mind to be boisterously good-humoured.

"Well," he said, and smacked Geli's bottom. "What's for lunch, eh?"

"Roast lamb. But I wish to talk, first." Geli led him into the lounge and turned to face him.

"What's this all about?"

"Oh, Hans!" She went to him and he held her close.

"Something is troubling you."

"Something. Would you like a drink?"

"I will get it." He went to the bar, opened a can of beer. "For you?"

"No." Geli sat on the settee and waited for him to sit also, opposite her in an armchair.

"Well?"

Geli licked her lips. She still had no idea how to go about this. "Hans . . . Walther Schmidt is dead."

"Is he? Good Lord! But we knew it had to happen some time pretty soon. He was past eighty wasn't he?"

"Yes. But . . . he was tortured to death, Hans."

Hans raised his head, frowning.

"At least, that is what the police in Switzerland think happened," Geli said.

"Do they know why?"

"I do not think so. Not yet."

"Well, I am sure they will find the murderers. I know you are upset by this, Geli, but how do we know what Uncle Walther was mixed up in? All we know about him is that he administered your mother's trust fund. Well, I suppose there may be a problem with that. We shall have to get in touch with his nephew."

"I have already spoken with his nephew," Geli said.

Hans raised his eyebrows.

"And there will be no trouble with the fund. In fact Walther Schmidt Junior wishes to wind it up and pay the capital to me."

"Can he do that?"

"Yes. Apparently it should have been done years ago. Uncle Walther was using the money for his own purpose."

"By Christ, the rascal. I'm not surprised he was murdered if that's what he's been doing with all his clients' funds. Is there a lot involved?"

"Ah . . . more than three million Deutschmarks."

Hans put down his beer glass as he sat up. "Did you say three million?"

"Yes," Geli said.

Hans gave a low whistle. "I never knew I was married to a millionairess."

"I did not know I was one until this morning."

"Well, I am glad you called me right away. You know I'm sorry about poor old Uncle Walther, but if he was a crook . . . I think we should open a bottle of bubbly. Three million Deutschmarks . . ."

"Hans . . ." Geli drew a very long breath. "Uncle Walther was an agent for the SS."

Hans was on his way to the bar. Now he stopped and slowly turned.

"You never asked me where the trust fund came from," Geli said.

"Why . . . I had supposed that it was set up by your grandparents. The SS? But that was a very long time ago."

"Some things are never a long time ago. You are close to being right, the trust fund was set up on behalf of my father, for the use of my mother."

"He must have been a wealthy man."

164

"I believe he was. Once upon a time he held the whole world in the palm of his hand."

Hans ignored what he obviously considered was a flight of fancy, to concentrate upon the essentials. "And he was a member of the SS?"

Another long breath. "My father was Adolf Hitler, Hans."

Hans stared at her, some of his normal high colour fading. "Why are you saying this?"

"Because it is the truth. My mother was one of the women taken to Rastenberg for . . . what is the word they use? Comfort? She was the only one who became pregnant."

Hans sat down: his knees seemed to give way and he collapsed on to the nearest chair.

"I never knew my father, as you know," Geli went on. "I was four months old when he died, and by then we were already in Istanbul. I do not know if Hitler ever knew I existed. Mother had her doubts about that. We were sent from Germany by Himmler, who had already set up the trust fund for us. Obviously, when he did that he was hoping to survive himself, and perhaps re-establish the Reich at some future date, at which time having Hitler's child available would presumably give him some aura of legitimacy. You know what a dream world all of those people lived in towards the end."

"My God! My God!" Hans muttered. "How long have you known this?"

"Mother told me when I was eighteen."

"And you married me when you were twenty. But you did not tell me."

Geli's shoulders hunched defensively. "There seemed no point. Hitler and Himmler, all of them, had been dead for twenty years. The Reich was never going to rise again. It was ancient history. It was something both of us wanted to forget . . . and Mother was dying. I think she only told me because she knew that."

"And you were afraid I would not marry you if I knew," he accused.

Geli stared at him. "Yes, Hans. I was afraid of that. We were both afraid of that."

"So you deceived me. For twenty-six years you have deceived me."

"Have I not been a good wife to you for twenty-six years?"

"Twenty-six years," he muttered. "And all that time you have been receiving blood money."

"Blood money?"

"Where do you suppose the SS got their money from?"

Geli bit her lip: she had never allowed herself to consider that. "Do you wish me to refuse to accept the fund?" She knew her husband too well to suppose he would ever turn his back on three million Deutschmarks, no matter how bloodstained.

"I don't know . . . I will have to think . . ." Then he looked up. "My God! The people who murdered Schmidt could be connected with you. With the SS. With the Reich."

"I think they are," Geli said quietly. "The man Brauer, who was murdered on Friday night, he had uncovered some secret to do with Himmler. Do you not remember?"

"My God!" Hans said. "My God!"

"And from Brauer, these people must have traced Mother to Uncle Walther. They must have been questioning him about her, about me, when he died."

Hans swallowed. Geli had never seen her husband look so frightened.

"I don't know if they found out anything or not," Geli went on. "But . . ."

"They could be on their way here now. To kill us all."

"We do not know they wish to do that. Why should they wish to kill us?"

"They have already killed two people."

"People who knew about me."

Hans was frowning. "They wish to find you. Why?"

"There could be several reasons," Geli said. "They *could* wish to kill me, although I cannot see why. They don't even know I know who I am. It would have to be some very weird revenge group. On the other hand, they may be after the money. Three million Deutschmarks."

"Yes," Hans said thoughtfully. "There could be another reason."

"What?"

"You have said that Himmler sent your mother and yourself out of Germany and arranged for you to be taken care of because he hoped to be able to use you one day, when the Reich rose again."

Geli's jaw dropped and she hastily closed it again. "Himmler has been dead for forty-seven years."

"Maybe, but we do not know who is alive and in whom he confided. We do know that there is still a Nazi Party. There has always been, no matter how well it has been disguised. Now that Germany has been reunited, is it not possible that the Party may be thinking of making a comeback? And would it not be useful for them to have Hitler's daughter as a figurehead?"

Geli clasped both hands to her neck. "I should never agree to that."

"I am sure you will not. But these people do not know that yet. And they are killers."

"But they can hardly wish to kill me if they intend to use me as a figurehead."

"Geli, we don't know what they want. All we know is that they are highly dangerous and they are looking for you."

"Then we must get out of Istanbul. Pack up and go."

Hans was astounded. "Just like that?"

"Hans, it is not only me and you. What about the children?"

"Geli, I cannot just walk away from my business. What would we live on?"

167

"We have three and a half million Deutschmarks waiting for us in Zurich."

"Oh, yes? And what happens when we go to collect it? Do you not suppose the killers are waiting for us to do that?"

"You mean we are not going to touch that money? I promised young Schmidt I would call him back with instructions this afternoon."

"Three million Deutschmarks," Hans muttered.

"What are we to do?"

"Let me think. Let me think." He got up and paced the room, shoulders hunched. "Why in the name of God did I ever marry you?"

"For God's sake," she shouted. "I thought you loved me."

"There is no need to shout. What to do . . ."

Geli watched him in consternation. She had always supposed him the strongest of men.

"Well," she said. "The first thing we must do is tell the children."

He turned to face her. "Tell the children? No, no, we must not do that."

"How can we not do that? They are involved. If my life, our lives, are in danger, are not theirs?"

"Do you wish your children to know that Adolf Hitler was their grandfather? Do you wish to ruin their lives?"

"My God!" she shouted. "I am trying to save their lives."

"That is not the way to go about it."

"Then what is? I wish to know what we must do."

Hans took a couple more turns up and down the room. "You must leave Istanbul."

"Is that not what I have been saying? Where will we go?"

"*We* are not going anywhere. You are the one who is at risk. Besides, were we all to leave, they would track us down very quickly. You are only going to leave Istanbul temporarily. You will just disappear."

168

"Disappear? Where?"

"Some place no one will ever think of looking for you."
He snapped his fingers. "I have it. You will join a tour."

"A tour? Going where?"

"Some place in Asiatic Turkey. I will arrange it this
afternoon. There are always tours going into Cappadocia
or even further, and at this time of the year they are
never fully booked. Listen, pack a bag and wait for my
telephone call. I will arrange the tour and book you into
a hotel under an assumed name. It will be supposed that
you have just flown in from Germany or somewhere to
join this tour. You will leave the house, go into Istanbul
and just disappear. I will book a hotel room for you. And
tomorrow you will have entirely disappeared when you
leave on the tour. Don't you see? For the next fortnight
you will have vanished totally in the middle of a crowd of
tourists."

"Fortnight?"

"I think a fortnight would be best. By the end of that
time this business will have sorted itself out. The police
will have caught the murderers and, well . . . it will have
sorted itself out."

He wants me away, Geli thought. But not necessarily
because he is afraid for me. Perhaps he is afraid *of* me.
Perhaps he is afraid that after all I will succumb to the
temptation of publicly declaring myself to be Hitler's
daughter. Perhaps he is afraid of so many things.

"What will you be doing during this fortnight?" she
asked.

"I will hold the fort here. It is you they wish. If you are
not here, well, they will have to go away again. And once
they have come, I will inform the police who they really
are. It is better that I am here to attend to them. This is
man's work."

He had either recovered his courage very quickly
or he was lying to her. Hans, lying to her! He had
never lied to her in his life before. But how did she
know that? He supposed she had never lied to him,

169

and her entire life had been a lie from his point of view.

The trouble was, she wanted to believe him. She wanted to run away and leave him to cope. She wanted to lean on his strength, as she had always leaned on his strength.

But . . . "What about the children?"

"What about the children?"

"They will be in danger as well."

"I do not think so. Anyway, the boys and I can take care of ourselves."

Now he was boasting.

"And what of Helene?"

"We can take care of Helene, too."

"I wish her to come with me."

"How can she do that? She has to go to school."

"No, she does not. When she comes home this afternoon I will tell her what we are doing . . ."

"But not who you are!" His voice was high with anxiety.

"I will not tell her who I am," Geli assured him. "Since the thought of it disturbs you so much. I will concoct a story, and as you say, we will then disappear to this hotel and tomorrow on this tourist bus. You will telephone the school tomorrow morning and tell them Helene has been taken ill and will be away for about a fortnight."

"Lies," Hans grumbled. "Suddenly I am surrounded with lies." He glanced at her. "But I have always been surrounded with lies, it seems."

"Do you wish to divorce me, Hans?"

"Of course I do not. I . . ." He was trying to choose words. "I am thinking only of your safety. Now I must be off to make arrangements. Do not forget, act as soon as you receive my call."

"I cannot leave here before six o'clock, Hans. I have to wait for Helene."

"You do realise that every minute, every second, may be a matter of life or death?"

170

"Yes, Hans, I do realise that. I will be leave here at six o'clock."

"Oh, very well." He hesitated, then stopped and kissed her forehead. "I must hurry." He went to the door, lunch apparently forgotten. But there he checked again. "The money!"

"I had supposed you wished to abandon that."

"I spoke without thinking. Your news upset me. No, no, we cannot abandon three million Deutschmarks. It is money we may very well need."

"What do you wish done with it?"

"I think you should telephone young Schmidt, tell him to liquidate the trust, as he seems to wish to do anyway, and place all the money, in Swiss francs, in a numbered account. There will be only two signatories on the account, you and me."

"You and me," Geli said thoughtfully.

"Well, my love, I feel I must have signing rights as I do not know what is going to happen."

"Oh, quite," Geli said, more thoughtfully yet. "But . . . a numbered account? Will that not attract negative interest?"

"I am not sure. But whether it does or not, we are not going to leave it there for more than the next fortnight. As soon as this business is sorted out we will move it somewhere better. Now, you do that right away. I will get on and make all of your bookings."

He wants me gone while he has control of my money, she thought. And once he has that . . . perhaps he will never wish me to return again. It would be a simple matter to let the people who were seeking her know where she had gone.

The shock of understanding that this man was her husband made her feel sick. But the sickness was already being submerged by anger. He thought she was a frightened fool. Well, she was frightened but she was not a fool.

"No," she said.

171

He had opened the door. Now he again turned.

"I have changed my mind."

"What?" he shouted.

"I think your plan is an excellent one," Geli said. "But I think it would be best if I made all the arrangements myself."

Hans stared at her.

"That way," Geli explained, "there will be no possibility of anyone finding out because not even you will know."

Hans considered. But there was logic in her argument and he knew how stubborn she could be. The important thing was that she was going.

"How will you pay for your tickets without revealing your real name?"

"I will do it. Just leave it to me."

"And you will be gone, and I will not know where you are?"

"I will telephone you when I am on the tour."

Another consideration. Then he nodded. "But you will not forget to make the arrangements about the money?"

"I will do that now," Geli promised.

Geli sat still for several minutes, staring at the wall: she no longer felt like lunch, either.

She had always been afraid to tell Hans the truth, for fear of his reaction. Well, perhaps once upon a time his reaction would have been honest: honestly amazed, honestly angry, perhaps even honestly frightened.

She thought that he had, for a moment, been honestly frightened just now. But the fear had very rapidly been overtaken by calculation and consideration.

By the end of her marriage. Because that was certain, no matter what happened in the future. She had suddenly become, on the one hand, an enormous liability, and on the other, an enormous asset. Hans' problem was how to separate the liability from the asset, retaining the one and . . . burying the other?

If anything was going to happen, it was going to happen

in the next couple of days. But he wanted her gone for two weeks. Time enough to secure the asset. And whatever he did with the money, his story would be entirely plausible: it would have been to save it from these people who were looking for her. Then when she came back, he could reassess the situation . . . because if, having appropriated the money, he then threw her out, it was hardly likely that she was going to take him to court . . . for Nazi money!

Obviously he considered her a complete fool. But there was much in his plan to recommend it. Whatever reason these people had for seeking her, it was her they wanted. Her signature on the release for the trust fund, or her support for a revival of the Nazi Party in a re-unified Germany, or only her body, either to be assassinated or placed on trial as being by the link of blood a war criminal. If they tracked her to Istanbul and she was simply not there, they would not know where to look.

But she needed more help than Hans was prepared to give – because Hans was not really giving any help at all. And there was only one direction she could turn, whatever her promise.

She went up to her bedroom and called Zurich.

"I'm sorry, Frau Littler," the girl said. "But Herr Schmidt Junior is not available right now. He is very busy."

"With the police," Geli suggested.

"He is very busy," she repeated.

"He asked me to call him," Geli told her. "As soon as possible. It may not be possible for me to call him again for a day or two. I will therefore have to give my instructions to you. Will you copy them down and convey them to Herr Schmidt?"

The girl hesitated. "But how can I know you are who you say you are. Frau Littler?"

"By telephoning me back, right away. I will not give you my number. You have it on file. I shall await your call."

She hung up started to pack. Amazingly, whereas before her talk with Hans she had been aware only of fear and a rising panic, now she felt quite cool. Because now she knew that she was only going to get out of her predicament by her own efforts.

Ten minutes later the telephone rang.

"This is Herr Walther Schmidt's secretary speaking," the voice said. "I would like to speak with Frau Geli Littler, please."

"I am she," Geli said.

"I believe you have certain instructions for Herr Schmidt, Frau Littler."

"Yes. It concerns the trust fund he has been handling for me. I wish you to write down what I have to say."

"Of course."

Geli gave the woman her instructions.

"These will have to be supported by a letter, Frau Littler."

"I will write the letter now," Geli promised. "And mail it this evening. It should be with you in three days. Now, I have some other instructions for you which I should be most grateful if you would carry out immediately."

"Of course, Frau Littler."

"I wish you to telephone the Europa Hotel, in Istanbul, and make a reservation for a double room for tonight for a Mrs Anna Petrov and her daughter, Elizabeth. I wish you to tell the hotel that Mrs Petrov and her daughter are flying in from Germany this evening, and will arrive at the hotel around seven. At the same time, I wish you to ask the hotel to book Mrs Petrov and her daughter on a Cappadocian tour. I not not mind which company it is or what it costs, but it must leave tomorrow and should last a fortnight. When you have made the booking, I would like you to telephone me back here and confirm. Can you do this"

"Well, of course, Frau Littler. But . . . are you not in Istanbul yourself?"

"It is necessary for me to disappear for a while, Fraulein. Therefore I would like you to put the hotel booking and the tour booking on either your own or Herr Schmidt's

174

credit card. You can recoup whatever it costs from the fund. Will you do this?"

This time the woman hesitated. Then she said, "Yes, I can do this, Frau Littler. I will have to check with Herr Schmidt, of course."

"I understand," Geli said. "I am most grateful. You may add whatever service charge you think suitable to the bill. But this must remain absolutely confidential."

"Of course, Frau Littler. And you will not forget the letter?"

"I will write it now," Geli promised.

Geli wrote the letter and then packed a second bag; she dabbled in amateur theatricals and possessed some useful aids to disguise.

Then it was just a matter of waiting.

Walther Schmidt's secretary called back at half past three to say the booking had been made at the hotel and for Fascination Tours, leaving Istanbul the following morning at ten o'clock.

Hans telephoned at four: Geli had no idea where he was calling from. "Have you managed to make all your bookings?"

"Yes."

"So . . . I will wish you a pleasant holiday. Oh, by the way, did you make the arrangements about the money?"

He asked so casually. She responded just as casually.

"Of course."

"No problems?"

"None at all."

"Well, then, have a good holiday. And do not forget to telephone me."

Helene came home first, just after five.

"I would like you to pack a small bag, just holiday things," Geli told her. "You and I are going away for a couple of weeks."

"I can't just go away in the middle of term, Mummy."

"Yes, you can. Your father is going to explain it to your headmistress."

"Then will you explain it to me?" Helene requested. She was a positive young woman.

"Yes, I will. When Herrmann and Paul get home. Just go and pack."

Helene obeyed; she had never known her mother be quite so positive, either.

Geli walked up and down while she waited for the boys. They arrived together half an hour later.

"I wish you to listen to me very carefully," Geli told them. "What I have to say may come as something of a shock."

They raised their eyebrows but sat down and waited. Helene sat between them.

"You have never asked about your grandfather," Geli said.

"Grandpa was killed in the war," Herrmann said.

"Yes, he died in the war," Geli agreed. "And I have always led you to believe that he was an officer in the German army. Well, I did not lie to you about that. He was an officer in the Wehrmacht. He was its commander-in-chief. His name was Adolf Hitler."

She gazed at them, and they stared back.

"You all right, Mum?" Herrmann asked at last.

"Of course I am all right."

"I don't think that's very funny," Helene remarked.

"I did not mean it as a joke. It is the truth."

There was another brief silence.

Paul broke it. "You are trying to tell us that you are the daughter of Hitler?"

"I am telling you that I am his daughter, yes."

"Does Papa know about this?"

"I told him this morning. He is not very pleased."

"Not very pleased," Herrmann grunted. "Jesus Christ! What are we supposed to be?"

"Your father did not wish me to tell you," Geli went on, refusing to lose her concentration. "He felt it would

176

upset you. Well, of course he was right. But I felt I had to because it will necessarily affect all of your lives. You may even be in danger."

"How come this has suddenly blown up?" Paul asked. "If Hitler is our grandfather, he's been our grandfather all of our lives, and it's never been a problem before."

"It has suddenly blown up, as you put it," Geli said, "because a German journalist found out about it two days ago. Or at least, he was murdered for finding out, two days ago. Until then the secret was known only to my mother, myself and my Uncle Walther in Switzerland. But this journalist found out. I don't know how. When he started looking for us, for me, I suppose, he was murdered."

"Murdered?" Herrmann's voice went up an octave.

"Yes. And then, through him, these people, whoever they are, got on to Uncle Walther and murdered him too." She decided against telling them about the money; they had enough to digest for the time being.

"But . . ." Helene stared at her mother. "Do you think they wish to harm you?"

"I don't know what they want of me," Geli said. "All anyone knows is that they appear to be very unpleasant people."

"The police . . ." Paul began.

"Have not yet made an arrest and the police in Turkey are not yet involved. Nor will they be, until after these people have come here and shown their hand. That may be too late for us. For me."

"But what can they *want*?" Herrmann's voice was plaintive. He did, Geli thought regretfully, take after his father. "I mean, you can't be guilty of any war crimes."

"Whatever they want, your father feels it would be better if I was not here when they get here," Geli said. "So Helene and I are leaving tonight. I'm not going to tell you where we are going: it is better that you do not know."

"What about us?" Hermann's voice was even more plaintive.

177

"Your father feels you should remain here with him. Obviously he cannot leave the business at a moment's notice. In any event, it is me they are looking for. I will simply disappear for a few days. In that time, if they come here, if they manage to find out where I am living, which is unlikely, they will find out nothing more because you know nothing of where I shall be, and they will have to go away again. By then the police will certainly be closing in on them and this whole thing will be over."

"Except that you will be known to be Hitler's daughter," Paul pointed out. "There is no hope of keeping that secret if they find out where you are."

"I have said that is unlikely," Geli reminded him. In fact she hadn't really considered what the future might hold – she wanted only to be rid of the immediate crisis.

"It's certain to happen," Herrmann said. "Hitler's grandchildren. My God!"

"Are you afraid of that?"

"Well . . ." He got up, went to the bar, poured himself a beer. "It'll make it impossible to live a normal life."

"Hitler had many relatives, all of whom have managed to live comparatively normal lives," Geli argued.

"Maybe. They weren't his direct descendants."

"Well, whether the fact that you are a direct descendant is to your advantage or your disadvantage will depend very largely on yourself," Geli told him.

"But why are you taking Helene and not us?" Paul wanted to know.

"I do not wish to be alone," Geli replied.

To lie to one's own children. And perhaps abandon them to danger . . . but she had to believe that Hans would be capable of at least looking after the boys.

"Now we must be going," Geli said. "Herrmann, you will come with us to bring the car back."

"I will come too," Paul decided.

The four of them drove into Istanbul. Geli stopped the car

178

about half a mile away from a taxi station. "We will walk from here."

"Here?" Herrmann gazed at the rain, the scurrying passers by. "This is not a very good neighbourhood."

"No one is going to trouble us." She fastened her raincoat, raised the hood, picked up her umbrella and got out. "Come along, Helene."

Helene followed her example. Whatever she was thinking about the situation, the girl had said very little.

"Now I wish you to go straight home," Geli told Herrmann, "and wait for your father. And then do whatever he tells you to."

They drove away, somewhat reluctantly. Geli and Helene walked along to the taxi station.

"Mummy, where are we going?" Helene asked.

"I will tell you later." Geli led the way through the throng into the toilets, opened her second valise and handed Helene a blonde wig and a pair of dark glasses. "Go into one of the cubicles and put these on."

"Oh, really, Mummy," Helene commented.

"Just do it," Geli told her, and went into another of the cubicles. She took off her raincoat and dress and placed against her stomach a small cushion. She had used this prop several times before: it had its own straps to fit round her waist and secure firmly, rather like the lower half of a life jacket. Then she put on her dress again, and her raincoat. She had a blonde wig for herself as well, carefully tucked the last dark curl out of sight, put on her dark glasses and went outside.

Helene had already put on her wig and glasses. Now she stared at her mother in consternation, and Geli watched her mouth begin to pucker.

"If you laugh, I shall hit you," she promised.

"You look, well . . ."

"Realistic?" Geli suggested.

Helene considered her. "As a matter of fact, you do. At least six months pregnant. But honestly . . ."

"I am trying to protect us," Geli reminded her, and

went outside to summon a cab. They were driven to the hotel. Geli sat Helene down and went to the desk.

"You have a reservation for Mrs Anna Petrov and her daughter," she said.

"Made today," the clerk commented.

"Yes. We were double-booked at the other place. You should also have our coach tickets for tomorrow."

"Here they are, madame. I'm afraid you have missed the tour of Istanbul, the Topkapi and the Blue Mosque."

"What a pity," Geli said. "Perhaps it will be possible to do them when we return from Cappodocia."

"Perhaps," the clerk said, and handed her the key as well as the envelope.

After leaving the golf club, Hans Littler went to his office and telephoned Zurich.

"My name is Hans Littler," he said importantly. "I believe my wife, Mrs Geli Littler, spoke with you earlier this afternoon."

"That is correct, Herr Littler."

"Good. Have her instructions been carried out?"

"It is in the process of being done, Herr Littler."

"Good. Good. Now, what I would like you to do is send me here, by express delivery, all the details of the account."

The girl hesitated. "I think you should speak with Herr Schmidt's secretary."

"I will speak with Herr Schmidt himself."

"I am sorry, sir, but Herr Schmidt is not here. I will put you through to his secretary."

Hans frowned at the telephone as he waited.

"Herr Littler?"

"Yes, that is me."

"Fraulein Clausen, Herr Littler. I am Herr Schmidt's secretary. I understand you are enquiring about the instructions given us today by your wife."

"Yes. I wish full information about the arrangement, as quickly as possible."

"I am afraid there is no arrangement, Herr Littler. At least, there is no arrangement concerning you."

"What did you say?"

"Frau Littler issued certain instructions regarding funds which we are holding here for her. These instructions are private and confidential, and cannot be released to anyone except on the authority of Frau Littler."

"The funds are to be paid into a joint account," Hans said patiently. "Of which I am co-signatory. I have every right to know where they are."

"I am sorry, Herr Littler. Frau Littler made no mention of a joint account."

Hans stared at the telephone. "I am her husband, you stupid woman," he bellowed.

"I am sorry, Herr Littler. I must obey the instructions as given me by your wife. May I recommend that you obtain a letter of authority from your wife, instructing me to release the information to you, and then I will be happy to do as you ask?"

Hans slammed the telephone on to its rest. The bitch, he thought. The little bitch! Then he grinned: she wasn't quite as stupid as he sometimes thought she was.

But then, she never had been. Hitler's daughter, and keeping it close to her chest for twenty-six years! Now she was playing some game of her own, pretending to be scared out of her wits but still retaining enough sense to make sure no one could touch her money.

She'd never go along with being erected as a figurehead, she had said. Perhaps she had been telling the truth. But that did not mean she would refuse to be erected, or elected, as a leader! Hitler's daughter!

It occurred to him that he did not know his wife well enough. After twenty-six years, he still did not know her at all. He hadn't been sufficiently interested before.

It was his next step that concerned him. Because he didn't even know where she was.

*   *   *

181

"There's a belly dancing show in the restaurant tonight," Helene said. "Can we go?"

"I've ordered dinner in the room," Geli told her. "I think we should spend the evening up here. We have a long day tomorrow."

"Oh, Mummy! Where are we going?"

"On a tour of Cappadocia."

"Cappadocia?"

"To look at all the Greek temples. Haven't you always wanted to do that?"

"Well . . . but now? You're running away, aren't you?"

"I told you that was what I was doing," Geli said.

"And you don't want anyone to know where you have gone?"

"There wouldn't be much point in running away if everyone knew where I was going, would there?"

Helene sat beside her. "Are you scared, Mummy?"

"Yes," Geli said. "I'm scared."

"Of what, or who, specifically?"

"I don't know," Geli said thoughtfully. "There are so many things to be afraid of."

*

"I have told you exactly what happened," Hunt said. "My friend and I came to Istanbul for a little holiday, and we were set upon by these thugs."

"Who were obviously in league with your taxi driver," Inspector Mendelik pointed out. He was a precise little man with a precise little moustache and somewhat sharp features. He spoke perfect English.

"I'm afraid it seems as though they were," Hunt agreed.

"Who was not a taxi driver at all," Mendelik said. "But who you took from the airport."

"Well, he seemed all right to me," Hunt said.

"Which hotel are you staying at?"

"I have no idea."

"You came to Istanbul without making a booking?"

"It was all rather a rush," Hunt explained, and glanced

182

at Leni. "My friend's husband is such a bore. But actually, I have a friend here in Istanbul who I am sure will put us up until we can find a hotel."

Inspector Mendelik raised his eyebrows. "A lady friend?"

"No, no," Hunt said. "A man friend. A Mr Hans Littler. Well, I suppose I should say, Herr Hans Littler." He studied Mendelik as he spoke; had his expression reacted to the name? He couldn't be sure. But the Zurich police had certainly had lots of time to contact him if they were going to.

If they were going to follow up the lead of the telephone calls, they would certainly have done so.

"I see," Mendelik said. "Perhaps you should telephone him?"

"I shall, as soon as you let us go. Really, old man, anyone would think we were the criminals."

"I apologise, Mr Hunt. Why do you not use my phone? Do you know the number?"

Hunt hesitated, very briefly. But he could not allow himself to be pushed around now. "Are you holding us for any reason whatsoever, Inspector?"

"Mr Hunt, a man is dead. I believe you when you say that he was accidentally knifed by one of his friends in the course of their attack upon you, but at the very least you will be required to give evidence at the inquest. I wish to know where you will be staying. You will also be needed to identify the rest of these hooligans when they are caught."

"I see. Well, I will promise to let you know where we are staying as soon as we are staying there, if you follow me."

"At Herr Littler's house?"

"I shall have to see. He may already have houseguests. But I am sure he will find somewhere for us."

"But you will not telephone him?"

"I will telephone him," Hunt said. "But I would prefer my call to be private."

"If you wish I shall leave the room."

"Oh, come now, Inspector. I wasn't exactly born yesterday."

"Very well, Mr Hunt. You wish to go your own way. But may I make something very clear? You do not wish to tell me the true reason why you are in Turkey. You have, as yet, committed no crime and therefore I have no grounds for insisting that you do so. However, there can be no doubt that there is some force, here in Turkey, which is opposed to you and which this evening intended at least to beat you up, if not kill you. Now, my police force has a great deal to do. If you walk out of that door without co-operating with me, you are on your own. I can offer you no protection. I wish you to understand this."

"Oh, I do, I do," Hunt said. "But you see, Inspector, you have got hold of the wrong end of the stick. Those thugs weren't after me. They were after Miss Angstrom. It's her legs, you see. Irresistible."

Mendelik gave a cold smile.

"Listen," Leni said. "You and I have to have a little chat."

"Soon," Hunt promised, peering from the doorway of the police station at the rain.

"Like now?"

"When we've got to Littler."

"Hunt, the way things are going, we are not going to get to Littler. I am going to say nothing about being soaked to the skin and certain to catch my death of cold. I am going to say nothing about being dragged from that car and having my private parts massaged by a bunch of hoodlums. What I am saying is that whatever you are doing, there is at least someone who knows you are doing it and is prepared to stop you. We were just lucky that policeman turned up when he did, or we could be in dead trouble."

"Let's go!" Hunt lifted his valise, turned up his collar and ran on to the pavement. He had spotted a bar on the other side of the street.

Leni hesitated for a moment, the hefted her own bag and ran behind him. "Hunt!"

Hunt gained the shelter of the bar, leaned on the counter. "You speka da English?"

"Doesn't everyone?"

"You serva . . . we want raki!"

"Of course, sir." The barman looked past him at Leni struggling in the doorway, dripping water. "For two?"

"For two."

"Hunt!" Leni was beside him. "I want to know what's going on."

"Something very fishy," Hunt said, and drank deeply.

"You mean because the taxi was a plant?"

"The taxi, darling, was arranged by me."

"Sorry, you'll have to say that again."

"We'll have two more of those," Hunt said.

The barman frowned at them. "You know what they say of raki, sir."

"Surprise me," Hunt suggested.

"Well, after one raki a man loves his wife."

"Absolutely," Hunt said, looking at Leni.

"After two rakis, a man hates his wife."

"Absolutely," Hunt agreed, continuing to look at Leni.

"And after three rakis, a man knows his wife hates him."

"Absolutely," Hunt said. "You'd better make that two more. And may we use your phone?"

The barman pointed.

"Back in a flash," Hunt said.

"No way," Leni said. "I want to hear every word."

They huddled together in the half-booth while Hunt dialled and fed in the coins.

"Yes?" said the voice at the other end of the line.

"Herr Littler?" Hunt spoke German.

"Yes."

"You do not know me, but I am in Istanbul on a matter which may be of great interest to you."

"Ah," Littler said. "I have been expecting you."

185

"Have you? That is very good."

"Where are you calling from?"

Hunt looked out of the window across the rainswept street at the lights of the police station. "That is not relevant."

"Ah. I think I should tell you that my wife is not here at present."

"Your wife?"

"It is my wife you wish to see, is it not?"

"If you feel what I have to say would be of interest to her," Hunt agreed. "But you say she is not there."

"She is not in Istanbul. So your journey has been a waste of time."

Hunt looked at Leni, and Leni looked back at him.

"It is you I wish to see, Herr Littler," Hunt said. "I would like to come out and see you this evening. Would that be possible?"

"If you wish," Littler said. "Do you have the address?"

"I know you live in Telibaba, and the street and house number."

"Let me direct you. When you enter the village, turn up the hill and take the second road on the right. We are the fourth house on the right."

"Thank you," Hunt said.

"How soon will you get here?"

"I would say . . . forty-five minutes."

"I shall expect you. But you have not told me your name?"

"Schmidt," Hunt said, and hung up.

"How do you explain that?" Leni asked.

"It's very simple. It's possible our girl has been reading her newspaper, and has decided to do a bunk."

"Then our journey really has been fruitless. Bang goes our scoop."

"You give up too soon. It's equally possible that her husband may just have been saying that, with her standing at his elbow. Either way, we have to find out. And who

186

knows, friend Hans may turn out to be an accommodating fellow."

"Why?"

"That depends on how much Fraulein Hitler, or Frau Littler, has told him about herself." He went back to the bar, drank his second raki. "Is it possible to obtain a taxi from here?"

"Of course."

"Recommend one," Hunt suggested. "We weren't too lucky with our last one."

*

Hans replaced the telephone and looked at his sons: they had arrived home only just before him, in a state of some agitation, but he hadn't yet had time to ask them about it – he was too agitated himself. "We are to receive a visitor."

"The men from Switzerland?" Paul asked.

Hans frowned at him. "How did you know about that?"

"Mum told us. You did not think she would go away without telling us?"

The vixen, Hans thought. She had kept not one of her promises. But as the boys knew . . . he was actually somewhat relieved. He had meant to tell them an invented reason for what was happening. Now he was overtaken by events. But he was glad of their support.

"Well, it may well be the people from Switzerland," he agreed.

"In which case they are murderers," Herrmann said. "They will murder us."

"There is no reason for them to murder us. It is your mother they are after, which is why I have sent her away to safety."

"Where have you sent her?" Paul asked.

"It is better that you do not know that. That way you cannot tell anyone."

"We must call the police," Herrmann insisted.

Hans pulled his nose.

187

"We have the gun," Paul said eagerly. "We can take care of ourselves."

Hans pulled his nose again, and the telephone jangled again. All three of them looked at it for several seconds before Hans picked it up. "Hello?"

"Herr Littler?"

This was a different voice. A Turkish voice.

"I am he."

"Ah, Herr Littler, this is Inspector Mendelik from the police. We have met."

"Yes," Hans said. "I remember. What can I do for you, Inspector?"

"I would like to ask you if you know a man named Hunt. He is an English newspaper correspondent."

"Hunt," Hans said. "No, I do not know this man."

"I see. Well, it is very possible that he may attempt to contact you either tonight or tomorrow morning."

"What about?"

"That is what I am hoping you will be able to tell me, Herr Littler, as soon as you have spoken with him. He has come to Turkey to see you. I believe, but he will not tell me why. However, I must warn you that someone has tried to stop him getting to you, and that therefore he might be described as a dangerous man, at least to those close to him. What I would like you to do, therefore, is telephone me here the moment you receive any communication from this man. By all means agree to meet with him, but make sure that I know of it so that I may make certain arrangements."

"I received a telephone call from a man not ten minutes ago," Hans said.

"From Hunt?"

"I do not know. He said his name was Schmidt, but he was most definitely English."

"What did he want?"

"He said he wished to speak with me. He is on his way here now."

188

"That is almost certainly Hunt," Mendelik said. "Very good. I will make my arrangements."

"Inspector," Hans said. "I believe this man to be involved in two murders."

"Would you repeat that, please?"

"I believe this man, Hunt, you say is his name, murdered a German journalist name Brauer last Friday night, and then a Swiss lawyer named Schmidt later the same night."

"Go on." Mendelik's voice had taken on an edge.

"Well, now he wishes to speak with me."

"Are you connected with these people, Brauer and Schmidt?"

"Ah . . . indirectly."

"Herr Littler, I think you and I need to have a chat. And in view of what you have said, I need to have another talk with Hunt as well. Listen. I will have armed policemen at your house within fifteen minutes. They will not interfere unless they have to. That is, they will allow Hunt to enter your house. This is necessary because I wish him to commit himself. There is nothing for you to be afraid of. Keep him talking until I get there, which will be thirty minutes from now. Are you prepared to do this?"

"Of course," Hans said. "But I must tell you that I am armed and am also prepared to defend myself. If this man Hunt attempts to kill me, I will shoot him."

"Of course," Mendelik said. "But try not to kill him until I get there."

Hans replaced the receiver. "We have him," he said with some satisfaction. "But we will take no risks. Paul, fetch the gun. Herrmann, fetch that big knife from the kitchen. Keep it concealed, but be prepared to use it."

Herrmann licked his lips anxiously. "Should we not call the police, Dad?"

"That was the police, you silly boy. They are on our side and will be here in a few minutes. This man is walking into a trap. And after he has been arrested, why . . . we will be able to bring your mother and sister home. Will that not be ideal? Hurry now, the gun and the knife."

He armed himself with a hatchet which he concealed under the cushion of his chair. Herrmann did the same with the kitchen knife while Paul put the pistol in his pocket. Hans was quite excited, and so was Paul. Herrmann was merely nervous.

"Now," Hans said. "We wait. Paul, switch on the television. We must not make this man suspicious."

Paul got up. As he did so they heard the sound of a car in the drive. All three of them looked at their watches.

"He said forty-five minutes," Paul muttered.

"He was fooling you," Herrmann said. "He must have telephoned from the village. What are we going to do?"

"Bah," Hans commented. "We can take care of Mr Hunt until the police get here. Mendelik said it would not take longer than a quarter of an hour; he is obviously summoning a patrol car by radio. Are you ready?"

"Ready," Paul said.

Herrmann hesitated and then nodded.

The doorbell rang.

"Well," Hans said. "Here goes." He walked to the door, opened it, stared at the woman in surprise. And then looked past her at the man behind her. As he did so, he inhaled. The scent was very strong: Adoration.

CHAPTER SIX

"Do you think we could have a little chat now?" Leni asked. As the taxi pulled away from outside the bar into the rainswept night.

"As long as we keep it clean. This Achmed probably understands both English and German."

"You said you had arranged that earlier car. How did you do that?"

"I used the telephone, darling."

"Okay. Tell me why."

"Because I didn't like what was going on."

"You mean you like what's going on now?"

"No. But at least we're on our way to see Littler."

"And the woman?"

"You heard what he said. But I would expect to pick up a lead."

She considered for a few moments. Then she asked, "What didn't you like about earlier?"

"The way you and Corinne got shacked up together. It offended my sense of propriety because I come from a long line of heterosexual males. I think you should tell me the truth about that."

Leni considered some more. "Suppose I told you I have my own reasons for wishing to find Frau Littler?"

"And they have nothing to do with a story. Because you aren't actually a journalist, are you?"

"How did you work that out?"

"You mean apart from the fact that you do not look like a journalist, speak like a journalist, think like a journalist . . . and that you are not Leni Angstrom?"

191

Leni gulped. "I seem to have made rather a mess of things. How did you find out about Angstrom?"

"Darling, I have friends in the business. Next time you pick someone else's identity, you should at least check whether she is left- or right-handed."

"Oops. That *was* careless. Then you know who I am?"

"I know your name. It's on your spare passport, remember? Leni Weiss. But I do not yet know who you are."

"Well . . . what's happening?"

The night was filled with screaming sirens and flashing lights. Their driver obligingly pulled to the side of the road and the two police cars hurtled past, disappearing into the rain.

"Must be a murder," Hunt remarked.

"God! For a moment I thought they were after us."

"They have nothing on us, darling. Better yet, they don't even know where we are. Now, you were going to tell me something very important, I think. Do remember I've had three rakis, and that is undoubtedly going to colour my judgement."

"Well . . . actually . . . I work for the German Government."

"You mean you're the equivalent of MI5, or some such thing? Sent to keep tabs on me?"

"Not at all. Sent to find Hitler's daughter. You just seemed to be the man most likely to succeed, so I was told to tag along."

It was Hunt's turn to consider. "How did you know about it in the first place?"

"Brauer approached several editors, looking for backing for his search. One of then is a good German and telephoned us. Simple as that. Unfortunately, by the time I had been briefed and told to insinuate myself into Brauer's pattern, he was dead. My superiors got on to the Hamburg police to discover if there were any other leads, and were given your name."

"So you insinuated yourself into my pattern instead. I'm not grumbling: it was rather fun. But your methods

192

were a bit dangerous, weren't they? I might really have hurt you."

"I can take care of myself."

"Meaning you deliberately let me take you apart. Okay, maybe I'll buy that one, although I think we should have a rematch some time. And when you told all this to Corinne, she decided to co-operate?"

"Well, she insisted on telephoning my superiors first, for confirmation."

"Sensible girl. So, are you allowed to tell me your plans? Do you mean to arrest Frau Littler? What will be your charge? Just because she's her?"

"I wish to speak with Frau Littler. What happens after that will depend upon what she has to say to me. Obviously we do not wish anyone related to Hitler returning to Germany and stirring up a political storm. I mean, think of the trouble the Nazis are stirring up, anyway. But everyone agrees they're just a bunch of thugs. Having a Hitler appear, especially if, just suppose, she is both attractive and forceful, would really put the cat amongst the pigeons."

"Hm," Hunt commented.

"Look, I'm not going to interfere with your scoop in the least."

"That is the most confused thinking I have ever heard, Leni. It's my business to plaster Frau Littler's name and face and ancestry over the front page of the *Globe*, from whence it is going to be plastered over the front page of every newspaper and the screen of every television set in the world. You don't think that's going to put the cat amongst the pigeons?"

"I don't think it should, if we secure an undertaking from Frau Littler that she will never return to Germany. In fact, warn her that she will not be allowed to return. She has Swiss nationality. She has no *right* to return."

"Her Dad had Austrian nationality, as I recall. He didn't become a German until after becoming Chancellor."

"We will keep her out."

"Until and unless there is a coup in her name."

"Oh, really, Hunt, this is 1992."

"Don't remind me."

"Well," she said, a trifle defiantly. "What are you going to do about it, anyway?"

"Think," he said. "Let's talk to Littler first."

The taxi was entering the village and now it turned up the street from the waterfront, and then to the right.

"Oh, oh," Leni said, gazing at the flashing lights and the policemen. "I think we should get out of here, Hunt."

"Too late. Anyway, we need to find out what's going on, remember."

"Just don't, under any circumstances, blow my cover," she warned him.

The taxi stopped and Hunt got out to face several revolvers. And Inspector Mendelik.

"Well, Mr Hunt," Mendelik said. "And the delightful Miss Angstrom. You are under arrest."

"What have you got against us, Inspector?" Hunt asked politely.

"And do you think we could get out of the rain?" Leni requested.

"Yes, that might be an idea," Mendelik agreed. "Search them," he told his aides.

Hunt and Leni gazed at each other as wet hands riffled through their clothes and over their bodies.

"Nice work, if you can get it," Hunt said to the man who was handling Leni, quite literally, but the policeman didn't appear to understand English. "What about the taxi?" he asked Mendelik.

"You can pay him off."

"How do we get back to town?"

"We will take you back, Mr Hunt."

"That's very nice of you." Hunt paid the taxi driver and their valises were removed from the boot, to be immediately appropriated by the police. Hunt followed

Leni up the front steps and into the house: the door was open. As she checked on entering the lounge, he bumped into her, looked past her at the two frightened young men: one was having a rather ugly head wound dressed by a policeman, the other seemed unharmed, but looked as if he had seen a ghost. A chair remained overturned and there was blood on the carpet.

"You will see that your friends were here, Hunt," Mendelik said.

"Have I got any friends?"

"Probably not. But the charge is kidnapping."

"You'll have to explain that, Inspector."

"Tell this gentleman what happened here tonight, Mr Littler," Mendelik invited.

Hunt's nostrils were already twitching. There were a great many odours in the room, but one still hung on the air, as it had been created to do.

"There was a middle-aged woman and a younger man, with a beard," he suggested.

"We do not know," Paul Littler said. "They wore masks. But there was a woman and a man, that's right. They were looking for my mother. They took us by surprise: we were not expecting a woman, and they were so violent." He looked at his brother. "They hit Herrmann with the butt of a pistol, then the woman held us here at gunpoint while the man searched the house. They were very angry that my mother was not here. When they asked Papa where she was, he said he did not know. They were going to make him tell them, I think, but then we heard the police sirens. So they left, taking Papa with them."

Hunt looked at Mendelik.

"They got away," Mendelik said.

"With Littler? I think you'd better find them in a hurry, Inspector, if their track record is anything to go by."

"I am hoping you will tell me where they will have taken him, Mr Hunt."

"Me? You have got to be joking. Listen, these are the

195

people who have already committed at least two murders, to my knowledge."

"I know this. Herr Littler told me this when he spoke to me on the phone an hour ago."

"Littler called you?"

"No. I called him, to let him know you would be contacting him. You had just spoken with him, in fact, and he had no doubt that you were one of the assassins from Zurich and Hamburg. That is when I sent my people out here. But it seems I underestimated you, Hunt. I did not realise that you already had your people here in Telibaba."

"Inspector, you know that has to be nonsense."

"Why? Because you happen to be a famous newspaper correspondent? Even newspaper correspondents can be criminals."

"Oh, for God's sake! Why don't you ask Miss Angstrom?"

"Ask her what? She is your accomplice."

"Well . . ." Hunt looked at Leni, who shook her head.

"Leave me out of this, Hunt. I'm just along for the ride."

Hunt glared at her, but his position was not yet serious enough to warrant bringing her out into the open.

"Inspector," he said. "You will never, ever, prove that there is the slightest link between the people who have kidnapped Hans Littler and me, save that we are both looking for the same person: Mrs Littler. May I suggest that the most urgent task we face is to find the lady? She is in the gravest danger."

"You would not say that Herr Littler is in danger?"

"Indeed he is, but we do not know where he has been taken. We do know where his wife is."

"Do we?"

"These young gentlemen will tell us. You must tell us," he said to Paul. "It is your mother's life at stake."

"I do not know where she is," Paul wailed. "Neither of us know. We drove her and my sister downtown this afternoon, as instructed by her. She got out of the car at a taxi station and walked away."

"With your sister?"

"Yes."

"Was she carrying a bag?"

"Yes. They each had a small hold-all. Mother had two."

Hunt looked at Mendelik.

"They could be on a plane going anywhere in the world," the Inspector said.

"Or they could still be in Istanbul."

"It is a big city."

"You will have to put out a call over radio and television. Someone must have seen them. You have a description." He turned back to Paul. "Give us a description."

"Well, Mama is about five feet four inches tall, dark-haired, slender . . ."

"Pretty?"

"Well, yes, she is pretty, I think."

"Can you think of anyone she looks like?"

"Well . . . no. Only herself."

"Okay. Now your sister?"

"Taller, also dark-haired . . ."

"How old is she?"

"Seventeen."

"How old is your mother?"

"I'm not sure . . ." Paul looked at his brother.

"Mother is forty-seven." Herrmann mumbled.

"Right. There are your descriptions, Inspector," Hunt said. "I would get them out on TV right away."

"I will do that. But you are still under arrest." He looked at Leni. "Both of you."

"Telling you that you are making one hell of a mistake won't change your mind?"

"No," Mendelik said. "Will you come with us now, please?"

"Just one moment," Hunt said and turned back to Paul

197

Littler. "Did your mother say anything about going away before this afternoon?"

The boy shook his head. "No. No one knew anything of it until we came home, and she told us to drive her and Helene into town and then return here."

"Can you give us a list of your mother's close friends, anyone she might have gone to?"

"My mother has no close friends," Paul said.

Hunt looked at Mendelik, who raised his eyebrows.

"No close friends at all?"

"You say she was in danger, and knew this?" Paul asked. "There is no one in Istanbul she would have gone to for help."

"What about Freya Hartmann?" Herrmann mumbled. "She and Mother were always telephoning each other and playing bridge together."

"Freya Hartmann is the last person Mother would have gone to if she was trying to hide," Paul argued. "She is the biggest gossip in Istanbul."

"Freya Hartmann." Menedlik made a note. "I will check this. Now, Mr Hunt . . ."

"Do you think it might be possible for me to see your mother's room? Where she spent most of her time."

"Now look here, Hunt," Mendelik said.

"I'm not trying to get away," Hunt protested. "I'm trying to find out where Mrs Littler has gone."

"And you think that you will discover that here?"

"Who knows? Mr Littler?"

"Well . . ." Paul hesitated, looking at Mendelik.

"Oh, very well," Mendelik said.

Paul got up and went to the stairs. Hunt and Mendelik and a policeman followed: Leni made to do so, but was checked by another policeman. She looked as if she was going to protest, then changed her mind.

"This is my mother and father's bedroom," Paul explained.

Hunt looked around him. It had been searched, that was obvious, and was in a state of considerable disorder:

198

the drawers in the bureau had been emptied on to the floor.

"My men have also looked here," Mendelik pointed out.

"And did this?"

"This is as we found it."

Hunt considered the piled clothing, wondered what Geli Littler might have kept in her closet other than undies.

"Then through here is what you might call my mother's boudoir, I suppose," Paul said. "Where she sewed and, well, where she spent a lot of her time."

This too had been searched. There was a bookshelf and the books had been taken out and tumbled on the floor. Save for one which lay on the table, open. Hunt stood above it. "Did you put this book here?"

"No. I have touched nothing."

"Did your people put it here, Inspector?"

"No," Mendelik said. "It was on the table, just like that, when we came in. Either your friends left it like that or Mrs Littler had been reading it this afternoon."

"Yes," Hunt said thoughtfully.

"I do not see that it is important," Mendelik said. "I have turned the pages and there is nothing to be found. If there was anything, the kidnappers took it. But I do not believe there was ever anything in the book. You have been reading too many detective novels, Mr Hunt. This is simply a book on the ancient Greek civilisation in Cappadocia."

"Yes," Hunt said again. "Is your mother interested in history or archaelogy, Mr Littler?"

"I do not think so. she has never mentioned it to me."

"Yes," Hunt said a third time.

"We have wasted enough time," Mendelik said. "You will come with me now. Mr Hunt."

They were driven back into Istanbul in separate cars. Mendelik himself drove with Hunt.

"I hope you're not going to be rough on the little girl," Hunt said.

"She will have to go through the normal procedures. perhaps she will be more co-operative than you."

"I don't see how she can be as she knows even less about this business than I do."

"We shall have to see."

"And when will we be released?"

"When we have arrested the people who abducted Herr Littler and have established that you are not guilty of that crime. If such a thing can be established."

"I see. In England an arrested man is allowed to make a telephone call. Is that the law in Turkey as well?"

"You may make one phone call if you wish, Mr Hunt. When we get to the station. But I am hoping that before then you will tell me what this is all about."

"What?"

"Who is this Mrs Littler, and what makes her so important that you and your people are prepared to kill to find her?"

"Inspector, believe it or not, but those people, the middle-aged woman and her minder, are trying to stop me from reaching Frau Littler. I suspect it was them hijacked my taxi earlier this evening."

"Tell me about Frau Littler and I may begin to believe you."

"I will do that, Inspector, when the lady turns up."

Mendelik sighed. "You are making life very difficult for yourself, Mr Hunt. But . . . it is your decision. Will you not at least give me a description of the two people we are looking for?"

"Not a very good one, I'm afraid. I only know that the woman is over fifty, maybe even sixty, and the man wears a beard. The woman also uses Adoration."

"Adoration?"

"It is a very expensive perfume with a very expensive scent."

200

"I see. I am sure there is much more you could tell us about them if you wished."

"Only that they seem to have a weakness for burning people with cigarette lighters and then killing them."

Mendelik gave him a cold stare.

The car drove into Istanbul and to the Central Police Station. Hunt looked for Leni but she was not to be seen.

"Where is my fiancée?" he demanded.

"Your . . . ah, the young lady. They must have got held up in traffic."

"Inspector, if you are having that little girl knocked about you are going to be in deep trouble."

"I would not dream of knocking your fiancée about, Mr Hunt." Mendelik showed him into the same office in which they had earlier been interviewed.

"There are many different forms of inflicting torture," Hunt told him. "In the case of Leni it is food, or rather, lack of it. She needs to be fed every couple of hours and we haven't eaten since getting off the aircraft."

"I will see to it," Mendelik said wearily. He picked up his telephone, held it out. "One call."

Hunt began to dial. Mendelik watched him with interest. "Where are you calling?"

"London, England."

"Then why are you using the international dialling code for Germany?"

"Ah . . . my mistake. I'll try again, shall I?"

Mendelik placed his hand on the bar. "You are allowed one *local* call, Mr Hunt."

"Big deal. Well . . ." He checked his diary, dialled Roger Trenton at home. "Listen," he said, gazing at the attentive Mendelik. "I am calling from the Central Police Station where I'm in all kinds of trouble, principally because things got fouled up at this end, for which I am inclined to blame you. Now you get hold of your local lawyer or whoever and get me out of here, tonight."

"Well, I'll see what I can do, of course, Mr Hunt."

"You do that. And listen, there's a plane due in any moment from Zurich. On board will be a Mrs Corinne Grundy. You'd better meet her and put her in the picture, and tell her I need to have a chat with her at the earliest possible moment."

"Will do, Mr Hunt."

Hunt replaced the phone, gazed at Mendelik. "That was our Istanbul correspondent."

"So I gathered. And this Mrs Grundy?"

"Also works for the *Globe*. And therefore, on this assignment, for me."

"Very good. Now you will be charged."

"With what?"

"I think withholding vital information from the police with regard to the kidnapping of Hans Littler will do for now."

"Inspector, you know you cannot make that stick."

Mendelik smiled. "Of course not, Mr Hunt. But there is also the little matter of the handguns smuggled into this country, hidden in your luggage. I'm afraid that is a grave offence, Mr Hunt. It could even indicate that you are a member of a terrorist organisation, and here in Turkey we take this very seriously. But no matter what you are charged with, at least I shall know where you are, tonight. And hopefully, by tomorrow morning we will have found both Herr and Frau Littler, arrested the kidnappers and proved your innocence. If it exists. Then you will be able to fly away from Turkey and perhaps not come back. Will that not be pleasant for us all?"

The cell turned out to be empty, which was a relief. But by the time he got there Hunt had had to submit to a strip search, which was sufficiently unpleasant, and had had his belt and tie removed, together with all his other personal belongings, as well, of course, as his valise. This left him ruffled and aggressive, feeling very dirty, unshaven, and generally unhuman. He had also not enjoyed his meal;

he did not care to consider Leni's opinion of Turkish prison food.

Yet he knew he had to submerge his emotions and do some serious thinking.

He was careering forward into a situation which was increasingly out of his control. He did not like that one little bit.

He had asked for a back-up and been given one; and she had apparently gone over to the enemy without a moment's hesitation. He had asked for support here in Istanbul and been sold a pup . . . or someone had got in before him. Both those facts, he had no doubt at all, were intimately connected with Leni.

He was now reduced to depending on Trenton for help without any idea whether or not the man was working for him at all.

He also had the small problem of how Adoration and her friend had known to come to Istanbul, and what information they might at this moment be extracting from Hans Littler . . . he did not doubt they would be extracting something, which would leave them that much closer to their quarry than himself.

And he had supposed them out of the race!

As for whether or not Leni was actually a German agent, he was inclined to disbelieve her there too, but Mendelik had prevented him from checking that out. On the other hand, if she *was* a German agent sent to find Geli Littler, it was impossible to believe she was entirely on her own. She would have a back-up as well, who had not yet materialised but who was likely to do so at the most inconvenient possible moment. What had to concern him was whether her back-up was connected with Halliday's endorsement of her claim to be a journalist. Which could mean he was facing really enormous odds . . . including Corinne, whenever she arrived. But he suspected that already.

The truly annoying thing was that he had virtually invited her to come along. Of course his reasoning had been sound. Having established where he was and how much he knew, she would have followed him anyway or had him followed . . . but he could have got rid of her more easily on the way, had he known just where the way was going to lead him.

There was no point in crying over spilt milk. The true fact to be considered was that thanks to whoever had done him the dirty over that taxi driver and caused that quite unnecessary delay, he had failed to reach the Littlers before Adoration and her friend. They had Littler, and through him they would very soon have his wife.

And that would be that.

The cell started to fill up as the evening went on, and by dawn there were six men sharing the small space. Three of them were drunks, the other two were extremely unsavoury-looking characters and it occurred to Hunt that the removal of all his worldly goods by the police had been an act of sound judgement – at least there was no risk of him being robbed. He wondered how Leni was faring.

He even managed to sleep for a while, and awoke stiff and feeling more dirty than ever, with a two-day growth of beard.

He contemplated his five companions in distress, and the full slop bucket, and discovered he was getting quite angry, when the cell door was opened by two armed policemen.

"You," one said, pointing at Hunt. "Nobody else."

"Hate to go," Hunt smiled at them as he was taken into the corridor.

He was escorted up the stairs and into Mendelik's office. Unlike him, the Inspector was freshly bathed and shaved, and wearing a recently pressed uniform. However, Leni, seated in a chair on the far side of the desk, entirely lacking make-up and with her clothes crushed, looked as decrepit as Hunt felt.

"Are you all right?" she asked.

"I will be. How about you?"

"I've spent better nights."

"I am sure you will both feel better for a hot bath," Mendelik said. "You are free to go. Here are your valises, and your other personal belongings. Will you kindly check through them and make sure that nothing is missing, and then sign these receipts?"

"Are you trying to tell us you've caught the kidnappers?" Hunt asked.

"I am trying to tell you that you are free to go," Mendelik repeated.

"Then you've located Mrs Littler? You mean she was with this woman Freya Hartmann, after all?"

"I would buy a newspaper on the way out," Mendelik suggested.

Hunt looked at Leni, who shrugged. "Never look a gift horse in the mouth, I'd say, Hunt."

"Not even a Turkish one." He checked his valise. "There are certain items missing."

"We felt you would be better off without them," Mendelik said.

Hunt looked at Leni, who had been checking her bag as well. She shrugged again: clearly the pieces of her pistol had also been removed.

Hunt signed the receipt. "Are we being deported?"

"My dear Mr Hunt, why should I wish to do that?" Mendelik asked blandly. "As a matter of fact, while my actions in arresting you were entirely justified in view of your refusal to co-operate, I am willing to admit now that you are in all probability innocent, at least of kidnapping. Thus I have booked you in to the Hotel Berlin. They take credit cards, so you should have no difficulty." His smile drifted to Leni and back again. "I have booked a double room. I assumed this would be what you wished."

"Absolutely," Leni said.

"Well, then . . . the hotel is waiting. One of our cars will drop you off."

205

Hunt gazed at him. "Just what the hell is going on, Inspector?"

"Ah, Mr Hunt, I suspect you will have to ask the devil that. Good day to you."

They sat together in the back of the police car.

"Have you ever had the feeling of being totally, completely and finally fucked?" Hunt asked.

"I hate to shatter your male ego, but no," Leni said. "No man has ever yet accomplished that. Although one or two have tried," she reminisced.

She was in an excellent humour. Presumably she was thinking about breakfast. While Hunt's brain was so confused he thought he was going to burst. He did not like being confused.

The Hotel Berlin was expecting them and they were hurried up to their room before any of the other guests could see them: by this time it was nine o'clock and Istanbul was awakening.

"Breakfast," Leni told the bellhop in German. "We want an English breakfast. Eggs, lots and lots of eggs. Oh, I think eight. Poached. And bacon. And tomatoes, and mushrooms. And fried bread and toast and marmalade and about eight jugs of coffee. Got that? And make it fast." She closed the door. "You hungry, Hunt?"

"Do you eat that sort of breakfast in Germany?"

"Worse luck, not very often. Who's first for the tub?"

"You go ahead." He watched her go into the bathroom, sat down with the telephone. He began with Trenton.

"Oh, Mr Hunt," Trenton said. "I'm working on it, but I'm not getting very far. It's the guns, you see. Smuggling guns into Turkey is a very serious offence."

"So I understand," Hunt commented. "You mean I have to sit in this stinking cell for the rest of my life. Tell me, did Mrs Grundy get here?"

"Oh, yes, Mr Hunt. She's working on it too. Would you like her to come down and see you?"

"I'm afraid these aren't very salubrious surroundings,"

Hunt said, leaning back on the leather armchair and watching Leni emerge from the bathroom. She was naked and the room was suddenly very comfortable indeed. "Now, Trenton, tell me what's been happening overnight."

"Mr Hunt?"

"What's the current news headline here in Istanbul? Any fires, big robberies, murders?"

"Well, sir, there is at least one murder every night in Istanbul."

"Oh, quite. Anyone important?"

"It does not appear so, sir. But there is one item of interest. On the television news last night, and on the radio, the police put out an urgent call for them to be contacted by a Frau Geli Littler, or by anyone who has seen Frau Littler. She is apparently a middle-aged dark-haired woman who may be accompanied by her seventeen-year-old daughter, also brunette."

"Did the police give a reason for wishing to find this woman?"

"No. sir. They merely said it was most urgent they find her."

"But she hasn't either turned up or been spotted?"

"Apparently not, sir. The message and description were put out again this morning."

Leni was waggling her eyebrows and various other things at him. "I'm just getting in," she mouthed. "Sign for breakfast."

He nodded, waited for her to withdraw.

"All right, Trenton. Where is Mrs Grundy staying?"

"I have booked her in at the Europa Hotel."

"Right. I'll contact her there." His brain was still racing as he tried to analyse what he had just learned. Geli Littler had disappeared, taking her daughter with her, therefore she was definitely running. Despite her sons' pessimism, she might just have gone to her woman friend, Freva Hartmann. But if she had done that, the police would have found her last night; as they had considered it necessary to

207

put out the APB again this morning, it seemed that they had not found her.

He was actually inclined to regard that as a lucky break. Had they found her, she would now be under police protection and twice as difficult to get at.

But if they hadn't found her, where was she? And had Adoration found that out? It was possible that Hans Littler had told her where to find his wife, but equally he might have held out, like Walther Schmidt, to the last.

Might still be holding out, to the last.

The important point was that the decision to run had been taken fairly recently, and fairly suddenly. Geli had not told her sons about it beforehand, nor had she told them where she was going. She and her daughter had taken a valise each . . . and undoubtedly they had also taken some kind of disguise, hence the fact that no one had as yet turned them in. She had managed to disappear, utterly and completely, with a snap of her fingers.

"Mr Hunt?" Trenton asked. "Are you there?"

There was also the disturbing thought that Mendelik, who after the discovery of the guns could have held his prisoners virtually for as long as he liked without bringing them to court, had suddenly let them go in a most open-handed fashion. He had therefore been told to do so. By someone who also wanted to find Hitler's daughter, and who felt that Hunt was the best person to accomplish that?

But finding the lady was still his number one priority. He would have to deal with any lampreys which might have attached themselves to him when the time came.

"Yes," Hunt said. "I'm here. Listen, Trenton, I have a job for you."

"Anything you say, sir."

"I want you to try every airline and every travel company, and find out if there has been any booking made, somewhat suddenly, in the last forty-eight hours or so. This would have been for two people, a mother

208

and daughter. You'll have to cover trains and ships as well as planes."

"You mean, you wish me to find out if this Mrs Littler and her daughter have left the country."

"Yes."

"Are they that important?"

"Yes."

"With respect, sir, the police will have covered the possibility of their having left. As I said, they put out a description of Mrs and Miss Littler over the television last night, and I am sure they will have put a watch on all airports and seaports and border crossings."

"I know they did," Hunt told him. "But they were looking for the wrong people."

"Sir?"

"I think we are looking for a *blonde* middle-aged woman, and a blonde daughter."

"But . . . that is exactly opposite to the description given out by the police."

"Quite."

"I see, sir. Well, I will do what I can, but if the police have not traced them . . . I mean, even if they are disguised, they would still have to present their passports . . ."

Hunt snapped his fingers as he suddenly remembered: if Geli Littler was indeed Hitler's daughter, by a member of one of Germany's premier families, she would be a highly intelligent woman who would know that it would be very simple to trace anyone attempting to flee a country by plane or boat or train, and have someone waiting at the disembarkation point. Crossing borders, with all the checks that entailed, was the tricky part. Therefore it was safest not to cross borders, if one just wanted to disappear . . . and just before leaving her house, to disappear, Geli Littler had been studying a book on the ancient Greek civilisation in Cappadocia. Why would a woman who must have been terrified out of her wits by the news of Walther Schmidt's death sit down with such a book at such a time,

209

especially as her sons had said it was not a subject she was particularly interested in? "All right, Trenton, forget that. As you say, the police will have covered that angle. Listen, I want you to check all internal tours instead. Concentrate especially on those concerned with the Greek temples in Cappadocia. A yellow-haired woman and her daughter, who would have made a late booking – possibly as late as yesterday. Got me?"

"Greek temples in Cappadocia, sir? That covers a huge area."

"I know that, Trenton. That's why they do tours. Check that out, first thing."

"Yes, sir. I'll deal with that right away. Can I reach you in prison?"

"No, you can't. I'll call you in an hour."

Hunt replaced the telephone, got up and strolled into the bathroom. Leni was submerged beneath a mass of foam, which was a pity, but she was firmly ensconced.

"Breakfast here?" she asked eagerly.

"Not yet. This is Turkey. How long are you going to be?"

"About ten minutes. This feels so good. Or it would be good if I wasn't so hungry."

"Well, when you're done, draw me one, will you?" He went out again, apparently carelessly closing the door behind himself. Then he dialled.

"Franke."

"Hunt. This is urgent. Leni Weiss, German passport holder, claims to be Government agent on trail of you-know-who. I need that checked out."

"Where are you?"

"Hotel Berlin, Istanbul. But I may be leaving later on today. I also need help. Have a couple of people standing by. I will tell you where I want them when I want them. They should be armed and they should carry a spare pistol, with ammunition. Understood?"

"Understood. Stay until lunch. I will get back to you by then."

210

Hunt hung up, contemplated calling Halliday and changed his mind. Something had gone dramatically wrong at that end. As far as he was concerned, Halliday and Corinne could screw themselves.

Breakfast arrived, to the great delight of Leni who was just out of the tub. Hunt joined her in an eating orgy, then left her still eating, shaved and settled into his own tub: he did not think anything had ever felt so good. Presumably he should be worrying about who or what had got them out of goal so promptly, but he just wanted to relax for fifteen minutes.

Leni joined him to sit on the loo with her second cup of coffee. "What do we do now?"

"Wait."

"For what?"

"Something to turn up."

"Sometimes you drive me to distraction. What you mean is, you've blown it."

"Whatever makes you say that?"

"Don't you think that by now Littler has told those people where his wife is?"

"Let's hope he hasn't."

"But whether he has or not . . . we've lost her."

"Perhaps. And perhaps not." Hunt got out of the bath and towelled himself dry.

Leni returned to the bedroom for a third cup of coffee. "What do you think they're after, Hunt?"

"If I knew that, I'd be laughing."

"So . . . we're completely in the dark."

"It's darker than you think. Why are we here, Leni?"

She raised her eyebrows. "We're looking for Geli Littler."

"You're supposed to be quicker than that, darling. Mendelik arrested us last night on suspicion of being connected with Adoration and her boyfriend, and therefore implicated in the kidnapping of Hans Littler. He also had a charge on which he could have kept us locked up

211

until this time next century: the guns. But we are promptly released."

"Well . . . maybe they managed to arrest Adoration and her boyfriend and they confessed that we had nothing to do with them."

"If you believe that, you'll believe anything. Anyway, if the police had picked up Adoration, everyone would know about it."

"So what are we going to do?"

"As I said: be patient. Are you fully digested?"

"That depends on what you want me to do."

"You don't have to do a lot. I was thinking of bouncing up and down on your stomach for a few minutes. It's something I have wanted to do since we first met. I have been frustrated several times, and I'm at the age when a beautiful naked woman wandering around me induces a certain chemical reaction which prevents coherent thought unless assuaged."

"That's been obvious for the past half hour," she pointed out. "And I do appreciate the compliment. I suppose I'll have to go along with you. However, no one is bouncing on my stomach right now. That would be a disaster. On the other hand, if your stomach can stand it . . ."

How he hoped he would not have to kill her.

Five minutes after Leni rolled off him, Hunt was fast asleep.

It seemed only thirty seconds afterwards that she was shaking his shoulder.

"Telephone. I asked him to give a message but he wouldn't."

"Probably my boyfriend. He is telepathetically jealous." Hunt took the receiver. "Hunt."

"Franke. My contact informs me that there is no Leni Weiss serving with the German Secret Service or the German police, in any shape or form."

"Was the cover complete?"

212

"My contact has access to the central computer."

"I see. Thanks very much, old man. What about the other matter?"

"That is in hand. Where do you want them?"

Hunt smiled at Leni, standing six feet away. "I'll have to let you know." He replaced the receiver.

Leni looked at him, and he looked at Leni.

"That was a German," Leni remarked. "He spoke to me in English but he was a German."

"Oh, quite."

"Are all your second cousins German?"

"That fellow is on the staff of our German office. I called him earlier to see if anything had turned up there about Adoration and Brauer's murder."

"I see," Leni said. "And nothing has?"

"I'm afraid not. But they do seem to have fingers in a lot of pies."

"Then what now?"

"More patience."

He lay down again, his eyes shut, listened to her moving about the room. Leni Weiss, he thought. She wasn't a journalist and she wasn't a German agent. So what, or who, the devil was she? Apart from being a deliciously attractive blonde who knew how to take care of herself? And who also knew how to stick closer than a leech?

And who had also been able, apparently, to turn Corinne from someone who heartily disliked her into someone who wanted only to help her.

And he was stuck with her, at least in the short term. Mendelik was just waiting for him to step out of line. Were he to do what he should, which was to lay her out, tie her up and walk away from her, he'd have every policeman in Turkey on his tail.

He sat up, looked at his watch. Eleven o'clock. Time enough.

Leni had been gazing out of the window. "You won't believe this," she said. "But it's stopped raining."

"Things are getting brighter all the while." He picked

213

up the phone, dialled. She watched him with interest.

"Well?"

"Oh, Mr Hunt," Trenton said. "I may have what you want."

"Good man."

"There was a late booking for the Fascination Tour of Cappadocia. It was made yesterday afternoon for a Mrs Petrov and her daughter."

"That could be the one."

"Well . . . it's a little puzzling. The reservation was made from Zurich in Switzerland."

"Now I know it's the one." It occurred to Hunt that Geli Hitler was even more intelligent than he had supposed. And therefore, more dangerous? "When does this tour depart?"

"It left an hour ago, sir. For Gallipoli."

"Ah. Have you the whole tour itinerary?"

"Ah, yes, sir. Would you like me to read it out?"

"You said it was Fascination Tours. There'll be a brochure in the lobby of most hotels, won't there?"

"Oh, indeed, sir."

"Then I'll pick one up."

"Yes, sir. But . . . aren't you still in gaol?"

"Don't worry about it, old man." Hunt hung up.

"They've gone on a tour," Leni said. "Brilliant."

"So long as only they, and we, know about it."

"Which tour?"

"Fascination. We'll pick up a tour brochure downstairs. Right now, let's get dressed and see about hiring a car."

"You aim to chase them?"

"That would be a little obvious. We never can tell which set of nasties are still trailing *us*. I think we'll study that itinerary over lunch, and choose our point of interception."

"What about our friends?"

"Well, the situation is rather similar to Switzerland. If Hans Littler has coughed up then they have at least

214

a twelve-hour start. So there's not much we can do about that."

"That's what you said about Walther Schmidt. And he was dead by the time we got to him."

"I'm more optimistic about Geli. These people seem quite happy to kill to get to her, but I'm not sure they mean to kill *her*. At least, not until they have got what they want out of her. Besides, once she's on that coach she's surrounded by happy tourists. And I'm pretty certain she got on the coach. So it would seem that Hans is still holding out, stout fellow. I think they've missed the bus."

"I seem to remember one of your prime ministers once saying that, somewhat prematurely," Leni remarked. "Let's eat."

*

Out of Istanbul, the tour bus took the main road along the north side of the Sea of Marmara.

Geli and Helene were early at the assembly point, the Grand Hotel, having walked along from the Europa after settling their small account with cash. The room had been prepaid from Zurich. Nobody paid them any attention.

Geli had spent a sleepless night after watching the news broadcast in which descriptions of Helene and herself had been put out, with the urgent message that they report to the police as soon as possible.

Geli was sure of what had happened: Hans had panicked and gone to the police. Whether this had been blind panic, pique because she had told the children, or because he had got on to Zurich and been told she had not after all placed the money where he could get at it, she did not know. It could even have been that some member of the group who were looking for her had got in touch with him. But whatever the reason, it was not good enough. He had let her down.

But had she not known he was going to do that? Hence the wigs and the glasses and the cushion.

Even so, it was an enormous temptation to ring the police, or ring home, to find out what was going on.

215

But her business was to disappear, and she intended to do just that.

"Do we have to wear these dreadful things again today, Mum?" Helene asked as they dressed.

"Yes."

"And you intend to carry on with that pregnancy charade?"

"Yes," Geli said.

And now at last she felt she could relax. They had been accepted as the late tourists they had pretended to be. The tour guide, a cheerful, black-bearded character whose name was Semih, had greeted them most courteously, if a trifle anxiously when he had realised Geli's "condition", and once they were on the bus had introduced them to the other members of the group. These consisted of some dozen couples, all of whom Geli estimated were over forty, and half a dozen unattached females who were even older. There were no unattached males of any age, save for the driver, Tensit, and Semih himself. It was going to be a long trip for Helene.

The girl's expression indicated that she had worked that out for herself.

Apparently all the other tourists had arrived two days previously and had spent yesterday on an all-day tour of Istanbul and its environs, visiting Topkapi and St Sophia and the Blue Mosque as well as various ancient Christian churches.

"You will be able to do that tour when we return, Frau Petrov, if you wish," Semih said kindly; he spoke perfect German. "Now, ladies and gentlemen, as you know, today we are going to drive along the coast of Marmara until we reach Gallipoli. There we will lunch before crossing the Dardanelles. This afternoon we visit the ruins of Troy, and tonight we stay at a hotel on the eastern shore of the Dardanelles before we leave for the south tomorrow. Now, we are going to be together for a fortnight and it would be best if we come to some arrangement about the

216

seats. You may prefer to make your own, but the method we have used on previous tours, and which seems to work very well, is that at every main stop, that is, for lunch or overnight, everyone moves forward one seat. Thus those who are now seated in the front of the bus will move to the rear after lunch, and the ones behind them will move to the front, everyone else moving up in turn. I hope this meets with your approval?"

He looked from face to face, and when everyone had nodded, grinned at them. "Then . . . let's go."

The bus rolled away from the kerb.

"Do you realise how hot we are going to be in these wigs, down south?" Helene whispered.

"We can take them off at night," Geli said. "Besides . . . maybe we won't have to wear them the whole way."

Helene giggled. "It'll cause a stir if we suddenly turn dark."

"If we can take them off," Geli promised her, "we won't give a damn."

The drive was soporific, so much so that Geli fell asleep, awaking from time to time as they took a particularly sharp bend or some passing car blared its horn. There wasn't very much for Semih to tell them about on this first leg of the journey, and he let them get on with settling down. From time to time she woke up and found herself wondering what was happening at home, what Hans was doing after his call to the police. What the police were doing. But she could not escape the feeling that she and Helene had got clear away. As for Hans . . . her mind was slowly hardening against him. She only worried that the boys were still in Telibaba. But Herrmann and Paul could take care of themselves. At least, Paul could . . .

The coach turned inland at Tekirdag, to avoid the Tekir Daglari massif. The sea was left behind them, and they drove through the low hills until they suddenly emerged at Gallipoli. As they rumbled down the narrow road towards the little ferry port, with the sea now close on their left,

217

Semih told them about the British and Australian and New Zealand landings during the First World War, and the stirring defence conducted by the Turks under the command of the immortal Mustafa Kemal, which had resulted in a resounding Allied defeat.

"Weren't they actually commanded by a German officer?" Helene whispered.

"Yes," Geli replied. "Liman von Sanders."

"Shouldn't we remind him of that? He hasn't mentioned von Sanders once."

"No, I don't think we should remind him of that," Geli said. "We are here to be inconspicuous."

The coach rolled into Gallipoli itself and they disembarked to have lunch at a café situated on the very edge of the Dardanelles and close to where the ferry from the Asiatic shore actually docked. The lunch consisted of a buffet but the food was quite good. Geli and Helene secured their plates and found themselves at a table with a middle-aged couple from Stuttgart, who introduced themselves as Herr and Frau Freilinger, both in their fifties.

"Anna Petrov," Geli said. "And this is my daughter, Elizabeth."

"Ah," said Frau Freilinger, casting a surreptitious glance at Geli's stomach.

Geli smiled at her. "If I do not holiday now, it may not be again for a long time."

"Ah," said Frau Freilinger again. She was obviously dying to ask more questions about the whereabouts of Herr Petrov, but was clearly deciding that as there were still two weeks to go on the tour, she would find out everything she wished to know during that time. "I hope it will not prove too much for you."

"I never felt better in my life," Geli asserted.

Helene was tucking away. Although the coach party had taken over virtually the entire restaurant, there were a considerable number of other people present, some just waiting for the ferry, others actually having a meal. Now Helene raised her head.

"What's that marvellous smell?"

Geli wrinkled her nose. "It's a perfume. A very expensive perfume."

"It's just gorgeous," Helene said. "Do you know what it's called?"

"Oh, yes. Hans bought me some once. It's called Adoration."

CHAPTER SEVEN

Geli and Helene left their table to stand with the others and watch the ferry berth, with much growling of diesels and shouted commands.

"You will walk on to the ferry, please," Semih told them as he joined them. "The coach will drive on later." He paused next to Geli. "The journey is not proving too much for you, Frau Petrov?"

"No, no," Geli said. "I am enjoying it."

"It can be very hot in the south," he said. "But the coach has air-conditioning. If there is anything else you need, just let me know."

"I shall, and thank you."

"Have you ever had a baby delivered on one of your tours?" Helene asked disarmingly.

"Not yet, Fraulein. Not yet." Semih smiled at the pretty girl and walked on.

"I don't see how you can bear to have that thing strapped against your stomach all the time," Helene remarked. "You must be sweating like a pig."

"I am," Geli agreed, and led the way to the gangplank. She climbed to the upper deck, followed by Helene, and from there could watch the other passengers boarding, as well as the coach driving down the ramp, followed by several cars. Once all were on board, the ramp was raised and the ferry began to chug back across to the Asiatic side.

"Didn't Lord Byron swim across here?" Helene said. "He must have been an awfully good swimmer."

"It was further south, where the strait is narrower," Geli told her. She was still looking down at the passengers getting out of their cars. One of the women was striking: middle-aged – Geli put her down as perhaps sixty-five – but tall and slender and elegant, beautifully dressed, her iron-grey hair held in a snood. Her companion was considerably younger than herself, clean-shaven, and he too was well-dressed. Mother and son, perhaps? Geli wondered. Or rich bitch and toy boy? Then she gave a little start. Presumably she now qualified as a rich bitch herself. Once this was over. And supposing she could decide what to do.

The woman looked up and gazed at Geli. Their eyes held each other's for some seconds, then the woman looked away. But Geli was aware of a most peculiar feeling, as if somehow they had communicated. But she didn't know what had passed between them.

Her more immediate problem was Helene. The girl had been wrapped up in the excitement of their flight, but the long hours in the coach had given her time to think as well. When they arrived at their evening's destination, a motel set in wooded country on the east bank of the Dardanelles, after having spent the afternoon wandering around the ruins of Troy and being regaled by Semih with a potted version of the *Iliad*, she could restrain herself no longer.

Carefully she locked the bedroom door behind them. "Mum, you and I have to have a talk."

"What about?" Geli stripped off her sweat-wet clothing and gratefully unstrapped the cushion: her stomach was soaking. As was her hair when she removed her wig and laid it on the table to dry.

"Well . . . about everything."

"What everything?" Geli went into the bathroom, did a double-take when she discovered that there was an electrical wall plug exactly under the shower head – new hotels were springing up all over Turkey and not all of them were of the highest standard – then shrugged and turned on the water, standing with her face up to the lukewarm flow, allowing it to cascade from her shoulders and down her body. It felt so good.

221

"Oh, really, Ma." Helene had also undressed and removed her wig. Now she leaned in the doorway, her towel slung on her shoulder, nudely elegant. "You. Me. Hitler. The people we are running from."

Geli switched off the water and wrapped herself in her towel. Helene took her place. "Right now all that matters is the people we are running from."

"We cannot run for ever."

"Hopefully, we will not have to do that. Hopefully, these people will either give up when they cannot find me, or be arrested."

"But suppose they catch up with us?" Helene also wrapped herself in a towel and the two women stretched out on their beds.

"They cannot catch up with us because no one knows where we are, or what we now look like."

"But . . ." Helene raised herself on her elbow. "You do not even know what they want. It might be something of importance."

"I am quite sure it is important, to them," Geli said. "So important they are prepared to kill to get it."

"You don't know that," Helene argued. "You don't even know for sure that the people who murdered Great-uncle Walther are connected with you at all, or that they know you live in Istanbul. And even if they are looking for you, you only know that they are prepared to kill to get to you, not that they mean to harm *you*."

"And you seriously think I should have waited for them to arrive? So that I could ask them, do you mean to kill me? What do you think I should have done if they had said yes?"

"Oh . . ." Helene discarded the towel and sat up, arms clasped around her knees, chin resting. "Aren't you curious as to why they wish to find you?"

"Yes, I am curious. But not sufficiently curious to wish to risk my life."

"But it must be to do with the fact that you are Hitler's daughter."

"Sssh," Geli said. The bedrooms to either side were occupied by other members of the tour party.

"No one can hear us in here. Mum . . . what do you feel about that?"

"What am I supposed to feel?"

"Oh, Mum! You are the daughter of probably the most famous man of the twentieth century, and the most famous German of all time."

"The word is infamous."

"How can you say that of your own father?"

"Because it's true. You know what he did."

"Well . . . Napoleon caused a lot of deaths."

"He didn't suffocate millions in gas chambers," Geli reminded her.

"Oh, all right, Mum, but that was so long ago."

Geli stared at her daughter in horror.

"Forty-seven years," Helene pointed out. "Before either of us was born."

"Just what are you trying to say?" Geli demanded.

"Well . . . if you *are* Hitler's daughter, well . . . you're a historical figure. Aren't you?"

Geli just looked at her.

"I mean, suppose you were the daughter of the Queen of England, you'd have a historical responsibility to be that daughter. Wouldn't you?"

"I am not the daughter of the Queen of England. I am the daughter of a power-mad megalomaniac who committed every possible crime. Just for example, do you suppose the children of Mustafa Kemal have a historical right to proclaim themselves, and that they would accomplish anything if they did?"

"They might have done something to help Turkey out of the mess it's in."

"Or they might have made that mess a whole lot worse," Geli declared.

"I still think that perhaps you should try to find out what these people want, what the people of Germany want," Helen said.

"And where do you suppose that will leave you? And Paul and Herrmann? Branded with a name and a reputation of which you knew nothing until yesterday?"

"Mum," Helene said patiently. "We are stuck with it now, no matter what happens. We can't forget that now."

"You are only stuck with it if you let it become known, and if you let it influence your lives."

"Oh, really, Mum, do you honestly suppose something like this can be kept secret?"

"It was kept secret for forty-seven years," Geli said fiercely.

"That was pure luck. Now your luck has run out."

"Then I shall just disappear. And if you like, you can disappear with me. And the boys."

"You are in cloud-cuckoo land if you think you can do that," Helene said. "Anyway, what would we live on?"

"I have come into a substantial inheritance," Geli told her. "Which is just waiting to be picked up."

"From Grandpa?"

"From . . . how can you refer to a man like Hitler as Grandpa?"

"Because he is my grandpa. Isn't he?"

"Oh, my God!" Geli muttered.

"And it's his money, right?"

"Well . . . I suppose so."

"And you're happy to take it. You want to take from him everything you can that you think may be of value to you, but you won't accept the responsibility of being what you are."

"You are making me wish I had left you behind," Geli told her. Yet she knew the girl was being uncomfortably logical, and putting into words all the considerations she was afraid to examine. She got up, began to dress. "Let us go across to the restaurant and have an aperitif before dinner."

"Are you going to call home?"

Geli considered. But Hans had now done the dirty on

224

her twice. He would have to stew in his own juice for a while longer. "No," she decided. "Not tonight. Maybe tomorrow."

As they strolled across to the restaurant, she found herself thinking of the elegant woman on the ferry. She and her companion had driven off on the Asiatic shore and disappeared. She did not expect ever to see them again. Yet she could not forget that look.

*

Hunt obtained a brochure for Fascination Tours from the desk and sat down with it and a drink before lunch.

"Like to take a drive into Asia?" he asked Leni.

"Something I've always wanted to do," she remarked. "Is that where our bird has flown?"

"I think so. Right now she's probably at Gallipoli. Tonight she's going to be at a place called Tuhan, on the Asiatic side."

"So that's where we're going?"

"No," Hunt said.

"You've lost me," Leni confessed.

"We don't want to frighten the lady by charging along behind her like the US cavalry. I think we want to just turn up at one of her stops and suss out the land before we tell her who and what we are."

"Supposing we knew where she is going to be."

"But we do, darling." Hunt waved his brochure. "It's all here. Tomorrow she's going to Selcuk, and she's going to be there for two nights. I think that's our opportunity. It says here that tomorrow, for instance, the group have the afternoon at leisure. Once we've identified our quarry, that would be the time to move in, don't you think?"

"You sound like a hunter looking for a kill," Leni remarked.

"I'm a newspaper man looking for an exclusive scoop. Don't you see, darling, especially in view of everything that has happened, I want not only to put Frau Littler under exclusive contract to the *Globe*, but I also want to get her away to some place where she'll be safe."

"Hm," Leni commented. "Don't you think she's going to become very agitated when she learns that her husband has been kidnapped?"

"How is she going to do that when the news has not yet been released?"

"But you propose to tell her."

"Well . . . if it appears the right thing to do. Oh, of course I am going to tell her, but we'll pick our time. We have to discover just what kind of woman she is before we do anything. Is she as tough as nails or as soft as butter? Is she secretly glorying in the knowledge of who she really is, or does the thought terrify her? As I said, the worst thing we could do is scare her off."

"You've obviously given it a lot of thought. And what do you think our friends are doing all this time?"

"They have, as I said, missed the bus. Kidnapping Littler was a booboo, as I believe he has nothing to tell them."

"I feel quite sorry for him. But they know we're here."

"Do they?"

"Well . . . what about last night?"

"I'm brooding on that one. Let's eat." He got up and checked. "Oh, shit!" he commented.

Entering the hotel lobby were Inspector Mendelik and Corinne Grundy.

"Hunt," Corinne said, "just what the hell is going on?"

"She always greets me like that, Inspector," Hunt pointed out.

"You were supposed to contact me," Corinne said. "And I thought you were still in goal."

"So you went along to visit me and were put right by the Inspector. Care to join us for lunch?"

"Thank you, no," Mendelik said. "But I wish to speak with you. Can we go somewhere private for five minutes?"

"Well, I don't know. It's at least three hours since Leni

226

last ate. You'll have to make it no more than five minutes."
He watched Leni and Corinne looking at each other.
There was some movement of eyebrows, and certainly
an unspoken message had been passed between them.

Which placed him in a difficult position because now
there could be no doubt that the two women were working
together, and that was very bad news given that Leni had
twice not turned out to be what she claimed to be. Then
was Corinne what she claimed to be? But Corinne had
been on the staff of the *Globe* for a dozen years!

But then, he reflected ruefully, he had been on the staff
of the *Globe* for a lot longer than a dozen years and no one
even suspected where his real interests lay.

The point at issue, however, was what he was going
to do with them. Neither could be allowed to interfere
with his plans once he found himself face to face with
Geli Littler. But he had tried ditching at least one
of them once before, unsuccessfully. Easy to remind
himself that then he had been trusting Corinne. He
would not do that again. That didn't alter the fact that
ditching the pair of them was going to be twice as
difficult. Unless he was prepared to be very ruthless
indeed.

He liked them both. He could almost say more than
that about Leni.

"I think we'd better go up to our room," he suggested.
"That way we can be sure of privacy."

They rode up in the lift and Hunt hung a "Do Not
Disturb" sign on the door.

"Well, Inspector?" he asked.

"We have found the body of Hans Littler."

"Ah."

"It was in the boot of a car abandoned in an alleyway.
It was not a very pretty sight."

"I can imagine. Tell me, did he die under questioning
or was he murdered afterwards?"

"He was murdered when they had finished with him,
Mr Hunt." The Inspector studied him as he spoke.

227

"And you have no idea as to the identity of his murderers?"

"No. Save that they would seem to be the same people responsible for the deaths in Zurich and Hamburg. They are obviously very dangerous."

"That is the understatement of the year."

"The question is where are they now, and what are they doing?"

"Am I still under suspicion, Inspector?"

Mendelik gave a delicate shrug. "You were in my cell when the murder was committed. But I still feel that you know more about them than you have been prepared to tell me. I think that now you should, how do you say? Come clean? These people must be caught. I need to know what they are really after, so that I may form an opinion as to where they might be now. I can tell you that I am sure they are still in Turkey, because from the moment I heard of their existence I put out an all points bulletin to every seaport, border crossing road or railway, and airport, using the descriptions you gave me. I know your descriptions weren't very detailed, but I still feel sure they would have been picked up had they tried to leave the country."

"You also put one out for Mrs Littler and her daughter and weren't too successful. These people are following Mrs Littler."

"Therefore I feel that Frau Littler and her daughter are still in Turkey, Mr Hunt," Mendelik asserted. "So, will you now co-operate, please?"

"If you will answer one or two questions."

"Willingly, if I can."

"Well, firstly, why did you release us this morning?"

"My dear Mr Hunt, I am a police officer. I have my duty to do but I also have my duty to be fair to the public, whoever they are. In all the circumstances, I felt I had no option but to lock you up. But equally, in all the circumstances, I felt it my duty to contact the Zurich police and they assured me that you could not be one of that group of assassins. So I let you go."

He and Hunt gazed at each other as he spoke. Mendelik could have no doubt that Hunt knew he was lying. What he could not do was stop his eyes from straying, ever so slightly, to the two women seated nearby. This might have been politeness, to include them in the conversation, but Hunt did not think it was.

"Inspector LeCompte said that, did he?" Hunt said. "What a nice man. My other question is: has the news of the discovery of Littler's body been made public?"

"Not as yet. As you will know, we did not even release news of his kidnapping. However, I am on my way out to Telibaba to see the two young men now, and I am afraid it will have to be made public very shortly. My superiors will insist upon it."

"It would probably be helpful if you could suppress it for as long as possible."

"Helpful to whom, Mr Hunt?"

"Why, to you, Inspector. Obviously the murderers will move much more openly if they believe Littler's body has not yet been found. I'm sure your superiors will appreciate that."

"Hm. I will consider that, although in any event I do not believe it will be possible to keep the secret for more than twenty-four hours. For example, I cannot prevent the two boys from speaking of it."

"I certainly think you should try to persuade them not to. Can you not take them into protective custody? They might well need protecting."

"That I shall have to see. Now, Mr Hunt, tell me what these people are after."

Hunt had been considering while he spoke. He had to come to a decision, and the decision had to be based on an estimation of who knew what. This took him back to the Littler sons. He had formed the impression the previous night that they knew who their mother was. Then they had been determined to keep their secret. But would they continue to do so when they learned of their father's death? By refusing to co-operate with Mendelik he would be buying himself not more than a couple of hours, and that was insufficient.

"Whatever I tell you is in the strictest confidence, of course."

"Of course. Except in so far as it might endanger the security of Turkey, or prevent me from catching up with these criminals."

"Oh, quite. Well, then, we believe that Frau Littler may actually be the daughter of Adolf Hitler."

Mendelik's face creased into a frown. "You expect me to believe this?"

"It happens to be a well-substantiated rumour. Listen." He outlined all the evidence Brauer had been able to accumulate. It was also the first time Corinne had heard the whole story, so far as he knew: she certainly acted as astounded as Mendelik himself.

"So," Mendelik said when he had finished. "Your newspaper is looking for an exclusive interview?"

"Correct."

"And what are these assassins looking for from Frau Littler?"

"I wish I knew the answer to that."

"But this makes it more imperative than ever that we find this woman before they do."

"I'm sure it does."

"So where is she?"

"I have no idea. But then, neither do the assassins."

"How can you be sure of that? They held Littler for several hours. He must have told them."

"I do not think he knew where his wife is, Inspector."

"You believe her children?"

"Yes. Yes, I do."

"You think she would have just taken off without telling her husband?"

"Without telling her husband where she was going, yes. I think they would have agreed that she should do that.

That was safest for both of them, don't you see? They could have had no idea that they were dealing with cold-blooded killers who are prepared to murder their way to her."

"What a situation. I do not understand why my people have not turned them up. The descriptions were put out on the television last night . . ."

"They would have disguised themselves. Wigs, glasses, anything else they could think of. And they would have kept a very low profile."

"But still, two women, one middle-aged, the other young, they would have been stopped for questioning at any border station or airport. Anyway, my people have checked with all the airlines for such a booking made within the last forty-eight hours, and have found none."

"Then, as you said just now, they are probably still in the country. Still in Istanbul."

Mendelik stroked his moustache. "Then what are you going to do, Mr Hunt?"

"Be patient, and hope that you find them before the assassins."

"I see. You will be remaining in this hotel?"

"Well, as I'm here I may take a look at some of your beautiful country. But yes, I intend to make this hotel my base."

Mendelik looked at Leni. "With Miss Angstrom?"

"Where I am, there you will find Miss Angstrom, Inspector."

"And Mrs Grundy?"

Hunt smiled at Corinne. "I imagine, as we have come to a dead end, at least temporarily, Mrs Grundy will be returning to England."

"Oh, yes?" Corinne enquired.

"We shall talk about it over lunch," Hunt promised.

"Well, I shall leave you," Mendelik said, and stood up. "I have an unpleasant duty to perform, telling the two sons what has happened to their father. I will be in touch." He brushed the peak of his cap with his swagger stick and left.

"Hunt," Leni said. "Don't you think it would have been better for us all if you had just told the Inspector where Mrs Littler is?"

"You mean he knows?" Corinne asked.

"Of course he does. Or he thinks he does."

"When I catch up with her, I will see that she is adequately protected," Hunt said. "But, quite honestly, I believe she is far better off where she is than in police custody – then the whole world will know where she is."

"But if Adoration and her friend got it out of Littler . . ."

"We don't know they did. We don't even know if Littler knew where his wife was going. As I told Mendelik, it would have made sense for her not to tell him. Now, we have a lot to do . . ."

"After lunch," Leni pointed out.

"Oh, quite."

"Just where do I fit into all this?" Corinne enquired. "If you think I'm going back to England now . . ."

"I think you and I need to have a chat. Leni, I know you're ravenous. Why don't you go downstairs and order lunch, and in fact start? We'll be there in five minutes."

Leni hesitated, looking at Corinne.

Who shrugged. "He is the boss."

Leni left the room.

"Now, then," Corinne said.

"Now, then," Hunt agreed. "Just what's up with you and her?"

"I'm entitled to ask the same question. You told me to come here as your back-up. So when I get here, you don't want to know, any more than you wanted to know in Switzerland, until the chips were down. I have an idea you were planning to sneak off and abandon me. If I hadn't had the sense to go to the police . . ."

"When I asked you to come here, darling," Hunt reminded her, "I was under the impression that you were

232

going to dump Leni for me. Instead of which, you sent her after me. I should put you across my knee."

"It's a deal," she said.

"Later. Tell me what she told you to have you eating out of her hand."

"I don't think I can do that. She made me promise I wouldn't tell anyone."

"So tell me this: are you working for the *Globe* or for Leni Angstrom?"

"Well, of course I'm working for the *Globe*, Charles. It's just that . . ."

"Right. You're on the next plane out."

Corinne sighed and played with the top button of her blouse as if she was considering vamping him. "Oh, very well. Leni is an agent for the German Government. It's absolutely vital for the peace of the world that she find this Mrs Littler."

"Ah. She told you all about that, did she?"

"Yes, she did. Which is more than you did."

"Quite. And you checked out her credentials, I take it?"

"Well, of course I did."

"How?"

"I called London and asked them to have it checked."

"Who did you call in London?"

"Well . . . actually. I called Mr Halliday himself. After what she had told me, I realised how hush-hush it all was."

Hunt gazed at her. If only he had the slightest idea of whether or not she was telling the truth. If she was . . . then Halliday was wading in some very murky waters indeed – but he had sufficient evidence of this already. On the other hand, if she was not telling the truth, and he trusted her again . . . but if he insisted she go back to London, she would merely report to Halliday . . . and somebody else would appear, perhaps not quite so attractive.

Another decision had to be made. But if Halliday was trying to surround him, he had a few resources of his own.

233

"So Halliday told you Leni was genuine?"

"Yes. He did."

"So on that basis you went ahead and put her requirements in front of mine?"

"I was told to do so by Halliday," Corinne pointed out.

"Oh, quite. Well . . . suppose I told you she's not?"

"Come again?"

"I checked her out as well, when she gave me that story."

"You mean Halliday has changed his mind?"

"No, darling. I went direct to Germany. I have quite a few contacts there, you know. And their answer was . . . don't know the girl, either as Leni Angstrom or Leni Weiss, which appears to be her real name. Did you know that?"

"Yes," Corinne said. "She told me. But . . . my God, Hunt? What's going on?"

"If I knew that we'd both be laughing."

"But Halliday . . ."

"Our esteemed Halliday, editor of the year and all that, the wonderman of British journalism, may not be all he appears."

"Oh, Hunt! What are we going to do?"

"You on the level, Corinne?"

"Oh, Hunt. Of course I am. I'm working with *you*."

"I very recently took a resolution that I would never, under any circumstances, trust any woman again. You are asking me to break that resolution."

"Just tell me what to do."

Hunt told her.

Corinne gulped. "You mean to, well . . . take her out?"

"If I have to, Corinne. We know she's not a journalist, and we know she's not a German agent. That can only mean she's after Geli Littler on behalf of some group which does not intend to have Hitler's daughter resurfacing. If that is the case, she has to be stopped. Geli

Littler is not only our pigeon, she is also our responsibility. Right?"

"But you say Leni is not working with the people who murdered Littler?"

"I don't think she is. There are too many inconsistencies. But that doesn't mean there is only one group who would be embarrassed by having a Hitler reappear to claim a political heritage."

"But just to set out to kill her . . . Hunt, I'm scared."

He grinned at her. "Join the club. Now let's get moving. I believe we've ditched Adoration or to put it another way, they've ditched themselves by their weakness for cigarette lighters. But now that I've been obliged to tell Mendelik what's going on, he's going to redouble his efforts to find Mrs Littler. We want to be there first."

She nodded, stood up. "Hunt, give me a hug."

He did, and her lips found his.

"Hunt, when this is over let's you and me just go away some place, like the Seychelles, for a week. We are both going to need a rest."

"Absolutely," Hunt said. "But if I go away with you, Corinne . . . am I going to have a rest?"

"Silly boy," she said, and kissed him some more.

*

"I'll say goodbye," Corinne told Leni who was well into her second steak.

"Goodbye?"

"Hunt is insisting that I go back to England."

"Oh, really, Hunt. That is absurd. I think we are going to need everyone we have if we run into Adoration and her mob."

"We aren't. And anyway, she's two-handed. So are we. If we do run into her, I'll take care of her and you can have the chap with the beard."

"I really am sorry to run out on you," Corinne said and looked beseechingly at Hunt.

"You have a plane to catch," Hunt told her.

Corinne leaned over Leni and kissed both cheeks. Hunt

watched her hand stroke up and down the side of Leni's pants suit as they embraced. That figured: Corinne had been to the loo before leaving the bedroom and would have had the time to scribble a message.

They really both deserved whatever was coming to them.

But that meant Leni would now know he had discovered she wasn't a German agent and that he intended to use executive force, if necessary, to get rid of her. But she wasn't armed and he had a weapon, and a reliable second string, waiting for him wherever he wanted it . . . and she didn't know *that*.

"Take care, Hunt," Corinne said and departed.

"You really are a bastard," Leni told him.

Hunt sat down. "I'm spending company money. There's a limit. Did you order steak for me too?"

"It's here. I hope your teeth are in good order. This cow certainly didn't die yesterday."

"That means it's been well hung."

"Like certain people I know," she commented.

"Been?"

"It'll be that if Adoration gets her hands on your knackers. What are we going to do after lunch?"

"I told you, hire a car and go for a drive," Hunt told her. "But first I simply have to go to the loo."

He returned to the room, locked the door and made a long distance telephone call.

"Selcuk," Franke repeated. "How do you spell that?"

"S-E-L-C-U-K, but there's some kind of Turkish cedilla under the C, so that it sounds like CH."

"Got it."

"Have you arranged support?"

"It will be waiting for you in Selcuk."

"There's been a change of plan. Send one to Selcuk, and the other to a place called Pammukale."

"I know Pammukale. It is a tourist resort."

"Aren't they all, nowadays?"

"Pammukale is special. It has hot springs."

236

"Well, your boy is not going there to take the waters. He is going to keep an eye on a Mrs Corinne Grundy. She is five foot ten inches tall, weighs about a hundred and forty pounds, has long back hair and a big nose. I don't want her interfered with. I just want him to tail her and prevent her, should the occasion arise, from interfering with me. However, should Mrs Grundy become physically involved with a third party, he is to lend her all the assistance in his power. As a casual passer by. Understood?"

"This is becoming very complicated, Hunt."

"I am dealing with a very complicated situation," Hunt told him. "I need all the help I can get, and they have to be capable of executive action."

There was a brief silence. Then Franke said, "You understand that we wish to avoid all publicity, at least at this time."

"If it can be done quietly, it will be done," Hunt assured him. "How soon can your people be in position?"

"By tomorrow afternoon."

"Not a moment later," Hunt requested.

Leni was banging on the door. "Tummy upset?" she enquired when he opened it.

"Must be something I kissed," he told her.

"What's the quickest route to a place called Selcuk?" Hunt asked the girl on the desk.

"You wish to go by car?"

"That was the idea."

"Well, sir, the most direct route by car is along the north coast of the Sea of Marmara to Gelibolu, cross the Dardanelles by ferry and then take the coast road south."

"Right. By Gelibolu I assume you mean Gallipoli."

"Yes, sir."

"Right. How long should it take me? I'd like to be there by tonight."

The girl looked at the clock. It was just after two. "That is impossible."

237

"Why?"

"Because it is twelve hundred kilometres. Allowing for the ferry, it is at least a fifteen-hour drive."

"Damnation." Hunt realised he had been careless in not looking at a map.

"But sir," the girl said. "There is an airport at Menemen, just north of Izmir. Smyrna," she added, this time making allowance for his being English. She took out a timetable. "There is a flight leaving Istanbul at three o'clock. You will catch it if you go now. And it will land you at Menemen in three hours. From Menemen it is only a hundred kilometres to Selcuk: we can arrange for a hire car to be there to meet you."

"Good girl. Will you do that? And will you also telephone the airport and reserve me two seats on that flight?"

"Of course, sir."

"I will also need a hotel in Selcuk."

"Of course, sir. I will book one for you and have the name waiting for you at the Airport Information Desk at Menemen."

"Are there many hotels in Selcuk?"

"Oh, several, sir. It is a popular tourist centre, you see, because of its nearness to Pergamum and Ephesus, and the Temple of Diana. But at this early stage of the season there will be no difficulty."

"Thank you," Hunt said, and collected Leni. "Let's go catch a plane."

The THY (Turk Hava Yollari) internal flight was in a 737. It left Yesilkoy just after three, and touched down in Menemen just before five, exactly on schedule.

"I'm so glad we flew instead of driving," Leni said. "That was one of the pleasantest flights I have ever been on. And the scenery. God, are those mountains rugged."

"And was that water blue," Hunt pointed out. "I wonder if we shall have a chance to swim in it?"

238

"Well, Ephesus was a seaport, wasn't it?"

"Two and a half thousand years ago, darling. The reason it went out of business was that the sea kept going away until it went for good."

"Mr Hunt?" asked a uniformed young woman. She hadn't had any difficulty spotting them: Hunt was clearly the only northern European male on the flight, just as Leni was the only blonde. "I have a car waiting for you, and your hotel is the Metropole. Here is a map, and I have marked the route."

"Excellent. I say, this Metropole isn't one of those ghastly places used by the tour buses, is it?"

"No, sir. You are thinking of the Hillview."

"Ah. Good. But . . . presumably we're not next door to each other, or anything like that?"

"No, sir," the girl said patiently. "The Metropole and the Hillview are at least five blocks apart."

"Thank God for that. I cannot abide tour parties."

The girl raised her eyes to heaven.

"Tell me about Smyrna," Leni suggested as they drove through the very crowded streets round the ancient harbour.

"Its principal claim to fame is as the site of a horrendous massacre in 1922. When the Turks finally defeated the Greeks, remember?"

"I'm sorry, I was minus forty-one at the time."

"Impossible to visualise. Well, as you may know, just after the First World War the Greeks thought they could overrun all of Turkey that they felt like having. The Ottoman Empire was in a state of total collapse and the idea looked good. And in fact the Greeks did conquer all of Anatolia up to the Sakarya River. Then up popped Mustafa Kemal, to reorganise the Turkish armies and beat the hell out of the invaders."

"Which is why he is the hero of his country."

"Absolutely. Well, the Greeks were actually at the end of both their line of communication and their tether. Once

239

they lost the decisive battle, they turned into a rabble and fled, with the Turks behind them. There were atrocities on both sides. The disaster left the very large Greek community in Smyrna up the creek. Their sole idea was to get out. But of course there weren't enough ships, and there was total confusion, with the result that when the Turkish army reached here, very few of the Greek civilians had left. What happened next depends on whose history book you happen to be reading. But whether the Greeks determined to defend their section of the town, or whether the Turks were just told to go in and clear them out, the fact is that a couple of days later the Greek quarter of Smyrna was a burned out shell and there was quite literally blood running down the streets."

"Sounds like fun."

"You would probably have enjoyed it," he said. "Ooops."

"What's happening?"

They were through the town now and driving south down a relatively empty highway.

"That bus up ahead. That's Fascination Tours."

Leni glanced at him: he looked quite agitated.

"What do you aim to do?"

"Get past it and drive like hell."

"It seems to be stopping at that estaminet, or whatever."

"Their last comfort stop of the day, I would say."

"Then shouldn't we stop as well? I could do with a bit of comfort."

"Have you no control over your internal organs at all?" Hunt enquired. "You went on the plane."

"I'd pretend, stupid so you could at least ascertain that our friend is on that bus."

"She's on that bus," Hunt said.

"Well, then, you could make your move."

"In front of another forty people? When I talk to Geli Littler I want it to be just us."

"And me."

"Of course," Hunt said, and put his hand on the horn as he pressed the gas pedal down.

*

The bus left the hotel at eight thirty. Geli had slept heavily and well, and was in fact feeling more relaxed than for a long time – certainly since before the news of Brauer's death. It gave her an enormous feeling of security to be a totally anonymous woman in the midst of another thirty-eight totally anonymous men and women.

Of course Eva Freilinger was probably going to be a nuisance. The Freilingers had insisted on sitting with Geli and Helene at dinner the previous night, and Eva had told them all about herself and her husband, how he was an industrial engineer in Cologne and how this was their first holiday in three years because he had been so busy.

She then told them all about their four children, looking meaningfully at Helene and then at Geli's stomach as she spoke: whatever was down there had to have been the afterthought of all time.

She had then paused, awaiting a response. But Geli had smiled sweetly and said, "We're for an early night. In my condition this driving is quite exhausting."

Helene would obviously have preferred to stay up and perhaps flirt with one of the waiters, but she had dutifully accompanied her mother to bed. However, as they were having two nights in Selcuk, with the whole of one afternoon off. Geli realised she was going to have to prepare herself for a real onslaught – she couldn't spend the entire tour in her bedroom when not on the bus.

She also, she knew, needed to do some serious thinking because Helene had raised some very pertinent points the previous evening. Ever since the news of Gustave Brauer's death she had been in a state of terror, and the terror had been compounded by the certainty that something had happened to Uncle Walther as well. But, she was beginning to realise, she had actually been in a state of terror all of her life, while always refusing to admit it. Because Mama had always been afraid, and she had transmitted her fear to her daughter.

Well, presumably Mama had some reason for fear if what had happened over the past few days was anything to judge by. But equally, presumably, the people who were attempting to find her would themselves be found, as they were being looked for by the police of several countries. They might already have been found and the immediate crisis over.

She was strongly tempted to telephone home before leaving the hotel. But equally, she didn't want to be drawn into the more lasting crisis of her identity, and her relationship with Hans, until she had worked it out for herself. That was the real reason for this total cut off.

She *was* Hitler's daughter. Ever since the age of eighteen, when Mama had told her the truth, she had lived with that fact as she might have lived with the fact that she had diabetes or TB or malaria, something which was going to be there for always, weakening her – if she let it – but private to her alone. She had never attempted to think through the problem because Mama had never done so.

Everything had been very logical, up till now. Hans would not have married her had he known. Once she had elected to keep it from him, the secret was there for ever. But it was there no longer. Helene had been right about that.

Thus she had to decide where she went from here.

She had firstly to accept that her marriage was over. Her twenty-five years of deceit had ended in disaster, but also in the knowledge that the husband she had always respected and admired had feet of clay. Even if he now magnanimously decided to forgive her for never trusting him in the past, she would have to believe it was only that he could get his hands on her money.

Then there was the money itself. Again, Helene had put her finger on a point she had always refused to consider. Hitler himself had been a wealthy man because *Mein Kampf*, as required reading in every German home, had

242

earned him a fortune. But there was none of that money involved in the Swiss fund. To believe that would be to begin deluding herself all over again. That money had been placed there by Himmler for the use of himself and his agents as became necessary. Therefore it was at the very least money which had been stolen or confiscated from SS victims, and at the very worst money which had been extracted by blood.

Yet if she left Hans, it would be all she had to live on.

Therefore, if she did not come out into the open and admit who she was, she would virtually be a thief and a murderess herself.

But if she did . . . she would have to be absolutely sure in her mind what attitude she was going to adopt, how she was going to react to the millions of people who would instinctively revile her – and perhaps even more important, to the handful who would instinctively wish to worship her because of her name!

She didn't know if she could handle that.

On leaving the hotel, the bus drove slowly down the coast to the town of Bergama, where they stopped for lunch after looking at some ruins. Fortunately the Freilingers were a good dozen seats away from Geli and Helene, and as Semih insisted everyone stick rigidly to his advancing principle, there was no way they could get any closer, while the people actually seated close by did not seem particularly interested in the pregnant woman and her companion.

The drive, which was uninterrupted save for the occasional comfort stop, gave Geli more time to think, and she knew she had to concentrate on the immediate problem rather than the distant one. She hadn't made up her mind whether to invent an entirely fictitious background, which would have to be taught to Helene and remembered by them both, or just to tell the Freilingers to mind their own business, when they made their luncheon stop.

Or just avoid them. This she managed to do by rushing

off the bus and finding Helene and herself seats at a table for four, where there was already a pair of elderly ladies.

Close to Bergama are the ruins of the ancient Greek city state of Pergamum, and this they explored after lunch, Geli even climbing down into the huge amphitheatre despite the suggestion of Semih that it might be too much for her. But Eva Freilinger had already announced that she was not risking life and limb, and it was a splendid opportunity to get as far away from her as possible.

They regained the bus tired but happy, and duly advanced another two seats.

"According to my calculations," Helene said, "we shall have the front row in four days' time."

"That'll be perfect," Geli remarked. "By then we'll really be in Cappadocia, where the scenery is something."

From Bergama they drove down to the seaport of Izmir, and Semih told them all about the fighting there during what he called the Turkish War of Independence. The stories of Greek massacres, he explained, were greatly exaggerated. The driver fought his way through the rush-hour traffic and they emerged on to the open road for the last forty kilometres to Selcuk.

"Would anyone like a final comfort stop?" Semith asked.

"Oh. Yes," all the women chorused. "Then we can have some more of that delicious apple tea."

The bus was just about to pull off the road into the yard of a wayside bar when there was the blaring of a horn and a car rushed by.

"Tourists!" Semih commented in disgust. "Crazy fools."

They reached Selcuk and the hotel just on six. It was a pleasant hotel, not quite as comfortable as their previous one but it had a swimming pool into which Helene promptly plunged. It was obviously impractical for Geli to join her: the cushion would hardly fit into her swim suit,

244

quite apart from the impossibility of drying it afterwards, but in any event she was glad of the opportunity to be alone. She had decided after all to telephone home.

It took her some time to get through, but then she listened to the telephone buzzing. It was just before seven, on a Monday evening. Everyone would be home by now. But the telephone just buzzed and buzzed.

Where was Shiera? She seldom left before seven, and she would certainly never leave the house until at least one member of the family had come home.

Geli waited until the phone had rung for several minutes before she replaced the receiver and stared at the wall, shoulders hunched. Of course the most obvious thing to have happened was that Hans and the boys had gone out together. It was just the sort of thing that Hans would do.

But he had known she meant to call him. Although she hadn't actually stated a date and time.

What it meant was that he was bidding for the boys' support in the coming matrimonial quarrel.

But it could also mean so much more than that . . . and there was nothing she could do about it.

Anyway, it was useless to panic. She'd call again tomorrow morning, before they set out. Certainly Shiera would be there then.

But how she wished she had called this morning.

She showered and dressed. By then Helene had also come in from her frolic.

"Things are looking up," she announced as she showered in turn.

"Not a Turkish waiter?"

"Oh, Mummy, what a suggestion. No. he's a German."

"A what?"

"Well, for Heaven's sake, everyone on the coach is German. Save for Semih and the driver."

Geli frowned. Save for Semih and the driver there was no man on the coach under fifty. And save for herself and Helene, no woman, either.

245

"He's staying in the hotel," Helene explained. "He's on a private tour with his aunt."

"All right, my darling, tell me about him."

"Well, he's in his middle twenties, I suppose, good-looking . . . He's very quiet and gentle, but he has a tremendous physique . . ."

"Which you have managed to scrutinise already."

"Well, he was bathing in the pool with me." Helene waggled her eyebrows. "He likes my physique too."

"I see. Does this paragon have a name?"

"Josef."

"Josef. And do I get to meet him?"

"Of course, Mummy. Now. He and his aunt are waiting for us in the bar." Helene tucked her arm through her mother's. "I just know you're going to adore him. He's so charming, so elegant, so . . . well, rich as well, I suppose."

"How do you know that?"

"Well . . . he wears a massive gold chain round his neck, and a massive gold Rolex watch . . . and he even has a massive gold cigarette lighter."

CHAPTER EIGHT

Geli's nostrils twitched as she entered the bar: Adoration!

She gazed at the tall, elegant, middle-aged woman who was rising to greet her. "Frau Petrov! This is a great pleasure."

"But . . . you were on the ferry from Gallipoli," Geli said. "I saw you."

And I must have smelt you, she thought, at the restaurant.

"Why, yes, so I was. And you . . . of course, the woman on the upper deck. I remember now. And this is your so charming daughter. Josef has spoken of you."

The heavily built young man stood beside his aunt, all smiles as he kissed Geli's hand and then ordered drinks.

"I have never been on a tour," Ilse Bruening said. "But I am wondering if it is not better than attempting to see things on your own. Josef and I, we have a map and we have the guide books, and yet I am sure we are missing a great deal. May I ask where you are going tomorrow, Frau Petrov?"

"According to our schedule, we are staying here tomorrow, but we are spending the morning at Ephesus. Apparently it's just along the road."

"Ah, Ephesus," Ilse Bruening said. "I believe it is the most perfectly preserved of the old Greek cities. I should hate not to see it. I mean properly. Do you suppose that if I asked your guide he would let us join your party? Just for tomorrow, of course."

"Why, I sure he would," Geli said. "I suppose . . . there might be a charge."

"Oh, of course," Ilse Bruening said. "I should not dream of coming otherwise."

They approached Semih right away, and Semih was perfectly agreeable: there were spare seats on the bus. Then they ate together, quite shutting out the Freilingers, and after the meal talked over their brandies. Ilse Bruening was both informed and sophisticated, vivacious and, best of all, uncurious. She spoke of her own travels – apparently she was a wealthy widow and her nephew Josef was her only living relative – and even of her girlhood, which had been spent in Germany during the war, and immediately afterwards, when she had all but starved. Unlike Eva Freilinger, she never asked a single question in return, not even when Geli, warming to her as she had never before warmed to any woman, broke the rule of a lifetime and said, "My mother had a personal maid named Ilse towards the end of the war. I often wondered what became of her."

Ilse Bruening merely commented, "It was a bad time."

Both the older women wished to retire early: Helene naturally wished to stay up with Josef, but Geli had no objection to that – she had never liked people so immediately. Actually, she felt so relaxed she telephoned Telibaba again, and again no one answered the phone. But, she reflected, if they had gone out together they would hardly be home yet. She sat up with a book for over an hour, at the end of which Helene came in looking flushed and happy.

"Well?" Geli enquired.

"Well, what?"

"Do you still like Josef?" Geli asked carefully. Over the past year she had not delved too closely into Helene's sexual habits, once the crisis of whether she would or would not go on the pill had been resolved – in Helene's favour. Her only prayer was that the girl would not wind up with a Turk.

"Oh, yes, Mummy. He is an absolute charmer."

"You did remember not to tell him anything about us, I hope."

"He never asked." Helene switched out the light and was apparently asleep in seconds.

Well, Geli reflected as she switched off her own light, she could do a lot worse.

We could do a lot worse.

Next morning Geli awoke early and telephoned: if she got them out of bed, so much the worse for them. And listened to the phone ringing.

She sat up, suddenly feeling quite cold.

But what could have happened, for all three of them to leave home so suddenly?

She had left home just as suddenly. Were they fleeing? Or was it some ghastly plan concocted by Hans? And what had happened to Shiera?

And what was she going to do about it?

The first thing was to fight back the rising tide of panic which was threatening to overwhelm her yet again. There had to be a reasonable and logical explanation for whatever had happened. Her only problem was how to find out.

She did not have Shiera's address with her, but in any event she knew that Shiera did not have a telephone. She did have Freya's address and telephone number in her address book, however, and this she now called.

This telephone also rang for several minutes before being answered.

"Hello?" muttered a sleepy woman's voice.

"Freya? This is Geli."

"Geli? Geli? My God, do you know the time?"

"It is seven o'clock," Geli said severely.

"Seven . . . it is the middle of the night."

"Look out of your window," Geli recommended.

"Geli . . . what is the matter? I telephoned you yesterday and was told you had gone away."

"You telephoned . . . when was this, Freya?"

"Yesterday morning. About nine o'clock."

"And who did you speak with?"

"That maid of yours, Shiera. She said you had gone away."

"Well, I had. I have had to go away on business."

"Then where are you calling from?"

"Did Shiera say anything else?"

"No, just that you had gone away. Where are you, Geli?"

"That's not important," Geli told her. "I am glad you telephoned, Freya."

"I was going to ask you to play bridge. But now you have gone away . . . where are you calling from?"

"A hotel bedroom. Freya, I would like you to do something for me."

"Well . . . what is it?"

Freya was clearly put out at her friend having left Istanbul without confiding in her, to which could be added Geli's refusal to confide in her now.

"I promised to call Hans this morning, but the confounded telephone seems to be out of order. Will you get hold of him and ask him to see that it is put right, and tell him that I will call him . . ." She checked the brochure. They were spending the entire morning at Ephesus, but were returning to this hotel for lunch, after which the afternoon was free. "At five o'clock this afternoon."

"At the office?"

"No, no. I wish to call him at home. Tell him to go home early and I will call him there at five o'clock."

"Will he do that?" Freya was also married to a German.

"Yes," Geli said. "I am most grateful for your help, Freya."

"Yes, but Geli . . ."

"I must go now," Geli said. "I have somewhere to go." She hung up and looked at Helene, who was looking at her. "Well," she said, "we do have somewhere to go. After we have had breakfast." She went into the bathroom.

* * *

250

She had to be patient and wait. Freya would stir things up, at the least. She would discover exactly what was going on that afternoon.

Ephesus was a magnificent ruin. It had once been a thriving seaport and the docks remained . . . now several kilometres from the sea. But there were also many public buildings in an excellent state of repair, as well as a recently excavated private house which was almost in the class of Pompeii. The ruins spread over a large area, and it was a long and exhausting morning, during which the tour party split up into several groups as one lot wanted to linger longer than another.

Geli attached herself to the Bruenings, a manoeuvre which naturally met with Helene's entire approval. Eva Freilinger was visibly put out, but if she was getting the message that Geli wished no more têtes-à-tête with her, Geli was well pleased.

She began to flag as the day became hotter, however, and decided against climbing one very steep flight of steps cut into the hillside to gain some vantage point or other.

"I will stay with you," Ilse decided. "Let the young ones explore on their own."

Josef and Helene went off happily together, and Ilse and Geli found a flat stone on which to sit, their sun hats pulled well down.

"It is very brave of you to bring your daughter on a trip like this, when you are pregnant," Ilse remarked.

"Well . . . it is her last chance before she returns to Germany," Geli explained. She was becoming a perfectly natural liar. But of course she had made a mistake.

"Ah. She is going home. I am sorry. I thought Germany *was* your home."

"Well . . ." Geli's brain raced. But this woman was so friendly and so, she was sure, trustworthy. "Actually my husband works in Istanbul."

"How delightful," Ilse said. "Do you mean you live in the city?"

"Well, no. We live at Telibaba. It's a village at the north end of the Bosporus."

"The best of all possible worlds: out in the country but with the city at your fingertips. Have you lived in Turkey long?"

"All of my life." Geli gulped. "Well, not really. I was born in Germany, of course, but my mother moved to Turkey when I was very small."

"And you decided to remain there and married a . . . forgive me but Petrov is really a Baltic name, is it not?"

"Ah . . . yes," Geli said. "My husband is in business in Istanbul."

"And now your daughter wishes to return to the fatherland. Good for her. But surely she will stay with you until after the birth?"

"The birth? Oh . . ." Geli flushed. "Well . . . yes, I am sure she will."

How she wanted to trust this woman, so much older and obviously experienced, and kind. Why, she could be her own mother, she thought, only far more successful.

"Here they are, returning now," Ilse Bruening said brightly.

The coach got back to the hotel just before one, and they all trooped into lunch. As usual, the Bruenings and Geli and Helene sat together and chatted contentedly, sharing a bottle of wine.

"What are you going to do this afternoon?" Ilse asked.

"I think rest up," Geli decided. "I gather we have a long ride tomorrow, all the way to Pammukale."

"I think that is very wise," Ilse agreed. "I will do the same."

"Josef and I thought we might take a walk around Selcuk," Helene said.

"Of course. Amuse yourselves. We will see you again when the heat has left the sun." Ilse Bruening got up, went to the desk. "You wouldn't have a newspaper, would you?"

"Of course. The newspapers came in this morning, while you were at the site." The clerk gave her one.

"Bother," Ilse said, having scanned the front page. "This is in Turkish."

The clerk raised his eyebrows. "You are in Turkey, Frau Bruening."

"Do you not have one in German?"

"I'm afraid not."

Ilse turned round. Geli had got up to join her. "Do you read Turkish?"

"Of course."

"Would you like to read this paper for me?"

"If you would like me to. Is there something particualr you were looking for?"

"It is just that a firm in which I am interested is in the middle of a takeover bid," Ilse Bruening explained. "I would very much like to know what is happening about it."

"Do you think it will be in a Turkish paper?" Geli asked doubtfully.

"It could be. There is a financial page, and it is quite a big merger. I should be so grateful if you would look for me."

"Well, I shall, of course. Let us find somewhere quiet to sit down."

"But you wish to rest," Ilse protested. "You need to rest, my dear Geli. Listen, why do you not go to your room and lie down, and have a nice leisurely read of the paper? If you find anything which might interest me you can tell me this afternoon. The firm I am interested in is called Uta Bruening. Shall we meet at . . . four o'clock for a cup of tea? Josef and Helene may well be back by then."

She was such a nice person, Geli thought as, in the privacy of her bedroom, she thankfully stripped off the cushion and lay down: she had become quite used to the wig, so she left it on. Obviously this merger meant a good deal to her – Geli had observed that Ilse was really far more agitated than she pretended when she had glanced at the paper and discovered she would not be able to read it, and clearly, from its name, the firm was connected with her husband's family – but she would do nothing to inconvenience anyone else.

It would be a pleasure to help her, Geli thought. But actually it was a pleasure to read the paper. She had been so determined to cut herself off entirely from the outside world that she had not picked one up since leaving her home on Saturday night. Of course, that was only three days ago, but still . . . she looked at the financial page first, but there was no reference to the Uta Bruening company.

She returned to page one, idly read the various international news stories of the day . . . and then sat bolt upright as she came across an item towards the bottom of the page, in the Stop Press column.

"GERMAN BUSINESSMAN MURDERED.

"THE BODY OF HERR HANS LITTLER. MANAGING DIRECTOR OF SCHILLER AND COMPANY AND WELL-KNOWN IN ISTANBUL BUSINESS AND SOCIAL CIRCLES, WAS THIS MORNING FOUND BY POLICE IN THE LOCKED BOOT OF A CAR PARKED IN GALATA SUBURB. THE POLICE ARE TREATING HERR LITTLER'S DEATH AS MURDER."

That was all: the item must have been released late last night or very early this morning.

Hans, dead! Murdered! It could only be by the people who were hunting her.

For a moment her brain went blank, then she discovered she was trembling, shaking from head to foot, even lying in bed. She felt she could hardly breathe, got up and walked to and fro rapidly for several minutes, willing her heart to settle down.

Her husband! Dead! So perhaps during the past few days she had begun to have reservations about him, but to

think of him being killed and stuffed into the boot of a car
. . . what kind of people would do something like that?

The people who were after her. She broke out in a fresh
bout of shuddering, sat on the bed, her fists so tightly
clenched her nails were eating into her palms.

Hans, dead . . . Then what about the boys? No one was
answering her telephone. Were they dead too?

She felt physically sick.

Freya . . . but of course Freya's paper would not have
arrived when they spoke that morning . . . and she had
given Freya no means of contacting her. Desperately she
scrabbled at the phone and dialled, waited through the
normal succession of clicks and bumps.

"Freya!" she shouted. "Is that you?"

"Geli!" Freya cried. "Listen. Do you know what has
happened?"

"I just read it. But . . ."

"It was dreadful, I believe," Freya sobbed. "Oh, dreadful. They are saying he was tortured. Poor Hans. But
poor Geli!"

"Where are the boys?" Geli asked, fighting to keep her
voice under control. "Are they all right?"

"I don't know. I have not been able to find out. The
house is locked up. I believe the boys are in police custody,
but they will not admit this."

"Police custody?" Geli shouted. "Why are they in police
custody? Surely the police do not think they murdered
their father?"

"I do not believe so," Freya said. "I think they are in
protective custody. There is a rumour that Hans' death is
connected with some other murder, in Switzerland."

"Oh, my God!" Geli muttered. "Oh, my God!"

"Geli, where are you? The police wish to know. They
are most anxious about you. Geli, you must tell us where
you are."

Geli stared at the phone. I am only alive, she thought,
because I have told no one where I was going.

"Geli?"

"I cannot tell you where I am," Geli said.

"But the police want to know!"

"Then they will have to find out."

"But Hans is dead," Freya waited. "Aren't you coming back for his funeral? Your husband is dead, Geli!"

Geli replaced the receiver, a sudden thought having crossed her mind that the police might have put a tap on Freya's phone and be tracing the call.

But what was she to do? Freya was right. Her husband was dead. Even if they had suddenly become virtual strangers, Hans had still been her husband for twenty-six years. She could not just turn her back upon his dead body.

Nor could she abandon her sons.

But to go back would be to risk her own life. And that of Helene.

If only there was someone to whom she could turn for advice . . . and suddenly she realised there was. Right here in the hotel. It would mean telling Ilse the truth, of course . . . but if there was anyone in the world she felt she could trust, Ilse Bruening was that person.

She scrambled out of bed, pulled on her dressing gown and ran out of the room and into the hall. At half past two in the afternoon there was not even anyone at the hotel desk. She went along to the door of Ilse's room and knocked.

"Yes? Who is it?"

"It is Geli. May I come in?"

"Of course, Geli." A moment later the door was unlocked. Ilse also wore a dressing-gown, but yet managed to appear as elegant and freshly groomed as ever. The scent of Adoration hung on the air.

"I didn't wake you?" Geli asked anxiously.

"No, no. I was awake. Did you find something about my company?"

"No. May I come in?"

"Of course." Ilse stood to one side to allow Geli to enter the room, then carefully closed and locked the door. "What is the matter? You look as if you have seen a ghost.

256

And . . ." She stared at Geli's suddenly flat waist. "My God! You have hurt yourself."

Geli sat on the bed. "No. I have not hurt myself. There never was a baby."

Ilse sat beside her. "My dear, I am so happy for you. Your time for babies was long ago. But something is the matter. You must tell me what it is."

Geli pulled off her wig.

Ilse blinked at her. "Do you know, you look quite a different person? I'm afraid I do not understand."

"Ilse . . ." Geli held her hands. "I am in the most terrible trouble."

"Tell me, my darling," Ilse invited.

"How I want to. But . . . you will be shocked."

Ilse smiled. "I stopped being shocked many years ago. I want you to tell me everything, Geli. Then I will be able to help you. Begin at the very beginning."

When she was finished Ilse took her in her arms and stroked her hair, as if she were a baby.

"You poor darling," she said. "What a life you have had. How I admire your courage. But now . . ."

Geli raised her head. "What am I to do?"

Ilse kissed her nose. "There is only one way to deal with problems like this, or with people who are trying to kill you." She spoke in perfectly matter-of-fact tones. "You must face up to them, and face them down."

"Oh, Ilse. But they will kill me, as they killed Brauer and Uncle Walther . . . and Hans."

"No, they will not," Ilse said firmly.

"How do you know that?"

"Because Josef and I will be standing beside you. And the police will also protect you, of course."

"But Ilse . . . I cannot possibly ask you to do that. I don't think you understand. These people are killers. Cold-blooded killers."

Ilse patted her hand. "I am not afraid of them. Now listen, we must hurry: we must get back to Istanbul

257

tonight. You return to your room and dress, and pack. For Helene as well. I will do the same and I will see to Josef's things also. Then we will tell Semih that we can no longer continue the tour because of a bereavement, and must leave immediately to catch a plane back to Istanbul from that airport north of Izmir. He will understand."

"But what about Josef and Helene?"

"We will find them. This is not a very large town."

"You are being so kind. So reassuring. If you knew how I have wanted to be reassured, for so long." Geli went to the door, and hesitated. "But what about . . . my identity?"

"Let us worry about that after these people have been arrested," Ilse suggested. "Do you still wish it kept a secret?"

"Do you think that is possible?"

"We will talk about it when we have left Selcuk. Now we must hurry."

*

"So what's the plan?" Leni asked over breakfast. "Do we go along to that other place and make ourselves known?"

"Not on your nellie."

"I thought we could perhaps ask if we could join in the tour to Ephesus. Just pretend to be tourists."

"We don't want to get too close to her," Hunt repeated.

"I don't understand you at all," Leni complained. "You nearly bust a gut to catch up with this female, and now you are within touching distance, you're backing off."

"I've explained all that. We are just going to sit tight until this afternoon."

"Well, I at least intend to go along to the Hillview and see if she's on board," Leni declared.

"After the coach has left."

They waited until ten o'clock and then strolled down to the Hillview, strangely empty and quiet with all the guests having departed for the day.

"Can you tell me if there is a mother and daughter with the party?" Hunt asked at the desk, in German. As this hotel catered for German coach parties, he didn't doubt the girl spoke the language. "The mother would be about forty-five, the daughter about seventeen."

"Ah, you mean the pregnant lady, Frau Petrov."

"The pre . . . yes, of course, that's her, Mrs Petrov."

"Is there a message for her?"

"Ah, no. I think she is the wife of an acquaintance of mine. I'll drop back later, after she has returned."

"Who shall I say called, sir?"

Hunt slid a ten thousand lira note across the counter. "I would prefer if you didn't mention me at all," he said. "I wish to surprise her."

They returned to the Metropole and had a swim. They were sun-bathing when a tall, thin-faced man emerged from the bar, looked at Hunt and went back inside again. Leni was lying on her face with her bikini top loosed, and did not even notice.

Hunt got up.

"Where are you off to?" she asked lazily.

"The loo."

"Again? You have got the trots."

Hunt went inside. The man was leaning against the bar. Hunt jerked his head and went down the corridor to the bedrooms, pausing by the window which overlooked the swimming pool. He could see Leni.

The man came up to him. "Hunt? Adolf." He spoke German.

"You're kidding."

"It is a good German name," Adolf protested.

"Indeed it is. You have something for me?"

Adolf took an automatic pistol from his pocket. "It is loaded. And here is a spare clip. And the silencer."

"Thank you." Hunt placed the gun, silencer and magazine in his pocket. "Is number two also in position?"

"I should think so." Adolf looked through the window. "Is that the woman you wish taken out?"

259

"Only if it becomes necessary," Hunt said.

Adolf looked at him.

"I do not know what her business is," Hunt explained. "It may be that she will not interfere."

"You have become fond of this woman," Adolf remarked.

"Wouldn't you, if you'd spent several days shacked up with her?"

Adolf smiled. "No. But I will enjoy taking her out."

"Now, you listen to me," Hunt said. "You are under my orders and you will do what I tell you."

"I have been told that she is dangerous. If I wait for orders I might wind up dead."

"If you don't wait for orders," Hunt told him. "I am personally going to cut off your balls and push them down your throat. You got me?"

Adolf looked Hunt up and down, then shrugged. "So what are your orders?"

"Frau Littler is at present on a tour of Ephesus. She will return about one, and the entire group will have lunch in the hotel. The afternoon after that is free. We will give them time to have their lunch and digest. Then I will go to the hotel, say about three o'clock this afternoon. Frau Littler is masquerading as a pregnant woman, therefore I expect that she will spend the afternoon resting. I will ask to speak with her, and hopefully there will be no problem after that."

"The woman?"

Hunt watched Leni roll over and adjust her bra. In only a few moments she'd be looking for him. "She will almost certainly wish to accompany me. When I meet up with Frau Littler, she will equally almost certainly show her hand. I therefore wish you to follow us when we go to the hotel and should I need you, I wish you to come in."

"And take out the woman?"

Hunt sighed. "If I need you, if I call for you or you hear a shot, yes. Take her out. Now beat it."

Adolf walked away. Hunt allowed him a few seconds

260

and then, as Leni was getting up, he sauntered back down the corridor and through the bar.

"You okay?" she asked.

"Just about."

"Well, you don't look too good to me. I suggest we have an aperitif and then eat."

"Why not?"

He studied her as they ate. Well, studying Leni was a great pleasure in any event. But just what was she at? He didn't really want anything as delightfully shaped as she was to be blown away. Quite apart from the problems that would thereby be caused with the Turkish police.

Not that he intended to let the problems, or Leni for that matter stand in the way of the completion of his mission. From his point of view, and that of a good many other people, what he had to do this afternoon might be one of the more important moments of history.

But it would still be far simpler if Leni were on his side.

"You shouldn't eat so much," Leni said, resuming her schoolmistress tone.

"Talk about pots and kettles," Hunt remarked as she commenced work or her third kebab.

"I meant, with an upset stomach. When you have an upset stomach you're supposed to starve yourself and take medication. I have some kaolin and morphine. Would you like a dose?"

"I come from a long line of devoted sufferers," Hunt said. "Nor can I afford to be drowsy. We have a busy afternoon."

"What's the form?" Leni asked.

"We stroll along to the Hillview and you wait outside while I have a word with Frau Littler."

"Oh, no," Leni said. "Oh, no, no, no, no, no."

"Darling, I want to sign her up. All you want to do is stop her returning to Germany, so you say."

"I need to be present when you speak with her," Leni said.

261

"Why?"

"Those are my orders."

They gazed at each other. She was such a lovely girl. And Adolf was just itching to get his hands on her.

It was beginning to look as if Adolf would have to be allowed to achieve his ambition.

"All right," Hunt said. "Providing you promise to keep absolutely quiet."

"I cannot promise to do that, Hunt. But I will promise not to interfere with your negotiations unless what you propose, or she proposes, happens to clash with my instructions."

Once again they looked at each other. Then Hunt ordered coffee. He felt that one of them was going to need it.

Hunt dawdled over the meal until he was quite sure the entire coach party would have been fed and dispersed for the afternoon. He was not too concerned as to whether or not Geli Littler had gone to bed or gone out on the town: Selcuk wasn't all that large, and he was sure he would find her quickly enough. The important thing was that Corinne had been got rid of and that Adolf was here.

He held Leni's hand as they strolled along the street. A quick glance behind him assured him that Adolf was some fifty yards behind them, pretending to look in shop windows. They reached the street in which the hotel was situated, saw the tour bus parked outside the main entrance, stepped back as a black Mercedes drove out of the gateway and turned on to the street they had just left. The car had tinted windows and he couldn't see who was inside.

They walked past the swimming pool where several guests were disporting themselves, and through the bar to the hotel reception. Adolf had also entered the hotel grounds, as nonchalantly as he did everything else, and was pausing to admire the bikinis in the pool.

262

"Hello," Hunt said to the girl on the desk. "Remember me? I was here this morning."

"Oh, yes," the girl said. "You're the gentleman who was enquiring about the pregnant woman and her daughter."

"That's right," Hunt said. "Are they in?"

"No, sir. Frau Petrov just left."

"Bother," Hunt said. "You mean they have gone for a stroll in the town?"

"No, sir. Frau Petrov has left Selcuk for the airport at Izmir. She has had to cancel their tour. A family bereavement." She smiled encouragingly. "You have only just missed her. She drove out of the yard not ten minutes ago."

"Oh, sh . . . not a black Mercedes?"

"That is correct, sir. Frau Bruening very kindly offered to drive her to the airport."

"Frau Bruening," Hunt said slowly. "Would this lady be about sixty-five, good-looking, and wearing Adoration perfume?"

"Why, sir, is she a friend of yours as well?"

"And she has a friend, about thirty and bearded?"

"No, sir. Herr Bruening does not wear a beard."

"Oh, shit!" This time he did say it, in English.

"Hunt, you have boobed," Leni said.

Hunt kept his temper with an effort. "This Frau Bruening," he asked the girl. "Is she one of the tour party?"

"Oh, no, sir. She is travelling separately, with her nephew. She arrived yesterday."

"Twenty-four hours," Hunt said thoughtfully. Adoration was also suffering from over-confidence. "And she and Frau Petrov were friends?"

"Well, they became friends," the girl said. "I do not think they had met before."

"And you say they left together? A family bereavement? How did they learn of it?"

"I do not know, sir. Someone must have telephoned. Frau Petrov was very upset."

"I can imagine."

"What are we going to do?" Leni asked.

"They're only ten minutes ahead of us," Hunt said. "Come on. We can catch them up."

He ran out of the hotel, Leni at his heels. Adolf stopped admiring bikinis long enough to stare after them in consternation. But there was no time to rebrief Adolf or to continue hiding him from Leni. Adolf had the back-up firepower he was going to need.

"Come on," he snapped. "Our girl has been nobbled."

Adolf ran behind them.

"Hunt," Leni panted.

"Later." Hunt pounded up the street, reached the Metropole, dashed into the carpark. As he unlocked the car he looked back, saw Adolf holding Leni's elbow to hurry her along.

He almost wanted to laugh.

"Hunt," Leni gasped as she got up to him.

"Later. You sit in the back, Adolf."

Adolf climbed in, and Hunt thrust Leni into the front passenger seat, then got in himself and started the engine.

"Hunt," Leni said. "Who is this man?"

"My second cousin, twice removed."

"Oh, shit," Leni commented. "And he has a gun."

Adolf had taken a rather large automatic pistol from a shoulder holster and was checking the magazine.

"If he didn't," Hunt told her. "I'd have left him behind."

*

Ilse Bruening turned the wheel sharply and the Mercedes slid down a side street. Then she made another sharp turn to go right again.

"What is the matter?" Geli asked, having been thrown left and then right.

"Those people, the big man and the blonde girl. Do you not know them?"

"I never saw them before in my life," Geli confessed.

"Ah. Well, I can tell you that they both belong to

264

an international group dedicated to destroying the last vestiges of Nazidom."

"Oh, my God!" Geli clasped her neck.

"They work outside the law, and are quite ruthless. The merest hint that someone was even connected with the Nazis is sufficient for them to go into action. Murder is their trademark."

"But . . . do you think they killed Hans?"

"And Schmidt, and Brauer? I am certain of it. They, or other members of their group."

"And now they are here. After me."

"And Helene," Ilse reminded her. "Which is all the more reason for leaving in a hurry."

"But . . . should we not merely go to the police?"

"That would be too risky," Ilse told her. "We do not know how many other members of the group are in Selcuk. No, no, we must make ourselves very scarce. We will change our minds about the airport at Menemen, just in case the girl at the hotel tells them where we are going."

"But what about Helene and Josef?"

"They are just here." Ilse pulled the car to a halt outside a café where Josef and Helene were sitting. She almost might have known they would be there, Geli thought. But she was too relieved to see Helene to worry about that.

"What on earth's happening?" the girl asked as Josef virtually pushed her into the car – again, Geli thought, as if he had been expecting his aunt.

"You had better tell her," Ilse said.

Geli drew a deep breath as the Mercedes whipped round corners and sought a road out of town. "Your father is dead."

Helene stared at her, her mouth slowly making an O.

"He was murdered," Geli explained. "By an anti-Nazi group."

"Who are now here in Selcuk," Ilse added.

"That is why we are trying to get away," Geli said.

"But . . . Daddy . . ."

"I know." Geli was practically hanging over the back

265

seat to hug her daughter. "We are going back there now."

"But . . . oh, God!" Helene burst into tears and buried her face in her hands. Josef out a protective arm round her shoulders.

"There is a map in the glove compartment," Ilse said. "Where is the nearest airport? Other than Menemen?"

Geli opened the compartment, took out the map. "Well, there is one at Dalaman. But that is well south. Right down on the coast."

"I had better look at the map." Ilse pulled in to the side of the road; they were now entirely clear of houses. She peered at the map. "Hm," she said. "That will do as well as any. But if you do not mind, Geli, we will not drive directly to it. One cannot be too careful. So . . . we will turn off at Soke, and go east along the valley of the Menderes, and round this mountain Besmarpak Dag, down to Yatagan and then Mugla, before coming back to the coast. Does that not seem a lonely enough stretch of country, Josef?"

Josef was leaning forward to peer over his aunt's shoulder. "That seems ideal."

"I don't know how to thank you for what you are doing," Geli said.

"Then do not try. We only wish to help you." Ilse gunned the engine and Jozef put his arm back round Helene's still shaking shoulders.

*

Hunt threaded his way in and out of the traffic as they entered Izmir, driving as fast as he could. Leni sat half-turned towards the back, looking at both men at the same time. Adolf had put away his gun but she was definitely agitated.

"I think you owe it to me to tell me what is going on, Hunt," she said.

"I wish I knew, darling. I can only suppose that, after all, poor old Hans knew something and coughed it up before he copped it, so that Adoration and her boyfriend

266

managed to get down here and persuade Mrs Littler to trust them enough to go off to the airport with them."

"I meant, I want to know how it is you have second cousins popping out of the woodwork wherever we happen to be," Leni said.

"Ah, well, you see, I belong to an international newspaper . . ."

"You mean *he* . . ." She looked at Adolf. "Works for the *Globe*?"

"Of course. He is one of my back-ups."

"I thought Corinne Grundy was your back-up?"

"She is. One of them."

"She thought she was the only one."

"We simply cannot let Corinne know everything that's going on. She drinks."

Leni considered that inarguable point while Hunt got through Izmir and put his foot down on the open road.

"But," she said at last, "she didn't recognise your friend Carl in Zurich."

"Well, of course not. She doesn't know everyone on the staff."

"But . . ." Leni began.

"This woman asks too many questions," Adolf remarked in German. "Would you not like me to . . ."

"Shut up," Hunt explained.

"Just what did he mean by that?" Leni enquired.

"Will you both shut up? I need to think."

They were on the open road now and it was quite a long, straight stretch. He had driven as fast as was humanly possible from Selcuk. But there was no black Mercedes in front of him. Of course, it was conceivable that he might have overtaken Adoration in Izmir, had she followed a different route through the town. But there was no black Mercedes behind them, either. He was beginning to get a very uneasy sensation.

He snapped his fingers.

"Forgotten your toothbrush?" Leni asked.

"That black Mercedes. We didn't see who was in it

267

because of the tinted glass. But whoever was in it, Adoration and her buddy, saw us and recognised us. Well, I mean, the boyfriend would hardly have forgotten you, now would he?"

"I would like to lay my hands on that character," Leni said. "In a fair fight."

"A match I look forward to refereeing. But you're straying from the point, as usual. Adoration was faced with a problem because she had already told the hotel clerk she was taking Geli and her daughter to Menemen Airport . . . and she had to assume the girl would tell us that."

"Ergo, she changed her mind and we are driving in entirely the wrong direction," Leni said. "Do you have a map?"

"There is one in the glove compartment."

Leni opened it out and peered at it. Adolf leaned forward from the back seat to look as well.

"Assuming she wouldn't have taken this road, then, the nearest airport south of Selcuk is at a place called Dalaman. That's a hundred and eighty kilometres away, right down on the south coast. Let's say a two-hour drive. Leaving the hotel at three, she'd be there at five. And the time is . . ." She looked at her watch. "Three thirty."

"That is supposing she means to go to an airport at all. If her business is to murder Mrs Littler, all she needs is to get her somewhere quiet." He glanced left and right. "There's a lot of them about in this country."

"But until she got to such a place, she would have to pretend to be going to an airport," Leni argued. "Or Frau Littler would get suspicious."

"That's a point. And it's all we have to go on. Shit!"

The Cumaovasi airport buildings were in sight. Hunt pulled off the road into the parking lot. "You speak Turkish, don't you, Adolf?"

"Of course."

"Well, then, nip inside and charter us a light aircraft

268

which will get us to Dalaman inside an hour. We'll just have to pray we're doing the right thing."

Adolf nodded and ran for the buildings.

Leni got out more slowly. "He seems enthusiastic."

"He is, about everything. Always have an Adolf in your hip pocket, I say."

"I'm inclined to agree with you." Together they hurried towards the building.

"Hunt . . . can we get to Mrs Littler in time?"

"I hope so," Hunt said. "If we're going the right way."

CHAPTER NINE

While the light aircraft was being fuelled and made ready, Hunt studied his map and made a telephone call. He was in the position of a general calling in all his troops to concentrate on an enemy whose whereabouts he did not know. Nor could he have any faith in the loyalty of the troops he was calling in, save for Adolf. But it was a risk he had to take, just as he had to take the risk of making certain assumptions based on very inadequate information.

But the more he considered the situation, as the chartered aircraft climbed into the clear blue afternoon sky and turned south, the less he liked it.

He had been utterly hoodwinked . . . because he had believed the two Littler boys. He still did not suppose they had been lying – they had been far too distraught – but it was possible they simply had been unaware of how much of their mother's plans had been known to their father.

Thus he had willingly given Adoration virtually twenty-four hours to play with, simply because he had supposed she was stumped and because he had considered it necessary to wait for his back-up to have time to arrive. Now she had neatly kidnapped Geli Littler and her daughter without kidnapping them at all – she had merely frightened them into going along with her. While he had been waiting to make sure of getting Geli by herself.

He had needed his back-up to deal with Leni!

He glanced at her, shoulders hunched as she peered down at the scenery. Adolf was sitting in the front beside the Turkish pilot.

The aircraft itself was not entirely reassuring. It was old

and it did not appear to have been serviced recently. It certainly had not been cleaned, inside or out, for some time – his shoes were resting on a carpet of discarded cigarette packets and plastic containers.

"Do you suppose he has such a thing as a parachute?" Leni had asked as they had boarded.

"He has two engines. One of them must work," Hunt had told her.

When they landed at Dalaman, the passengers for the evening flight to Istanbul were already assembling, although the aircraft had not yet arrived. There was no sign of Adoration, the man with the beard who was now apparently clean-shaven, or any two women who could possibly have been Geli Littler and her daughter.

But then, he had not expected there to be.

"What do we do?" Leni asked. "Wait? But what happens when they get here? This place is kind of crowded."

Hunt sent Adolf off to hire two cars, and then led her into the somewhat bare room that purported to be a waiting lounge, found a vacant table and spread the map on it. "Now let's think like Adoration. As far as she knows, she has shaken us and we are waiting hopefully at Menemen. She's driving south but she has no reason to break any speed limits. Therefore I would say she is at this moment within a radius of perhaps a hundred and twenty kilometres of Selcuk. That means that if she was coming here, she'd be about Mugla. Right?"

"I thought you said she was coming here?"

"Not necessarily. But if she is, you'll see there is only one road from Mugla to Dalaman, so that we are certain to bump into her by driving back towards Mugla. The one alternative she has is to take that small road to the right just south of Mugla, out on to the Cnidus Nova Peninsular. We are going to have to cover that as well, but that shouldn't take long."

"But now you think she may not be coming to Dalaman

271

at all," Leni complained. "In that case, she could have taken the main road east to Denizli. She'd be about there by now."

"That road is covered," Hunt promised her.

Leni raised her eyebrows. "Not another of your cousins?"

"Corinne, as a matter of fact. I didn't send her to England after all. I sent her to Pammukale. Just in case." As if Corinne wouldn't have told her that in her note.

"Hunt, you are either a genius or you have sixth sense. And it was Corinne you telephoned from Menemen."

"And told her to take to the road and look for a black Mercedes."

"And is she armed?"

"There was a gun in her bag. The police had no reason to search her."

"God, I hope she knows how to use it. So, you have all the main roads covered. But supposing Adoration simply turns back towards Selcuk?"

"Then we're sunk. But I don't think she has. Figure it out. She and her boyfriend have been tracking Geli Littler for nearly a week."

"And have been prepared to kill to reach her."

"Agreed. And if their objective was merely to reach her and kill her, then it's done. But I am not sure it is. I think Adoration wants to get hold of Geli to obtain something from her. Everything points that way. According to the girl at the hotel, Adoration was in Selcuk twenty-four hours ago. She could easily have got Geli to one side, put a bullet in her or strangled her, as they seem to like doing best, and departed in that time, if that was what she wanted to do. But she didn't. She palled up with her in a most public way; even the desk clerk noticed it. Then she soothes Geli when the news breaks about Hans and offers to drive them to the airport. It's my bet she never meant to go near any airport. She wants to take Geli some place where she can have her all to herself for a couple of hours, and put the screw on her in her well-known fashion. That

272

means it has to be some place in this rather desolate area around Madran Baba and Gok Tepe." He thumped the map. "That's where we are going to find them."

"That's one hell of a big area."

"But it only has one or two access roads and they are driving a Mercedes."

Leni hugged herself. "The idea of being at the mercy of Adoration for two *hours* . . . ten minutes was more than enough for me. But I would say this peninsular down here on the right below Mugla looks even more desolate. Suppose she takes Geli there?"

"Then we have her because, as I said, we are going to check that out and there is only one road in or out."

"Hunt, what are we going to find even if we do catch up with them?"

"I wish to God I knew," Hunt said, with feeling. He was now almost more anxious to catch up with Adoration than he was with Geli.

Adolf secured the cars, apparently with difficulty: neither was less than five years old and both looked and sounded it. Hunt put him behind the wheel of one and took Leni with himself in the other. There was no other way he could separate them, for Leni's sake. There were going to be an awful lot of pieces to be picked up over the next few hours.

Or put down.

They drove along the Mugla road, which was pretty well deserted. They passed two cars and three trucks: none of them was a black Mercedes. By the time they reached the sharp right hand bend which led to Mugla itself, it was half-past five and the sun was beginning to droop.

Hunt braked, and waved Adolf to stop. The road from Dalaman had followed a valley formed by two considerable areas of high land. Now they again looked at a branch of the sea, the Kerme Korfezi. On their right, the road began the fairly steep climb up to Mugla on the mainland, dominated by the height of Sandras

273

Dag, some seven thousand feet. To their left the bulk of Koycegiz Golu also rose starkly, but neither as high nor as dramatically. Beyond, the peninsular divided into two arms, the right hand leading out to the ancient ruins of Cnidus Nova, the left to the narrow jutting point which faced the island of Rhodes – as Hunt had seen on the map, there was only one road. This also divided in time, to follow each arm, but as the whole area was less than forty miles long he didn't anticipate much of a problem in searching it for a conspicuous car.

"Frau Weiss and I are going to check out the peninsular," he told Adolf. "You stay here. Should a black Mercedes come down this road, don't do anything about it, but tail it. If it takes the road out on to the peninsular, follow it as far as the bifurcation and wait for us there. If it comes down the road we happen to be on, we'll handle it. If it goes the other way, we'll combine forces and follow it. If it takes the road to Dalaman, you'll follow. When we return to this crossroad, if you aren't here we'll assume you are on your way back to Dalaman and follow as fast as we can. Understood?"

Adolf nodded and looked at Leni.

"Don't worry, I'm bringing her back with me," Hunt told him.

"That character gives me the creeps," Leni said as they drove off. "I have an idea he would like to get his claws into me."

"He's human," Hunt agreed.

*

The big black car hummed south along the road from Aydin to Mugla. No one said much. Ilse was concentrating as the road was narrow and winding and there was some traffic. Josef and Helene still had their arms round each other in the back seat. It might have been the most instant of romances but Geli was happy for the girl, for the time being. It was something to be sorted out later.

Geli was feeling her nerves slowly begin to settle down. Of course it was horrible to think of Hans being tortured to death, but it would be hypocritical to pretend she still loved him after the way he had behaved. The important thing was that the boys were safe, as she and Helene were safe, and surely the police would now soon catch these people.

In any event, once they regained Istanbul Geli had every intention of asking for police protection herself. That might involve telling them who she really was, but that was preferable to being hunted . . . and no one could possibly pretend she was guilty of any crime.

Mugla was a surprisingly large town and there were the usual hold-ups to permit the passage of donkey-drawn carts as well as a flock of goats. By the time they emerged on to the open road beyond the town it was nearly dusk.

Ilse switched on her headlamps as the car drove south down the slope to the sea, the mountain high and black on their left.

"Do you think we will get a flight this late?" Geli asked.

"Probably not. We will catch one first thing in the morning."

"Oh. I am worried about the boys. I mean, I know they are in protective custody . . ."

"We can telephone from the hotel," Ilse said.

"Will there be a hotel at Dalaman?"

"There will be a hotel somewhere around there," Ilse assured her. "The important thing is that we have thrown those thugs off your trail."

"Yes," Geli said. "I am most terribly grateful." She peered ahead, following the beam of the headlamps into the gathering gloom, and saw the road bend to their left and the sign: DALAMAN. To the right there was a narrower road branching away. Between the two, parked on the grass verge, there was a rather battered-looking saloon car; leaning against it was a tall, thin man smoking a cigarette.

Ilse had taken all this in too and without hesitation she swung the car to the right to drive down the smaller road.

"But . . . you've passed the turn-off," Geli protested.

"I do not like the look of that man," Ilse said.

Geli turned round, saw the lights of the stationary car come on as the engine was started.

"This is not the sort of country where strange men wait in cars at crossroads without some sinister reason," Ilse said. As I thought, he is following us, Josef. We will have to stop him."

Josef took his arm from round Helene's shoulders, reached inside his jacket and produced a large automatic pistol.

"Oh, my God!" Helene cried. "What are you going to do?"

"Stop that fellow," Josef said. "Hold her steady, Ilse."

"You're not going to shoot at him?" Geli asked in consternation.

"It's the only way, and this is a lonely stretch of road." Josef rolled down his window and leaned out, while Ilse slowed the Mercedes and held it as steady as she could on the somewhat bumpy surface. Josef levelled the gun while Geli and Helene gazed at him in horror. Then he squeezed the trigger, and again.

They stared through the rear window. The nearside headlamp on the pursuing car had gone out, and the other one was swinging from side to side. Ilse slowed some more, and Josef fired twice more. The one remaining headlight swung across the road again and then kept going into the ditch. The car thudded behind it.

Ilse braked. "Can you see?" she asked.

"Enough." Josef was out of the Mercedes and crouching by the rear left wing. "He's getting out. Armed."

"Down," Ilse snapped, seizing Geli's shoulder to press her to the seat.

"Helene!" Geli gasped.

But Helene had thrown herself on to the floor in the back with a reassuring thump.

And Josef was firing again, holding the pistol in both hands now.

"It is all right," he said.

Ilse opened the front door and got out. Geli got out the other side. Even in the gloom she could make out the crumpled body lying at the side of the road.

"My God," she said. "Is he . . ."

"I certainly hope so. You had better stay here."

But Geli followed her as Ilse went up the road, in turn following Josef as he advanced upon Adolf, his pistol levelled.

Josef reached the body and stood above it, then turned it over with his toe. Adolf was still bleeding from the bullet wound in his chest. Now he made a feeble attempt to reach the gun he had dropped. Josef kicked it away.

Geli caught up with Ilse. "He's alive!" she gasped. "We must find a doctor."

"Josef will attend to him," Ilse said.

Josef had reached into his jacket pocket and produced a silencer. This he screwed into the muzzle of his pistol while Geli watched, her numbed brain only slowly realising what he was about to do.

"No," she gasped, and attempted to run forward but was instead struck a swinging blow from the edge of Ilse's hand which knocked her right off her feet and sent her sprawling across the road.

She sat up and listened to the two somewhat dull sounds as Josef fired again. In that instant she knew that something was terribly wrong, that she had to get away . . . she looked back at the car, and Helene, who had also got out but was standing there, staring at what had been happening.

"Helene!" she screamed. "Run! Helene . . ."

Helene hesitated and Ilse acted very quickly. From her own pocket she produced a smaller pistol, in the same movement kneeling beside Geli, and gripped her hair to drag her head backwards, thrusting the gun mizzle against her neck.

"Do you want your mother to die?" Ilse called.

Geli tried to move but the pressure on both her scalp

277

and her neck was too great; she felt as if her spine might be going to snap at any moment.

Helene stood still, staring at them.

"Come here," Ilse commanded.

Josef had been stooping beside Adolf's corpse. Now he straightened, took out and pocketed the empty magazine clip, slapped a fresh one into the butt of the pistol. Then he began going through the dead man's pockets.

Helene had come right up to them. "Please don't hurt my mother," she begged.

"I would prefer not to, certainly." Ilse released Geli's hair and stood up. "Get up," she said.

Geli stood up in turn, massaging her neck. She had to swallow several times before she could speak. "Who are you?" she asked. "You killed that man in cold blood."

"He was becoming a nuisance," Ilse agreed.

"He is German," Josef remarked, using a small pocket torch to read the various cards in the wallet he had taken from Adolf's pocket. "Who sent him, do you suppose? Hunt?"

"I do not see how Hunt can have done that," Ilse said. "Anyway, it does not matter. He has failed in his mission, whatever it is. See if there is anything useful in the boot of our car."

Josef went back to the Mercedes and unlocked the boot. Geli looked at Helene, and Helene looked at her mother. But Ilse still held her pistol and neither of them knew anything about overpowering anyone. Their lives had been too sheltered.

Ilse smiled. "Just stand still, both of you. Or it will be very bad."

Josef returned with a short length of cord. "Just the one," he said.

"Use it on Geli," Ilse said.

Josef pulled Geli's arms behind her back and looped the cord round her wrists several times before tying it tightly. Geli tried to think of something to say, or do, but her brain had gone blank.

"What about the girl?" Josef asked.

Breath hissed in Helene's nostrils: only fifteen minutes before, this man had had his arm round her shoulder and had been kissing her.

"Do you wear stockings?" Ilse looked at Helene's pants-enclosed legs. "I suppose not. All right, take off your brassiere."

"What?" Helene took a step backwards.

"Do you wish Josef to do it for you?" Ilse asked.

Helene gasped, but pulled her shirt out of her pants and reached behind herself, under the material.

"You killed Hans," Geli muttered.

"When he had fulfilled his useful purpose, yes."

"You . . ." Freya had said Hans had been tortured. She swallowed again.

Helene had taken off her bra, slipping it down one sleeve of her shirt. Josef grabbed it, pulled her arms behind her back and secured her in turn.

"It is warm," he said. "And smells of you." He kissed her ear.

Helene stamped her foot in outrage.

"Now, just continue to stand there," Ilse advised. "Josef, cram that man's body into the boot of his car."

Josef took the keys from the ignition of the wrecked car, unlocked the boot and heaved Adolf's body into it. Then he closed and locked it, pocketed the key. "Shall I fire it?" he asked.

"No," Ilse said. "Just leave it. Anyone coming along will suppose he had a smash and has walked for help. They will not find him until tomorrow, when he starts to smell."

"My God, you are not human," Geli muttered.

"I can be very pleasant," Ilse reminded her. "But my life has not been conducive to excessive humanity. Back to the car."

They returned to the car and Helene was thrust into the back seat again, Geli into the front.

"May I?" Josef asked.

"Oh, if it will amuse you," Isle agreed. She started the

279

engine. "He is a sex maniac," she explained to Geli. "He can't even keep his hands off me, for God's sake, and I am old enough to be his mother."

"We are going the wrong way," Geli said as Ilse engaged Drive. "Dalaman is behind us."

"We are not going to Dalaman," Ilse told her. "We never were. We were always coming here."

Geli opened her mouth and then closed it again.

"Please," Helene begged as Josef unbuttoned her shirt.

"Enjoy it," Ilse advised as she drove away. "You may not have them all that much longer."

"Why torment her?" Geli snapped. "Is it not me you are after?"

"Of course. But she will encourage you to co-operate with us, don't you think?"

Geli listened to Helene gasping in the back seat. "What do you want from me?" she asked. "Just tell me."

Ilse glanced at her. "And you will give it to me?"

"Yes," Geli said. "Yes."

Ilse smiled. "That will disappoint Josef. There is time. Now both of you be quiet: we are coming to a village."

The village was called Marmaris. Ilse slowed the car as they entered the single main street. Desperately Geli looked out of her window, seeking assistance of any description. It was quite dark now and the tavern was doing a good trade, its customers sitting outside to smoke and drink. Children ran to and fro and waved at the big car, and a dog barked. But it was obvious no one had heard the shots.

Geli looked over her shoulder. Josef had closed up Helene's shirt and had drawn a wicked-looking sheath knife to hold against her side. In the darkness Geli could not make out her daughter's expression. She did not dare imagine what might be going through her mind.

The lights and houses fell behind, and a few minutes later they came to a divide in the road. Ilse took the left-hand lane, almost due south: the right-hand lane went to the west.

Now the road was even worse, but after another few kilometres they again saw lights.

"That is the last village in this branch of the peninsular," Ilse said. "It is called Bozburan."

"But if we go through it they may wonder what we are doing in the evening, driving to the end of the peninsular," Josef said.

"Oh, yes," Ilse agreed. "But we do not have to go through it." A few minutes later she swung the car to the left, bumping down a stony parapet to come to rest on the edge of a field, and out of sight of the road, certainly at night. In front of them there was a hill rising sharply to a considerable height.

"Now let us take a little walk," Ilse said.

The doors were opened and the two women were dragged out. Helene's shirt flapped in the breeze and she shivered as the chill struck at her naked flesh.

"Over there," Ilse said. "It will be quiet there."

She took a briefcase from beneath her seat, held Geli's arm with her other hand and pulled her forward. Geli stumbled on the uneven ground, but Ilse held her up. Behind her she heard Helene panting: she was being held up by Josef, in his own fashion.

"Isn't this a beautiful spot?" Ilse asked as they climbed, feet scuffing on the stones and pebbles they uncovered, but they were all wearing good walking shoes. Again, Ilse's remarkable fitness amazed Geli. "Look, there is the sea. And there is an early moon. Oh, it is so lovely."

She was in the best of humours, thoroughly enjoying herself, while Geli could only keep thinking what a fool she had been – after all her precautions, she had delivered herself into these people's hands. People who had murdered Hans in cold blood, and that man on the road, and heaven alone knew how many others. Just to get to her. Now . . . "Please tell me what you want," she begged. "I will give you anything you want. Please don't harm us."

"I know you will, Geli, dear Geli," Ilse said. "The

trouble is, I want so very much. From you. But I am sure you will give it to me. This is high enough."

They had reached a kind of ledge beneath the overhanging peak of the mountain. From here they looked down on the sea, which was just beginning to shimmer as the moon began to play on it. Across the water, less than five kilometres away, they gazed at a mass of lights.

"That is the international airport on Rhodes," Ilse told her. "So near and yet so far, eh, Geli? Sit down. You must be tired."

Geli collapsed on the ground, so suddenly she jarred her spine. She had forgotten she could not use her hands. She felt unutterably exhausted. And so afraid. She had lost all feeling in her arms.

"You sit too," Josef invited, and forced Helene to her knees. Then he pushed her over so that she lay on the grass and stones.

"Such a pretty girl," Ilse remarked. "She looks like her grandmother, you know, Geli. But you . . . you look like your father." She laughed. "Only you are much prettier."

Geli stared at her in the darkness. "You . . ."

"Oh. yes, you realised who I was from the moment of our first meeting, when you remembered that your mother had had a personal maid called Ilse," Ilse told her. "Only you could not believe it, so you discarded the idea." She sat down as well, beside Geli, watched Josef rolling Helene to and fro, listened to the girl panting and whimpering as his hands explored her. "I told you he was a sex maniac," she said regretfully.

"You knew me as a baby," Geli said desperately. "Why do you wish to hurt me and my daughter? Why did you kill my husband?"

"Why? Well, there are many reasons. But I wanted to tell you about myself, about how I was treated by your mother."

"My mother always regretted leaving you behind," Geli said. "Please believe that. It haunted her to her grave."

282

"And so it should," Ilse agreed. "I had nothing save your mother. She knew that I was destitute. And she, she was going to great riches. A million Deutschmarks, in Swiss francs, waiting for her in Zurich. I overheard Himmler telling her this. She was going to great wealth. And I . . . oh, she said something about taking me. But he refused. 'No one must know,' he said. 'And that girl knows too much as it is.' I was only a girl then, you see. I was eighteen, a year older than your Helene is now.

"Your mother said, 'But as she already knows . . .' and he replied. 'That is all the more reason why she must be eliminated.' I could not believe my ears. I had worked for your mother for two years: we were more than just mistress and servant – I thought we were friends. I waited for her to refuse, absolutely. I waited and then she asked, 'How will it be done?' Nothing more than that. 'How will it be done?'"

Geli stared at her with stricken eyes.

"Himmler laughed," Ilse said. "That funny little laugh of his. 'My men are not monsters,' he said. 'A pistol shot in the back of the neck. It will not even hurt.' When I heard that I could keep still no longer. I threw myself into the room, at my mistress's feet, and begged her to save my life. She was sitting there with her babe at her breast. You, at her breast, Geli. Himmler called his guards to take me away. I screamed and begged her. And do you know what she said? She said. 'It will not hurt, Ilse. It will not hurt.' While you sucked."

The evening was filled with venom. Geli felt physically sick. "But you are alive," she whispered. "You are alive!"

"Yes," Ilse said. "I am alive. Himmler told his men to shoot me the moment he, your mother, and you had left the house. Your mother did not wish to see it or know of it. But when they left, the SS men decided to amuse themselves. I was a pretty girl, and up there in the Bavarian mountains they had not had a pretty girl to themselves for too long. They took me into one of the barns and amused themselves. There were twelve of them, and each of them had me twice. Do you know that up to the first one, I was a virgin?"

"I am so sorry," Geli said. "So terribly sorry. But . . ."

"Oh, they intended to kill me when they were finished. They told me so, several times. 'Enjoy it, Ilse,' they said as they laughed. 'It's all you'll ever know.' And then there was a miracle. I thought so at the time. An RAF bomber bombed the farm. I think it was unable to find its proper target and just decided to let the bombs go anyway. The first lot hit the farm and killed everyone in it. The SS men ran outside to see what had happened. The second lot landed in the yard, on them. The barn was not hit at all. But they had torn my clothes to shreds and when the bombers had gone, I was naked, in April, in the Bavarian mountains."

"And you survived?" Geli was incredulous.

"Oh, yes," Ilse said. "When you have been raped twenty-four times in two hours, when you are sufficiently angry, you can survive anything. When you want vengeance badly enough, you possess an enormous strength of mind, as well as body. And I wanted vengeance."

"On me?" Geli shouted. "I did not rape you!"

"The vengeance I sought then was on your mother, for abandoning me. But I wished to destroy you as well because you were a loathsome thing, a product of those loathsome loins." Ilse still spoke quietly but her voice was loaded with anger. "And I wanted the money. It was owed to me for what I had suffered. But first it was necessary to survive. I warmed myself by the flames of the burning farmhouse, and when they died down I hunted amongst the dead bodies and wrecked furniture. I found some of my clothes which were wearable, and I came down from the hillside into the village. I became a refugee. All Germany was full of refugees then.

"I was taken by some American soldiers and raped some more. It became so every time I saw a man in uniform I expected to be raped: it didn't seem to matter any more.

284

Then I was sent to a camp but that was terrible. I got out of the camp and made off on my own. I thought, if men so enjoyed raping me, why shouldn't they pay for the privilege? I lived off my body for three years."

Even Helene was still now. Geli dared not look at her, partly because she did not want to know what Josef had been doing to her and partly because she was too ashamed.

"Then, do you know, I met Bruening? He used me, and paid me, and apparently enjoyed me so much he wanted to set me up as his mistress. I was not going to refuse that. He was a black marketeer and had a lot of women. But he liked me best. Sometimes I think he loved me. I worked hard to make him love me, Geli. Have you ever had to work to make a man love you? It means you have to suppress every bit of your own personality, be everything he wants and nothing you want. But at the same time, you must never be a doormat. Then he leaves you. It is a difficult role to play. But I did it so successfully that when he became legitimate, he married me. He was rich, very rich, by then. I enjoyed being his wife. But I enjoyed being his widow more."

"You killed him?" Geli found she was panting.

"Well, he had served his purpose once he had left everything to me. He drowned in his bath. No one knew we had been making love in the bath, and when he had come and was gasping for breath, I simply pushed his head under. It was very quick. The police were puzzled but he had definitely drowned, and there were no signs of violence."

"Do you hate everyone in the world so very much?"

"Well, not everyone. Do you think I hate you, Josef?"

"Sometimes I think you do, Ilse," Josef said thoughtfully.

"Well," Ilse said, "there it was. I think I have good reason to hate everyone. All I have ever had from the world is hate."

"You said Bruening loved you," Geli said desperately.

285

"He loved my body and my subservient self. But he was a loathsome man. However, he left me quite well off. But not rich. And I still had a lot to do with my life. I wanted to track Helene von Uderstadt down. I wanted to watch her die, but before that I wanted to force her to give me that million Deutschmarks."

"I will give it to you," Geli said.

"Of course you will, my dear. But finding you, or rather, your mother, that was the problem. I spent nearly forty years on that search. I made friends with a newspaper reporter, Joachim Allendt. Well, I let him sleep with me for nothing, in return for the right to examine his files. But I found nothing. I told him what I was looking for, however, and I promised him half of the money if he ever turned anything up. Still, as the years went by I started to despair. But Joachim had by this time worked his way up to be editor. And then, just a week ago, Gustave Brauer went to see him with the story of how he thought he could find your mother. And you."

"And this man told you?" Geli whispered.

"Well, as I have said, he is my lover. Even now he is my lover. Joachim understood, of course, that I did not wish the whole business brought into the open, as would have had to happen had he agreed to finance Brauer's quest. Brauer wanted so much money it would have had to be placed before Joachim's board. Of course it might have brought great profit to his newspaper, but little to himself personally. While I had promised him those five hundred thousand Deutschmarks. So he turned Brauer down and telephoned me.

"Then it was simply a matter of rounding up two of my friends and paying this has-been a visit to obtain all the information he possessed. This information, according to Joachim, was principally in the form of an appointments diary which had belonged to Himmler's secretary at the end of the war. I wanted this diary. But the swinehound had been negotiating with an English newspaper as well, and had done a deal. He had put the diary in his bank, with instructions that it was only to be given to this wretched man, Hunt. Can you believe it?

"I was very angry, I can tell you. I told Josef to question Brauer. Josef enjoys questioning people. It is his principal pleasure: had he been born before the war he would have been a most valuable member of the Gestapo. I am going to let him question Helene, just now, if you do not co-operate. He is very anxious to do this."

"I am going to co-operate!" Geli wailed. How she wanted to be able to hit this woman. And how aware she was of her helplessness.

And even of being sorry for her.

"We shall see. Anyway, locking up his diary didn't do this disgusting Brauer any good. By the time Josef had questioned him for ten minutes he was willing to tell us the name and address of the man who was in control of your mother's trust fund. So we went to Zurich."

"After killing Brauer? Why did you have to do that?"

"Well, my dear, we could hardly leave the poor old fellow with his balls burned black."

Geli gasped in horror.

"In any event, he would have told the police about us. No, no, he was better off dead."

"And then you killed Uncle Walther?"

"Uncle Walther," Ilse said. "How sweet. No, Geli, we did not kill Uncle Walther. The louse went and died on us. Josef was not even questioning him. We were merely trying to convince him to make the trust over to us. Do you know how much the trust has grown, Geli? It is now three and a half million Marks."

"I know. You can have it all. Please, you can have it all."

"That is very generous of you. I knew you would be generous. But you will understand that with Schmidt dying, there were only two people in the world who could transfer the trust: his nephew and partner, and you. The nephew and partner was obviously out of the question at the time Schmidt died. It was very nearly dawn and Zurich was waking up. We had to leave and decide what to do.

"My problem was, I did not know where you were. My only hope therefore was that Hunt would also come to Zurich, and that he would go to Schmidt's apartment and from there continue towards you. So we kept it under surveillance. Of course, the police went there first, summoned by the concierge, and there was a great to-do. Josef wanted to abandon the whole project. Didn't you, Josef?"

"I did not see how we could possibly progress," Josef admitted.

"But I have learned to be patient during the ups and downs of my life. And I was proved right: Hunt did appear, with his blonde sidekick. He couldn't get into Schmidt's apartment, of course, so he went to a hotel. We trailed him there and it was just a matter of gaining access to his room at an appropriate time. But before then, would you believe it, he was arrested by the Zurich police. I will tell you, then I nearly despaired myself.

"But then I realised that a man like Hunt, an internationally known correspondent, would be able to talk himself out of his arrest, especially, of course, as he had not committed any crime. And as I expected, back he and his little friend came soon enough. You liked that girl, didn't you, Josef?"

"If I had had another five minutes with her . . ." Josef said.

"I know," Ilse said sympathetically. "But the whole idea was a mistake. See, I admit it freely. Even I make mistakes, my dear Geli. I should never have tried to obtain what I wanted from Hunt and his friend. Not because I would not have succeeded, given, as Josef says, another few minutes, but because I had underestimated the resources Hunt had at his disposal. We were taken by surprise, and I have no idea what happened to poor Heinrich: I think he was killed by a madwoman. But Josef and I made our escape, utterly defeated, you might say.

"Except that as we descended to the lobby, I had a stroke of genius. I realised of course that despite what had happened upstairs, Hunt was unlikely to wish to involve the police because then he would have been held up in Zurich. Therefore we had no need to fear an immediate pursuit. But I also realised that if Hunt had all these resources, and the diary, he would almost certainly be able to find out where your mother had fled after Zurich. And equally, that he had probably already done so and was preparing to go. In which case . . . I merely stopped at the desk and asked if my friend Mr Hunt was leaving the next day, and where he was going. They told me without the slightest hesitation: he and his friend were booked on the first flight out to Istanbul!"

Ilse laughed. "Is life not really very simple, if you approach it in a straightforward fashion? What really made it amusing was that I have been to Istanbul, to Turkey, many times. It is one of my favourite countries. And to think you had been living here all of these years! Anyway, Josef and I drove down to Berne and caught the first available flight from there for Istanbul. It actually left at nine thirty, so we were in Turkey well before Hunt. As a matter of fact, he seems to have missed the ten o'clock flight and did not arrive until seven in the evening. So we had to wait but we used our time well, because I also have a number of useful contacts in Istanbul, old black market trading partners of Bruening. They haven't changed their ways, and they supposed I hadn't, either. Of course, I did not know where you were, or what name you were living under. But I knew Hunt was coming, and I knew that Hunt would have arranged everything because he is like that. It was simply a matter of getting my friends to ask the various drivers which of them was meeting a Mr Hunt, the famous correspondent. Then, when Hunt's driver finally arrived, it was an equally simple matter to invite him to have a drink before the aircraft landed, and dispose of him. One of my friends took over the car. His business

289

was to learn where Hunt intended to go, and then dispose of him also.

"Unfortunately, he and his friends failed to do this. But he did have the address Hunt gave him, and this he telephoned to where Josef and I were waiting. After that it was simple, save that you had already fled. But you had made the mistake of telling your husband what you were going to do. That was stupid. He was such a weak, frightened man. He told us very quickly. He didn't know which tour you would be on, but once we knew it was a tour, why, it was simple. Mother and daughter? Fair when they should have been dark, and the mother pregnant? I knew then we had you in our sights. So . . . here we are."

Geli drew a long breath. "But . . . this man, Hunt . . . you said he was a thug, after my life. Now you say he is a newspaper correspondent."

"Well, he *is* a newspaper correspondent. There can be no doubt about that. But for the rest of it . . . I do not know about Mr Hunt. Nobody is sure about him. He has some very odd friends, both in Germany and in other places. Obviously, it suits him to have everyone, especially the police, think that he is chasing you for an exclusive story . . . but if my information is correct, he is actually chasing you for a lot more than that. You do not want, ever, to trust Mr Hunt." Ilse smiled. "But of course, now you won't have to."

"No," Geli said. "Please . . . just tell me what you want me to do."

Ilse opened her briefcase and from it took another of the small torches. With the beam of this she sorted through several papers. "I have here various documents which I would like you to sign."

"If I sign them," Geli panted, "will you let us go?"

"After certain precautions have been taken," Ilse promised. "After all, we will require a considerable start. You will have to spend the night out here."

Could she be trusted? She spoke so reasonably. But

then, she had spoken so reasonably about the people she had killed. Yet there was no alternative if Helene was to be saved from further ill-treatment.

"I will sign the papers," Geli said.

"Josef," Ilse said.

Josef left Helene and knelt beside Geli to untie her wrists.

"Slap your hands together," he told her. "It will restore circulation more quickly."

Geli obeyed, and gasped in agony as the pins and needles commenced.

"You understand that if you attempt to attack us, or get away, we will hurt both you and Helene very badly?" Ilse said.

Geli wept as the pain grew, and then started to subside.

"You should be all right now," Ilse said. "There is no need to read the papers. All you have to do is sign them." She gave Geli a pen and the sheaf of papers, closed the lid of the briefcase and held the torch. "Just place them on that surface, and sign where I have marked."

There were six papers. Two of them were letters, Geli could tell at a glance, and one of the letters was addressed to Schmidt & Schmidt. She wasn't sure what the other four were. But she signed them all, one after the other. Presumably she was signing instructions for Walther Schmidt Junior to pay the entire trust fund over to Ilse Bruening, supposing that was her real name . . . but Ilse did not know that Walther Schmidt Junior already had instructions on what to do with the fund, and if he had acted on that first thing this morning, he would be unable to touch any of the money, no matter what he might be instructed to do.

Ilse was going to be strung up on her own efficiency.

Ilse inspected each signature. "That is very good, Geli," she said. "Very nice of you." She reopened the briefcase, put the papers into the lid-pocket.

"Now, will you take us to Dalaman Airport?" Geli asked.

"Now?" Ilse seemed quite surprised. "No, no, my dear Geli. Now we are going to kill you. But surely you knew that?"

"You . . . I signed the papers!" Geli screamed.

"Therefore you have fulfilled your natural purpose," Ilse pointed out. "And if you scream again, I shall gag you. In fact, I think you will have to be gagged anyway. Your daughter certainly will. Josef . . ."

"What am I supposed to use?" Josef asked.

"Oh . . . use their knickers. Cram them into their mouths."

"Oh, yes," Josef said enthusiastically, and returned to kneel beside Helene.

Geli realised that they were actually in tremendous danger. "Listen," she said urgently. "Those papers I signed – they are useless."

"Oh, yes," Ilse remarked.

"Listen," Geli said. "I wrote a letter on Saturday to Walther Schmidt Junior, giving him certain instructions as to what to do with the trust fund. This was at his request, and is perfectly legal. He will have received the letter this morning and acted on it immediately. He cannot dispose of any moneys now. Only I can do that."

Ilse gazed at her for several seconds. "If that is true, I would be very angry," she said.

"It is true. I am sorry. I did not know this was going to happen. If you must know, I was determined to keep the money from my husband."

"And now you think you can keep it from us," Ilse remarked.

"No. I will give it to you on condition you do not harm us. I will write to my bank and have the money transferred wherever you wish."

"But it will have to be a fresh letter," Ilse mused. "Very well. I have some good notepaper in my case. You will write the letter by the light of my torch. Now."

"No," Geli said.

Ilse raised her eyebrows.

292

"I will write the letter after we have returned to somewhere public."

"You must take me for a fool."

"Well," Geli said. "You obviously mistake me for one."

Ilse's lips twisted. "You are certainly not a coward, at any rate, Fraulein Hitler. But do you really suppose you can defy me?"

"I am not attempting to defy you. I am attempting to reach a bargain with you. If you wish my money, it must be in exchange for something."

Ilse smiled. "I do not admit your reasoning. I am going to take your money because it is owed to me by your mother, for the years of suffering she inflicted on me. I owe you nothing in return. Now, write the letter."

"After which you will kill us."

"Yes, very probably." Her teeth gleamed as her smile widened. "But painlessly. A shot in the back of the neck. Exactly what your mother promised me. You will not feel a thing, and the world will be rid of a monster."

"You are mad," Geli declared. "You think I will write any letter now?"

"I think you will. If you do not, you are going to watch your daughter die, very, very slowly. After all, we have all night. And Josef is so anxious to enjoy himself. Then, when he is finished with Helene, he will start on you. But you may stop the agony at any moment, simply by writing the letter. Think about this. But do not take too long."

Geli panted as she looked from Ilse to Josef and Helene. Josef was kneeling beside Helene, his hands on the waistband of her pants, just awaiting the command to strip her. Helene was clearly too terrified even to cry out.

Was she now going to watch that beauty destroyed?

They were going to die, anyway. Could she willingly inflict a horrifying death on Helene, if death was inevitable? For the sake of defying this true monster who sat beside her?

293

How she wanted to defy her.

"Very well, Josef," Ilse said. "You may commence. Gag her, and then burn between her legs. You will watch, Geli." She switched on her flashlight again, directed it at Helene.

Josef unfastened Helene's waistband.

"Mummy . . ." Helene said urgently.

Geli knew her brief attempt at resistance had been defeated. "Wait," she said.

"Ah," Ilse said. "Wait a moment, Josef."

Josef waited, his hands resting on Helene's thighs. They could hear the breath whistling in Helene's nostrils.

"You wished to say something?" Ilse asked Geli.

Geli licked her lips. "I . . . I will write the letter."

"Believe me, that is far the most sensible course to take," Ilse agreed. She opened her case again, took out a sheet of notepaper, handed it and the pen to Geli, closed the case again and shone her torch on it. "Although the moon is so bright it is hardly necessary. Now, you will instruct your bank to transfer the funds to the Bundesberg Bank, Hamburg, to an account in your name and that of Ilse Bruening. That will entirely allay their suspicions, except in so far as you may perhaps be gay. However, the account will be available to either signatory, by herself." She giggled. "That will convince them, eh? You have fallen in love, Geli."

Geli wrote the letter, trying to keep her hand from trembling. When she was finished, Ilse read it. "Very good. I thank you." She folded the sheet of paper and placed it in her briefcase. "Now, will you take off your pants and knickers, please."

Geli clasped her hands in front of herself. "But why? I have written the letter. You said you would kill us painlessly."

"Oh, I know I did," Ilse said sympathetically. "But Josef gets so peevish when he doesn't have his way. For forty-eight hours he has been dreaming about burning Helene. I could not possibly deprive him of that pleasure

294

now. But you are going to start screaming, aren't you, Geli? So you simply have to be bound and gagged. You do understand that? Josef, you had better come and give me a hand."

Josef got to his feet. As he did so, Helene made a tremendous effort and got to her feet as well. She tried to move away from him but the loose pants caught round her knees and she fell on to the lip of the edge before rolling down the hillside with a despairing scream.

CHAPTER TEN

After Hunt drove through Marmaris, he first of all took the left-hand fork on to the Daracya Peninsular. The road ended in the village of Bozburan, although there were another fifteen kilometres of rugged country before the end of the peninsular could be reached. By dint of a good deal of shouting and arm-waving, and some helpful sketches made by Leni, however, he determined that no large black Mercedes motor-car had been seen in the village.

"False trail number one," Leni commented as they turned and drove back towards the bifurcation.

"What you mean is, possibility number one has been checked and eliminated," Hunt told her. "You must learn to think positively."

He swung left on to the much longer road leading out to Cnidus Nova. After driving some twenty kilometres they came to the village of Yarimadasi. Here again, according to the map, there were another twenty-odd kilometres to the end of the peninsular, reached but what appeared to be a series of cart tracks. But equally, here again, they were able to establish that no large black Mercedes had passed this way.

"I hate to think critically," Leni remarked. "But if they have changed cars this is an exercise in futility."

"You are being totally negative," Hunt snapped, understanding that she could be correct. "Why on earth should they do that? As far as they're concerned, we're still at Menemen Airport."

"Ha," Leni commented.

By now it was quite dark. They drove back through

Yarimadasi, where the locals were enjoying themselves and the street was crowded.

"My, that smells good," Leni commented. "Hunt, do you realise it is five hours since we ate?"

"Chew the floormat," Hunt said bad-temperedly. "It could be another five hours."

They drove past the bifurcation, and through Marmaris.

"What are we going to do when we get back to the crossroads and find your friend Adolf still there, contemplating his navel?" Leni asked. "With not a black Mercedes in sight?"

"If you don't shut up, we are going to leave you on watch while he and I drive back to Dalaman for a five-course dinner," Hunt told her. "What the . . ."

Marmaris was ten minutes behind them, and on the side of the very empty road in front of them there was a car half into the ditch.

"That wasn't there when we drove down," Hunt said.

"Looks like one of the locals had a shade too much raki," Leni commented.

Hunt braked. "That's Adolf's car."

"Oh, really, Hunt!"

"Look, gorgeous, you may be a fake reporter. I happen to be the real thing. One memorises number plates." He checked his pistol, held it loosely as he opened the door and got out.

He walked to the car, heard Leni behind him. The moon had just risen and it was quite light; there was no difficulty in ascertaining that the car was empty.

"I'd say he skidded and went off the road, and has gone someplace for help," Leni opined.

"Good thinking," Hunt agreed. "Where did he go?"

"Well . . ."

"Mugla is about twenty kilometres north of us. Dalaman is about thirty kilometres east, after we reach the crossroad. Marmaris is about five behind us. Which way would you have walked?"

"Well . . . Marmaris, I suppose."

"So how come we didn't pass him?" Hunt pocketed his pistol, dropped to his haunches on the side of the road beside some dark marks. He stroked one of these with his finger, then scraped at it, lifted his finger. "This is blood. Pretty well dry. Maybe an hour."

Leni knelt beside him. "Sure you're not fantasising?"

"Try some for yourself." Hunt crawled back to the car, noting some more dark splodges on the road. "Mind yourself." He drew the pistol, aimed at the lock on the boot and fired. Tortured metal screamed, but the lock was smashed.

"You can be quite a guy," Leni remarked.

"Compliments will get you everywhere. Shit!"

He had thrown up the boot top.

"Oh, hell," Leni commented. "I never did like that character, but . . . you're sure it's him?"

Adolf's head was a shapeless bloody mass from the last two bullets fired into it at close range.

"It's him," Hunt said.

"What do we do?" Leni's voice held a distinct quaver as she looked right and left into the moonlight.

What indeed? Hunt wondered. He had lost his back-up, but he would definitely need help now. First things first.

"Go find Adoration. She has Frau Littler and her daughter, remember, and by now they must have realised who they're riding with." He went back to the car.

Leni scrambled into the seat beside him as he began to reverse. "But how do we know where they've gone?"

"Adolf was following someone, right? In accordance with his instructions. When they passed him, he was going to follow them as far as the bifurcation, and wait there for us. Only they cottoned on to him and did him before they reached the bifurcation."

"And then got the hell out of here."

"Why should they, if they were coming here anyway? So someone was sent to follow them. As far as they can possibly know, he was on his own."

"You said they'd make for the mountains."

"And you pointed out that this peninsular is even more desolate. Okay, you were right and I was wrong. The point is, now we know where they are. Because if they had come towards Cnidus Nova, we'd have met them. They've gone south, to Bozburan."

"We were there, Hunt, just over an hour ago."

"We were in front of them. When we were in Bozburan, they were here." He looked at the dead body, and then closed the boot again. "Settling with Adolf."

They drove back through Marmaris, this time attracting increased attention. Five minutes later they reached the bifurcation and turned south. Hunt was travelling slowly now, because for all the moonlight, they were surrounded by deep shadows while the mountain rose stark to their left.

But the road was empty.

They went on into Bozburan, stopped by the same little shop. By this time the proprietor knew what they were about and shook his head almost before they got out of the car.

"Looks like you goofed again," Leni suggested. "Unless you reckon this character has had his palm greased with Deutschmarks."

"I don't think he has. There is no way they could get anything other than four-wheel drive over that track." He reversed the car and drove back out of the village, north.

"So . . . back to Dalaman? You going to tell the cops about Adolf? Sooner or later they're going to reckon that wherever Hunt is, there is usually a dead body. Usually sooner than later."

"Sssh," he recommended, and switched off his lights. The moon was sufficient for him to see the road, if not the potholes, and there was no other traffic. "They're here, somewhere."

"Well," Leni began, and then squeezed his arm. "Hunt! Stop!"

He braked.

"I saw a gleam of light."

"Where?"

"Up there on the hillside."

"What kind of light was it?"

"A kind of flickering gleam."

"Like a lighter?"

"No, more like a flashlight . . . oh, my God, Hunt!"

"Let's take a look. Quiet now." He got out of the car, went to the side of the road, looked down the embankment at the clump of trees. "Prize time," he said.

Leni stood beside him, also saw the glint of the Mercedes.

"I think we need to hurry," Hunt said. "But let's see if we can avoid making any noise."

He needed her now, thanks to the elimination of Adolf. At least up to a point.

They jogged across the field and came to the rising ground. The wind was light and soughing faintly; beyond, the sea was restless, effectively hiding the sound of their feet. In the distance they could make out the huge glow of the Rhodes Airport.

They looked up, trying to see anything which might guide them, and heard a crashing sound somewhere to their right. Hunt ran in that direction and saw a body rolling down the hill towards him, legs flailing in the moonlight. From the way it was falling he thought for an uneasy moment that it was a corpse, but then it came to rest only a few feet in front of him in a clump of bushes and he discovered it was a girl with her hands tied behind her back, her shirt flapping open and her pants round her knees. For the moment she was breathless, but she stared at him with enormous eyes as she panted. Even in the gloom, he could see that she had suffered several nasty cuts and bruises from her fall.

"Hunt," Leni whispered as she crouched beside him.

Hunt looked up and saw the man hurrying down the

slope. He did not appear to have seen them, but he carried a drawn pistol.

Hunt had no doubt who it was and his opinion was confirmed by Helene, who had got her breath back.

"Please don't let him kill me," she gasped. "Please!"

"I don't like that fellow," Hunt remarked. "But one can't pot a sitting duck, I suppose." He stood up, his pistol levelled and held in both hands. "Stop right there, Fungus."

Even if he had shaved off his beard.

Josef checked, peering into the darkness.

"Here," Hunt said. "Throw the pistol in front of you."

Josef saw him and the girl at his feet in the same instant. He brought up his gun, and Hunt fired. The bullet struck Josef in the centre of the forehead, and he went over backwards without a sound. Hunt did not possess a silencer, however, and the noise of the shot echoed up the mountain.

"Hunt," Leni said, "that was cold-blooded murder."

"It was an execution. Not enough governments practise it nowadays, where people like that are concerned. How is the girl?"

Leni was untying Helene's wrists, and the girl was moaning as she was pulled clear of the bushes, scrabbling to pull her pants back up. "She is torn half to ribbons. What she needs is a drink."

"Don't we all?" Hunt climbed up the hillside to make sure Josef was dead, and pocketed his pistol. Then he returned to the women, took off his jacket and wrapped it round Helene's shoulders; she had managed to fasten the waistband of her pants, but the shirt had virtually disintegrated. "Who else is up there?"

Helene licked her lips. "My mother . . . and that woman. Oh, God, I hurt all over."

"We'll get help for you as quickly as possible. Can you stay here for a while? We'll come back for you."

Helene whimpered as the blood began to return to her wrists and hands. "She's armed."

"That figures. Now be a brave girl. I'm going straight up, Leni. You circle to the left. Adoration can't know how many of us there are. Can you shoot?"

"I have before."

"Well, we're not interested in bringing charges." He gave her Josef's gun. "There's only one safe place for Adoration, and that's six feet under the ground. So when you shoot, shoot to kill. And try to miss me and Frau Littler."

Leni made no reply, merely scuttled off into the darkness. Hunt decided to give her a few minutes, remained kneeling beside the girl.

"Will you save Mummy, please?" Helene asked. She was massaging her legs, smearing the blood which welled out of the myriad little rents her pants had suffered during her fall.

"I reckon."

"What they were going to do . . ." A long shudder seeped through her body.

"That's something you're just going to have to forget," Hunt advised. "Now you stay put."

He began scrambling up the path, but had not gone very far when he heard footsteps above him and saw the two women coming down. As far as he could see, one of the women also had her hands bound behind her back; she was being urged onwards by the taller woman, who was carrying a briefcase in her left hand and a pistol in her right.

Now the pair stopped as they saw the figure standing below them. Josef's body was an unidentifiable lump.

"Josef?" Ilse Bruening called. "Is that you? I heard the shot. Did you kill the girl?"

"My name is Hunt, actually," Hunt said.

"Hunt? Hunt!" Ilse's voice rose an octave. "My God! Where is Josef?"

"Somewhere around. He's not going to be too much help to you, though. He's dead."

Ilse peered at him, and presumably was looking left and

right as well. At last she said, "All right, Hunt. You have done well. Now tell me what you want?"

"I want Frau Littler," Hunt said.

"Well, you can have her in due course. Now listen to me, Hunt. I am coming down this hill with Frau Littler. My pistol is pressed into her back and if you attempt to stop me, I shall kill her. Do you understand this?"

"Yes," Hunt said.

Helene gave a little gasp.

"So what you will do is lay down your weapon and then empty your pockets."

"That kind of makes life easy for you, doesn't it?"

"I didn't ask you to come here. Do it, or watch Frau Littler die. I have all I want from her, anyway."

Hunt hesitated. What the devil was Leni doing? Slowly he laid the pistol on the ground then turned out his pockets, placing the items carefully beside the gun.

"It is your car keys I wish, Hunt," Ilse said. "Come here, with the keys in your hand."

Hunt moved slowly towards them. When he was about fifteen feet away from them, Ilse said, "Stop there and toss the keys to my feet."

Hunt drew a long breath and obeyed; Leni had had sufficient time to climb to the top of the mountain and back down again.

"Thank you," Ilse said. "Now, Geli, we will kneel together."

Geli Littler slowly sank to her knees. Ilse went with her, obviously intending to keep her as a shield at all times. But as Geli reached the ground, she suddenly turned, violently thrusting her shoulder against Ilse's arm. Ilse, suspended between standing and kneeling, lost her balance and fell over, and Geli got back to her feet.

"You stupid bitch!" Ilse snarled, and levelled her pistol, while Hunt started to move forward, sickeningly aware that he could not make it in time.

In that moment there was a shot. Ilse half-turned round, and then collapsed heavily.

Geli, just reaching her feet, tripped and fell also, and rolled away from her captor. Hunt was already bounding forward to reach Ilse as she attempted to regain the pistol, which had fallen from her hand.

Hunt picked it up instead, inhaled Adoration as he looked down at her. Her face was twisted in agony and blood was soaking her blouse; she had been struck between the shoulder blades.

Footsteps crunched beside him.

"I thought I told you to shoot to kill," Hunt remarked.

"I did, when I could be sure of not hitting Frau Littler. Is she . . ."

"She'll die if we don't get her to a doctor in about fifteen minutes. As we can't do that, and wouldn't even if we could, you could say she's dead, yes."

"Bastard!" Ilse whispered.

"It's a point of view." Hunt gazed at the tortured features. "Would you like to offer a prayer for the souls of Gustave Brauer, or Walther Schmidt, or Hans Littler? Or even your friends, Heinrich and the ex-Beard?"

"I will pray to meet you again in hell," Ilse muttered.

"Ouch," Leni remarked.

"She's dead," Hunt said, and stooped beside Geli, who had been a breathless witness of Ilse's execution. "Are you all right, Frau Littler?"

"My daughter . . ."

"Is all right. A bit battered. The important thing is you are both alive."

He gazed at Leni who gazed back. She had thrust the pistol into the waistband of her pants and was kneeling beside him to release Geli's wrists. She had no doubt now that they were partners, it seemed.

But Hunt had already had to come to a decision. He couldn't have done it without Leni . . . but he couldn't do anything more with her. Whatever she really was, whoever she was really working for, from this moment on he and she had to be enemies rather than rivals. He was really sorry about that.

304

And right this moment she had lowered her guard, was kneeling beside him, shoulder to shoulder, rubbing Geli's wrists to help restore the circulation.

Hunt moved. With one hand he jerked the pistol from Leni's waistband, and with the other he drew Ilse's pistol from his own, at the same time leaping to his feet and taking several steps backwards; he didn't wish to get too close to a Leni as angry as this Leni was going to be.

For the moment, she seemed more sorrowful. "I thought we had quite a relationship going."

"We did. And I wish we could keep it up. But . . . work before pleasure, remember?"

Geli looked from one to the other in bewilderment; she was obviously still in considerable discomfort from her hands.

"Don't be a fool, Hunt," Leni said. "Whatever you do, we are going to get you."

"Who are we?"

She thrust her chin at him. "That you are going to have to find out."

They stared at each other.

"You know something?" Hunt asked at last. "I ought to put a bullet in your gut. Or at least warm you up with Josef's cigarette lighter. But I guess I'm just a softy after all. Take off your belt."

Leni hesitated, then obeyed, held up her pants with her hands.

"Now, lie down on the grass, on your face," Hunt said. "Please remember that I am treating you much better than you once treated me."

Leni lay down. "Hunt, if you harm this woman you are going to be committing suicide."

"I am going to secure your wrists," he said. "You may think you were playing back in the Hamburg bedroom, but so was I, you see. If you attempt to move, I am going to break your neck. Do concentrate on that."

Leni appeared to consider, then she brought her hands behind her back. Hunt thrust the pistol into his waistband, pulled off his tie, and secured the wrists together. Then he used her belt to secure her ankles.

Geli stared at him with enormous eyes, obviously considering attempting to escape but knowing that she wasn't going to make it, and aware, too, of how exhausted she was.

Hunt rolled Leni on her side, flicked some dust from her hair. "It's been fun," he told her.

He went back to where he had emptied his pockets, replaced everything, then helped Geli to her feet, and then Helene.

"I don't understand about the woman," Geli said.

"Don't try to. Just trust me."

Geli appeared to consider. "If you hadn't come," she said. "They were going to kill us. In their own way."

"I know. What were they after?"

"My money."

"Well, that's a relief."

Geli stared at him with her mouth open.

Hunt grinned. "I'm not after your money, Frau Littler. Now let's get the hell out of here."

"Where?" Geli asked.

"Some place we can talk, in the first instance."

"Hunt," Leni said. "Don't do it."

He knelt beside her to check her wrists. She had already nearly worked herself free, so he retied them. But he didn't suppose he was going to have much more than an hour's start. On the other hand . . . He went through Ilse's pockets and found the keys to the Mercedes. He pocketed these, as well as the keys to the hired car, and picked up the briefcase.

"Mrs Littler," Leni said. "You are in great danger."

"She's a hysteric," Hunt told Geli. "Let's go."

"You mean to leave her here, with two dead bodies?"

"She'll wriggle free soon enough."

"But . . ."

"Like she said, Frau Littler, you are in great danger. But from her, not from me." He hurried them down the hill.

306

"Don't believe him!" Leni shouted. "He means to kill you. He . . ." Her voice was lost in the breeze.

But Geli had stopped moving. "What do you want with me?"

"My name is Hunt. I've a card somewhere."

"Hunt! Ilse Bruening spoke of you. She said you were a famous newspaper reporter."

"That was nice of Ilse. Yes, I am what you might call a reporter."

"She also said you were dedicated to killing anyone even remotely connected with the Nazis."

"Just let's say I'm a reporter."

"And you wish to speak with me?"

"Shouldn't I? I would say you have a great deal to tell me."

Geli signed. "I suppose there is no escape now."

"I'm afraid there isn't," Hunt agreed. "I don't think any of us can shirk our heritage." They reached the cars. "We'll take the Mercedes." He unlocked it and allowed Helene into the back seat. The girl shivered constantly; she was on the edge of a nervous breakdown.

"But all these people trying to kill me . . . and that woman . . . does she want to kill me too?"

"Quite possibly. You are a target, Frau Littler."

He started the engine and drove back on to the road.

"Are you always prepared to kill people for the sake of your story?"

"In this instance, yes. My paper is prepared to pay you very well for an exclusive."

"I do not need money," Geli said.

"In my experience, one can never have too much money," Hunt remarked, and slowed to drive through Marmaris.

"Where are you taking us?" Helene asked.

"Well, I thought first of all we should stop and have a bite to eat. In Mugla. That way we can park off the main street and be discreet."

307

"Eat," Helene muttered. "I could not eat anything. If I could have a glass of water . . ."

"You'll have your water. I am sure you'll find an appetite from somewhere. Then we should find somewhere for the night. I assume your bags are in this car?"

"Yes," Geli said.

"Well, I left Selcuk in rather a hurry; my gear is still there. And I still have a room there, too. Perhaps after dinner we could drive back there. We shouldn't be too late."

"And after that?"

"After that, well . . . I think we should disappear for a few days. Of course you will wish to let your sons know that you and your daughter are all right, but it would be best if they did not know where you are. With that pair of thugs dead, you at least know they are in no danger, but they will undoubtedly be closely watched by the Turkish police. We do not want them getting into the act."

"Why not?" Geli asked.

"Well . . ." Hunt watched the road. "There will be a lot of publicity and let's face it, there may well be other people after your blood. Leni – that's the woman we left back there – is certainly working for some organisation which wants to get their hands on you."

"Mr Hunt," Geli said. "You are all labouring under a grave misapprehension. All right, my father was Adolf Hitler. I never set eyes on him, and except for one brief holiday, if you can call it that, I have not set foot in Germany since I was three months old. There is absolutely nothing I can tell you that will be of the least interest to your readers, and there is nothing that I possess which can be of the least use, or the least danger, to any living human being. Oh, there is the money, of course. It is SS money, and therefore it is blood money. And there is quite a lot of it. But if they wish to take it away from me, well, they are welcome to it. Hans will have left me enough to live on. And that is all I wish to do, live my own life in peace."

Hunt pointed at the lights in the distance. "Mugla," he said.

He studied them as they ate. Helene was clearly still in a state of shock but she was eating, even if she snatched at her food and gulped at the wine. She was going to suffer agonies of indigestion.

But in any event, she was irrelevant.

He found Geli fascinating. She had been through hardly less of an ordeal than her daughter, and in addition it was easy to see that she was a very well-bred, old-fashioned woman who had been exposed in every possible sense. Yet she was allowing neither her fear nor her humiliation, nor even the relief she must be feeling that at least she was no longer in physical danger, as she would suppose, to overwhelm her, ate quietly, sipped her wine, and occasionally gave him an anxious glance.

Was she truly the woman he sought? There was no question that she was Hitler's daughter. Therefore a great deal of character probably lurked behind those soft eyes, character which indeed she had been revealing over the past few days, and certainly over the past few hours. Therefore why had he brought her here at all? His mission could have been completed out there on Cnidus Nova, with no witnesses.

Or was he still hoping, absurdly, that his mission need never have to be completed at all?

But at least part of the mission was getting to know her, understanding her . . . evaluating her and determining just what she was capable of . . . or not.

"That was a very brave thing you did on the hillside," he remarked. "Knocking Ilse Bruening over, I mean. You could have been shot."

"It was something I had wanted to do for several hours. Knock her over. Will you let me go?" she asked. "I understand that you wish a story. I have no story. If you feel that you must tell the world of how you found Hitler's daughter, then I cannot stop you. But as I cannot prove who I am, I am not sure the world will believe you. All you will have done is complete the ruination of my life. Are you that brutal a man, Mr Hunt?"

Hunt sighed. "I would like to speak with you, alone, Frau Littler. It is very important. But this is neither the time nor the place. You are very tired, and you have had a horrifying experience. Do you not think that any decisions should wait until you have had a good night's sleep, a chance to assess your position?"

"What you wish to speak with me about, it is not to do with your newspaper," Geli remarked.

"No, it is not. But it is far more important."

"You are asking me to come with you, to trust you. Ilse Bruening said you were not to be trusted. I know she wanted to kill me, but . . ."

"You think she may have been telling the truth. Yes, I take your point." He felt in his pocket, took out an object and laid it on the table. It was one half of an alligator nut-cracker.

Geli inhaled slowly as she gazed at the piece of brass. Hunt glanced at Helene, who was just finishing her meal. She looked at the alligator as well, but without great interest.

"Can you match that, Geli?" Hunt asked.

"Who are you?" Geli whispered.

Hunt shrugged. "Just a messenger, really."

"From whom?"

Hunt looked at Helene.

"Helene," Geli said. "I wish you to remain here until we return. Mr Hunt and I are going to take a little walk. Have some ice cream, and order coffee. We will not be long."

"I don't want to be left alone," Helene objected, and gave a little shiver.

"You are perfectly safe here," Geli pointed out; the restaurant was full. "And we will be just outside. Now be a good girl."

She led Hunt out of the glow of the lights and into

310

a small garden. Then she turned to face him. "Who sent you?"

"An organisation."

"The Nazi Party?"

"I'm afraid not."

She frowned. "Then . . . I do not understand. That nutcracker . . ."

"It was found amongst Himmler's personal effects."

"Forty-seven years ago? You were not born."

"True."

"Then . . .?"

"It was not considered important by the people who found it. Just a momento. But if I was not yet born, my organisation was then *being* born, and its founder members were interested in such an object. Half an object. Where was the other half? They managed to obtain this half, and then to obtain other pieces of information which related to it, from scraps of written evidence, from condemned men who had some inkling of what was happening in the last days of the Reich . . ."

"You mean your 'organisation' knew of me, years ago?"

"Let's say, we suspected your existence, years ago. But there were absolutely no leads, not a shred of evidence that you were alive, until Brauer."

"And now you know . . ." She licked her lips. "What happens?"

"That is up to you, Geli."

"But you were sent to find me?"

"Yes."

"Why?"

They gazed at each other.

"Oh, my God!" Geli clasped her hands round her neck. "You are as big a thug as Ilse Bruening."

"I hope not. We are trying to prevent a recurrence of the greatest tragedy which ever overtook mankind."

She peered at him. "You are not a Jew."

"No."

311

"But you work for them."

"I work for a Jewish organisation, yes."

"And they sent you to kill me? Then why did you not just stand back and let that woman do it? She was going to, you know."

"I know. And I agree, a lot of people wouldn't see my point of view. Put me down as a romantic fool. Death should be clean, and quick . . . and only when necessary."

She licked her lips. "But you still mean to kill me."

"That is up to you. Frau Littler . . . Geli . . . Fraulein Hitler, I have to know what you mean to do."

"I wish to be left alone."

Hunt studied her.

Her shoulders sagged. "I don't suppose that is good enough."

"Do you have not the slightest desire to go back, to adulation, fame, wealth . . ."

She shuddered. "The adulation of the neo-Nazis? The fame of being the daughter of the greatest mass murderer the world has ever known? The . . ." She hesitated.

"Suppose I said we were going to take that money away from you?"

She sighed. "I have no right to it. But I suppose I would simply have to get on with being a widow. Hans must have left me something. And the children will help me." She raised her eyes. "Unless you kill me now, and put me out of my misery."

"You understand, Hunt," Carl Uhlmann had said. "She must never return to Germany. Indeed, she must never make her true identity known. If there is the slightest risk of either of those things happening . . . then you will have to make sure they can never happen."

Kill this utterly attractive, surprisingly brave, strongly intelligent and untemptable woman?

"Why should I wish to do that?"

"Well . . . what *are* you going to do?"

Hunt considered. Her determination had affected him

312

more than he would have thought possible; it had never occurred to him that she might refuse the temptation of stepping on to the world stage. Suddenly he felt ashamed of himself and everything he stood for. Of everything he had always stood for in his fierce hatred of Nazism. "I don't really know. Confess to my employers that they sent the wrong man, I suppose."

"I am sorry."

"So am I."

"What about your other role?"

"That's a tricky one. But . . . with Adoration and her bearded friend dead, there are very few people in the world who have any idea that you exist. There's me, of course, and my editor, and unfortunately there's Leni."

"I do not understand your relationship with her," Geli said.

"I'm not sure I do, either. But I intend to find out. And there is another member of the staff of the *Globe*. Those can all be sorted out, I think. Then there is my employer, a man called Ulhmann. But he will simply know I have failed. As for Mendelik . . . I'll just tell him I was mistaken."

"Ilse Bruening spoke of a man called Allendt."

"Oh, yes. Joachim. However, I don't think he is going to be shouting it to all the world when the news of your friend Ilse's death becomes public. I intend to inform him of it myself, anyway. So you see it is a small number, of whom I would say only Leni Weiss matters. As I said, you may leave Leni to me."

"And?"

"Well . . . I would suggest that what we do is this. Can you drive?"

"Of course."

"Then we will drive up to Selcuk together. You will drop me there, and drive on with Helene. Where you go, or what you do, is up to you. I will wait in Selcuk for Leni. Because that is where she will begin her search for me."

313

Geli frowned at him. "You are not even going to write a story about me?"

"It would cause a lot of fuss, wouldn't it?"

"But it would bring you fame, and money."

"I don't actually need either, you know."

"I don't understand why you should do this."

"You know something . . . I'm not sure I do either. Maybe I'm just not used to meeting plain, straightforward, decent people. Maybe that's what *is* important in the world, more important than Fascism or democracy or governments, the fact that there are people like you around. That's certainly more important than newspaper stories. However, there is one problem left: your daughter. And your sons. They know the truth, don't they?"

"Yes. But I think, after all that has happened, I can persuade them it is best forgotten."

"You don't think one of them might one day feel the urge to earn some money? Quite a lot of money? All he'd have to do is telephone a newspaper."

"I will try to make sure that none of them ever feel that way. But if they do . . . whoever it is will telephone the *Globe*. Is that fair?"

"Sounds fair to me."

"And you will write the story?"

"If I'm still on the staff. I'm not sure about that, after this business."

"Oh. I should not like to think . . ."

"I can take care of myself, Geli."

"I know. I have seen you do it. Mr Hunt," Geli said. "Ilse Bruening said you were a bad man. So did Leni Weiss."

"Oh, I am," Hunt said. "Believe me. Let's get out of here."

They reached Selcuk just before midnight. By then Hunt had filled the Mercedes' fuel tank.

"Now," he said. "Just disappear, Geli Littler. The world is your oyster. I shall see to that."

314

Geli had got out of the car to come round to the driver's seat. Now she reached up and kissed him on the cheek. "I owe you my life, and a lot more than that."

He grinned, took her in his arms and kissed her on the mouth. "Maybe I owe you my sanity."

The Mercedes drove away, and Hunt went into the hotel.

"Mr Hunt," said the girl on the desk. "There has been a telephone call for you."

"I imagine it was a lady."

The girl smirked. "Oh, yes. She asked when you would be returning. I said I did not know."

"Well, if she turns up, show her in," Hunt said, and went along the corridor to his room.

He was exhausted, both mentally and physically, his brain deadened by the way his quest had turned out so differently to what he had expected. He didn't want to think until he had had a good night's sleep . . . and he had no doubt that when he woke up he was going to have to do a lot of very rapid thinking.

Hunt awoke with a start as the curtains were drawn and his bedroom was flooded with daylight. He sat up, looked from Corinne to Leni. They both looked rather tired, which figured as he did not suppose either of them had slept, and distinctly untidy. Nor were their expressions reassuring.

"I know," he said. "You want breakfast."

"Where is she, Hunt?" Leni asked, her voice like steel. And she was speaking English.

"I have absolutely no idea."

"Right. You are under arrest."

"Ah," Hunt said. "Wrong MI5, is that it?"

"Yes," Leni said.

"Ah. So that's why Halliday was prepared to back your every story, and why you found it so easy to persuade Corinne to obey you rather than me. I suppose it was also you, or your boss, persuaded Mendelik to let us go."

"That's history, Hunt."

"I really am rather flattered. Still, darling, this isn't England, you know. You can't pull any rank in Turkey."

"Inspector Mendelik is waiting for my call. His people will be here whenever I send for them."

"Ah," Hunt said again. He looked at Corinne.

"Well," Corinne said defensively, "when she told me who she was, and I checked and, well, she was who she was . . . I had to go along with her. Besides, the boss told me to."

"So," Hunt said thoughtfully. "I have been surrounded by British Intelligence ever since Hamburg."

"Anyone not quite so wrapped up in himself would have worked that out," Leni told him, starting to sound like a schoolmistress again.

"Is the condemned man allowed two questions?"

"The condemned man should get up and get dressed," Leni told him. "But you may ask your questions."

"Why did they send you, and not a bloke?"

"My boss felt you would be more susceptible to a woman."

"Your boss of course being Peter Layton. Jolly good. Now will you tell me whether you were actually looking for Frau Littler yourself, or just trying to stop me finding her?"

"Oh, we wanted to find the lady, Hunt. But we also wanted to stop you from suborning her. Or from assassinating her."

"Well, you seem to have failed."

"Yes," Leni said grimly. "But you are going to pay for it, Hunt."

Hunt got out of bed, cleaned his teeth, scraped his beard with his razor. The women watched him.

"I don't suppose it would do me any good to say that the lady is alive and well and sinking into obscurity, where she intends to remain?"

"I saw a pig flying on the way here," Leni remarked.

Hunt got dressed. "Look, Geli Littler is not interested

in bring Hitler's daughter. She told me so, and after we'd talked a bit, I accepted her point of view. As far as I am concerned she doesn't exist."

"Just like that?"

"If you must know," Hunt said, "I was the one who was suborned."

"Tell me another."

"Leni, you are too convinced that all the world is evil," Hunt said sadly.

"I'm quite convinced your part of it is, Hunt. You know, you were growing on me. But to kill that woman, and her daughter . . ."

They stared at each other . . . and the telephone jangled.

"Shall I?" Corinne asked.

Leni nodded, and Corinne picked up the phone.

"Yes?" She put her hand over the mouthpiece. "It's a woman, for Hunt."

Hunt raised his eyebrows.

"Ask her name," Leni said, "and tell her to leave a message."

"I'm afraid Mr Hunt is tied up right now," Corinne said. "He asks if you would leave your name, and a message, and he'll get back to you just as soon as possible." She listened, an expression of consternation slowly spreading across her face. "Yes," she said. "Yes. Hold on a minute." She put her hand over the phone and gazed at Leni. "It's someone claiming to be Frau Littler."

Leni frowned and looked at Hunt. Who shrugged.

Leni took the phone. "Frau Littler? Can you identify yourself?"

"Isn't that Leni? Oh, I'm so glad you're all right."

"Yes," Leni said. "I'm all right. Do you wish to speak with Hunt?"

"Yes. Yes, please."

Leni gave him the phone.

"Mr Hunt," Geli said. "We never decided what I should do with the money."

"Spend it," Hunt advised. "I think you deserve that."

"Oh. Would you like to know where we are?"

"No," Hunt said.

"Oh. I . . . I do not feel I have thanked you enough for what you have done."

"Okay," Hunt said. "I gave you my card, remember? If you still feel like thanking me again, when you've had time to think about it, you know how to get hold of me. Take care."

He replaced the phone.

"Well," Leni said, and pocketed her pistol. "It seems we owe you an apology, Hunt. I'm glad of that."

"So am I. But tell me, how did you two get back together?"

"Corinne let me know where she was being sent."

"Of course; the note she passed you at the hotel." He frowned. "But . . ."

"I've been to Turkey before," Corinne explained. "I knew which hotel I was going to stay at in Pammukale. I put that in the note as well."

"You were supposed to be on the road, looking for Adoration," Hunt said.

"I got fed up with that," Corinne said. "And went home. Luckily. I was there when Leni telephoned."

"From Bozburan, presumably?"

"It was a brisk walk," Leni admitted. "But that nice shopkeeper remembered me."

"And Corinne drove like the clappers and picked you up." Hunt wondered what the tail he had put on Corinne had thought about all that – but he had specifically told him not to interfere unless she got herself into trouble. "Well, what happens now?"

"I have apologised," Leni reminded him. "I will now leave you. With Corinne. You'll have to make your own peace with Mr Halliday. If Geli Littler does mean to maintain her anonymity, my job is over."

"Just like that," Hunt said regretfully. "I thought we had something going."

318

"Maybe we did, Hunt. Until you left me with two corpses to mind. They're still there, by the way. I haven't mentioned them to anyone. However, as you haven't turned out to be quite the villain we supposed, give me a ring some time. I'm in the book. Lesley White."

Hunt lay down again. "Wouldn't work. I'm too old for you, darling. I rather think I'll wait for someone more my own age group to call me. After all, she has the number."